Denny's Demons

by

Ivor McKenzie

We all have inner demons to fight, we call these demons, fear and hatred and anger. If you do not conquer them then a life of one hundred years is a tragedy. If you do, then a life of a single day can be a triumph.

Yip Man

Chapter 1

Petra sat on a bench at the bow of the ferry trying not to watch the white waves crashing against the side of the boat. She was eight months pregnant with her first born and unfortunately, she had suffered long term morning sickness for most of that time. The sickness and the sea sickness were making this an extremely uncomfortable journey to say the least. The thought of holding her baby soon kept her spirits up. Until her husband Lachlan wandered out to see how she was coping holding a mug of tea and a greasy Scotch pie. Whereby Petra angrily grabbed the pie and threw it as far as she could into the path of some seagulls that were following the boat. Although a bit stunned, he said,

"Never mind my dear at least the Sea Gods in the Straits of Durma are being kind to us today. It's like a mill pond out there is it not?"

Petra's face turned from ashen white to a bright raging red in a second.

"Lachlan it's a good job I love you or I will take immense pleasure in throwing you over the side. I've never seen a mill pond with three-foot waves. Now get out of my sight before I must explain your untimely demise. "

Lachlan new when he should retreat and wandered back inside. Petra kept her eyes fixed on the dot on the horizon that her husband had told her was their destination, but it never seemed to get any nearer.

She just sat there holding her bump and telling stories to her unborn child with a few tears thrown in.

"Hold tight my darling baby it won't be long now, "she said.

Petra had met Lachlan when they were both students in Edinburgh. She had settled in Scotland after the war studying Art and Design and receiving her degree with honours. It was in the last year of the course that she met Lachlan and they hit it off at once. A relationship had developed and eventually they rented a flat together in Leith. Lachlan was a few years older and was studying to be a Veterinary Surgeon. He was just waiting to hear if he had qualified and five long years were resting on the exam

1

results. When word came through, he was overjoyed as he had passed with flying colours.

Petra was a stunning looking girl with long black hair down to her shoulders and an hourglass figure. Standing at just under six feet she was at least three inches taller than Lachlan. With a temper not to be messed with. Everyone wondered what she saw in him with his large belly, rough beard, and his continuous wearing of the kilt. An immensely proud Scotsman indeed. The most mismatched couple you could ever imagine.

After several years of living in Edinburgh they both decided that a fresh challenge was needed. By a twist of fate, the British Veterinary Association had contacted Lachlan and enquired if he would be interested in taking up a post on the island of Durma as well as covering the islands of Yasil and Smore Isle. This was something he had wanted for a long time, and it would get them out of the rat race that Edinburgh had become. There was one massive consideration. Petra was pregnant and she was about twelve weeks gone. They had never married, but she was happy to be called Petra Foggerty and thought that one day it might happen.

A big decision had to be made and after many hours of discussion Lachlan had persuaded Petra that this was the big chance they needed and they should grab it with both arms. Petra didn't even know these islands existed, but trusted Lachlan's judgement.

Now the dot on the horizon had materialised and they were about to step onto the rock called Durma. Their new home.

As the ferry finally docked Lachlan grabbed the bags and stood waiting for them to disembark. Petra stood and looked at the port of Sea Haven in disbelief. Surely nobody could live in this God forsaken hole she said to herself. Little did she know worse was to come.

She kept her head bowed as she walked down the gangway. Maybe if I don't look at this place, I might feel better she thought. It didn't work as she walked along the dock the rain started, but at least it would wash her tears away so that Lachlan wouldn't notice. He did.

Waiting to transport them to Kismay was John McDonald, a man who never turned the offer of a job down when cash and the thought of a few whiskies in Scroggies bar afterwards was on offer. John was well into his seventies, but still with a mop of grey hair and unbelievably still having all his own teeth. With an islander's diet that was exceedingly rare indeed. Probably not as white as they might be though. Nobody could remember him having a change of clothes. A tweed jacket, corduroy trousers of a discernible colour and wellington boots held together with tape were his only attire. His trousers were held up with baling twine and replenished every so often. He was the go-to man if you ever needed anything transported on the island.

Nobody knew anything about him apart from the fact that he had taken over the croft from his grandmother and he had arrived on the island as a young boy. He had received a small amount of money when his gran died. However, he didn't care for lots of money as long as he had enough for food and his frequent trips to the pub he was happy.

John recognised them from the description the official from the Veterinary Association had given him. Petra stood there with as 'crabbit' a face that John had ever witnessed. Oh, this is going to be a fun journey John said to himself and gave a little laugh, but he felt there was something dark about the 'lassie'. Petra asked Lachlan if she could have a minute to take in what she was seeing before her. Drab weather, drab houses, drab looking people and even the water looked drab. Her entire world had turned to a very dark shade of grey and she thought the island was well named. She held her belly and said,

" Ich bin mir darüber nicht sicher mein Baby. "

John introduced himself with a little doff of his cap and said he would carry their bags to his vehicle. Lachlan said they were expecting another delivery the following week and would he be kind enough to pick it up for them. Pound signs were now in his eyes. He wasn't sure if Petra had turned her nose up at him or if it was permanently like that. When they arrived at his vehicle Petra's bottom jaw almost hit the ground. Here was a pickup truck that could be heard from miles away as John didn't believe in exhaust systems. It was held together with rust and wire and the wire was supported by even more wire and rope. The paint work had fallen off years ago. When she pointed out that the tyres were completely bald he said,

"Don't worry yourself 'lass' as we have only got about 20 miles to go."

He thought she was going to pass out. On the back of his truck was a homemade wooden cage which John used when transporting livestock, but it was highly unlikely that they would have survived long in that contraption.

They started their journey with Petra sitting in between John and Lachlan just bouncing around.

"I'm curious as to the purpose of the screwdriver sticking out from the dashboard Mr McDonald and do you think we could put the heater up on such a chilly day. "Petra asked.

"Well, 'lass' you must start the engine somehow as I lost the ignition keys about thirty years ago. As for the heater you would need a miracle for that to start up." he replied as a matter of fact. As they started the journey the road was beginning to get bumpy not helped by the fact that John had no springs on the truck. They had fallen off about fifteen years ago and he never felt the need to replace them. The way John's mind worked was that he would always weigh up his options. New springs or whisky? Only one winner there.

As they bounced along the road, he noticed Petra holding her belly now and again. John was inwardly pleading that the little 'bairn' wouldn't be making an appearance any time soon.

After a while Petra couldn't hold back any longer.

"Mr McDonald, what is that infernal smell in here?"

"Now Mrs Foggerty, I'm taking exception to your inferred accusation. I never pass wind when a lady is downwind from me, but if she is up wind then that is a different matter. Also, I had a bath last month albeit a quick dip in the sea off Rocky Point."

Lachlan had been chuckling at this conversation between the two of them. As they trundled on John had to keep pumping the choke to get as much petrol to the engine as possible. Suddenly, he started to slow the truck down. Very slowly as the brakes weren't in the best of condition. When the truck finally stopped John said,

"Bonnie 'lass' I owe you an apology as the smell you are experiencing is probably Badger and he is not keen on the water, a bit like me."

At that point Petra started to grab a hold of Lachlan and shout,

4

"Please don't tell me you have a badger in this cab with us?"
"Contain yourself 'lass' and keep calm. Take your time, turn round, and look behind your seat. "

Petra did as he suggested as did Lachlan only to see Badger a Border Collie of indiscernible age lying on the floor behind the seat. Slowly he lifted his head, took a quick look at the faces and as there was nothing for him to be interested in he went back to sleep, but not before having a good scratch at the fleas behind both ears. Lachlan started to laugh until Petra gave him a glare that sent a shiver up his spine. Badger had arrived at John's croft a few years ago and he had taken him in until he could find his owner. Although he asked around nobody came to claim him which to be honest suited John as he had become quite fond of him, so he took Badger everywhere he went. Even to the pub as he reckoned he smelled better than some of the fishermen that frequented the place.

The rest of the journey passed without incident with John telling them about the history of the island and whose croft was which along the way and what animals they had which was of interest to Lachlan. He had told them that when the youngsters on the island reached fifteen or sixteen years they were desperate to leave and the crofts were never passed on to the younger generation. A dying island. Not that Petra was a keen listener. She just sat there and very, very quietly sang lullaby songs to her unborn in a dialect that John didn't understand, and which left him a bit unnerved.

Finally, they came over the brow of the hill and there stood Kismay in all its glory. John stopped there for effect. Wrong move. Many a time people had said that this was the last place God had made with all the pieces that were left over from the rest of the world. Petra's face turned to a look of horror. All she could see was emptiness. Sea Haven was bad enough, but Kismay took the prize for the most run-down fishing village on any Scottish island. There was a look of resignation on Petra's face with another single tear starting to roll down her cheek, One of many tears to come.

John parked up close to the harbour and went into Betty May's shop. Betty was only five feet tall with tiny hands and thinning black hair, but with a temper and snarl that could blacken day into night. Everybody said she had been on the island since it had emerged from the sea. Nobody could recall her history and she never divulged it to anyone. Even the hardened fishermen had too much respect to mess with her. Her shop was just her converted living room and most of the island's provisions were kept in a large building out the back. People had said that stepping into her living room was like stepping back into the dark ages. She just sat there in her old armchair and knitted, mostly giving the knitwear to families who she felt needed it.

The whole of Kismay had to put their order for provisions in at least three days before the ferry left the mainland. An exceptionally large warehouse on the mainland catered for all the islanders needs. Anybody who had to go to the mainland had no problem in bringing back provisions for any villager who needed it. As for Betty's mark up well, she just made it up as she went along. If she liked you then fine. If not, it was a case of pay up and get out.

John came out with four large carrier bags and put them in the back. As he got back in he told them it was essentials provided courtesy of the islanders for their arrival. Petra and Lachlan thought this was a kind gesture. John had held a whip round in Scroggies bar the night before when most of the clientele were a few sheets to the wind and hadn't a clue what they were paying up for. John taking a few pounds for his services of course.

From the harbour it was only a few hundred yards to the large imposing four bedroomed house that was to be the Foggerty home for the foreseeable future. Stone built with a large upstairs window that looked out over the sea. Although Lachlan had briefly seen the house before he felt Petra might be a bit isolated being out of the village. Many years down the line Lachlan did purchase the house from the Veterinary Association as they were glad to get rid of it and he thought it would be a lovely legacy for the baby when the time came.

John said his goodbyes, but not before Lachlan had handed him a £20 note. John then headed off to the sanctuary of Scroggies Bar. Now he had the grand total £40 burning a hole in his pocket. £20 from the Veterinary Association and now £20 from Mr Foggerty. He could get used to this as now he felt like a millionaire.

6

Chapter 2

Daniel Rey Foggerty was born a few weeks later. A healthy 9lb 5oz baby boy. Little did he know that this was going to be the start of one hell of a journey. Even in these few weeks Petra had threatened to go back to Edinburgh several times, but Lachlan had consoled her each time and told her to think about the baby as they were going to make a new life for themselves.

Nobody could prepare you for living on Durma, but I suppose being born there helped as you never knew anything different and to you that life was normal. It was the loneliest place on God's earth at times. To live here was a feat of human endurance, but most people just got on with it and would never dream of leaving.

This was a cold, windswept rock in the Atlantic Ocean where sunshine was at a premium and the north winds blew constantly. Approximately thirty miles from the Scottish mainland. The islanders used to say it was thirty miles from civilisation. It measured only twenty-five miles by twenty- five miles with a population of about four thousand hardy souls. Most of them lived in or around the two villages and their harbours. Crofts were spread out over the island, but they were becoming exceedingly rare as a crofting life was now just becoming an existence. You couldn't survive on what you grew around your place or what animals you reared. The coastline was interspersed with small coves some which were accessible from the cliffs and some only from the sea. Several small beaches were dotted about, but rest assured they weren't meant for sunbathing on. The old fishermen used to say that if you fell into the sea then you only had five minutes to make peace with your God before you froze to death. Many of the lobster and crab fishermen couldn't even swim as they used to say what was the point.

Kismay had about forty crabbing and lobster boats at any one time with a couple of larger fishing boats that could go out further for the mackerel and stay out for a couple of days. The village was centred around the harbour and a constant odour of fish and diesel engine oil hung in the air. Most of the houses in the village were in disrepair as there was very little money to go around and

7

there was never any point in repainting your doors and windows as the harsh North wind stripped the paint off within a few weeks.

All the fishermen made a living, but only just. If you weren't into fishing or crofting, you scratched a living at anything you could lend your hand to. Most of the houses were in or around the harbour and a lot of the population were elderly just waiting till God had decided as to when they were ready for their demise. How they could spin a good yarn though. A few boat chandlers in the harbour were a necessary part of the fishing community as your boat couldn't be out of commission for any length of time. Their catch had to be transported daily to the larger Icehouse at Sea Haven ready for forwarding to the mainland. A few shops had survived over the years, but unless some investment was found to prop up the islands economy then most people felt that in several years Durma would just be a barren rock.

Scroggies bar in Kismay was the hub of the community. The older generation told you that they never knew what its real name was, but that the original owner was a Captain John Scroggland about one hundred years ago. If this place closed, then there would be a flotilla of boats of all description heading for the mainland for good. Although there was a pub at Sea Haven nobody from Kismay would ever dream of stepping one foot inside it. Scroggies was packed to the gunnels most nights as drinking was a way of life and how the islanders embraced it.

With drunken brawls breaking out now and again and although they could be brutal a few minutes after the altercation everybody was friends again. It was just a way of letting off steam. This is what the island did to you.

On the outside the bar was the dirtiest building you could ever imagine. You couldn't see inside and you couldn't see outside when you were in the place as the windows were caked thick with the salt from the sea when the wind was battering the front of the bar. Inside the walls were plastered with fishing memorabilia which was often just junk that somebody wanted rid of. In fact, the walls were being held together with everything that was hanging there. The toilets at the back had no windows so often you could have a conversation with anybody who happened to be passing while you were urinating. The serving bar was made up of old wooden flotsam and repaired several times over the years.

Heavy wooden benches and seats were the only décor in the place and sawdust was spread on the floor daily to soak up the spillages. No clock had ever adorned any of the walls for as long as anybody could remember. Throwing out time was when the sun started to rise, and the lock ins could last for days if the weather was stormy and the boats couldn't get out. The only alcohol available was whisky and beer, nothing else. You couldn't even get a soft drink or a packet of crisps. The stories that were told in that bar were so exaggerated and legendary that you would have thought that the fishermen had caught the Great White Whale where Captain Ahab had failed.

Daniel's early upbringing wasn't as normal as most other kids had as his mum couldn't be described as very maternal, and Lachlan wasn't very happy when she had decided she didn't want to breast feed him anymore. He knew the benefits of breast feeding, but he only knew about this when boxes of powdered milk were dropped off at their house. Maybe this was for the best as Lachlan had confronted her and asked if she had been taking alcohol. Petra had denied it, but he knew and several times he had sat down with her and asked her what was happening. Still, she denied it until he had found several empty bottles of vodka hidden behind the wood store at the back of the house. He was so angry that she was drinking while looking after Daniel. That precious little boy didn't deserve that.

He went down to Scroggies and asked if they knew how she was getting the alcohol, but the only answer they could think of was that somebody from the ferry was bringing it in for her. Her moods were getting worse, and she would often take to her bed for hours at a time. This left Lachlan to try and make sure Daniel was being looked after combined with his veterinary duties. Lachlan made up his mind that his main priority would be his boy, and if his mum didn't care for him then so be it.

At best Petra could be described as a functioning alcoholic and at worst just a drunk! His mum was strict and could often be heard shouting,

"Discipline, discipline Daniel you must have discipline in your life." when he misbehaved.

His dad would just take him out of the way when that happened and they would wander down to the small beach just along the road to play. Daniel loved those special times with his dad while his mum would go for a lie down. What Daniel didn't know at that delicate age was that his mum was well on her way to being an alcoholic by the time he was age to go to school. Though his dad would often look at him and think what a lovely little boy he was and how proud he was of him through these turbulent family times.

Soon it was Daniels's time to start school, and this was to be a very weird experience for him as he had never really mixed with any of the other kids in the village. Mostly at the insistence of his mum as she only strolled down to the village shop when it was a necessity and she had made it abundantly clear that she had no intention of mixing with the locals. However, Lachlan would occasionally take him into the village where all the children would gather behind the church and play games before being chased away by the Rev. McGlashan. It didn't matter to Daniel as he was just so happy to be in and around the other children. When they walked back home Daniel kept on asking his dad when he could go back again. Soon he would tell his son. Lachlan was glad that he would be going to school as at least somebody would be looking after him and he wouldn't have to worry about him.

This was the day that Daniel started school. All his school clothes had been bought by his dad and every piece of clothing had to be warm and hard wearing. His pencil case was lovingly tucked away in his satchel along with his lunch. His mother never even roused herself from her drunken slumber to see him off, but that didn't stop him from holding his dad's hand and skipping excitedly all the way to the playground. He looked at the big doors in wonderment then gave his dad a big hug and walked through the doors.

The school was the church hall and was set off from the main part. It was sectioned off into two parts as all the kids up to the ages of fourteen and fifteen years were taught here, and it had only two teachers to look after all the forty pupils. The building was rented from the Church, but no money was ever spent on it. It was like God had taken their money and ran. Furniture was sparse to say the least and the chairs and desks were basic with years of graffiti and names carved on them.

The teachers were Miss Glover and Miss ' Dizzy ' Lizzie

Bryant ably assisted by a classroom monitor. Miss Glover looked after the older pupils and technically she knocked them into shape. A very grim looking woman who never smiled and had big spectacles that could have been used as binoculars. Even the older kids were frightened of her, and she was never too shy to grab a pupil by the ear and drag them into the side room for a belting. She had a belt the size of her arm and wasn't afraid to use it.

Miss Bryant tutored the younger kids, but her nickname suited her to a tee. Never a day went by when there wasn't some sort of drama caused by her scatter brain. Nobody could ever understand why she had ended up on Durma. She had been asked out on a date on more than a few occasions but had turned them down flat. A strange creature indeed. Although she always had a soft spot for Daniel as he used her as a surrogate mother in some ways.

School days were haphazard for Daniel although he was always first there in the mornings. Not long after starting school he asked his dad if he could walk on his own to school and back each day. His dad thought that was a great idea. Any homework he had been given was overseen by his dad, never his mother. Even when he brought back his little projects his mother would barely look at them which really hurt him. He never had to spend too much time on his homework as Daniel had an extraordinary memory and even at a very young age he knew that things were going to happen before they did. Probably a sixth sense, but he was too young to understand why.

Playtime was special for him. Running about wild with all the children was so exciting for him and at times he was reluctant to go back to the class. Daniel was clever, very clever, but at times he became bored as he had to wait on the other pupils catching up. He was infatuated by one boy who was a couple of years older than him. His name was John Scougal, but he was only referred to as Scoug.

Scoug was a scoundrel through and through and always up to mischief. Invariably he roped Daniel into his goings on, but Daniel would often realise that whatever Scoug was up to might not end well. More than once, he asked him not to do what he was up to. Often there was a letter sent to their mums or dads, but Daniel's dad always intercepted his before his mother could see

11

it and start her usual ranting and raving and the shouting of, "Discipline, discipline Daniel you must have discipline.".

Daniel got the nickname Denny due to a young girl not being able say his name properly and what came out was Denny, so it stuck. His dad found that amusing but had told him he would always be Daniel to him and his mum. Denny and Scoug were as thick as thieves with Denny towering over Scoug by a good few inches which always seemed to rankle with Scoug.

John lived with his mum and dad in a cottage by the harbour. His dad was an abusive, drunken wife beater named Talisker Joe, a small wiry man with a loudmouth and an explosive temper. Everyone new about him but seemed to turn a blind eye to it all. Jean his wife stuck with him through the beatings for John's sake. She would never cover up her bruises and would often tell people she had fallen or had walked into something. To most villagers Jean was a lovely woman and they all felt ashamed that they had never intervened to stop the abuse.

Talisker lived for the whisky and although he didn't have a real job, he did all the odd jobs that nobody else wanted for the fishermen when they needed him. Joe spent almost all of his earnings in Scroggies, but when drunk he was a real pest. Often, he became so obstreperous that some of the men throwing him out of the pub became par for the course. Very little money went back to Jean and John, and they survived on her earnings from doing clothes alterations which she excelled at. Any money she earned was secreted away and Talisker could never find it despite inflicting beatings on his wife to try and make her tell. John often witnessed the violence and was upset by it all. Jean would just hold him and tell him that it would be better someday.

Denny and Scoug became the best of mates and often had each other's backs. However even from an early age Denny never fully trusted him. There was always that niggle in the back of his mind. Scoug always liked coming to Denny's house after school as Petra, when able, tried to feed Scoug up. Petra would often refer to him as her little waif from the village and felt sorry for him. Denny swore that he once saw Scoug licking his plate like a hungry dog and felt his mum cared more for Scoug than she did him. He had noticed that Scoug had been wearing some of his clothes that no longer fitted him. What he didn't know was that his dad had been taking them down to Scoug's mum when Talisker wasn't around. Denny never mentioned it.

To Denny school was something that had to be done, but by the time he was about ten years old it became a real chore and he couldn't wait for the end of the day. After school he would often run home and grab his dad's hunting rifle. Off he would go hunting rabbits. At that age he was a crack shot and rarely failed to hit at what he was aiming. If he did then he would try repeatedly until he got it right.

His dad nearly put a stop to his hunting when Denny had asked Scoug to go with him. He thought Scoug was a bad influence on his son but decided to let them go this time. It ended up in disaster when Scoug had for no reason turned the rifle on one of the crofter's sheep. Denny couldn't believe it and had run home and told his dad who had grabbed his Vet's bag and ran back to where the incident had happened. There was no sign of Scoug. Only the gun was lying there. Lachlan checked out the injury to the sheep, but after speaking to the owner it was decided to put the animal down. He took the rifle and shot the sheep in the head. He advised the crofter that he would pay for the loss of the sheep and the crofter could butcher the animal and keep the meat. Daniel felt sad about the death of the animal, but a strange feeling came over him and for a minute after the shot was fired a weird smile had come over his face. His dad told Daniel that on no account Scoug could go hunting with him again. No more was said between them.

Denny had decided that he wanted to explore the island more. So, most weekends he told his dad that he was going to take his small tent, sleeping bag, along with his rifle and he would be away for a day or so. Lachlan always packed some provisions in a rucksack and gave it to Denny with a little talk about staying safe.

Before he left for the first time his dad gave him a scope for his rifle. Denny didn't know it even existed, but he was so excited and couldn't wait to learn how to use it. While walking along the small path at the top of the cliffs he was using the scope to check out all the small inlets. Which ones he could get down to as he wanted to explore from the sea level. He found it absolutely fascinating as to what had been washed up into these small coves.

13

After walking for several hours, he climbed down to a beach. As he stood there trying to figure out the time of the tides he turned around and there was the wreck of an old lobster boat. He was slightly taken aback by this and although keeping an eye on the tide he slowly walked over to it. It was pretty bashed up. He looked inside but whatever had been there had been taken by the sea. The name was barely visible and after giving it a wipe with his sleeve he could make out SEA ROSE. He would ask his dad when he got home. Something didn't feel right though. There was an eerie feeling about the place, so he picked up his gear and headed back up to the top of the cliff.

As dusk fell, he pitched his tent and before eating he decided to try out the scope with the rifle. It didn't take him long to figure it out and he lay there as still as the night just waiting for the rabbits to appear. Here they come he said to himself. Taking his time, he slowly fired the gun, and the first rabbit went down, then the next until he had killed five. This was so easy with the new scope he thought. Now he knew it was impossible for him to miss. He smiled and smiled. He settled down for the night eating only a few biscuits from the rucksack and drinking from a flask of water his dad had filled for him. He felt extremely comfortable just lying there identifying all the sounds he was hearing. Some he wasn't sure about, but he wasn't scared being there by himself.

Next morning, he packed up and started to walk slowly back as he had been told to hang any rabbits on the gates of any crofter, he was okay with. He wasn't that far from home when he decided to hang a couple of rabbits on the gate of Hamish's garden. Hamish was a giant of a man, but there was always a debate about his surname. Hamish would suffice. The epitome of a highlander. He stood about six feet four inches with straggly, ginger hair and a bushy beard to match. A real man mountain and he was the only other person Denny had seen wearing a kilt each day. The villagers told stories about him, but Denny preferred to take people as he found them. He had just finished tying the rabbits on when the door of the old gypsy caravan opened.

"Get these filthy vermin off my gate Foggerty," shouted Hamish in a booming aggressive voice.

Denny didn't understand why he had to be like that.

"I'm just trying to be nice sir. Why are you saying that?"

Denny had replied.

Hamish started to walk aggressively towards him while threatening that Denny would be as dead as the rabbits if he didn't remove himself from his property. He pointed out to Hamish that he was standing on a coastal path and not his land which enraged Hamish even more. He stood his ground whereby Hamish started to shout profanities at him with an evil sneer on his face. Denny wasn't scared and when Hamish was getting too close he slowly took the rifle off his shoulder, cocked it, and pointed it at him. Hamish stopped in his tracks and said,

"You won't fire that gun as you're too scared because you're a Foggerty."

"Try me you freak of nature. I'll never be scared of you and I suggest you go back into your old Traveller caravan and stay away from me," Denny replied.

A standoff ensued with Denny never taking his aim of the freaks forehead until Hamish started to retreat to his caravan. Denny started to walk backwards never lowering his gun until he was far enough away from the caravan to be safe. He then stopped, took a big deep breath, and gave a smile that could be construed as being sinister. Today Denny had learned that it felt good when he had another human being in his sights and he knew that he could take somebodies life anytime he wanted to and depending on who it was, with pleasure.

Rain started as he was nearing home and although he was starting to get soaked through the feel of the rifle on his shoulder gave him a very calming effect. As he walked in through the front door his dad came out of his study and greeted him with a lovely smile. Denny knew there was something up. His dad told him to go up and change and come down as he wanted to speak to him. Denny changed and went to hear what his dad had to say. Lachlan sat him down and started to tell him what was wrong with his Mum. He had never heard of alcoholism before, but his dad explained it very softly to him. When Lachlan had finished Denny looked his dad in the eye and asked,

"Is my mum going to die dad?"

"Son, if she doesn't stop drinking and to be honest, I don't think she wants to now. In fact I don't think she can. I have tried to speak to her about getting help from the mainland, but she doesn't want to know. Please remember son she is still your mum and I know it's difficult to understand, but deep down she loves you very much."

Denny walked through to the lounge where his mum was sitting just staring into space. He sat down beside her taking the empty glass from her hand and gave her a long hug, but to be honest what he felt was just skin and bone. He started to cry with the tears streaming down his face. He felt he got a slight response from her but wasn't sure she knew what was happening.

"I love you mum and I don't want you to die," he gently whispered to her.

He left her sitting there as he couldn't think of anything else to say or do and wandered through to his dad and said,

"Dad this is the last time I'm ever going to cry."

Lachlan sat him down and put his arm around him and said,

"I blame myself Daniel for bringing her to this God forsaken piece of rock. I thought we could make a good life for us here, but your mum just couldn't cope and I can't find the person who is giving her the alcohol. If I could then I would not be responsible for my actions."

He then tried to take Denny's mind of his mum by asking about his overnight camping. Denny couldn't wait to tell him about the rifle with the new scope and asked if he could keep it. His dad had agreed, but only if Denny used it safely. He then asked his dad about the Sea Rose. He was told that the wreck had been there for a long time. A father and son had gone out in harsh weather and never returned. It was about a year later that the Sea Rose had washed up on the beach after a storm. No trace was ever found of the father and son. The unforgiving sea had taken them to their watery graves.

Denny broached the subject of the altercation with Hamish. Minus the gun being aimed at Hamish of course. Lachlan's face turned to a rage.

"Let me tell you about that horrible monster," said Lachlan and proceeded to tell him about Hamish's unwanted advances to his mum and how she had continually rebuffed him. This happened when he was out visiting crofts while doing his job and apparently it was happening all too often. Lachlan had confronted him, and he had denied it saying his wife was so far out of it that

16

she didn't know what she was saying. His dad had told Denny never to trust him and never to go near his caravan again. Denny was so enraged that he got up and grabbed his rifle. His dad stopped him, and Denny ran to his room, his face distorted with rage. His dad put the gun back under lock and key.

Chapter 3

Next day was school for Denny, but his dad had told him he would come for him at lunch time as he was going to a funeral. This was going to be a bit strange as he had never experienced this in his young life. When he asked who had died his dad had told him that it was John McDonald and told him how he had greeted his mum and him to the island. When he told him about his truck and Badger. Denny just laughed. After a boring morning which had been disrupted by Scoug playing up as usual he waited at the doors to the school for his dad and it wasn't long before they were walking the short distance to the cemetery with Scoug tagging along behind them.

Denny didn't know how a funeral played out, so he just watched and waited. After a while there was laughter and clapping from the people there which Denny found strange. It was the noise that made him look up to the road that ran down to the harbour. Here was John's pickup truck rattling down the road with the coffin in the back. Somebody wise cracked that if John wasn't dead before he was put in the truck he certainly would be now. Shaken to bits.

Most of the village was there and Denny walked to the graveside holding his dad's hand. Unknown to Denny, Scoug had sidled up and took Lachlan's other hand. The Rev. McGlashan was standing with his Bible and started to give another of his boring sermons with people wishing they were the ones in the coffin. Eventually John was put to rest in his grave and people started to move off. While they were walking back Denny turned to his dad and said,

"Is that it dad? When you die you get put in a hole and get covered in soil. That can't be right dad. Is there not a better way when you die?"

Lachlan had been a bit emotional and struggled to find the right words.

"Son there is nothing surer in this world than dying and it doesn't matter what happens at the end. Your soul leaves your body as soon as you have taken your last breath and that was no longer John in the coffin. Remember son your body is just a container for what is really important, you."

This threw Denny, but he thought his dad must be right. His dad was always right. Denny walked backed to the school with his dad and waved him goodbye.

Over the next few months, he noticed a big decline in his mum, and he had made up his mind that if she wouldn't give him a hug then he would give her one as often as he felt she could manage it. Often that one lonely tear would trickle down her cheek. She wouldn't even wipe it away.

Island life was getting to Denny, and it was getting him down. Every day at school was so repetitive for Denny with Scoug constantly playing up and giving Miss Glover a tough time. He felt sorry for her and often told Scoug to back off, but he knew Scoug couldn't care less.

Soon his life was to change forever. One day as he trudged into class there was a new girl sitting at the desk next to where he sat. Denny couldn't take his eyes off her. She was the most beautiful girl Denny had ever seen in his life. Lovely sparkling eyes and such a lovely smile. Miss Glover introduced her to the class as Helen Fraser and she had come from the mainland to stay with her gran. Her gran was Tinker Maisie who had a cottage just behind the harbour. Maisie's husband had died in a boating accident several years ago and she had survived by doing cleaning jobs which was a bit of a contradiction as Maisie was as black as the Earl of Hell's waistcoat. However, she did a wonderful job and the fishermen, especially the single ones, paid her well. He knew he wanted to get to know this girl, but Scoug had said she was going to be his. Several arguments ensued between them in the following days before Scoug had said some nasty words about Helen which culminated in Denny giving Scoug a good beating. After the beating he turned his back away from Helen who had been watching and smiled. He knew that it wasn't just about Helen, but all the other trouble Scoug had been causing, but why did he have to smile. Denny tried to distance himself from him, but sometimes Scoug would act as if nothing had happened between them.

Helen and Denny had become inseparable and often sat chatting during their school breaks with Helen offering him cakes that her gran had baked. He never refused. Helen had told him that she had ended up on the island because her mum and dad couldn't look after her after they had fallen on challenging times due to drug abuse. She didn't particularly want to come to Durma, but her life in a council estate was awful. She often had to look after herself and she had lost count of the times she had to run to the phone box on the corner of the street for an ambulance for either her mum or dad, sometimes both. She was hardly ever at school as she was having to look after her parents all the time and Social Services were of no use to her at all. Her mum had phoned her gran pleading with her to look after Helen as it was best for everybody. No matter what happened Denny wanted Helen to be part of his life.

Helen always thought how good-looking Denny was and he was beginning to fill out and stood much taller than anybody else in his class even the older boys. She wondered if you could fall in love at twelve years old although she was nearly thirteen. It didn't matter as she knew she loved Denny with all her heart. He always left the house early each school morning so that he could call in for her. Her gran always said the same thing from the cottage door each day.

"Please take care of my precious 'lass' Denny. "

"With my life Maisie, "he always replied. Hand in hand they would stroll to class.

One day a miracle of Biblical proportions happened in class. Miss Glover started a talk on being kind to animals. Little Tommy McCrorie interrupted her.

"Please Miss can I bring my dog to school each day and don't worry he is cleverer than half the idiots in this class?"

Well, the class erupted, and Jenny Boil started to shout,

"Miss, if he brings his dog then I'm bringing my crow as my dad says its far cleverer than me. "

Next up was a lad whose ferret was very clever at catching rabbits and one whose snail was so clever that it kept escaping from its box every time her dad was looking after it. Now the pupils were wanting to bring a menagerie to school each day. After the excitement receded the miracle happened. As they looked to Miss Glover for guidance, they found her laughing her head off at the thought of Durma's Travelling Circus arriving at school each day. The pupils were stunned as they had never seen Miss Glover smile never mind laugh. They all looked at each other and suddenly burst out laughing.

A few weeks after, Denny's dad sat him down and said,

"It's your thirteenth birthday on the thirteenth of Aug and your mum and I would like to give you a party where you can invite all your friends, what do you think? "

All Denny could do was to run over and give him a huge hug. He then ran through to hug his mum, but she wasn't in a clever way, so he just squeezed her hand and gave her a loving smile while kissing her gently on her cheek. He waited for the lonely tear to start coming down her cheek, but today it wasn't going to happen. His dad had said he would buy all the food if he and Helen would organise all the invites, but they had to restrict it to no more than fifteen friends. He was so excited that he ran down to Helen's house and told her what was going to happen. They walked back up to the Foggerty house and started planning. After school they would meet up and exchange ideas with each other. Denny really wanted the whole of his class to come, but he realised that he didn't know a lot of the older pupils apart from Scoug. Helen got the use of his dad's typewriter and printed off some lovely invitations, but Denny insisted that there wasn't to be any presents as he did not want the parents spending money that they could not afford.

It seemed like the days leading up to the party were dragging. One day Denny got a shout from his dad. When he came downstairs his dad was sitting in his study and asked him to sit down.

"I know you have your party coming up son and I don't want to spoil it for you, but I want to speak to you about your schoolwork. I have had a letter from Miss Glover saying that your work is not what it should be. I know the answer as to why that is son. Helen. You want to spend every waking minute with her."

The look on Denny's face said it all. His dad could see how hurt he was, so he quickly said that he did not want him to stop seeing Helen, but just put more effort into his schoolwork. Denny agreed and promised his schoolwork would improve.

This was Saturday the thirteenth and the day of the party. It had been the talk of the school for days. Helen had arrived late

21

morning and Denny and her had started to get all the party food ready. Everybody was to arrive at 1pm. To Denny and Helen something was missing until his dad came through with his Dansette Record player and a large box of single records. The preparations were complete and now all they needed were their friends. At about twelve forty-five they looked out the window and he could see them all coming along the road. They must have all met up at the harbour to walk to the party. Lachlan was looking out of his study and his heart felt so proud. Here were fifteen kids from diverse backgrounds smiling and excitedly laughing as they neared the house.

At the party they ate, danced, and played games, but most of them just laughed and enjoyed themselves like there was no tomorrow. As the party was coming to an end there was the final song and Helen and Denny danced slowly and held each other close as they didn't want to let each other go. After it finished a hush came over the room. Everybody stood stock still and looked towards the top of the stairs. Standing there was Denny's mum. Nobody uttered a word. She was wearing a long black lace dress and had let her hair drape down to her shoulders. Everybody could see what a beautiful woman she was. She walked slowly down the stairs and Helen thought how beautiful she really was. Denny had told her about his mum's illness, but Helen new all about it from her own experiences.

As she reached the bottom some of the boys and girls took a step back as this was the first time most of them had seen Frau Foggerty. Denny walked over, took his Mum's hand, and turned to the boys and girls and said,

"Everyone this is my precious mum and I love her very much."

As his mum squeezed his hand Denny looked round to see his dad at the door to the study with an ear-splitting smile on his face. He gave Denny a slight nod and his son reciprocated. It was time for everybody to go home, but not before the kids wanted to pay their respects to Petra. The first was Jinty Thomas. A wee lass that was as near to an imp as you could possibly get. Jinty didn't care who you were, and she said it like it was. She walked over to Petra and gave her a huge hug leaving a deposit of jam from the party cakes on her dress. Petra didn't mind at all.

"What's your first name Mrs Foggerty? "she asked.

"My name is Petra young lady, "she replied.

"Where did you come from before you landed here? "

"I came from Germany, "replied Petra.

"You came from Germany and yet you ended up on this 'shit hole' of an island Mrs Foggerty. "

Helen thought it might be time to interrupt and hustle Jinty to the side. One by one they came up to Petra and thanked her for the party. She even gave Scoug her little waif from the village a special hug. She always found him comical with his large ears and the big gap between his top front teeth. They all trundled off and Lachlan watched them laughing and joking on their way to their own houses. Petra had walked back up the stairs and when she was at the top Helen said,

"Mrs Foggerty thank you so much for Daniel. It may seem strange at my age, but I love him very much. "

Petra stood and smiled and then walked into her bedroom.

Lachlan had told Daniel to walk Helen home and come back to help him clean up.

On Monday at school the party was all the talk with everybody hoping that they would get a party on their birthday.

For the next few months life on the island was just the norm. Until a buzz went around the village. There was a woman coming to stay with Big Hamish. Everybody thought it was no more than a rumour as nobody knew who she was or really anything about her. To be honest nobody could really believe it. One day a car stopped outside Betty's shop and a beautiful young lady got out and the driver took her bags out of the boot and drove off. This girls face could have adorned the front page of Vogue magazine anytime. She was stunning. Long blonde hair and a slim body to die for. As she waited there it was as if time had stood still. All the fishermen stopped working on their boats and just looked in disbelief. Everyone around the harbour was trying to get a look at her. Where had this angel came from.

One of the fishermen, Ian 'Fish' McLeod, wandered over to her to see if he could help. He only managed to introduce himself and for her to tell him her name was Isla before a car came down the road with its horn blaring. When it stopped Big Hamish got out, grabbed her bags, and put them into the car. Once the girl was in the car and out of earshot Hamish had said,

"Keep away from this girl as she is going to be my wife so keep your leering eyes to yourself. She doesn't need your help so get lost McLeod. "

Ian was at a loss as to what had just happened. Here was a beautiful girl sitting in the front of a car driven by this monstrosity of a man. She could only have been mid to late twenties and Hamish had to be at least fifty if he was a day.

Ian had been nicknamed fish due to his uncanny ability of forever catching a large quantity of crab and lobster whenever he went out when most of the others failed. He should have been called crab but no doubt his nickname originated in Scroggies.

"I will tell you one thing Hamish this beautiful young lady will be a part of my life one way or another whether you like it or not. "

Ian had shouted this out aloud as the car sped away. He was approaching thirty-five years old and ruggedly handsome in his own way. Many of the local girls had hoped that they would get to know him but any relationships he had were just casual affairs. Why he had never left the island was anybody's guess.

Nobody ever saw much of Isla over the following months apart from when she was out walking along the coastal paths. Which was all she ever seemed to do. She did stop and talk to anyone she met though, but she was very reserved and almost shy. Nobody ever saw her in or around the village unless it was sitting in Hamish's car.

When she had arrived, she had been the talk of Scroggies for a while and anytime anyone asked her about where she came from, she tended to clam up. The one person she did willingly speak to was Denny as she often met him when he was on his travels along the cliffs. Once she had looked down to a small beach and Denny was sitting there just watching the sea. She had shouted to him to see if she could come down and sit with him. He just waved for her to come down. They talked for a long time and Denny gave her one of his sandwiches from Helen's gran which she thought was delicious. After a time of just sitting gazing at the sea Isla turned to him and said,

"Do you mind if I call you Denny. I know your real name is Daniel and I know you are only thirteen years old, but can I tell you a few things as I have nobody else to speak to apart from that brute of a man I live with. I have made a lot of mistakes in my life and a big mistake was coming to this island. I made this decision in haste to get away from my parents. They know Hamish and they told me I had to go and live with him to get my head sorted out. The mistakes I have made do not make me a bad person and I just probably needed a bit of love and attention in my life. Denny, please believe me. "

She sat sobbing with her head in her hands.

"Why can't you just jump on the ferry Isla and disappear?" Denny had asked.

"Because I know he will try and find me as he is so jealous. I can't even go down to the shops by myself. I don't want to keep looking over my shoulder all my life. I have told you enough Denny and I'm sorry to have burdened you with this."

Denny wasn't sure he wanted to hear any more as his blood was beginning to boil at the mention of Hamish. He also thought that he didn't want to be the guardian of her secrets and when she said that she was seeing Ian McLeod behind Hamish's back he knew nothing good was going to come from all this. After a while Isla had said that she must be off home and gave Denny a big hug which he found strange as the only female he had ever hugged apart from his mum was Helen. He waved her away and sat back down on the tree trunk they had been sitting on. This had been a lot for him to take in and he felt quite drained. He promised himself though that Isla's secrets were going to be his and his alone. What a strange encounter this had been, and he was going to head home too.

Next morning, he was up early and wandered down to the little beach down the road. He stood at the water's edge with everything that Isla had told him going through his mind. He knew there was nothing he could do and hopefully Ian and her could solve her problems. He thought about his rifle being aimed at Hamish's forehead, but he quickly dispelled the thought. Yet there was that smile appearing on his face again. Why did this always occur when something bad had happened or may happen. Time for school he told himself and headed back to get ready. After picking up Helen they strolled down to the school.

"What's wrong with you today, Denny? You haven't said a

word to me all the way. Just say if it's me that's the problem."

"It's not you Helen I promise. There is so much going through my head at the moment that it hurts. Just let me sort it all out. "

Chapter 4

When they arrived at the school there was a commotion and Denny could see that Scoug was in the thick of it. One boy was accusing Scoug of stealing his lunch pack with Scoug vehemently denying it. Everybody was starting to get anxious, and tempers were beginning to fray. Denny couldn't be bothered with all this as it was not a good start to the school day and his head still hurt.

He quietly walked over to Scoug and asked him if he could have a word with him behind the school. Scoug followed him until they were out of earshot of the rest of the pupils. Denny's sixth sense kicked in and he knew that Scoug had stolen the lunch pack.

"I'm only going to ask you this once. Did you steal that boy's food? I know you did, but I want to hear it from you and why did you do it? You could have always asked me if you were hungry."

"You don't know it was me Foggerty so just get lost and leave me alone."

Denny was foolish to turn his back as Scoug took a swing at him catching him on the side of his head.

"You shouldn't have done that Scougal."

Denny roared as an angry rage started to envelope him. He knew what was about to happen, but there was no way to control it.

He gripped Scoug's jacket and then put him down on the ground with a barrage of punches that would have floored a horse. It happened so quickly that Scoug didn't know what was going on. His nose was bleeding profusely, probably broken, and his eyes were puffed up and starting to close already. Denny kept the onslaught going until Helen and Miss Glover came running round the corner.

"Leave him, please leave him Denny, "Helen shouted.

Miss Glover was trying to pull Denny off Scoug without much success. Suddenly it was over as quick as it had started as Denny stopped and took a few paces back. He knew this was another episode he could not control, and he started to shake

27

uncontrollably. What made it worse, much worse, was the evil smile that came over him. This was beginning to tire him out. He felt Helen wrap her arms around him and hold him as tightly as she could.

"No more Denny, no more," shouted Helen.

"Take him home Helen and I will speak to him tomorrow, "said Miss Glover.

Helen started to lead Denny away, but she could feel him shaking and mumbling incoherently. When she got to the old bench outside Scroggies she sat him down. By this time, he was more himself, so she said,

"Denny, I don't understand what just happened back there. The look on your face was very sinister and evil looking. What is going on with you? I've never seen you in such a state before and to be honest I don't want to ever again."

"I really can't explain what comes over me Helen. It scares me witless, and I'm scared for everyone around me when it happens."

He started to tell her about all the incidents when these sinister looks and feelings came over him. She started to feel very afraid, but this was the love of her life so she just clung on to him as tightly as she could. After a while, the cold was getting to them, so they started walking towards Denny's house. As they stood on the front doorstep, he turned round to her and said,

"Don't worry Helen you'll have nothing to fear when you are with me. I will never let anything bad happen to you. Honest."

They reluctantly said their goodbyes and Helen walked slowly to her gran's house with tears streaming down her face. Denny slowly walked through the door and his dad's face said it all. He knew Miss Glover had phoned him. The look of disappointment was something he never wanted to see again. His dad asked him to sit down, and he would come through and speak to him in a minute. Lachlan knew that the adrenalin would still be surging through his son's body and it was best for Denny to calm down before approaching the subject. Denny couldn't sit still so he wandered upstairs and looked around the door of his mother's bedroom. She lay there very peacefully with her breathing ever so quiet, but shallow. He closed the door and went downstairs and sat with his head in his hands wondering what was happening.

Eventually Lachlan walked through with a glass of water, gave it to Denny and asked him to explain everything that had happened.

"I don't know what comes over me in these situations dad. I get so angry that I lose all control and can't stop. There have been a few incidents lately, but this has been the worst and why is it that an evil, sinister smile comes over me afterwards. It's like I'm enjoying it, but I'm not, I hate it."

Lachlan had no idea what was going on with his son and couldn't give him a rational explanation as to his behaviour. He told him that he should take a couple of days off school to get his thoughts together. He told him that Miss Glover was coming to the house tomorrow to discuss things over, but he would not be involved in the discussions. Denny realised the situation was bad but went along with what his dad had said. His Dad had also told him that he would be speaking to Helen's Gran and Scoug's mother. Denny spent most of the time over the next two days in his room only coming downstairs to eat. He had heard Miss Glover come and go and saw his dad walking down to the village. He was extremely nervous as to what the outcome might be, but whatever it was he would just have to accept it.

That night his dad had shouted him downstairs to discuss the events of the last two days. He explained to him that Miss Glover had said that if this happened again then he would effectively be expelled from school. This in turn would be the finish of their lives on Durma. Helen's gran had been most upset as had Helen. Her gran had said that she would not let Helen have anything to do with Denny in the future unless he could control himself. Jean Scougal had acknowledged that John could be a handful but was disappointed as to the viciousness of the attack. She also explained that John had threatened his dad with a knife that night when he had goaded him about being beaten up by a younger boy.

Lachlan had made a few phone calls to people he knew in the medical profession in Edinburgh to see if they could throw any light as to why his son was behaving like he was. Some had said they weren't sure, and others said it wasn't their field of expertise, but a couple had said they knew exactly what was wrong with Denny. Intermittent Explosive Disorder. It all made sense to Lachlan when he had sat down and thought about it. He decided that he wasn't going to tell his son about what was going on with him, but just hope it was something he would grow out of. Just hope for the best. Rightly or wrongly.

Denny and his dad had agreed that he would go back to school on the third day. That morning he had walked down to the small beach and threw some stones into the sea wondering how everyone would react to him at the school. Eventually he set off after giving his mum and dad a hug. As he approached Helen's house, he decides he would just walk on by as he didn't know how she was feeling. The wind was bitterly cold and blowing hard which matched his mood which got worse when he walked past her door.

"Look after my wee 'lass' Daniel," came a shout from behind him. He looked around and saw Helen giving her gran a huge hug and she walked towards him. She slipped her hand into his and they both started to walk away, but not before Denny turned round and said,

"I always will Maisie."

There was not a lot said as they walked to school, but Denny put his arm around her to try and save her from the wind. As the school gates approached Helen felt a slight hesitation in his step, but she squeezed his hand for reassurance. When they entered the classroom there were a few awkward glances, but the ice was broken when Jinty Thomas shouted,

"He bloody deserved it Denny, well done."

Other shouts started to reverberate around the classroom until Miss Glover entered and the class went quiet.

"I have got some good news for all of you," she said.

"Please tell us that Scougal is not coming back Miss," said Jinty.

"No, it is not that Jinty Thomas and please refrain from your outbursts. Contain yourself young lady. My news is that the Parish Council have decided to hold a pageant in the next few months. The school will choose their own Kismay Queen of the Sea and the activities will centre around the harbour and the sea that is so important to this island. I'll let you know the itinerary and dates as soon as I can. Now before we continue with the lessons are there any questions?" Suddenly a hand shot up. It was Jinty.

"Please Miss when did I become a young lady and what's an itinerary thing? "

All Miss Glover could do was to shake her head and walk away to her desk.

The whole school was excited about the pageant as was the village in fact. The pupils were eagerly talking about who their choice for the Kismay Queen would be. Denny was quite glad as this was a distraction away from him. He still couldn't get his head around what was causing his episodes, and felt his dad was holding something back from him. He decided that he needed to speak to someone other than Helen or his dad and after some deliberation decided to approach Ian McLeod and ask for his advice. One day after school Denny had told Helen that he had to speak to somebody, and he would see her tomorrow. She realised that he was struggling mentally after his fight with Scoug, so she had just smiled and said,

"Love you Denny and I can't wait to see you in the morning. "The weather had been foul over the past few days, so all the small boats were moored up and the fishermen were busy cleaning and doing maintenance. As he was walking, Denny thought he could never see himself doing that job. Scoug's dad was busy working on a boat's engine with more oil and grease on him than on the engine itself.

Denny eventually spotted Ian cleaning some lobster pots and gave him a shout. Ian hailed him over and asked him what was up.

"Ian, can you give me a few minutes of your time so that I can ask you for some advice please?" asked Denny.

"No problem, Denny. There is an old jersey in that box so shove it on and you can help me repair the pots while we talk. Ian started to show Denny how to repair them and before long an hour had passed. Eventually Denny had said,

"I'm sure you will have heard about the fight with John Scougal. Why do you think I am like that Ian? Is there something wrong with me?"

Denny told him about all the other incidents.

Ian continued repairing the pots and after a while he stopped and asked Denny to sit down on whatever he could.

"My answer is simple Denny. Yes, I do think there is

31

something wrong with you. The ferociousness of your outburst to young Scougal was not normal no matter if he had deserved it or not. My worry for you Denny is how easy these feelings come over you. I can tell you exactly what's wrong with you as I have a brother called Willie who lives in the Northeast coast of the mainland. Unfortunately, he has the same explosive nature as you have. "

"Will you please tell me what it is Ian?" said Denny.

Ian looked at him to see if he thought Denny could manage the truth. After a few moments Ian said,

"I am certain that what you have is Intermittent Explosive Disorder. Willie was diagnosed with it from an early age and struggles to control it. He still lives in the same village he was born in and to be honest people are very wary of winding him up. Hence his nickname is Time Bomb ."

Denny just sat there with his head in his hands and wanted to weep. Ian continued repairing the pots to let him have a minute or two to digest what he had just said. After a while Ian put his arm around Denny's shoulder and said,

"Look lad, there is only one person that can control this. That is, you. You must try and not put yourself in these situations where you can just explode. It won't spoil your life, but it may cause you a few problems in the future, but you must fight it, Denny."

Ian carried on with his work until Denny thanked him for his advice and started to walk off the boat. However, he stopped and told Ian about his talk with Isla. Ian said that he knew about it and thanked him for not telling anyone. As Denny jumped off the boat Ian shouted to him that Hamish was not long for this earth. Denny just nodded his head. He thought it best not to say anything to his dad. This was something he had to work out himself.

The next few weeks of schoolwork was drab for him but at least he had the pageant to look forward to. Finally, Miss Glover told them that she was going to announce who had been selected to be the Durma Queen. All the pupils were gathered in eager anticipation. This was the moment.

"The Kismay Queen is Helen Fraser with Jinty Thomas as her Lady in Waiting, "said Miss Glover.

The class erupted with applause and cheering. Helen came over to Denny, but he told her that this was her day and to enjoy it. Lots of hugging was going on and Wee Jinty was running around the classroom waving her satchel above her head. Miss Glover knew when it was time to make herself scarce.

As the pageant neared the whole village was starting to get in the mood. Lachlan had asked Petra if she would like to give Helen one of her white dresses for the day. It would have to be altered, but Petra was more than happy for that to happen. He took the dress to Helen and her gran and asked them if they would like to have it. They were ecstatic about it as it was such a beautiful dress and Lachlan had said he had already spoken to Jeannie Scougal about altering it. Jeannie was extremely willing to help.

The pageant was to be held at the end of June which was only two weeks away. Preparations were at fever pitch as something like this had never happened on Durma before and it rejuvenated the whole village. People were going to celebrate in their own way. Helen and Jinty had to attend some of the Parish council meetings to go over their part in the proceedings which they both found quite boring. This meant that Helen was not seeing that much of Denny, but they both understood. The school had organised for the pupils to form a choir to sing some of the songs they had learned at school which were mainly sea shanties. All of this down to Miss Glover and Miss Bryant. Petra had told Lachlan to go into the chest in the bedroom where he would find two white shawls that she had brought over from Germany, and she would like to give them to Helen and Jinty for their special day. When Lachlan took them to the girl's houses they were overjoyed. Both asked him to thank Mrs Foggerty very much.

Chapter 5

The day of the pageant had finally come and there was not one house that wasn't adorned with some form of bunting. All the colours of the rainbow were strewn across the village. Even Scroggies had tried to clean their windows for the day. Helen's gran had her kitchen table outside her door ready for the pies, cakes, and lemonade for anybody who wanted it. All the other houses had done the same and there was to be a veritable feast in and around the harbour for everybody.

Denny had walked to Helen and Jinty's house that morning to wish them well. Jinty was ' as high as a kite ' and she gave him a huge hug. As huge as it could be seeing she was a small impish girl. He thought she wasn't going to let go. As he started to walk back, he sat on the seat outside Scroggies. He looked over the village and marvelled at how they had pulled together for this day. While he looked at the bunting he wondered if some of the villagers would be going to bed with a patch out of their nightshirts that evening. It made him determined to forget about his own problems for a while. He then walked back to his house to get himself ready for the day.

His dad had explained to him that the festivities would start when the Kismay Queen arrived in at the harbour from around the headland. Denny prayed that the weather would hold as this morning only one sepia shower had started early, but now the sky was clear and holding. Denny decided that he was not going to wear all his new clothes as he felt this was not that type of celebration.

"I'll see you down at the harbour dad," shouted Denny.

He thought his dad must be busy as he never heard a reply. As he started to walk he felt a little spring in his step, but he was under no illusion that his problems had gone away. As he neared the harbour most of the villagers were starting to gather on either side the harbour wall or in front of the houses. A large banner was erected on the railings at the side of the school wishing Helen and Jinty congratulations from all the pupils at the school. The school choir stood next to it and several fishermen had come

34

along with their musical instruments to accompany them. Denny wondered if some of the instruments would make it past several songs. He felt a bit left out as most people were wearing their home-made novelty hats.

He positioned himself on the harbour wall so that he could see the lead boat with Helen and Jinty coming round the headland first. As he stood there, he felt an arm around his waist. It was Scoug's mum. In her hand she held a beautifully made novelty hat.

"I know you're having a tough time son, but I hope you will accept this hat to wear for Helen and Jinty's special day. "

Denny gave Jeannie a hug and told her he would wear her hat with pride. Jeannie started to walk away until Denny had asked her to stop and turn around. Here he was wearing his hat of every imaginable colour. Jeannie just gave a quick laugh and continued walking. A few minutes after she had left Denny heard a noise behind him. He turned to see Talisker Joe banging on the door of Scroggies looking for entry. Unfortunately for him it had been decided not to open until later in the day. Joe was standing cursing until one of the fishermen had walked up and told him to behave himself and go home. Reluctantly he had as this was one exceptionally large fisherman and not one to be messed with.

A few shouts went up that the Queen was on her way, and everyone was starting to get extremely excited. Denny's sixth sense was trying to tell him something, but what? He then turned to see his dad with his mum holding on to his arm walking towards him. Denny almost broke his vow of not crying but held the tears back. They stood there with Petra flanked by her two favourite 'boys' and for once in a long time Denny thought she looked happy. She stood there with her long coat and Cossack hat on drawing admiring glances from all around. Still having a beautiful presence about her.

"Love you mum, "said Denny.

"I love you more than you could ever imagine Daniel," said his mum.

Suddenly, a blare of some sort of horn, probably rams was coming from top of the cliff just past the harbour. Then a peaceful calm came over the village. Everyone just stood there waiting in anticipation.

The sound of the engines from the flotilla was all that could be heard. The first of the boats came into view. It was Ian McLeod carrying the Queen and her Lady in Waiting. Ian had rigged up a handrail so that the girls could hold on to in the event of harsh weather. The place erupted with everyone cheering, clapping, and waving their home-made hats and flags. The young kids were jumping up and down and yelling.

Helen and Jinty were furiously waving to everyone with Jinty still jumping up and down. Their dresses were beautiful, and Petra's shawls were the perfect accompaniment. The cacophony of noise was incredible for such a small village. It was as if somebody had released a valve of pent-up emotion and they were going to let it out, big style. All the other boats were now round the headland and they had all made a great effort to decorate them in any way they could. The noise seemed to get louder as the boats came into the harbour.

Helen had seen Denny as well his mum and dad standing on the banking. She waved and blew kisses to them. Petra let go of their arms and blew kisses back. As she took their arms again, she was smiling.

Denny hadn't seen that in an awfully long time. He too smiled. Ian's boat finally moored next to the steps and the girls walked up holding their dresses slightly up just in case any algae touched the bottom. Helen ran to her gran and held her in her arms and gave her a loving smile.

"Thank you for looking after me gran. I don't know what I would have done without you. "

Helen's gaze turned towards Denny and his mum and dad. She then held her dress up and ran towards them. She first gave Denny a kiss and hug, and then a hug for Lachlan. She stood in front of Petra and said,

"Mrs Foggerty, I don't know how you are feeling, but may I give you a hug please? "

"Of course, you may my dear and may I say how beautiful you look. Not just to today, but every day."

Helen then hugged her and kissed her on both cheeks. Petra had then told her that this was her day and to go and mingle with the crowds. Lachlan had said to Denny to go and enjoy himself as his mum was tired and he was going to walk her home.

The pageant lasted all day where they sang, played music, although not always in tune and ate enough to fill their bellies for a week. Denny had tried not to be with Helen all the time, but she was adamant that she wanted to see him that night. The fading light and the coolness of the early evening had ended the pageant, but as the crowd was leaving the harbour all talk was about how they could better it next year.

The next day Denny had asked his dad if he could take Helen camping in the future but reassured him it would be just for the day, not overnight. He asked if he could teach Helen to shoot. His dad had said fine, but only if she comfortable with it. However, the final say would come from her gran. One Saturday Helen arrived early at Denny's house with her backpack. Excited about going camping. Denny had everything ready, so they started to walk south on the path along the cliffs. Two young lovers oblivious to everything around them. Denny took the south path as that kept him away from Hamish's caravan. He couldn't trust himself. He kept pointing out the small coves and inlets that he had explored previously. Helen was fascinated by his knowledge of the area and weather especially the small caves that she couldn't see until he pointed her in the right direction and gave her the scope to look through.

It wasn't long before the rain started so they ran for a forested area just a bit inland. Denny quickly erected the tent and they both dived in. They both started to laugh and held each other. Their tops were damp, so Helen had suggested they take them off and put on dry ones from their back packs. As she did so she saw Denny looking at her breasts. Slowly she took her bra off and asked him to lie down beside her. She asked him to gently play with her breasts and caress her nipples. This was mind blowing for Denny and he felt a lovely feeling in his groin area, not really realising what was happening. After a while Helen got up and put her bra back on. She wasn't ready for it to go any further. Denny fully understood.

The rain had finally stopped so they both took the tent down and put their wet clothes in their back packs and started for home as the light was now fading. They talked and talked as they walked back, and they agreed they would go camping the following week where Helen might get the chance to try out the rifle. As they arrived at Denny's house Helen gave him a hand to spread out the tent for drying. Afterwards Denny walked Helen home as tomorrow was school for both. When he entered his house, his dad asked him how they got on. Denny had said fine, but his dad thought he was being a bit evasive, so he asked him what was wrong. Denny tried to tell him about him and Helen being intimate but felt embarrassed.

"Never be embarrassed about what you did Daniel as it's the most natural thing in the world. However, I knew this day would come. So, I could give you a talk about it son or you could learn from the book that's in my study. I ordered it from a shop on the mainland about a year ago. It is very educational, but if you don't understand any part of it then please just ask. Remember son you were not the Immaculate Conception. "

Denny took the book and decided he would read it from cover to cover. Whatever he was going to have with Helen then he wanted it to be as good as it could be. He decided not to tell Helen about it just yet. Just to learn as much as he could before he would learn with Helen.

"Dad, can I ask you a big favour please? Is there any chance you could buy me some books on survival techniques? I know I don't have much money saved up, but anything I have I can give it to you. Books that you think I might find interesting."

Lachlan was slightly taken aback hearing this.

"Why this type of book son? "

"Well, I have spoken to you before about how I sense things before they happen and a couple of times I have felt that at some stage of my life I am going to depend on having learned these arts and techniques. "

Lachlan was a bit stunned to say the least, but finally he said,

"Son, how about I get a magazine sent over and it would then be up to you to choose which ones you want from it? "

For Denny days rolled into weeks and weeks into months with no real change in his life. His life was just becoming an existence. Now he understood what the islanders had been saying about their lives.

It was a Saturday morning when Denny was woken up with heavy rapping on his bedroom door.

"Get your scope son and come with me. Isla is missing and

38

hasn't been seen for about a day and a half. The villagers are organising a search party as are the people in Seahaven."

Denny quickly changed and met his dad outside. His dad had told him to put the rifle back as it was only the scope that was needed for searching. Most of the men from village were being organised by retired policeman Mike Stewart. Most carried a backpack and binoculars. Helen wandered up to Denny and asked if she could walk with him.

Half of them were sent on the South coastal path and the rest were heading North. Both parties had flares in case they found anything. After about an hour and with nothing being found they passed Hamish's caravan. Denny quickly sensed something wasn't right.

"Where the heck is Hamish, Mr Stewart. Why is that freak not helping us?" asked Denny.

"Yes, where is he?" asked Ian McLeod.

It was obvious that both Ian and Denny were becoming a bit agitated.

"He felt emotionally drained and didn't feel he could join the search party, "shouted Mike.

Everybody just stood looking at each other with a look of disgust on their faces. Lachlan asked everyone to continue the search as this was not helping to find Isla.

Denny was constantly looking through his scope with Helen by his side. After another 20 minutes they were passing an inlet that Denny knew well. He stopped as there was that six-sense feeling again coming over him. Both Helen and he were being left behind. His dad came running back and asked what was going on. Denny told him that something wasn't right about this place.

"Daniel, we have all had our binoculars on this place and there is nothing to see. There is not even a cave or rocks down there where she might be. So, hurry and catch us up."

Denny took Helen's hand and reluctantly moved on. After several hours they met the party from Seahaven. Mike Stewart radioed into the parties on the South search, but there was no trace of her. All the parties agreed that as the light was beginning to fade, they would head back home and resume the search tomorrow morning.

At first light everyone headed out again. There was not a lot of enthusiasm as to whether they would find Isla alive. Last night had been very cold and if she had fallen into the sea and managed to scramble out then hypothermia would have got to her. There would be no hope for her. Still there was no sign of Hamish and the search party had walked quickly passed his caravan for fear of some sort of reprisal from one of the men. When they got to the inlet where Denny had thought there was something wrong, he stopped.

"Helen, I know there is something wrong about this place and I know we have twice had the scope on it, but my gut is telling me something. "

He was about to start down the old worn path when his dad came running back.

"Daniel if you're not going to keep up then I'm going to ask you to return home. "

Denny was about to argue, but he knew it was futile. His Dad was right.

They searched for most of the day and when they returned to congregate outside the Foggerty home they were exhausted, both physically and mentally. Really drained. Although this was not their first search this felt different. Mike Stewart had told them he was calling off the search. He thanked them for their efforts and would call the mainland and see what they were prepared to do. Denny walked Helen home, but before seeing her to her door they sat on their usual seat at Scroggies. Nothing much was said as Denny's brain was scrambled, and Helen was becoming emotional. It was time to call it a night.

A day later Mike Stewart visited his dad and Denny heard him say that two police officers would be arriving within a couple of days. Denny thought that at least they would interview Hamish and make him confess to what he had done. He walked down to the harbour where he saw Ian McLeod sitting on his boat with his head in his hands. Denny asked for permission to come on board. Ian just looked up and nodded. Denny sat down beside him. He could see he was hurting so he sat and said nothing. Eventually Ian had turned to him and said,

"It is my fault lad. Only a few weeks ago I gave Isla a necklace I had made the last time I went to the mainland. It was

40

a silver fish to remind her of me. I'm quite sure he must have found it and took his rage out on her. "

"Do you think he murdered her Ian and if so where is the body. Where is Isla? "

"There are plenty of places to hide a body on this island lad. I don't know if we will ever find her especially if he put her in the sea. "

Ian could see that a rage was engulfing Denny. He was mumbling things and Ian couldn't understand what was going on, but he knew it wasn't going to be good. He asked him to sit down, and it quickly dawned on Ian that this was exactly how his brother was before he kicked off. Ian left him sitting there and continued working on his boat. After a while Denny said he would like to go home. Ian asked him if he would like for him to walk him up the road. Denny thanked him but said no as he would be all right. Before he left Ian said to Denny that no matter how he felt please leave any retribution to him. A few minutes after he left Ian ran to the phone box and called Denny's dad. He explained what had happened and could he please lock his gun away. Lachlan thanked him very much.

A few days later a car appeared outside Scroggies, and Mike Stewart came up from the village to meet the two people in it. The driver headed back to Seahaven. Standing there were Dc Kevin Keltie and Pc Brian Ronaldson.

"You took your time getting here," said Mike Stewart.

"We just missed booking the ferry after our trip from Inverness. It seems we are booked into this filthy pub by the look of it."

"Let's get this straight the pair of you. Your here to investigate a suspicious disappearance, not on a bloody jolly. Have you got that?" said Mike.

Over the next two days they made very little effort to find out what had happened to Isla. Preferring to spend most of their time drinking in Scroggies. This annoyed the villagers including Denny. On the third morning Denny couldn't take it any longer. At his lunch break he had walked up to the pub and straight over to the pair who were drinking again and said in a loud voice,

"If you two would stop drinking and start doing some detective work instead of sitting on your backsides then you

41

might find out what has happened to Isla. Go and speak to the freak living in his caravan."

The constable stood up and said,

"Look little man just leave us alone and let us do our jobs. "

Denny quickly replied,

"Don't you ever call me little man again, you hear me? "

Ian who had been sitting over by the window quickly got up and hustled Denny out of the door.

"Sit down on that bench and don't come in again. Wait for me please."

He walked back into the pub and stood in front of the two incompetent officers and said,

"Wipe that smile off your face. He's right. You've done nothing to solve this case. All you've done is fill yourselves with whisky. Never even getting your shoes dirtied by walking along the cliff top paths. Oh, and if you value your facial features never tangle with that boy again. I suggest you leave this village as soon as possible. "

A hearty cheer went up.

Ian walked out and told Denny to go home and forget about the incident. Denny did as he was asked, but later he told his dad about the incident. His dad wasn't too pleased, but he thought that the only good thing that came out of this was that Daniel didn't lose control. Denny lay in his room wondering if he had done the right thing in confronting the officers.

Mike Stewart came to the house a couple of days later saying he had been contacted by the Dundee Police. They were not making Isla's death suspicious, and they were filing it as misadventure.

Over the next few months both Helen and Lachlan had found Denny to be very withdrawn. No matter what they said to him didn't seem to bring him out of it. He was spending more and more time with his mum in her room. Often when Lachlan crept up stairs the door would be ajar, and he could see Denny holding his mum. Any conversation was one way. He had to phone Miss Glover to explain Daniel's behaviour and she said she would keep an eye on him. The only time that Denny felt happy was when he went camping with Helen. He found Helen to be an excellent student when it came to learning about shooting. Allowing for the wind and trajectory was something she picked up easily although she had said she wouldn't kill an animal unless it was absolutely necessary.

One day before they left for camping Helen had said,

"Denny, can you bring the Sex Education book that your dad gave you and we can read it together, but can we please be sensible about it."

She could see Denny looking at her quizzically.

"How do you know about the book Helen? "he asked.

"It was when I was waiting for you last week. Your dad inadvertently told me about it. It was a mistake so don't be cross with him. "

Denny decided to leave it at that and was happy that she had suggested bringing the book along. He thought that they should walk south along the cliff top path as something was still bothering him about the inlet North of Hamish's caravan. The weather was starting to get brutal, so they started to head inland a bit and after finding the only bit of shelter in some trees they hitched the tent. They sat and happily talked about anything except Isla. No amount of talk would bring her back. She was gone for good.

Helen had brought all the food and lemonade. Her gran had made some mutton pies and Denny found them to be delicious. After they had finished Helen suggested that they start reading the book together. Before they got started, she suddenly said,

"Denny, please don't think that every time we are together in the tent or in your house alone, I'm going to take my top off for you as I want each time to be special. We are nearly fifteen so the more we know the better it will be when we do finally make love. "

Denny said he was fine with that. They started to read the book which gave them quite a few surprises. Denny was starting to get aroused, but knew he had to hold back no matter how difficult it was. The difficulty was that Helen had cuddled into him and he could feel the warmth from her body. After about an hour of intense reading they lay back and cuddled. It wasn't long before they fell asleep in each other's arms. When Denny awoke, he looked down at Helen and thought how much he loved her. However, he knew that at some point it was inevitable he was going to leave her behind.

He knew that his future wasn't on this island. He didn't know if it was the island or him that was cursed, and he had already had one demon hanging over him. On speaking to his dad, he had said that due to his uncontrollable bouts of rage it was best if he left so that when these bouts happened then there would be nobody there who he loved to see them.

Chapter 6

A short memorial service was held at the church for Isla.

Although most people hadn't known the girl, they turned out in their numbers to pay their respects. The service was quite moving, even for the Rev. McGlashan. The mood of the villagers changed when the doors opened and in walked Hamish. He just stood at the back. Head down not making eye contact with anyone. A considerable number got up and left the church as Hamish stood there sobbing into a dirty handkerchief. As they walked past him, they just turned their heads away.

Denny, who was standing with his dad watched this charade play out until he couldn't stand it anymore.

"You're not fooling anyone with your crocodile tears you freak. The whole island knows you have murdered Isla. Have the decency to tell us where the body is," he shouted as he passed.

"This is the House of God. Please be respectful," shouted the reverend.

"This is just four walls with a leaking roof over them. God left us a long time ago," came a comment from one of the villagers.

Lachlan thought it prudent to take Denny out of the church before anything kicked off. The church emptied very quickly. Even Miss Glover left giving Hamish her evil eye on the way past. Everybody dispersed and headed to their own homes. Helen was tearful as she would have liked a nicer memorial service for Isla. Denny took her up to her house and told her not to worry as he was certain Hamish would come to an untimely end.

"Denny please tell me you are not going to do anything stupid, "said Helen.

He tried to tell her about Hamish's unwanted advances to his mum. Helen's whole demeanour change in a second. There was actual rage in her eyes.

"I hope when he meets his end it will be long and painful Denny," she said.

Denny had never seen her like this, so he just held her until he felt the rage subside. He knew what that was all about.

Next day word went out that Hamish was leaving the island. For how long nobody knew, but they guessed he was running from his actions. Ian had been waiting since dawn as he had found out Hamish was booked onto the ten o'clock ferry at Seahaven.

At about eight he could see his car coming over the brow of the hill. As it was passing Ian picked up one of his lobster pots, ran forward and threw it through the passenger window of his car. Hamish swerved but corrected it. He knew better than to stop the car and engage in anything with Ian. His car was last seen heading toward Seahaven. A call was made soon after to the Harbour Master to make sure he was on the ferry and to let Kismay know if he ever returned. He never did.

Two days after, Ian and a few fishermen had gone up to his caravan, cleared the stones from the back wall, set it ablaze and pushed it over the cliff. Calm came over the village and people started to get on with their lives.

Over the next few months, the only thing that was different was Betty May's health had started to deteriorate. Her son had arrived on the island to try and persuade her to leave and come and stay with him and his family. The villagers were surprised due to the fact that nobody knew she had a family. Betty had finally conceded that she really wasn't up to it anymore. She then told the Parish Council that she would give them three months to find someone else.

Over the next few weeks Denny became quite close to Ian. He liked talking to his dad but speaking to Ian was like speaking to a brother he didn't have. He and Helen were out with the tent most weekends and agreed that they would try experimenting on each other with the help of the book. Denny thought it wouldn't be long before they finally made love. All their experimenting was concluding, and they were happy that they had waited. He made up his mind that he would never have sex with a lady, always make love to her no matter what.

One day while out walking Helen told him that she intended leaving school to take over her gran's job of cleaning and baking for the villagers as her gran wasn't keeping very well. He told her that he was expecting it and was glad as he knew she hadn't been enjoying school anymore.

"I'll still be expecting you to come in and see me in the morning and when school is finished," she said.

As they hugged Denny said,

"It will all work out Helen trust me. "

Denny knew he had to decide on his own future. It was okay sitting talking to his dad about it, but he needed to act on it. First thing in the morning he would speak to Miss Glover and Miss Bryant. To ask for their guidance. It would be a start.

The one thing that Denny did know was that he was going to leave this island. It now felt claustrophobic to him. However, he always thought that nothing could frighten him, but leaving the comfort and security of the island might well do. Next day he spoke to them. Both teachers agreed that they had gone as far as they could with his education. Legally at fifteen years he didn't have to attend any more. Miss Glover did make a suggestion. That until he knew what he was going to do then why didn't he use the extensive school library and if he wanted different books then he should ask his dad to buy them for him. She said it might be an idea to use one of the rooms in the school to work his way through the books and she would be there if he had any difficulties.

"Daniel you're an intelligent boy but try not to let your demons drag you down. At times you have been a breath of fresh air to this school," said Miss Glover.

He thanked them both for giving him something to consider.

The books that he had asked for had surprised his dad to say the least. The two books on explosives surprised him the most. Denny had sat down with him and explained that one of his choices was to enrol in the army. So, it made sense to get a head start. His dad had told him that whatever he chose to do would be fine by him and his mum. Denny was becoming frustrated though. Trying to work out what he really wanted in life. The thought of him staying on the island and ending up a fisherman like Ian did not appeal to him one bit. He knew he had only a couple of years before taking the plunge and heading off into a new, but very scary world.

He had started to exercise more by doing a lot of running in all weathers. The exercise was making him fill out and with his hight of six feet and still growing it made him a very imposing

47

figure indeed.

He had only seen Scoug on a rare occasion. When he did it was a bit awkward between them. With often just a glare coming from Scoug or a nod at best as they passed each other. He had often wondered what Scoug had been doing with himself since he hadn't been at school. He knew it couldn't have been easy with a dad like him. Joe had been making an absolute menace of himself while touting for work around the harbour and especially in Scroggies when scrounging for drink. The weather had been foul over the last few weeks and the fishermen were hardly making money so buying Talisker Joe drink wasn't an option.

Lachlan knew it would only be a matter of time before his son left the island. He didn't want him arriving on the mainland for the first on his own so he had concocted an idea to ask him to go to Edinburgh to pick up some Veterinary supplies that he could not trust any supplier to deliver safely. He had asked Denny to come into his study one night and mentioned to Denny to see if he could help him out by going to Edinburgh the following week for three days.

"Are you sure about this dad as I am still only fifteen. I don't want to let you down," said Denny.

His dad pulled his chair next to him and said,

"Daniel, I promise you won't let me down. I have the utmost confidence in you."

Denny had thought about asking if Helen could go with him but knew she wouldn't leave her gran. He knew that being tied down looking after her would be a problem at some stage. He then asked his dad a question that no fifteen-year-old should have to.

"Dad how long do you think my mum has to live? "

"I can't give you an exact length of time Daniel, but I can tell you I found out who was supplying her with the alcohol. It was one of the workers on the ferry and he had asked his mate who lived in Kismay to deliver it to her. Neither of them has a job on the ferry now and the guy who lives in Kismay was asked to leave the island a month ago. She no longer drinks, but the alcohol has taken its toll on her organs, and they will never recover. They will slowly shut down and that will be the end for your mum. "

Denny just sat there staring at his dad before getting up and going upstairs. He popped his head around the door and was surprised to see her sitting up on the bed.

"Come and sit beside me for a while Daniel. I'd like to tell you about a few stories from my youth when I lived in Germany. "

Denny propped up the pillows and sat down beside her. Holding her hand, she told him about her time living in the Bavarian Forest with her family. This had surprised him as he had never heard her talk about it. He knew she was German, but she never talked about her family. He asked if she had any brothers or sisters.

"One sister Daniel, but she left our family a long time ago. You see our family was on the 'wrong' side during the Second World war. Our family made a choice, the wrong one according to the rest of Europe. My grandfather wasn't a nice man for reasons I don't want to talk about. It would pain me too much. I really hope you can one day go back to where I grew up. See our log cabin in the woods. I certainly hope Max our family caretaker is still living there. "

Denny thought her mind was beginning to wander and her eyes were beginning to close. He laid her back, put a pillow under her head and pulled the covers over her. Before he left, he kissed her gently on her forehead and whispered good night.

When he got downstairs, he asked his dad if they could have a chat. He asked him about where his mum came from and about the log cabin in the forest. His dad explained that his mum's family were very wealthy after the war, but it had caused a real upheaval within the family. It was just politics as some members did not want to receive help from money made during the war. There is a large family house in Zwiesel and a beautiful log cabin close to there.

"Your mum's family were quite wealthy in their own right before all the goings on. I can tell you this Daniel. Your mum and I have made provisions to leave you a very, very considerable sum of money when you reach twenty-five years old. It is lodged with a bank in Edinburgh and on your twenty fifth birthday they will contact you to see what you want to do with the money. "

"I don't know where I'll be in ten years dad so how will they know where to find me?"

"Don't worry about that son they will. "

Tomorrow would be Saturday so Denny, although it was late, walked down to see Helen to ask her what they were going to do. Helen had said why don't they go camping, but what she said next both surprised and excited him.

"We'll have a lovely day camping, but we don't need to take the book with us. "

He knew what might happen, but also knew he had better not get too excited. The book was adamant that getting over excited would make it less enjoyable.

It was eight o'clock when the sun poured in through the crack in the curtains of Denny's bedroom. He got up and washed before going down for some breakfast. Helen would be here in half an hour. He had to get the tent ready, but today he was leaving the rifle and scope at home. After some toast Denny went out and sat on the doorstep waiting for Helen. She was running late, but he just sat there letting the sun rays hit his face. Sun on this island was a bonus so he was going to enjoy it.

Eventually he turned to see Helen walking up with her backpack. He gave her a kiss and a hug then they walked holding hands towards the coastal path going south. He still couldn't walk past the inlet where his sixth sense had kicked in during the search for Isla.

"Denny, do you know a secluded beach we can go to today and pitch our tent? "

"We're about half an hour from a lovely little cove but be careful as the path down is not very stable."

"I'll be fine as I know I have you to help me. "

It wasn't long before Denny announced they had arrived. Helen really couldn't see anything at all until he took her hand and walked over to the edge of the cliff. On looking down she saw the most beautiful beach imaginable. She never thought that this place could ever exist on Durma. He took all the bags and lead her by the hand to a very rough path leading down to the beach. They both had to be careful not to lose their footing until eventually they stepped onto the beach. The sand was so fine and silvery with absolutely no flotsam having been brought in by the tide.

Denny pitched the tent and put all the bags inside just in case.

This was a beautiful sunny day for the island, but the weather could change in a heartbeat. Helen suggested that they eat what provisions she had brought, courtesy of Helen's gran. They sat there just eating and looking at the sea. Both giving the occasional glance at each other. Both thought that if this was love then they wanted increasingly more of it.

Helen suddenly got up and said,

"Let's go for a paddle Denny. Don't just sit there."

He couldn't believe what he had just heard.

"Are you mad the water will be freezing. "

He watched her run down to the sea, so he stood up and thought why not. Just as he had got his socks and shoes off, he looked up to see Helen at the water's edge stripping all her clothes off. He couldn't take his eyes away from the beauty of her nakedness with the sunlight bathing her in a golden glow. He couldn't get his clothes of quick enough, but Helen laughed when his foot caught in his trouser leg, and he fell over. As he waded in it was as he had expected, freezing. She was oblivious to the cold. She was laughing and splashing, and Denny thought she looked deliriously happy. She walked over to him and put her arms around him. He held her tight and felt her hard nipples against his chest. It was beginning to get cold and not very complimentary to his manhood. He was beginning to lose the circulation in his feet, so he led her out of the water and guided her towards the tent.

They sat rubbing their bodies with the towels to get some heat into them. Afterwards the sand was next to be cleaned off from their feet. The look between them said it all. After all the days sitting in the tent reading the sex education book, they both knew what was about to happen.

They lay back holding each other and started to kiss. Denny could feel a nervous energy coming from Helen and she was holding him tighter than she had ever done before. He started to gently fondle her breasts before lightly kissing her nipples. There were slight murmurs coming from Helen and she put her leg over his. He put his hand down between her legs to find her as wet as she could ever be. Helen shifted her hand down to hold his hard penis and they both knew it was time.

She pulled Denny on top of her and after a bit of fumbling and awkwardness he very gently entered her. She only gave a few groans and tensed her body ever so lightly, but she was determined to give her whole body to him. He wanted to make love to Helen not have sex with her, so he slowly started to rock back and forward. He knew by the look on her face and the quiet moans she was giving out how much she was enjoying it. He couldn't believe how natural this felt to him.

After a while Helen started to move her body in rhythm with his and their love making starting to become a little more energetic. It made them feel so alive. Eventually Helen started to climax with gasps of pure joy. Her nails digging into the skin of his back. She had never thought how good this could be. Denny climaxed soon after and on feeling this Helen wrapped her legs around his waist tightly not wanting to let him go.

Denny eventually pulled out and they lay beside each other not saying a word as neither could believe how wonderful it had just been. It didn't matter how much the temperature was dropping in the tent as all the heat they needed was coming from their bodies.

As they lay there Denny turned to her and said,

"Helen, I think we've just made a big mistake. "

"Denny, what are you talking about, didn't you enjoy our lovemaking? "

"Of course I did Helen it's just that don't you remember what the book said was the most important thing. We had to use protection and we didn't."

She took his head in her hands and said,

"Oh Denny, my beautiful boy don't worry yourself. My gran and I visited Doctor Henderson at Seahaven several weeks ago to ask if I could go on the contraceptive pill. I never told you as I didn't want you getting anxious and rushing this beautiful moment that we have just had."

He had never felt so relieved in his life. As the sun was starting to disappear Denny knew that the cold was going to end their memorable day, so he suggested that they clean themselves with their towels and start packing up. Neither of them spoke much on the way home. Helen felt as if she could float all the way. Denny dropped off the tent with his rucksack at his house and walked her home. Plans were made to see each other the next night as she wanted to spend a bit time with her gran throughout the day.

The next day Denny spent a lot of time with his mum who seemed to be at her happiest when she was regaling him with her tales of Bavaria. It tired her though and she would often fall asleep before she finished the story.

At seven o'clock Denny started to walk down for Helen, but his mind was in a turmoil. He hadn't been sleeping well lately and was beginning to be plagued by really awful dreams which often culminated in nightmares. What he wasn't looking forward to was how he would tell Helen that at some point he was going to leave the island. When he arrived at the harbour, he saw Helen sitting on the bench just down from Scroggies. As he sat down beside her he leaned over and gave her a long lingering kiss.

"Denny, do you mind if we just sit here for a while and watch all the boats dancing up and down on the water? "

He was quite happy with that as he thought it would have a soothing effect on his mind. He decided not to tell her about his thoughts on leaving the island as yesterday had been wonderful. They were not sure how long they could stay there as the light was nearly gone and the sky was heavy with rain clouds. Denny thought he could hear the slight rumble of thunder out in the Sound and told Helen they might have to run for shelter at any moment.

Just when they thought it best to leave, they heard an almighty commotion coming from Scroggies. They could just about make out shadows through the windows of what looked like people fighting, but they weren't too concerned as this was a common occurrence. Suddenly the doors to the pub were thrown open and someone came flying through them landing on the ground. Helen was about to go and help him, but Denny's instinct was to hold her back. Somebody came out and grabbed the man, hauled him up and gave him a punch in the face.

"Don't you ever steal my whisky again you lowlife," shouted the man.

Denny didn't recognise the large man, but he did recognise the man he had punched. It was Talisker Joe. Scoug's dad. His nose was lying to one side and his lip was split. Blood was coming from both injuries. Denny's sixth sense told him that something bad was going to happen.

Denny shouted,

"Let him be now as he's finished. Please don't hit him anymore."

The man glared at Denny and was about to walk towards him until Denny took a few steps forwards. The man could see how formidable Denny was, so he backed off and went back inside.

Denny knew he should intervene, but Helen was shocked and had started to cry. He put an arm around her and was about to walk her home when laughter started up in the bar. Talisker was standing unsteadily on his feet. He was crying. Having been humiliated in front of all the people he knew.

Slowly, Talisker walked and opened the doors to the pub. He just stood there wiping the blood from his mouth and nose and flicking it onto the sawdust on the floor.

"You all think I'm a joke, don't you? Just because I don't have a boat of my own you think you are better than me. Well just watch."

The fishermen were still laughing and one or two of them were shouting at Talisker to go home. He staggered down the cobbles towards the harbours edge. Denny was getting worried when he saw him jump onto one of the lobster boats. Suddenly the boats engine roared into life. Talisker, having worked on most of the boats knew where the men kept the spare key hidden. Denny started shouting at him to stop while he ran up and into the pub.

"Please help as Talisker is intending to take a boat out. Quick."

Silence descended over the pub and when they heard the noise from the engine, they all scrambled over each other to get out of the doors. Denny then told Helen to start going home and not to look back. They all stood there in disbelief at the sight of Talisker starting to take the boat out towards the harbour entrance. Some were saying that he would bottle it soon and turn the boat around. To Denny nobody was doing anything, but there wasn't anything they could do. Suddenly the boat slowed down and they all thought he was about to turn around, but Talisker turned, faced everyone, and gave them a defiant two finger salute.

He revved up the boat's engines again just as the rain started to come down in 'sheets' with the wind starting to get wild.

Denny was pleading for the fishermen to do something until a hand gripped his shoulder. It was Ian.

"There is nothing anybody can do Denny. He is not thinking straight as he is full of whisky. Let's hope he turns around." They stood there watching and shouting for him to come back. Some were bent over with their head in their hands. Others had run to the sea wall to shout to him. Talisker had not put any lights on and managed to scrape the harbour wall as he headed for its mouth. From the harbour it was straight out into the Scarra Sound and then the Atlantic Ocean. With no lights and a moonless night, they were finding it difficult to try and pinpoint where he was.

An almighty crack of thunder startled them all. This was Talisker's only hope now. That the imminent thunderstorm would drive him back. Quietly the men stood on the sea wall until nobody could hear the boat's engine. Only darkness lay before them. The blackness of their mood matched the colour of the sky. Ian walked over to Denny and said,

"Every man, woman and child know the weather forecast both day and night son. It appears he has a death wish. There is always a very slight chance he may be able to turn the boat around but remember Denny he doesn't even know how to sail a boat. Go home son. We will keep a vigil for the next few hours."

"No Ian I want to go and tell Jean and John. They need to hear it from someone they know."

Denny started to run to their cottage. When he got there, he stopped. He didn't know what he was going to say. After a few minutes he got himself together and knocked on the door. Jean didn't answer the door right away. She asked who was knocking and he said it was Denny. Slowly the door opened, and Jean stood there and said,

"Mercy your soaked through son what is going on? "

"Jean I'm sorry, but I have some shocking news for you and John. "

Denny told her what had happened and how all the men had tried hard to get her husband to turn back and that they were keeping a lookout for him.

Slowly a large smile appeared over her face. Denny felt a bit unnerved by this.

"Go home Denny and give your mum and dad a hug and get

yourself changed into something warm. I'll tell John when he comes in."

Denny couldn't think where John would be on a night like this. As he walked away, he turned only to see Jean looking towards the harbour with the same broad smile on her face. He ran back to the sea wall where some of the men were standing. They had all gone to their boats to retrieve their oilskins and stand their watch. There was nothing he could do so he decided to head home.

As he trudged past Scroggies the doors were open and he could see all the men waiting for their turn to be lookout. Obviously, there were copious amounts of whisky being consumed, but there was no merriment and everyone was just sitting in silence. When he got to the small beach before his house he could see the waves being dashed against the rocks. He started to feel the bitterly freezing wind seep into his bones. He quickly tried to put Talisker out of his mind.

When he arrived home his dad was shocked at his dishevelment and before Denny could explain his dad told him to go up and change before coming down and then tell him what was going on. Lachlan had made some sweet tea and gave Denny a steaming mug full. After a while Denny felt he was all right to tell everything to his dad. Lachlan was pretty shook up, mainly due to the fact that his son had been witness to this.

Suddenly Denny jumped up, ran, and picked up the phone. He had forgotten to call in on Helen. Eventually her gran answered and told him she was tucked up in bed sleeping. Denny just wanted to cry, but he had made that pledge to his dad that he would never cry again. Lachlan suggested that he finish his tea and head off to bed.

Not a lot of sleep came to him that night and when it did the awful nightmares were quick to start. Denny thought that he was cursed, and his demons were beginning to consume him.

He was awoken the next morning by voices downstairs. He got himself dressed and went downstairs, but not before popping his head round his mum's bedroom door. She was sleeping peacefully. When he went down into the living room Ian was standing there speaking to his dad. Ian had all his wet weather gear on, and he looked like he didn't get much sleep last night either. He asked Denny how he was and if he was up for coming with several of the men to walk round the cliffs in the off chance that Talisker's boat had made it back to land. Denny had agreed, but Ian had warned him that if, and it was a big if, they found anything then it might not be very pleasant.

The men started walking, but their body language said it all. This would be a fruitless search. They were very meticulous as they walked. If they spotted any bit of wreckage, then they climbed down to inspect it. When Denny passed by the small inlet where he had felt that strange feeling on the search for Isla, he wasn't expecting anything as before. However, there it was, more intense than ever. He tried to blank his mind from it.

After another two hours of walking Ian called a halt to the search. All the men stood silently looking at the sea in what seemed to be an inaudible prayer. Three hours later they had dropped Denny off at his house and dispersed to their own homes. He couldn't settle so he decided to walk down to the harbour. As he approached, he saw Scoug standing on the harbour wall looking out to the sea. He wondered if he should go over and say something. That decision was taken away from him as a hand gripped his arm. It was Jean, Scoug's mum.

"Leave him to grieve in his own way son. He wasn't the best dad, but he was still his dad. You might never see John again as he leaves for the army next week. "

This didn't surprise Denny as he felt Scoug was a lost cause with a tormented soul. Something inside him thought that he might end up like that too.

Chapter 7

Over the next few months Denny's world had become confusing for him. He became agitated very easily and struggled to concentrate on anything he did especially reading at the school. His dad knew something was wrong, so he said it was time to go to Edinburgh and pick up his veterinary supplies which they had talked about. Denny immediately said he would as he needed to escape this island.

His dad made the arrangements and told Denny that he would drive him to Seahaven the next morning. The night before he left, he had been out walking with Helen and before they said good night, Helen had said,

"Denny please don't take this the wrong way, but I have a feeling that at some stage soon you are going to leave the island and leave me. You don't have to say anything as I understand. I love you more than life itself and I would do anything for you, but our lives are going to go in different directions and there is nothing we can do about it."

For once Denny was lost for words. He kissed her and told her he loved her. Helen held back the tears until she had started to walk away and had her back to him.

By eight o'clock the next morning Denny and his dad were on their way to catch the early ferry. He felt quite excited about it, but was also very apprehensive as this was the first time he had done this journey of such magnitude on his own. The ferry docked in the port of Mayfort and from there he would get a bus overland to Inverness. He had come to the mainland a couple of times with his dad as a youngster, but this was a completely different ball game for him.

The journey was awful as the rickety bus seemed to stop at every small village for anybody standing on the side of the road with their arm out. This was not going to be the great adventure he thought it might be. Fortunately, he had brought a new book which his dad had purchased for him. So that kept him busy for a while, but at times he thought that he might have to get out and help push the bus up some of the hills.

After sleeping for a while he was woken up by the bus driver shouting that they had arrived in Inverness. His dad's instructions were clear. Get to the train station and purchase a ticket to Edinburgh. The walk was further than he imagined, and he had to ask several times to make sure he was going in the right direction. When he entered the station, he knew he had to find the ticket booth for his purchase. There it was. Sat behind the booth window was a guy who didn't really want to be there and after a bit of surly banter with the guy Denny had his ticket to the Capital city. He was going down the east coastline. He was prepared for another long journey, so he took a window seat and sat back. There was no sleep for him this time as the marvel of all the scenery blew him away. He had never seen such beauty. People were walking about with short sleeved shirts and shorts on. The sun looked like it was splitting the sky. He thought he was on a different planet. Beautiful beaches with lots of kids playing games and some were actually swimming.

After several hours Denny's train arrived in Edinburgh. When he exited the station he turned right and walked towards the road where all the people, cars and buildings were. The map his dad had given him said this was Princes Street. He was awestruck. He had to hold on to the railing that was around a huge garden. Denny couldn't comprehend why a huge garden was in the middle of the city.

He had to sit on one of the benches and just take it all in. He felt so out of his depth that he put his head in his hands. It only took a few minutes for him to come to terms with what was happening around him. Whatever this was he wanted to be a part of it. His instructions easily took him to the small hotel his dad had booked for. Denny ate in the hotel that night, and afterwards decided to go for a walk. He wasn't sure this was entirely safe, but he needed to see more of this city.

He just walked and walked taking in the sights, but always keeping Princes Street within eyesight. He kept himself to himself until he came to a place named Rose Street. He had never known a place so busy. Single people walking alone and then you had the couples and the groups of both males and females. Music came out of every pub and the noise was overpowering. He couldn't believe how little clothes some of the ladies were wearing. If they dressed like that on Durma then they would die of exposure in no time. He was tired and decided to walk home. Just as he came to the end of the street three lads were starting to hassle a young lady who had been leaning up against a pub window.

She was asking them to leave her alone, but they were drunk and started to touch her breasts. One of them tried to put his hand up her skirt. She shoved him away but got a backhanded slap for her effort. Denny's sixth sense told him to walk away, but he couldn't. He knew it wasn't going to end well for them. He walked towards them and said,

"Please leave her be. As you can see you are upsetting her. "

The three of them turned round and faced Denny. The smaller one in the middle looked like he was pushing his chest out knowing he had his big mates either side of him. He was covered in gold rings and chains. Slicked back hair and a gold tooth in the front. Denny could tell he was the weak link of the three. He really didn't want anything to do with this, but he felt he had no option.

"Go fuck yourself. Do you know who I am? Thomson is my name and after we've given you a right good kicking, you'll remember it in your dreams 'dick head.' "

Denny started to feel the rage coming over him, but he was trying hard to control it.

"I really don't care who you are with your pathetic gold tooth, girly necklaces, and big watches. You are beginning to annoy me so please just walk away or the three of you will regret it."

The two taller guys kept looking to the middle one for guidance until Thomson shouted,

"Get him boys and make it good. Make him remember my name."

The two started to come at Denny but the one on the left gave a slight hesitation. This was what Denny had been waiting on. His rage was now upon him, so he took a couple of steps, deflected a swing from the guy, and punched him so hard it lifted him off the ground. He lay prone on the cobbles as the one on the right moved in, but with no real conviction. Denny feigned to hit him with his right and as the guy tried to duck out the way Denny hit him with a left uppercut that took his bottom teeth out. With his rage in full flow, he started to pummel the faces of the two lackeys until they were just a bloody pulp. Thomson looked frightened but produced a knife from under his coat and ran at Denny but this guy was a loser, the proverbial coward. He quickly grabbed his arm and let a powerhouse of a punch go at his nose. His nose spread over his face, and he lay on the ground whimpering. Denny wasn't finished with him yet. He started punching his penis and testicles time after time until he felt arms go around his waist. He was in such a state he thought this was Helen grabbing him, but when his focus came back, he realised it was the girl the three goons had been hassling. The girl had said he had better leave quickly before the police arrived but thanked him for thinking about her.

As he started to leave sweat was running off his face. He was smiling and wondered if anybody who had witnessed the incident had seen him smile and that they thought he was evil. Maybe he was. He took a quick glance behind him only to see Thomson lying vomiting on the ground. Denny's chest started to heave up and down and at times he struggled for breath. He walked for a while until he found a low wall where he could sit for a moment. Blood was all over his scraped knuckles, so he quickly tore his handkerchief into two strips and wrapped them tightly around his hands and put them in his pockets.

He had no idea how long he had been sitting there when the sound of sirens gave him a bit of a fright. He sat low making himself less conspicuous. This was the first time he had ever seen a police car, or an ambulance and he marvelled at the speed at which they were travelling. Denny knew exactly where they were going so, he thought it best to head back to his hotel.

He lay on top of the sheets with his clothes on that night as he knew there would be no sleep for him. The guy Thomson was right though. Denny couldn't help remembering his name as the incident played out repeatedly in his head all night. He thought that his demons had followed him to Edinburgh. In the morning he bathed and patched up his knuckles the best he could.

When he came out of the bathroom there was a knock on his door. It was the owner telling him breakfast was ready. After dressing he walked down to the breakfast room.

"I took the liberty of making you a full Scottish breakfast

with lashings of toast and butter, "said the owner.

As he placed the plate down, he noticed Denny trying to hide his blooded hands. However, he left him to eat his breakfast in peace. When Denny had finished the owner walked through and sat down at the table.

"You can tell me to mind my own business son, but I take it you were in a bit of bother last night. On the radio at six o'clock this morning the Scottish news reported a disturbance in Rose Street where three guys had attempted to assault another guy. I say attempted as the tall guy kicked the 'shit' out of them. The three are in hospital and although their injuries are not life threatening, they will have facial disfigurement for the rest of their lives. Oh, and one of them won't be planning to have a family soon, if ever. Unfortunately, one was the son of the biggest crime boss on the east coast primarily based in Dundee. Thomson is his name. "

The hotel owner was Robert Trapp and he had gone on to say it was best that Denny did his business for his dad and leave Edinburgh earlier.

"Don't worry son. Nobody will come looking for you as they will think its gang related and by the time the guys in hospital can even speak, they won't remember a thing. Now here's the thing Daniel I knew both your mum and dad very well from their time in Edinburgh so do I phone and tell them what happened, or do we keep it between ourselves? "

Denny said that keeping it between them would be much appreciated and he was going to pack and leave Edinburgh as soon as possible. When he went down to pay Robert had refused his money.

"You've not had a particularly good introduction to our Capital city have you son, so you don't have to pay me. When you get to Inverness try and find a lovely gift for your mum who I believe is not very well. "

Denny had asked Robert where the location of the veterinary supply company was and fortunately it was only two streets away. After collecting his dad's parcel, he headed back up to Princes Street, crossed over the road and walked along beside the gardens. This was a rare pleasure for him as nothing seemed to grow on Durma except wildflowers and grass. Just before he turned down the road to the station entrance he stopped for a few minutes and looked all around him. This was truly a magnificent city, and he knew he would be back. However, it had been too much for him on this occasion.

The train journey to Inverness was uneventful. In one way he was sad to leave Edinburgh, but relieved in another way. As they passed through Dundee a shiver went down his spine. When the train arrived in Inverness, he had time to spare before catching the bus, so he headed into the street market to look for a present for his mum.

A lot of the stalls were just rubbish in his eyes, but he spied a beautiful silver broach with a small piece of heather encased in glass. He hoped his mum would like it. He had phoned his dad from the hotel to say he was coming back and could he book him on the ferry as soon as possible. Lachlan said he would do it right away and for Denny to phone him in half an hour. His dad asked him if there was anything wrong, but Denny reassured him that everything was fine.

By four in the afternoon, he was back on Durma. He couldn't say he was happy about it as Edinburgh was continually in his thoughts. When he got to his house, he quickly showed his dad the broach he had bought for his mum and asked if he could go upstairs and show it to her. Lachlan thought that would be nice and then he should come downstairs and tell him all about his trip.

Denny quietly went up to his mum's bedroom just in case she was sleeping. When he put his head round the door, she was sitting up sipping a glass of water. She noticed him and said,

"Come in my beautiful boy, sit on the bed beside me and tell me all about Edinburgh "

Denny propped some pillows behind her and told her about how he had found it to be a marvellous city. He missed the bit out about the incident but asked her how she and dad knew Robert.

"Robert was a dear friend to your dad and me. He was at our university, but his dad needed help running the hotel which you stayed at, so he cut short his studies to help him out. His dad died a few years back and now Robert owns and runs the place himself. "

She started to tell him about the times his dad and her had

during their courtship in the town. Stories of the student pranks they got up to. Some that were a little bit illegal at times.

"Daniel, I have always loved your dad from the first time I met him and always will. I know I have made a mess of all our lives and for that I am terribly sorry. No boy should have been put through that. "

"Please don't get upset mum as I know it was hard for you to come to this place. Now I want to get off the island as it's stifling me. I have already talked to dad about it, but I don't want to leave you both, you especially. "

"Come close to me Daniel and listen carefully. I know I don't have a long time left to live. Maybe a few months, maybe a few years, but not long. I accept my fate. You will make mistakes in your life, but don't dwell over them. Make a choice and stick to it. "

Denny then gave her the broach he had bought for her. Petra was overcome and tears were flowing down her cheeks.

"It's beautiful my lovely boy. I'll treasure it for ever. "

He gave her hand a gentle squeeze and left her alone to go and speak to his dad. He wasn't looking forward to this as he had seen his dad looking at his hands. Lachlan asked him about how he had found Edinburgh and what he had thought of his host Robert. He had waited till after Denny had waxed lyrically about the place before bringing up his skint knuckles. Denny had made up his mind to tell his dad everything. He wasn't going to hold anything back.

After he had finished, he couldn't tell what the look on his dad's face said. Was it disappointment, disgust or was it plain and simple bewilderment? Denny didn't like being put under the scrutiny by his dad and he was feeling angry at it. Denny started to say with a raised voice.

"Do you know what dad I felt awful and embarrassed about it especially for you and mum, but I am getting fed up feeling like that. I'm sorry for shouting at you and getting angry, but what I am angry about is that I had to find out for myself what is wrong with me. It took Ian to tell me what condition I have and that there was no cure other than not putting myself in these situations. "

His dad couldn't come up with anything to pacify him but said,

"Son, I never told you about your problem because if you make it public then it can ruin your life. You will never get into the army, police, or any other government departments. You will just end up here working on a boat. A dead-end job son. "

"When I'm away from this island I won't be anybody's problem. The sooner the better. It's cursed. "

Denny stormed out of the room before his dad could reply. Lachlan new it couldn't be easy for him with his mum's condition worsening, but he really didn't know how to placate him. If the Edinburgh incident was anything to go by then he felt his son was becoming increasingly angry, even hostile. He was resigned to the fact that Daniel would have to live with what he had, but hopefully the army might be the solution he needed. If he joined up.

For Denny, the weeks passed into months without any respite from the island boredom. He was tending to train even harder and would often be found on one of the beaches lifting rocks, or maybe some tree trunks that had been washed up. His training included schedules that he thought might be beneficial if he went into the army. Denny could run all day but had decided he needed speed. So, he would choose a long beach and do repetitive sprints until his legs wouldn't carry him anymore. He was fit, very fit with a sculpted body, but it wasn't his body he was worried about it was his mind.

He thought it was time to send for his application papers for both the army and the police force as getting off this island was paramount to him. He told his dad and Helen what he was doing, and both had said he was doing the right thing although deep down he knew Helen was hurting inside. It would be a while before he received any papers, so he just put it to the back of his mind and spend more time with Helen and his mum and dad.

Helen knew that time with him was going to be precious so she decided to dedicate as much time she could to being with him. She loved their time away just walking and pitching their tent so that it was just him and her. Their lovemaking in the tent was becoming increasingly intense as she found Denny had become a very athletic lover. Partly down to the fact that he had been given a book called the Kama Sutra, from Ian. Helen found herself making love in positions she didn't think was possible, but she certainly wasn't complaining. Out with the lovemaking they tended to talk a lot more, but Helen had tended to steer clear when the talk veered towards their futures.

A week of storms had battered Durma. It had been relentless. Fifty mph winds had lifted everything that wasn't tied down. Even part of the church roof had been taken off. The boats were securely tied up and nobody was venturing outdoors as debris was being thrown around like confetti. The school had been closed and the only hive of activity was Scroggies which was going like a fair. Denny had not seen Helen for a week and could only speak to her on the phone. On the seventh day the wind had eased, and Denny had walked down to Helen's house to see her. He was invited in by Maisie which wasn't a common occurrence as she was very guarded as to who got through her door. Helen was busy baking, and the aroma was tantalising. He asked her if she would like to go for a walk tomorrow first thing. Denny always enjoyed when the storm had ended as he would often walk the coastline to see what the tide had brought in.

Denny was still in his bed when Helen started knocking on his door. He opened the window and shouted for her to come up and wait as he wanted to speak to his mum. As she climbed the stairs, she could hear him and his mum speaking. She slowly put her head around the door. Petra immediately turned her head, gave a loving smile, and said,

"Come in my lovely child. Please sit on my other side and tell me what you two have been doing. Daniel does tell me, but my problem is that I tend to forget. "

Denny left to get changed. As Helen lay beside her Petra took hold of her hand. Helen was shocked as to how skeletal it felt. They both lay talking about everything and anything, but Helen was surprised as to how alert she was for being ill. The door opened and in walked Denny. His mum quickly said,

"What a hunk of a boy you are son. How tall are you? "

"I'm six feet two inches mum and according to dad I may have another two years of growth in me."

"Do you know you are dating a giant Helen? "

Petra had said laughing.

As they both got to the door she said,

"Oh, can I just say before you leave that if you're not having sexual relations yet then you bloody well should be."

They both looked at each other and laughed. Petra started to lie on her side and Helen ran over and put a pillow under her head.

As they walked towards the coastal paths Helen stopped and said,

"Denny, I have never really asked you as to the extent of your mum's illness. I hate to ask this, but is she dying and if so, how long has she got? If you don't want to speak about it, then fine."

"It's okay Helen I don't mind telling you that she will be lucky to have a year left. Although I'm not sure I should use the word lucky. Her organs are slowly shutting down and I know she is in a lot of pain."

Helen just stood and wept.

"I'm so sorry Denny I didn't realise how bad she is. I feel bad for you all."

He walked forward, put his arms around her and held her tight until she stopped crying.

"Let's not spoil the day by thinking about things we can't do anything about. "said Denny.

They strolled onto the coastal path and started to walk North. He was continually looking at the inlets, beaches and the damage a seven-day storm had done to the coastline. The variety of flotsam was incredible. He could make out everything with his scope. The sea was still thundering up against the bottom of the cliffs and he stood at times marvelling at the destructive powers of the sea. He wondered how many people had lost their lives being out in that God awful storm. Never to see the light of day again. Helen brought him out of his thoughts by asking if she could use the scope.

They walked on sharing the scope with Denny pointing out things that she had missed. He was anxious to get to the small bay where the wreck of the Sea Rose was.

When they arrived, Denny walked cautiously to the top of the rough path and looked over. At first, he was a bit mystified as he couldn't see it, but when he put the scope to his eye, he realised that the storm had brought the sea right up the small beach and the waves had done the rest. Smashed it to pieces. Small bits of boat timber still lay scattered around, but nothing to let you know that once a wreck of a boat was marooned there.

Denny was determined to walk quickly past the inlet where his sixth sense had kicked in while he had been helping to search for Isla. As he approached it, he quickly shouted for Helen to come and help him.

"What's going on Denny? Please don't frighten me like this. It's not nice. "

"I'm not pretending Helen an awful feeling has come over me and my legs aren't working properly. "

As she ran back to him, she could see the colour had drained from his face. She held him as best she could while he sat down on the grass shaking.

"Helen please don't think I'm losing my mind, but there is something seriously wrong down on that beach. I need to get the feeling back in my legs and then I'm going down. "

"Please don't go Denny as you are not looking well and you might endanger yourself, but if you're sure you must then I'm going with you. "

They both sat on the grass for a while until Denny felt better. As he stood up, he asked her for the scope and walked forward to the edge of the path and looked down. His legs weren't still back to full function, so he asked Helen to hold on to his trousers at the back. The storm had taken a lot of the sand away from the beach and holes had appeared all over, some quite deep. He was about to start down when something caught his eye. At the far end of the beach something was glinting. It was very faint and even with scope he couldn't make out what it was. He knew he had to get down there, so he had turned to Helen and said,

"If you're not sure about the path down Helen then please just wait here. "

"I'm coming Denny so please don't try and change my mind."

The path was crumbling as they descended with Denny leading in case Helen stumbled so that he would be there to catch her. When they got their feet on the sand Denny immediately walked towards where he had seen something glinting. He started to walk quicker, effectively leaving Helen behind.

"Slow down Denny please," she shouted.

However, Denny wasn't slowing for anybody and kept on walking until he came to the end of the beach. He stood for a moment to get his bearings. He looked up to get an idea where he had looked down from. There was nothing here. He didn't understand it. Had he just imagined it. He just knew he hadn't imagined it. His head was thumping as he walked around looking and looking. He was about to give up when a solitary ray of sunlight came through from behind the dark clouds to let him see what he was looking for. It was something glinting. As he walked over, he knew he was in for a shock, so he shouted,

"Don't come any closer Helen please. "

"Whatever it is Denny I want to know. I'm not afraid. "

He leaned over and took the object that had glistened in his hand and found it to have a small chain and it was attached to something. He couldn't make out what it was at first as it was covered in sand and seaweed. After using his jersey to clean it up he suddenly fell to his knees feeling nauseous.

"Oh God please no. Why had it to be me? "

Helen had come over wondering what was happening. She found Denny kneeling with his head bowed and uttering something incoherent. As she stood over him, he was shaking. She asked what he was holding. Denny opened his hand and showed her. It was a silver pendant of a fish.

Helen didn't see the chain attached and was wondering why it so disturbed him. He then told her to whom it had belonged. Isla. Although he didn't want to as his hands were shaking, he started to brush the sand away from around about it. All of a sudden, a skull came into view and Helen got the fright of her life, screamed and fell back scrambling on all fours away from what she had just seen.

Chapter 8

Denny quickly came to his senses and picked her up but made sure she had her back turned to the skull. Helen was in shock, so Denny walked her away from the scene. He felt her shaking and wished he had never brought her down to the beach. He then asked,

"Helen are you okay to run back to my house and tell dad what has just happened. Also, for him to get Mike Stewart and a few able bodies to come as fast as they can. Are you sure you can do this? "

Helen had said she would do it so off she went with Denny keeping an eye on her as she climbed the path. When she was out of sight, he sat down on a large rock next to the body. He wasn't sure what to do. Should he uncover all the body by moving the sand or just leave it for Mike to look at. He noticed the sea was getting a bit choppy and suddenly he knew what he had to do. If another storm was brewing then a high tide would come with it and there was a chance they wouldn't be able to remove the body.

He started to lift some large heavy stones and place them all round the body doubling up on the seaward side. Sitting down again on a rock he found himself talking to Isla. Why, he didn't know, but it made him feel calm. He noticed the tide starting to creep up the beach and the clouds were becoming ominous. He was starting to feel cold, so he got up and started to do some exercises to get the blood flowing through his body. The wind was getting a bit stronger, and a gust blew some sand from around the body's head. Denny looked closely and could see a large hole at the top.

"I know he has done this to you Isla. I should have shot him when I had the chance. Please believe me when I say he will get what's coming to him and it won't be pleasant. Ian will be here soon. "

It was just then that a shout came from up on the cliff top.

"Daniel are you all right, it's dad. "

Several faces then appeared looking down on him. He warned them about the state of the path before they started down. Some

70

of the men had ropes and one had a tarpaulin. He could see Ian walking with his head down and looking morose. As they walked across the sand Denny intercepted Ian.

"Ian if you don't want to do this then everyone will understand. It's not very pleasant. "

"I have to son. It's the least I can do. "

Mike Stewart took over the recovery of the body. Bagging anything, they felt relevant. He told everyone to try and work at a fast, but sensible pace. Like Denny he feared the creeping tide. It took them an hour working meticulously before they had everything in bags and the body wrapped in the tarpaulin. Denny watched as the men stood still and gave their usual silent prayer. At the top of the cliff Denny saw that they had managed to bring a small truck with them, so everything was placed on to the flatbed at the back. Most of the men stood holding on to the headboard with the rest sitting down. Denny and Ian had decided to walk home. As they watched the truck disappear Denny turned to Ian and said,

"I'm sorry this is the way it has turned out Ian, but at least she can finally be put to rest. I never really knew her, but from what I did she seemed a lovely woman."

"Thanks Denny. I do appreciate how you stuck by your convictions which lead to Isla being found. You have a gift that way son so it will put you in good stead throughout your life. However, when it's telling you to walk away from something that is happening then do it."

They walked in silence for a while until Denny reluctantly said,

"Ian, did you see the injury to the top of Isla's head? "

"I did son, but rest assured that the evil monster that did this to her will die a slow painful death at my hands. I have no confidence in the police ever finding him, but I have put out feelers all over Scotland. I don't think he would go anywhere else as he would stick out like a sore thumb. Time Bomb has been making a lot of enquiries and God help him if my brother finds him. I'd just leave him to get on with it. "

Not much else was said for the rest of their journey and when they came into the village Ian had said he would walk down to the Icehouse where Isla's remains would be kept. As they approached Helen's house Denny had said he would keep in touch with Ian. As Ian walked on Denny walked to her door and knocked. Maisie opened the door and said,

"Come away in son she is through in the living room. She is a bit shaken up so please tread carefully. The pair of you are going through a demanding time of it just now. "

He went into the room and Helen was just sitting there staring. The colour hadn't come back to her face and he thought she was still in shock. Denny sat down and held her for a while until she was responsive enough to speak to him. He had tried to make her laugh but was failing miserably so he kept the conversation light hearted. Eventually he thought it would be best if he left so he gave her a kiss and told her he would pop in and see her tomorrow.

Next day, Denny had heard his dad on the phone to someone in the morning. It had been Mike Stewart telling him that the relevant authorities had been contacted and both the police and a pathologist were on their way. He didn't know how long it would be before they got here. After the last debacle they wouldn't be in any hurry. Several days past before word got around that they were on the ferry to Seahaven. The sea that day was like a boiling cauldron and there wasn't a passenger who hadn't felt the effect of sea sickness. Mike Stewart had organised for himself to pick up the three individuals and transport them to Kismay.

There was a lady pathologist, Dr Neala Belmont and the two stooges that were here when Isla had disappeared. Probably sent back as some sort of punishment. The pathologist was dressed for her visit to the island with a long herringbone coat, jeans which were tucked into her boots and a woollen knitted hat. The other two had their double-breasted suits, slip on shoes and the obligatory long summer coats. It was obvious to Mike that because it was Durma the authorities on the mainland just couldn't care less about the islanders. He just hoped that the pathologist knew her stuff.

When he looked in the rear view mirror, he noticed the two incompetents were a bit green about the gills and their breath stank of alcohol. So much so that Dr Belmont had rolled the window down. Preferring the strong wind in her face rather than the stale smell of alcohol coming from the back.

"How long have we got to go Mr Stewart? "she enquired.

"About fifteen minutes doctor and please call me Mike as this won't be a pleasant time for any of us. Apart from the two incompetent sleeping beauties in the back who you'll struggle to get out of our only pub."

"Just watch me Mike. "

Mike dropped them off at their accommodation. The officers at Scroggies and Dr Belmont at the house of schoolteacher Liz Bryant who had kindly offered to put the doctor up for as long as she would be here. When the police were being dropped off Dr Belmont got out of the car and told them she expected them down at the Icehouse for the autopsy within twenty minutes. She also advised them that if they felt inclined to go into the bar for alcohol then they would be on the first ferry home with a disciplinary procedure hanging over them. Their faces said it all when she said that they had better have brought warm clothes with them as they would be visiting the site where the body was found.

Mike had asked the doctor if she would mind if Lachlan could be at the autopsy. That was fine by her. The body was laid out on an old work bench which has been scrubbed and a clean sheet put over it. She told everyone that as there were no scrubs to go around then they had to keep their distance. The skeleton was remarkably intact considering the circumstances. When she started to remove all the sea bugs from the skull that was when Dc Keltie had to rush out to throw up.

"If you feel like doing the same Dc Ronaldson then make sure your far away from this table."

He tried to put a brave face on it, but he simply couldn't. He was even quicker exiting than his counterpart. After a while she asked if she could speak to the boy who found Isla. Lachlan had told her it was his son, and he would phone the house and get him down. Fifteen minutes later Denny started to walk through the big wooden doors of the Icehouse. His dad had intercepted him and explained that it wasn't a pleasant site and if he needed to leave then that's fine.

"I'll be fine dad, trust me. "

"Come a little bit closer please son. What do I call you Daniel or Denny? "

"Denny will be fine doctor. "

73

"When you were observing the removal of the body by Mike and his men, can you tell me how they did it? "

"They removed most of the sand carefully by hand, but can I point out that I did the same to expose the chain not knowing what it was attached to. When most of the sand had been removed, they put any boards of timber they could find under the body and lifted it up on Mr Stewart's say so. "

"Now think about this carefully Denny please. When the body was lifted, did you see if the left arm fall from the torso in anyway? "

"Definitely not doctor as all the men treated her with the utmost respect. "

Dr Belmont thanked him for his help and asked him if could help even more tomorrow by taking her and the police to the place she was found. She also asked Mike if all the men who recovered the body could be available to help as well. Mike had said they would all be there at the time she specified. However, he explained that Denny's girlfriend wouldn't be there. He told her she was still in shock. The doctor was okay with that. Next day they all convened at the Icehouse and the same flatbed truck was there to transport them to where Isla's body had been found. Dr Belmont had noticed that the two police officers were worse for wear from their night in Scroggies. She made a mental note to have a stern word with them both.

Before they descended to the beach, she asked everyone to wait a minute while she spoke to Denny.

Denny told her about the times his sixth sense had kicked in every time he came near to this beach, telling him that something wasn't right down there. He had been walking with Helen and using the scope before spying the glinting object.

"You feel you have a sixth sense Denny, do you? That's very unusual is it not? "

"It might seem unusual to you doctor, but if we had listened to him a year ago then we would have found her then," said Ian.

"From the information I have gathered, you are Mr Ian McLeod, and you were in a relationship with the lady. So, the officers will want to speak to you to make statement."

They started off down the slippery path with Denny leading

while holding on to the doctor. Although it was a sombre time there was a bit of amusement when the two officers were continually falling on their backsides due to their slip-on shoes. That scenario even drew a wry smile from the doctor.

The wind started to get up and Dr Belmont felt the cold coming through her jacket. She thought what a foreboding place this was and that nobody should have died here. She asked Denny and then the men to show her exactly how they recovered the body. She got down on her knees, sifted through the sand, and bagged a few bits of what she thought could be clothing, but the sea had rotted most of it away.

After a while she announced that they were finished here and thanked everyone for their help and the police officers would take statements from them all as a matter of course. Denny had made sure that she got up the path safely albeit having to lift her several times. As the two officers slipped and slithered at the back she shouted,

"Officers, you have two minutes to get in this truck or you will be left. "

They managed it with seconds to spare although they were battered and bruised and covered in quite a bit of Durma mud. Mike asked her how long before she would come to her conclusions.

"Not long Mike as I'm finished and I've only some paperwork to finish off tonight, but can you do something for me please. Miss Bryant has talked so much about Scroggies being the heart of the community I'd like to see inside it before I leave. "

Mike was taken aback by this but agreed to take her in that night. When they were in Kismay the men had their statements taken at the Icehouse by the two officers who seemed impatient to get it finished as no doubt they wanted to get to Scroggies. At about eight o'clock that night Mike had called in to collect the doctor to take her up to the pub, still not sure it was a clever idea. As they neared the doors, he thought about warning her about the state of the place and the clientele but thought better of it. Best let her see how we live here on Durma. He kindly opened the door for her and in she walked. Suddenly there was silence as all the men either stood or sat there watching her. Then the whistling and cheering started up. Dr Belmont was a very good-looking woman, and this was a rare treat for the men.

She had obviously just missed the fight as two of them were wiping the blood off their faces with their sleeves. She thought that if the world came to an end, then this is what it would look like. As she manoeuvred herself past the puddles of blood, she spied an empty seat at the table Ian was sitting at and asked if it was okay to sit down. While ignoring the two incompetent police officers standing at the bar. Ian asked her what she wanted to drink explaining it would have to be either whisky or beer. By this time Mike had left them to their own company.

"Beer will be fine Mr McLeod, thank you."

"A pint and a half of beer, "Ian shouted to the barman.

As Ian started to walk to the bar Dr Belmont shouted over the din,

"I hope the half pint is for you Mr McLeod. "

Ian stopped in his tracks and looked around to see her smiling. He burst out laughing. It had been a long time since he had smiled never mind laughed.

Next day the inquiry party gathered at the Icehouse ready to be transported to Seahaven. When Mike arrived and got out of the car Dr Belmont took him aside.

"Mike, I shouldn't tell you my findings before I give them to the relevant authorities, but I'm declaring it as foul play. No surprise to anybody here on Durma I presume. The damage to the skull was by a blunt object, a hammer or similar. Another fact is that the left arm had been broken in several places which leads me to think that this girl had been dragged to the place of her death by somebody far more powerful than her. "

This shocked Mike, but the doctor had asked him not to say anything until the official findings were published. Before they left, Denny and Ian had walked down to see them off.

"Ian if I'm ever in a need of a quiet place for a holiday I'll give you a call. Not sure about Scroggies though. As for you young man please make sure that your sixth sense is used to help you and if it's telling you not to do something then make sure you don't do it. Oh, and we will contact her parents who will hopefully collect her remains and take them back home for a decent burial. "

Both Ian and Denny gave her a smile and a little nod. They waved goodbye and the party were on their way to Seahaven. As they walked home Ian had told Denny not to get too wrapped up in thinking about revenge for Isla. He would find him no matter how long it took. They said goodbye and Denny walked to Helen's house and knocked. It was Helen who answered it this time and at once threw her arms around him.

"Oh Denny, I'm sorry you had to go through all that. It couldn't have been nice. "

"It had to be done Helen and now I think we should all move on."

He never mentioned about Ian's efforts to find Hamish and knew he would never tell a soul. They agreed that they would meet up most nights and weekends. They both new at some point their relationship would end when he left the island, so they were going to make the most of it.

During the day he decided to get as fit as he could. One day he took off and ran or walked as quickly as he could around the whole of the island. Ten hours later he arrived home. Tired but none the worse for wear. Every second day Denny would just wander around the coastline. Often just sitting on the promontories that were jutting out into the sea. His mind wandered from one thing to another. About his rage problem, his mother, Talisker, Isla, Helen, and his desire to get off the island. Sometimes it would be all too much for his brain and then he had to lie back and see if any beautiful dreams came to him. Not very often unfortunately. He often wondered if fate had anything to do with him being on this cold, barren, desolate rock he has had to call his home for seventeen years. Thinking about how other people of his age were making decisions about their future.

The more he thought about the army the less appealing it was becoming. The police force wanted him but had said it was best that he waits a couple of years and then reapply. They wanted him to get more experience of life. It was so confusing to him. He had often thought that he might ask Helen to go away with him to the mainland and tour Scotland. See the beautiful sights his dad had told him about, but he knew she couldn't leave her gran. Thinking like this just made his brain more scrambled than it was. No matter how many times he told himself to get a grip of

77

himself it never seemed to work. He felt he had no purpose in his life and each morning was the same. He had no identity.

Chapter 9

Over the next week he had sat down with his dad and had several meaningful talks with him about his future. His dad was always a major source of inspiration to him. The island at this time of year never put anybody in the right frame of mind. It was very, very wet and the wind was particularly savage so as the boats weren't getting out as much as they wanted, and money was scarce which affected the whole island. Twice the ferry couldn't make it over which lead to people's moods becoming worse. Denny knew he had to make up his mind over the next few months as to what he was going to do.

One night Denny was lying awake just staring at the ceiling when an idea came into his head. He dismissed it repeatedly. By the time morning had come he had finally made up his mind. He was going to Zwiesel in Bavaria to see where his mum had lived. There was time enough to get a career so for the present he wanted to just enjoy himself. He dressed and walked through to his mum's bedroom. She opened her eyes and asked him to come in and lie down beside her. She always seemed to perk up when he did this. He couldn't wait to tell her about his decision.

"Can I ask you for one thing though Daniel and that is to wait for a few months. I can't explain but you would be doing me a lovely favour by waiting. "

Denny didn't like to ask her what she meant, but instead put his arm around her and gave her a hug. He was shocked as to what he felt. His mum had a very pronounced rattle in her chest. He laid her back on the bed and within no time she was asleep. He phoned Helen and told her that he wanted to speak to her tonight. His dad finally arrived home and went into his study. When Denny went in, he could see consternation on his face.

"What's the matter dad? I can see by your face something is troubling you. "

"Did you give your mum her usual hug today Daniel and if you did then what did you surmise. "

"It was the rattle I could hear in her chest that shocked me a bit. Dad does this mean what I think it does."

"I'm afraid so son. It's been getting worse over the last month and the outcome is inevitable, so you had better prepare for the worst."

They sat there without a word between them until Denny said, "How long dad? "

"Not long son. I am mentally preparing for your mum's funeral and it's difficult for me. Regardless of what she has put us through she is still your mum and my wife. "

Denny thought it best not to bring up the subject of Germany quite yet, so he went to prepare tea for tonight. Neither of them ate very much that night. Denny had told his dad that if he needed any help with the funeral preparations then he was just to ask. His dad had said no as he felt Daniel had enough going on in his head at the moment.

That night as Helen and him were out walking he decided to tell her about his plans. He told her they had changed He was no longer going to the army, and that he was going to fulfil his mum's dying wishes and visit Germany. He asked her not to mention anything to his dad as he had not told him. This came as a massive surprise to her. She asked him how long he was going for, but he was non-committal and said it was just an idea at the present. He decided to tell her about his mum's health. It wasn't long before the tears started trickling down her cheeks and she put her arms around him.

"I am so, so sorry Denny. You told me it was going to happen, but when the time comes it's difficult to accept."

"I have got to be strong for my dad Helen as he is going through a tough time emotionally just now. "

As the rain started to pour down it just compounded their moods and they felt it best just to say goodbye and head back to their respective homes.

The next day Denny spent a lot of the day just lying beside his mum and speaking to her although at times he felt she didn't know he was there. After a few hours, his dad came into the room and suggested that Denny could help him out by being with her when he was out working. He was extremely happy to be with her. The next day was the time for Betty May to leave the island for ever. Nobody thought this day would ever come. Most of the villagers had popped in to say farewell over the last week and give her a gift, no matter how small. Her son had told the Parish Council that she would be leaving about ten o'clock in the morning.

As Betty came out of the house, she almost left the island in a wooden box as all the villagers started shouting and cheering in unison. What a fright she got. She put a hand on the car to steady herself so that she could look around and try and see everyone. She was resplendent in a vibrant blue dress and matching hat which was at once blown off, only for one of the youngsters to chase and retrieve it before it took a dive into the harbour.

She walked around the car aided by her son to cast her eyes on the people she had lived with for the last sixty years. Many whom she had helped to bring into this world. The fishermen had congregated together just near their pots and as a mark of respect to her, had delayed their days fishing until they had waved her away. Betty slowly, but unaided, walked towards them and with the most heartfelt smile on her face shouted,

"Thank you, my brave, hardy boys. Be safe and don't let that cruel sea take you. God bless you all. "

One of the fishermen started to cry whereupon Betty in her own inimitable way shouted,

"Give it a rest Brian. I'm only leaving the island not dying for God's sake. "

This left the rest of the boys laughing. Just then Denny had walked forward with a large bouquet of flowers which his dad had organised from the mainland. He had to bend down to give them to her which the people found amusing, only for her to grab him around the neck and whisper,

"I know you will come back for that bonnie 'lassie' someday son."

This blew his mind as he had never told anyone out with Helen about his plans. She then walked towards the car as she was starting to feel the cold, plus the tears were about ready to flow. As the car slowly moved through the village, Betty waved and waved and never once felt the need to wipe away the tears. She wanted to show what the island and the people had meant to her. Eventually the car had disappeared. Betty was gone, but never to be forgotten.

The Parish Council had made plans well in advance and it was

Lachlan who had proposed that they ask Jean Scougal if she was prepared to take over the running of the village store. She had said yes as this was a wonderful opportunity for her since her husband had disappeared. Jean had asked Helen if she might be able to give her a hand for a few hours each week just until she got used to it. Helen said she would be glad to do it, plus the chance to earn a few extra pounds was always welcome.

Denny sat down with his dad one night and told him about his thoughts on visiting Germany. This was a bolt from the blue for Lachlan. He knew his son would leave the island, but just assumed it would be the army. Lachlan had asked him the reasoning behind it. Denny explained that he felt he wasn't ready for the army or the police force for that matter. He wanted to experience a bit of life off this island and didn't want any constraints on him. Also, the rage factor was still playing havoc with his mind. His dad had told him he couldn't go through life thinking and worrying about that.

Lachlan had asked him if they could talk about this after his mother was gone. While not wishing her away. Dr Henderson had paid her a visit from Seahaven and told Lachlan that it might only be a matter of two or three weeks and to get everything in order. Denny had understood and said he would leave it until his dad wanted to bring it up again.

Life had to continue, and Denny spent as much time as he could looking after his mum. She was no longer eating very much, and his dad had told him that she would eventually stop all together and that would be the time. At times, as he lay beside her, she would often scare him when her breathing would stop just for a few seconds and then resume.

He would lie there telling her about all the fantastic ideas he was going to do with his life and how proud he would make her. Helen would come round when she could, and they would both lie beside Petra and tell her about all the lovely times they had as they had grown up. They hoped that she could hear them, but they doubted it.

Over the next few weeks, it was just a waiting game. When Denny was lying on the bed beside her, he would often see her grimace with sharp rasping noises emitting from her lips. More often than not, whatever he or his dad had brought her to eat had not been touched. One day as he was looking at her face it was as if she was wearing a death mask. He just had to look away. She was still his mum and preferred to remember her as she used to be. The tall, beautiful, and proud lady from Bavaria.

At times during the day, he would walk down to Scroggies to sit for a while and speak to Ian, if the weather had prevented the boats from going out. He found it comforting speaking to him. He felt he could open up more to him than he could with his dad. It was one afternoon that he found himself in the bar waiting for the boats to come into the harbour. It was the worst and saddest point in his young life when he had gone to the bar and asked for a pint of beer. He just wanted to know why people were partaking in the drinking of alcohol.

He was enjoying it when the fishermen walked in.

"What the hell are you playing at Denny? "

The shout came from Ian. He was angry. In fact, he walked over and grabbed the pint glass and took it back to the bar. He saw the rage in Denny's eyes. It wasn't a nice sight. Pure evil. It reminded him of his brother Time Bomb.

"You shouldn't have touched my pint, Ian. You had no right. "

The bar went deathly quiet, and everybody just looked at each other waiting for the situation to explode. Ian walked over and pinned Denny's arms down on the table and said,

"Don't you dare think about trying to tackle me, Denny. I'm not intimidated by your stature or your reputation. You may overpower me and give me a right beating. However, here is what would happen afterwards. I would take immense pleasure in shooting you right between the eyes and dropping your body overboard in the Sound. Never to be seen again. So, make up your mind. "

Denny sat there with his eyes transfixed on Ian. He was shaking. It took fifteen minutes for Denny to come back to reality. He sat and shook his head.

"I'm sorry Ian. You know I would never try and hurt you. "

"Denny, given the circumstance you could hurt anybody. There is one thing though son. It would be some spectacle if you and my brother teamed up. "

Ian started to laugh as did Deny and the situation calmed itself down. Denny wanted to stay out, so he just sat and listened to all the exaggerated stories of their day's fishing. He did admire their imagination, however.

Later, Denny intended to walk home, but walked on past his house until he came to the coastal path. He sat at the edge of the cliff and stared at the sea. The clouds were black with a sense of foreboding. What a God-awful place this is he thought. Surely a prison cell would be easier. The demons must have heard him as the thunder and lightning started with the rain starting to soak him through. He roared a harsh, guttural sounding cry and thumped his fist into the ground repeatedly until it bled. Denny never knew if there was a God, but at that moment he believed somebody was punishing him. He stood up, arms wide, looked up and shouted,

"Why am I like this? Can't I just walk off the edge of the cliff and be done with it. "

Denny sank to his knees and stayed there until the rain was running off him. Eventually he slowly rose to his feet. He was trying to put one foot in front of the other but failing terribly. Gradually the feeling was coming back into his legs, so he kept pushing himself forward to try and get home. Soon his house came into view, and he saw his mum's bedroom light was still on, as was his dad's study light.

He thought he would get away with not seeing his dad, but Lachlan walked out of the kitchen as Denny entered the house. He was shocked at his son's dishevelled appearance.

"Please go and change son then come down and I'll make you a hot drink. You can tell me what has been going on. "

They sat and talked into the early hours of the morning before Lachlan finally told Denny that he should get away from the island as soon as it was possible. Denny lay on his bed knowing that he wouldn't get any sleep. His mind was churning and churning, and his sleep patterns were becoming so mixed up that every morning he felt exhausted. When sleep did come, it came with bad dreams and nightmares. Bad enough that they really scared Denny at times. His mood swings were getting worse, and he felt he was being short with everyone, especially Helen. He wondered if it was the fact that he knew he was going to miss her, and it was just him taking it out on her.

He decided the following day that he wouldn't take his moods out on anybody. He wandered down to the harbour and found Ian hard at work mending his pots next to his boat. He never looked up, but just said,

"Son, make yourself useful and make us a tea would you please. You'll have to hunt around in the cupboards to find what you need."

Denny asked if he could go aboard, and Ian gave him permission. He walked down the stairs and started to look around for the small stove. He eventually found everything, but his eyes were being drawn to what looked like a long cabinet that ran the length of the boat's interior. Only it didn't have a handle or visible hinges. He should have left it, but that wasn't his way. A shout came from Ian asking if the tea was about ready. Denny was so intrigued by the cupboard that he never replied. It was only after running his hand along the bottom that he finally heard a click and the cabinet door slowly opened downwards.

Denny got a real shock as displayed in front of him were a shotgun and what looked like a sniper's rifle. Two handguns which he couldn't recognise the make of. Filling up every other bit of space were knives of all descriptions. They were stunning. Denny knew then he was being watched and turned round to see Ian standing at the top of the stairs. Denny never uttered a word as Ian walked down.

"I see you've found the armoury then Denny. I hope you've not been shirking your duties and that the tea is ready. "

Over a tea Ian explained that the shotgun was there just in case he had a problem when out fishing. He often met boats of different nationality, and a couple of times he had felt a bit threatened when they had asked him about his catch. When they started to get aggressive Ian had decided that the discharge of both barrels towards the other boat did the trick. He told Denny that he had always collected knives since he was a youngster and had bought and sold dozens and dozens over the years. Their beauty had always captivated him.

"Ian, can I ask about the high-powered sniper rifle and scope. It doesn't seem to me that you would have much call to use it on the boat or even on the island. If you blasted a rabbit with that then there wouldn't be much left of it. "

85

"Your right son. However, it will be satisfying to see the bullet go between the eyebrows of Hamish McLure when I find him. The pistols, well they will be used if it must be done close up. Either way I will get retribution for Isla. There is a warrant out for his arrest, but I don't hold out much hope of the police finding him if the two idiots that came here have got anything to do with it. "

As they sat there drinking their tea Denny couldn't kept glancing at the rifle. Ian noticed and said,

"I believe you're a crack shot with your dad's rifle Denny. Well, here is the story lad. If, and it's a big if, you are ever in need of that rifle then as long as I'm still around then just take it. The ammunition is in a small drawer at the side. However, in case of that happening then please don't bring it back here. Get rid of it."

Denny couldn't imagine why he would ever need such a powerful rifle, but he thanked Ian for his offer. Ian then asked him why he was leaving to go to Bavaria which seemed an odd choice for him. Denny told him why and let him know about his mum's family. Even about the choices they had made during the war. None of this surprised Ian, but then again nothing did. Denny explained about his state of mind now and why he had to go even at the expense of his relationship with Helen.

"Go with your gut feeling son and when you decide then follow it through. If you fail, then it's nobody's fault but your own."

Denny thanked him for his advice and left to head home. He was only a short distance away when he heard Ian shout,

"Remember son, watch the drink "

Denny just waved and gave him the thumbs up. Back home he saw Dr Henderson's car outside the door. He ran in and found him talking to his dad. The doctor then excused himself and Lachlan asked Denny to sit down for a chat. His dad had told him that his mum wouldn't last more than a day or so. No matter how many times Denny had run this scenario through his head it still almost floored him. One consolation was at least death would end his mum's suffering.

He slowly and hesitantly walked up to his mum's room. He still felt the need to knock and when he lay down beside her it was then that realisation hit him. This wasn't him mum lying with him. Whoever or whatever it was wasn't his mum. She was back with her family walking through the forests of Bavaria. Laughing and singing with her sister. As he went out, he stopped, turned, and said,

"Oh, mum why did you do this to yourself. Why. Why? "

He was up early next morning. Sleep had given up on him, so he wasn't disappointed when none had come that night. His dad had shouted for him to come down and get something to eat. Denny had replied that he was going to lie beside his mum and eat later. Lachlan had told him that he was only going to attend emergency calls for the next few days so that they could both be with her. As he lay with her, he found himself singing songs, mostly sea shanties to her. Songs which he had learned in school. Her breathing was becoming shallower and shallower.

He held her as tight as he could, but knowing she was virtually skin and bone he didn't want to hurt her. At about eleven am he thought he felt a slight squeeze on his hand and then her breathing stopped. She was gone. He shouted on his dad and when he came running to the top of the stairs Denny said,

"Don't rush dad, mum has gone."

Lachlan at once broke down. Denny went and held him. They both walked to the edge of her bed and brought two chairs and placed them so that they could sit either side of her to hold her hands. His dad started to tell Denny about when he first met his mum. About all the fun they had together for which he was eternally grateful. Stories that made Denny laugh.

After a while, his dad had said he had better phone for Dr Henderson to come before the pub opened. He then phoned the Icehouse for them to bring up a body bag to take Petra down for embalming. No matter how much he had prepared himself for this moment, he was struggling. He went up to Petra's bedroom and got her long black lace dress and any bits and pieces of clothing he thought might be needed. The silver broach which Denny gave her was carefully attached to the dress. The two acting undertakers arrived soon, and Petra was taken down to lie in rest.

Word had got round and there was a continuous procession of villagers offering both Denny and his dad their condolences.

Helen had been the first through the door and she had hugged both Denny and his dad through floods of tears. It was an awful time for the three of them.

Helen took charge of looking after both Denny and his dad. Preparing something to eat and bullying them into eating it. She went home and packed a few clothes so that she could stay with the Foggerties. She wasn't going to be put off by their protestations. It was a very sombre next few days, but Helen had kept herself busy by doing her own work with her gran and looking after Denny and his dad. All preparations for the funeral had been made and it was to be three pm on the Friday so that if any of the fishermen wanted to attend then they had time to go out early so they could get back.

Helen had to go home on the Thursday to get her work up to date and make sure her gran was feeling okay and not overdoing it. When the Friday morning had arrived, Lachlan sat down with Denny and told him that he had phoned Max the housekeeper at the estate where his mum had lived to give him the sad news. Max had been terribly upset but had regained his composure when Lachlan had asked him if Denny could come and visit when the time was right. Denny would have been excited if it had been any other time, but not today. He was finding it hard to get his head around how the day would play out. The day was overcast with swirling black clouds up above. The wind was light just now but give it ten minutes and it could be a howling gale. After Helen had brought something for them to eat Denny had said to them,

"Dad, Helen, I really think we should walk to the church no matter the weather. Let us not use the van as other people will be walking. The weather is part and parcel of the island we live on so let us just get on with it."

They were all in agreement. There was a knock on the door and when Lachlan opened it Ian was standing there. He asked if there was anything he could do to help. Lachlan invited him in and thanked him for his offer, but everything was arranged. Helen made tea for them all and they sat about chatting with Ian trying hard to keep their spirits up by telling them amusing stories of the fishing community.

Hours had flown by and now it was time for them to get ready. Lachlan had asked Ian if he would like to walk to the church with them. Although he had said it should just be the three of them Denny had said they would be glad of his company. Ian was already changed although on Durma changed often meant putting on another pullover. Ian however had put on clean jeans, leather jacket, and what looked like a new shirt.

At about two forty-five they set off from the house and they could see lots of people heading towards the church. As they walked Ian had said,

"Don't walk with your head down son. Keep it high and be proud that she was your mother. We are going to celebrate her life not her death. "

Denny gave a small smile and did what he had suggested. As they walked through the big doors to the church Denny recognised some people, but others he didn't. The whole village had turned out. Even his ex-school friends had wanted to be there. The four of them moved into the front row of pews and Helen had faltered a bit as she saw the coffin, but Denny held her hand tight and then put his arm around her. Most people would never have met Petra, but out of courtesy to Lachlan and Denny they wanted to be there. Lachlan had told Rev. McGlashan that as Petra was not a religious person then he did not want the service to be morbid and keep the religious side to a minimum. He had suggested that any music be uplifting and for the Rev. to decide what he thought would be appropriate. The service had started and after a while the reverend had said that there would now be a eulogy. This was baffling to everyone until Denny walked toward the pulpit. Helen and Lachlan were mystified, but what they didn't know was that the reverend had paid a call to the house looking for Lachlan to ask if there was to be a eulogy. As he was out on an emergency call it was Denny who he spoke to, and he had said he would be doing it and not to trouble his dad.

Denny took his time to look around at everyone.

"Thank you all for coming today as it means a lot to us. I'm going to try and say a few words about my mum. I say try, not because I am too emotional, but to be honest I never really knew her. "

There were a few looks of surprise on people's faces.

"It doesn't matter how much I knew about her, but what I do know is that she loved me and my dad very much. She came to this country as Petra Albach from Germany to start a new life with my dad. Lately she told me about growing up in the forests of Bavaria and what a happy childhood she had. This island was not for her though as it seemed to rip out her soul. Towards the end mum had her troubles and no matter how hard dad tried he couldn't get her to accept help. Again, thank you for coming and paying your respects. "

Denny walked down the few steps, took a few steps forward and kissed the head of the coffin. Both his dad and Helen looked like they were in a bit of a shock. Ian just gave him a smile as he came back to his seat. None of them knew what was happening next as Denny and Helen's schoolmates started to walk to the front of the church. Jinty couldn't help herself as she stopped when passing Denny and came up and threw her arms around him with tears running down her cheeks. He kissed her gently on the cheek and she walked to where the pupils had formed two rows. Two guitarists stood at the back of them, and the reverend had asked the congregation to sing along if they knew the tune. It was a sea shanty called Wellerman which Helen and Denny had learned at school although it wasn't particular to Durma, but then no sea shanty was. They belonged to anywhere there was a sea.

The guitarists and the choir started up and within no time the whole congregation were clapping to the beat of the tune and singing. Lachlan was a bit taken aback, but he just looked at Denny who had a slight grin on his face when he looked back. Lachlan wanted a non-religious service and that's exactly what he got. The Rev. McGlashan then told everybody that they would now be going to the graveside. On that note Ian, Denny and four of the fishermen walked forward to the coffin and started to lift it on to their shoulders. Again, Lachlan was lost for words as he hadn't realised the extent of his son's involvement in the preparations.

Slowly they walked out of the church with everyone following them. As they walked to the graveyard Helen was amazed how many people had waited outside. She thought that most of them never knew Petra, but they knew Lachlan and Denny and that was the island way. One grieved, everybody grieved. At the graveside, the reverend gave a short sermon before her coffin was lowered into the grave. The villagers, one by one, moved forward and threw some wildflowers into the grave. The last was Helen. Her gran had handed her a beautiful bouquet of assorted wildflowers from around Kismay. They had both worked on them two nights ago after asking Denny to collect them. This was to be from her, Denny, and Lachlan.

After everyone had went home the three of them stood looking into the grave. Lachlan had held up quite well, but then he broke down setting Helen off. Denny stood in between them and held them tightly. Eventually Denny had asked Helen if she could take his dad home as he wanted to sit at the grave for a while after the workers had filled it in. The filling in of a grave on Durma had to be quick in case the rains came. The workers worked tirelessly. When he had the graveside to himself, he sat down beside his Mum and said,

"I would rather be anywhere than sitting here today. I'm not sure if things could have worked any different. This island gets a grip of you and won't let go. All you are left with are demons. They destroy your soul, and it feels like they just break your heart. Today they have. I hope you don't take this the wrong way mum, but I hope that I never have to come back to this grim, ghastly place again. You never know I might see you and your family playing in the forests near Zwiesel. Love you mum. "

Denny patted the ground, blew her a kiss, and walked away.

Chapter 10

When he got home, he went up to his mum's room for the last time. He would never set foot in there again. Helen had made something for their tea and now she was heading home to be with her gran. When they met up a couple of nights after Denny needed to speak to her about his imminent departure from the island. This scenario had gone through Helen's mind for ages. She had made up her mind to accept it and get on with her life.

"I really wish I could come with you Denny, but it's not going to happen for reasons you already know about. There is one thing Denny, I'll never forget Daniel Rey Foggerty and I'll never stop loving you. She gave a big smile and put her arms around him and hugged him like there was no tomorrow.

Over the next few days Denny made sure he looked after his dad who at times seemed really down. He didn't want to bring up Bavaria until he felt his dad was in a better place. He had strolled down a few times to the harbour to speak to Ian.

"I can tell your getting frustrated Denny, but for your dad's sake try and be patient and give him as much support as you can "

"I'm really trying for his sake Ian, but I just want to be away from this island before it gives me any more grief. Why do you stay here? "

Ian explained to him that it was just a way of life for him. He had never known anything different. However, he said that if Isla had still been around then he may have chosen to make a life elsewhere for the both of them. Denny said he understood, but deep down he wasn't sure he did. He made up his mind that he would be off the island within the next two weeks whether his dad agreed or not. He didn't want to make his dad feel any worse, but for his own sanity, or what was left of it, he was going. Plus, it wasn't fair on Helen not knowing what was going to happen.

Ten days later, Lachlan had called Denny into his study and told him that all the preparations were in place for him to go to Bavaria. His dad at once saw a change in his son. They sat down and started to go over all the travel arrangements and to say

Denny was excited was an understatement. His dad told him that he would be going in two days and to pack and say his goodbyes to anyone he needed to. The next day he thought it prudent to walk down to the school and say goodbye to Miss Glover and Miss Bryant. Miss Glover had hugged him and cried. Something he never thought would ever happen.

"Thank you so much for teaching me and looking after me at school. I couldn't wish for a better schooling from the both of you, "said Denny.

"If you are ever back here Daniel please pop in and see us, "Miss Bryant said.

However, both knew that they may never see Daniel again. He walked back to the harbour where he saw Ian. He told him what was happening.

"Well Denny, I wish you all the luck in the world and if I ever see you again, I feel it may be a long time. If you ever get to the Northeast coast of Scotland, there is a small town called Helmsford. Please look up my brother Willie and tell him I was asking after him, but whatever you do don't wind him up. If the pair of you get into a fight, then the whole of Scotland would feel the earth shake. God speed son and remember to listen to your sixth sense. "

"Thank you for being a good friend Ian and please make sure my dad doesn't get into any fights in Scroggies."

They both laughed as Denny walked away wondering if he would ever see Ian again. Denny met up with Helen that night and told her he would be leaving the next morning. She was inconsolable, but after a while she said,

"Whether you want it or not I'm coming to the ferry with you, and I won't take no for an answer, and you had better write and call as often as you can. "

Denny agreed but knew how hard it would be for both of them. Next day Denny was up early ready for his great adventure. At breakfast he said to his dad,

"Are you sure you'll be okay dad? I will worry about you. Oh, and I've asked Helen to pop in now and again to make sure your fine. "

"Daniel I'll be fine, trust me. If Helen does come up though I hope she brings some of her pies, "he said with a large grin on his face.

It was time to leave, and his dad gave him a huge hug and told him how much he loved him. He made him promise to write and phone as often as he could. Denny almost broke his vow of not crying and gave his dad a hug that almost squeezed the life out him.

Helen was standing outside when Lachlan locked up. He could see she had been crying. Probably all night. They started off to Seahaven. As they were just coming to the harbour Denny saw Ian sitting on his pots giving him the thumbs up. Denny smiled and reciprocated with his own thumbs up. He thought this was the end of an era and wasn't sure what the next one would bring. Every time he turned to look at Helen, she gave him a smile, but thought it was a little bit forced. Both knew that today would be the last time they saw each other for a very long time, if ever. The first thing they saw when approaching the harbour was the ferry. Just sitting and waiting to take people away from this miserable rock they call an island. Denny didn't want any long goodbyes so when the car stopped, he quickly got his bags out and gave his dad another hug. Lachlan had said he would wait in the car while Denny and Helen said their goodbyes.

"Helen, I love you more than words can say, but for both our sakes I must go. There is one thing though Helen, at some stage of my life I will come back, but please don't hang around waiting for me. "

Helen just choked back the tears and gave him a kiss. She knew she would struggle to get over him. Denny then walked over and on to the ferry, put his luggage into a safe place and walked to the bow of the boat. The ferry was starting to move, and he knew he would soon be out of sight from his dad and Helen. He assumed as good a position as he could and gave them a wave. The boat was turning and soon they were gone.

This journey was no different from the last and Denny knew he had to prepare himself for a long laborious trip to Edinburgh Airport. In the bus and train, he passed the same landmarks he had seen before and was never as glad as to when he came into Waverley Railway station in Edinburgh. His dad had organised for him to stay at Robert Trapp's hotel, so it wasn't far to walk.

When he walked through the door of the hotel Robert came

and met him.

"I am terribly sorry to hear about your mum Denny. She was a very bonnie lassie and I had great regard for her. "

Denny thanked him and shook his hand. He asked Robert if he wouldn't mind if he could just go to his room as he was very tired. He felt the last two days had taken it out of him. After a couple of hours Robert had shouted on him to come down for something to eat. There on the plate was a steak that was hanging over the sides with barely enough room for the chips. After tea Denny had told Robert not to worry as he wouldn't be going out tonight. This came as a relief to the hotel owner.

"Robert, can you tell me if there were any repercussions from the last time I was here? "

"None that I know of son. The only thing I do know is that none of them could give the police an identifiable description of their attacker. Although I did hear that the ring leader's dad, Thomson from Dundee, had made enquiries, but to no avail."

Denny didn't need an alarm clock as his usual sleepless night had brought some bad dreams, so he was awake for most of the time. After breakfast Robert was taking him to the airport. They set off and as they neared the airport Denny could see the planes both taking off and landing. He was nervous as this was going to be the first time in an aeroplane. At the terminal entrance he thanked Robert who again had refused any payment for his overnight stay. As he walked through the doors Denny shouted,

"I promise I'll see you again Robert. Take care. "

Little did Robert know that the next time he would see Denny it would be in a different light.

Denny found the entire process of going through baggage check in and passport control was a bit unnerving. It was made worse when he forgot about the coins he had left in his pocket and the x-ray machine had started beeping. When that was sorted out, he made his way to the gate he was to leave through.

He just sat there, and people watched. Groups going on holiday, all with their nervous energy about them. People rushing to get to their gate, running late with their bad planning. He could have sat there all day just watching however the call went out for his flight to Munich. He walked out on to the tarmac and went up the steps at the front of the plane. Once seated he just put his seat belt on as instructed and tried to relax.

His dad had told him it would be a very uneventful experience and smiled when he said just to pray that all the propellers kept turning. So just enjoy it. Lachlan had laughed when he told him about the turbulence but didn't elaborate so Denny was none the wiser. He realised his dad was right, there was nothing to this flying until they were over French air space and the turbulence started. As a first-time flyer Denny thought the plane was going to shake to bits so he just grabbed the arm rest very tightly and shut his eyes. After twenty minutes everything calmed down, so he went back to the book he was reading. The plane was getting noisier with children now becoming agitated and bored.

Three hours in an enclosed tin can was becoming enough for him. There was one thing that Denny wondered about and that was the miracle of getting this metal 'giant' up off the ground and into the air. He thought how sheltered he had been living on Durma.

The announcement came over the tannoid that they would be landing in twenty-five minutes so please fasten your seatbelts. Once landed he made his way to the arrivals lounge where hopefully Max would be waiting. All the instructions his dad had given him were spot on. He looked around till he spotted a small wiry man holding up a card with Denny's name on it. When he went over to him Max grabbed his arms, looked up at him, smiled and said in his near perfect English,

"Daniel, I would have known you anywhere as you are the perfect likeness to your mother, even the height. "

Max laughed as did Denny and they knew they were off to a good start.

Max was driving an Opel off road jeep. It didn't look much, but when Max turned the key and the engine roared into life then Denny knew this was an impressive piece of engineering. Max was pointing out landmarks and what areas had been heavily bombed during the war.

"Daniel before we travel any further may I point out that some people in Germany are still loyal to the old Nazi Germany or the Third Reich so it's best not to have an opinion on it when discussing it in company. The subject is taboo where you will be living for reasons I'll explain after you've been here for a while."

96

Denny sat back and both threw questions at each other and by the time they were approaching Zwiesel he felt he really knew Max. As they travelled through the town Denny thought it was bigger than his mum had said it was. He felt a sense like he was coming home, and a sense of excitement lay in the pit of his stomach.

Chapter 11

They arrived at the Albach town house which took Denny's breath away. Here was a house with countless windows and it had a turret on either side of the roof. He was later to learn it had eight bedrooms, each one bigger than the whole floor space of his house back home. Several bathrooms with a lounge and opulent dining room. The décor was something to behold. Portraits of men and women adorned the walls, and he was walking on carpets with a pile you could lie down on and easily disappear into.

As much as all of it impressed Denny he couldn't think who the owner of this 'castle' could be. Both his mum and dad had been very conservative with their description of the house and ownership was never mentioned.

"Daniel you must be hungry so would you like to come to the kitchen and meet my wife and daughter. This is my wife Elke and my daughter Maria. Our surname is Bauer, and we look after the house and shooting lodge for the Albach Trust. "

Elke and Maria gave Denny a hug and asked him to sit down and have some of the sauerbraten Maria had prepared this morning.

"Thank you all for making me most welcome and please call me Denny. I'll tell you why sometime although it's not very interesting. All this has been hard to take in as mum and dad never really told me much about mum's side of the family. It always was such a secret that they were trying to keep. It was only days before mum's funeral that I found out her maiden name and only because I saw her birth certificate on my dad's writing desk. Maybe you will be able to tell me why. "

Max and Elke gave each other a concerned look but were saved by Maria who had started to serve Denny with the sauerbraten. She must have thought Denny had an appetite to match his body as the plateful she gave him was absolutely heaped with what seemed like half a loaf of sourdough bread on the side to mop up the gravy. They all sat around the table eating and drinking. This was Denny's first taste of wine, and he was surprised how much he enjoyed it. Suddenly Max turned to Denny and said,

"Denny I'm sorry, but I should have asked if you were okay drinking wine after what your mum went through. It was amiss of me not to think of it. It is something we have with our daily main meals. "

"Don't worry Max I came to terms a long time ago with what mum was going through and why she was doing it. It was the demons on that cursed island we live on that drove her to do what she did. As for the wine I found it genuinely nice thank you and yes it was my first. "

The Bauers gave each other a fleeting look and left it at that.

"Denny after you've eaten why don't I take you for a walk around Zwiesel so we can both get some fresh air and see what the town is really like. But beware as you are such a good-looking boy, I'm going to pretend that you are my Scottish boyfriend to anybody who asks. "

Everyone just burst out laughing before Denny said,

"I would love that Maria and I'm more than happy to go along with your plan. "

Denny said he would like to lie down for an hour and then he would come down for her after a quick shower and change of clothes. He didn't sleep as there was so much going through his head. After a quick shower and change he was ready for what Maria could throw at him. She was an incredibly beautiful girl and he thought she might be a year or two older than him, but he was so looking forward to being in her company. His thoughts drifted to his dad and Helen and as much as he loved them both he could not be thinking about them if his new life was about to begin. He made a mental note to phone them within a couple of days.

Maria shouted on him to see if he was ready, and he walked down the grand staircase to meet her. They started off walking and Maria linked her arm through his and both felt good. Denny was both impressed and confused as it seemed like the place was new and when he asked Maria about it, she explained that a lot of this area had been bombed during the war due to the fact that there had been a munitions factory a few miles away. Hence the whole area had to be rebuilt.

Denny had heeded what Max had said in the car, so he left it alone. They talked and laughed as they strolled and after walking for an hour Maria had suggested they go into the nearest kneipe for a coffee. She explained a kneipe would be the equivalent to a Scottish pub. The thought of Scroggies serving coffee made him laugh. She asked why he was laughing, but he told her he would explain over a coffee. As they entered the kneipe he was quite surprised as to how busy it was even though it was only late afternoon. The image of Scroggies again came to him and a smile came over his face.

He enjoyed being in Maria's company and opened up a lot about how harsh it was living on Durma. She couldn't believe some of the things he was telling her. It felt easy talking to her and just like Max, he could ask her anything. There were a few young lads at one table and Denny thought he heard the name Albach being mentioned but wasn't quite sure. Maria was sure what had been said so she asked Denny if they could please leave and continue with their walk. As Denny stood up, he looked over at the lads and stared, then walked backwards not taking his eyes off them for a second. When they were outside, he said,

"What was that all about Maria. Were they offending you in any way? "

"Just leave it Denny as I'm sure my father will explain everything tonight, but please don't mention this to him."

Denny reassured her that he would keep it to himself, so they turned for home with Maria linking her arm through his. When they were home Maria had said she had to help with supper, so Denny wandered out to the back of the house and into the extensive gardens. He had never seen such a large privately owned garden. There were trees, bushes, and flower beds everywhere for a couple of hundred yards anyway. The lawns were beautifully manicured. Max came from behind what looked like a log shed and asked him what he thought of the town. Denny said he had been so impressed with it, but found it so different to Durma, to say the least.

Max asked him what his intentions were but told him he could stay for as long as he wanted.

"I haven't given it much thought Max, but what I want to do is earn my keep and hopefully there will be jobs around the house or garden I could undertake."

Max told him he didn't have to do that, but he would appreciate the help. Denny said he would start by chopping the logs that were stacked high against the shed. He stripped his shirt off and set about chopping them. Max had never seen such a ripped body on one so young and within no time Denny had finished the task. As he looked up at one of the windows, he saw Maria watching him, so he smiled and gave her a wave. Max had suggested they go in and clean up before supper. Denny agreed but asked him if he could make a couple of phone calls back home. Max had told him to help himself and to give all their regards to his dad.

Denny had showered, changed, and came downstairs. He asked where the telephone was, and Maria showed him. He phoned his dad first and told him all about the journey and Zwiesel. He then apologised for not asking how he was. His dad said he was coping fine, and that life just goes. Denny mentioned that Max was going to tell him all about the Albach Trust after supper.

"Daniel, I want to give you a warning. What Max will tell you will be mind blowing so get yourself prepared. "

"Dad what can Max tell me that is so significant about the name. After all it was mum's name. "

"Just wait son and Max will explain everything and if you want to call me afterwards then please do. "

Denny came off the phone wondering about the significance of what his dad had just said and decided to put it to the back of his mind. He was a bit apprehensive about phoning Helen but thought she deserved at least a call. After a while Helen answered the phone. He thought she would be so glad to hear from him, but she sounded subdued. After a while of small talk Denny had said he had to go as this was Max's phone. As he was about hang up, he told her he loved her.

"Denny please don't be hurt by this, but please don't say that as it hurts me, and we both know you won't be coming back to Durma. If you feel a need to call, then please do so and a letter now and again would be nice. We both know we are moving on, but not together. "

When he came off the phone, he felt a bit dismayed, but fully understood what she had been saying. As he entered the lounge, the ever-smiling Maria met him. He suddenly realised her striking features were genuinely like his mums. Prominent cheek bones, tall, blue eyes, and a light complexion. He thought he would like to get to know this girl better even if it was just a platonic relationship. Denny sat down, but before he did, he shouted on Elke to see if he could help with the supper.

"No sit-down Denny and have a glass of wine with Max as it's not the men's place here in Bavaria to help with the food. "she replied.

Max poured him a wine and they sat talking about life on Durma as Max was interested to know where his friend Petra had gone to live from Edinburgh. After their second glass of wine Max had said he was a bit shocked as to the life that his mum and dad chosen for themselves.

"I had never known anything else until I went to Edinburgh for a few days. Such a beautiful city. That visit confirmed to me what had been going through my mind for a long time. I needed to escape Max and now here I am.

The food was then served, and another heaped plate was put before Denny. This time it was ' kaesespaetzle ' which he could see was a pasta dish. It was delicious and quite different from his dad's culinary repertoire. Maria had asked him if he wanted more, but he had to decline for fear of not being able to move afterwards. After supper, the ladies left to clean up the dishes and it was about half an hour afterwards they all sat in a room with a log fire going. There were even more portraits and oil paintings on the walls, but one stuck out for Denny more than any of them. It was a stunning painting of a white stag set in a forest location with mountains as a backdrop.

Max thought he had better get his talk with Denny over first, so he asked him if he wanted Maria and Elke to be present. Something came over Denny at that point. He wasn't sure what was happening. He was very apprehensive but told Max that Maria and Elke were fine to be there. Max started by explaining the history of the Albach Trust. How during both wars, the Albach family had made their fortune from arms and munitions. Most of the profits were ploughed into businesses and property all over Germany after the Second World War had ended. A large part of Munich and Zwiesel was owned by the Trust. In fact, the business interests of the Albach family were now spread worldwide and controlled by a consortium of solicitors in Munich. Denny was struggling to see what this had to do with him. Max then continued saying,

"This is where it concerns you Denny. Your grandfather and grandmother who you never knew died at the end of the last war and left two siblings. Your mum and Aunt Anna. Your uncle Hans Albach took them in and cared for them like his own as he had no family of his own. He adopted them and gave them the Albach name. Both girls left when they were in their late teens after Uncle Hans died. Anna was killed in a motor accident in South Africa. It was said she had been under the influence of alcohol. Petra your mum ended up in Scotland but unfortunately died recently."

Max then asked Denny if he would like to continue. He had agreed but wasn't sure he wanted to hear what was coming next. Denny just sat there waiting in suspense.

"Daniel Rey Foggerty, you are now the sole heir to the Albach Trust. "

Denny's head dropped into his hands, and he started saying,

"No, no, no this can't be real. I'm just Denny Foggerty from Durma. I don't know anything about running a business that involves the amount of money you have intimated to me. "

Elke got up and went over and put her arm around him. They sat in silence until he said,

"Max, I would like to phone my dad if you don't mind. "

Max had told him to continue and don't rush the call. Denny wandered through to the phone and called his dad. Lachlan could tell by the way Denny had greeted him that Max had told him everything.

"Daniel your mum and I decided when we met that if we had a family, we wouldn't tell them about this until they were older. Until they could manage it. However, the death of your mum has brought this to the fore. Your mum didn't want anything to do with the Albach Trust, but remember it does a lot of good as well "

"Dad you were right it is mind blowing. What do I do about all this? "

103

His dad told him he had made preparations to come over to Bavaria to see him in anticipation of Max telling him and he would be there in a couple of days. He would get Max to pick him up in Munich, but under no circumstance was he to worry about all this. Denny had made him promise not to let anybody know what had just been spoken about. His dad had said it was a given.

When he ended the call after telling his dad he loved him he wandered through to where Max and his family were sitting. He told them that his dad would be here in a couple of days, and he would phone them to get things organised. He then asked Maria if she would like to go for a stroll with him so that he could clear his head. She gladly accepted and she said she would show him another part of the town. Just before they walked out the door he turned and said,

"When I come back, I think it's important that I tell you about myself and my demons. "

The Bauers suddenly looked at each other with a slight look of worry on their faces. It was a beautiful night and he loved having Maria hanging on his arm. Every so often she would give it a slight squeeze. A few older people stopped and spoke to Maria about the tall, ruggedly handsome man she was with. When Maria told them that this man was from bonnie Scotland they wanted to know more, but Maria felt it unfair as they were conversing in German. One old lady who was about ninety had told her that if she ever got bored with him then send him round to her house. When Maria translated for Denny, he burst out laughing.

He couldn't think of a better way to clear his head. After a while Maria suggested they head back even although Denny was up for going to the kneipe they were in before. She seemed very guarded about going so he just left it and walked home with her.

That night, as he lay there all the information that he had been given was just swirling around in his head. He knew he didn't want to have anything to do with this Albach Trust, but he would just wait until his dad arrived and speak to him. Over breakfast Elke had said,

"Denny you are quiet this morning is everything okay? Please let us know if there is anything troubling you. "

104

"You have been very welcoming Elke, you all have, but I need to tell you about myself, "said Denny.

He tried to tell them about what a hard few years this had been for him.

"More importantly folks I would like to tell you about a couple of personal problems I have. I suffer from Intermittent Explosive Disorder which is something I can't control other than not putting myself in the situation. Another thing I have is what I can only describe as a sixth sense that tells me not to be involved in something, but it can help in certain circumstances. However, both are a terrible burden to carry around with me. I will try and explain what they are. "

Denny sat and told them all about his problems. He didn't hold anything back. When he finished, they all looked a bit shocked.

"Don't worry you are perfectly safe with me as these things only kick off when I am goaded, feel I am being backed into a corner or when my friends or family are threatened. Apart from that I'm just an ordinary young lad. "

He sat there waiting for a reaction until Maria said,

"Denny, it seems like you have had a tough time of it culminating in the death of your mum. We won't treat you any different and we sure as hell won't goad or wind you up. "

She started to laugh which set everyone else off.

Over the next few days, he made himself as useful as he could around the house and garden grounds knowing only too well that at some stage his time in Bavaria would come to an end.

When his dad arrived, he was so glad to see him, but gave him a bit of a ribbing about his growing belly. Asking him if Helen was bringing some of her homemade pies up to the house for him. The two days his dad was there seemed to pass very quickly. They had both sat down and discussed all the ins and outs of the Trust. They agreed that Denny would wait until he was twenty-five before he would investigate it in more depth. It was soon time for Max to take Lachlan back to the airport. As they were waiting, he and his dad were looking at all the paintings on the wall. Eventually they came to the white stag.

"Ah the famous white stag of Bavaria. Your mum had talked about it. Beautiful isn't it, "said Lachlan.

Denny asked him if he knew the story of it, but his dad had

105

said no and suggested he asked Max about it.

"Dad before you leave, I was wondering if I could stay here for a year, maybe two and then it's my intention to try and get into the Police Force in Edinburgh. "

"Daniel, I think that would be a great idea as there is nothing for you to do on Durma. "

Max peeped the horn, and they embraced then Lachlan left for the airport. After he waved his dad away Denny felt a real emptiness in the pit of his stomach. Maria came and linked her arm into his and told him not to worry as he would keep popping over to see him.

That night as they sat around the fire Max had opened a few bottles of beer and although Denny had really enjoyed them, he found them to be strong. Next morning when he woke up, he felt no ill effects of his drinking beer for the first time. He had wondered what all the fuss was about. As they worked out in the garden, he asked Max about the painting of the white stag. Max had told him that the animal and its blood line had roamed the forests and woods near where the Albach shooting lodge was for a long time. It was protected and nobody was allowed to take aim at it never mind shoot it. He told him that it was truly a magnificent beast, and the painting didn't do it justice.

"After you have been here a few weeks we will take a trip up there to the lodge. Can you shoot Denny? "

"As well as any man Max. I spent a lot of time shooting with my dad's rifle. I'll look forward to the trip. Oh, by the way who owns the lodge, and will we be welcome? "

"I hope so Denny. You own it. "

More mind-blowing stuff for him to digest. From being a young lad on Durma with not needing very much to a lad who owned half of Germany. He decided that he had to forget all about it and concentrate on enjoying himself while he was here.

During the hot summers days after he had finished his chores, he often found himself visiting the kneipe that he and Maria had first went into. He started to really enjoy the German beer and would often sit or stand at the bar and have a few. He was getting used to the strength of the beer now so from having one or two he would end up having several each time. There was often the same crowd of young lads in the bar who always seemed to be a bit worse for wear and a couple of them were very loud, but they didn't bother him so they could get on and enjoy themselves.

One night he and Maria were out walking, and Denny asked her to have a beer with him at the Alma which was the first bar they had a coffee in. Although not that keen, she said she would go in for one. When they entered, he noticed the same bunch of lads where they normally sit. Maria and Denny sat as far away from them as they could at the window. They were on their second drink when Denny noticed them pointing to Maria and laughing.

"Okay Maria please tell me why these people are laughing and pointing at you? "

Maria had said that one of them, the tall one with the blonde hair had asked her out once and when she refused, he had been abusive every time he had seen her. Denny waited to see what his sixth sense was telling him, but he couldn't wait. So he got up even though Maria asked him not to and walked over to where the five of them were sitting. They were all full of beer, so Denny decided to be very tactful.

"Can any of you speak English? "

One of them had asked if he didn't mean Scottish while making out as if he was Highland dancing. They all started to laugh.

"Okay you've had your little joke so I'm going to ask you politely. Not to be disrespectful to my friend again whenever you see her. "

"What could you do about if we did as there are five of us sometimes six, "came the reply from the same guy as before.

"Well let me tell you a story about what would happen. I will take you out one by one or all of you at the same time. Not a problem to me so I'm asking you again, stop trying to torment my friend. Please remember her name is Bauer not Albach. I'll leave you to enjoy yourself now. "

Just as Denny was leaving one of the crowd put two fingers up to him. Whereby he immediately grabbed them and took immense pleasure in breaking them in several places. The squeals from the guy made the landlord of the bar come running over. He immediately told Denny that this lad was the son of a prominent businessman in Zwiesel. Denny walked right up to his face and

107

said,

"Well, I am now the rightful heir to the Albach Trust. I think I've just beaten you on that one. "

The landlord didn't know whether to believe him or not, but Denny just stood and looked at him. The man thought better than to challenge what he had just said. As he walked back to Maria the usual smile came over his face. They both left the bar with Maria holding his arm very tightly.

"Sorry you had to see that Maria, but if that's all you ever see then I'll be glad. "

Chapter 12

Over the next few weeks Denny had tried his best to integrate into the Bauer family. He had tried to ask Max more about the Family Trust, but most times it just sailed over his head. The incident in the bar hadn't put him off having drinks in some of the bars. Just keeping himself to himself. A couple of times he had asked himself if he was drinking too much but dismissed it as ramblings in his head.

One morning Max had collared him in the garden.

"Son, I heard about you in the Alma. I do appreciate you trying to protect my precious daughter, but you must be careful as not to ostracise yourself from the village. It wasn't Maria that told me, but an old friend who was sitting at the bar. He has the gift of not being seen. Ask him how he does it sometime but beware it will cost you in Jägermeister. I also appreciate you keeping your rage in check. "

"What I would like to ask you Denny is would you be up for going to the shooting lodge for a few days at the end of next week? "

"I would love to Max, but don't be upset if my shooting skills put you to shame. "

You can wipe that smile of your face young man as it won't be me you'd be hunting with. It will be Otto and if you think you can shoot then wait till you meet him."

For Denny, the days before the shooting trip were beginning to drag and it was only the time he spent with Maria that kept him going. He felt he was growing close to her, but equally he didn't want to get too close and ending up hurting her as he had Helen. He had taken Max's advice and took the opportunity to seek out Felix. Max's friend who frequented the Alma bar. Max was right about the Jägermeister and Denny wondered if he had hollow legs as he didn't know where he was putting it. Felix was the type you would never know was there. He told Denny he worked undercover for the British Intelligence during the latter part of the war. Felix was small with a hooked nose, and you felt you could blow him over as he was that thin. He gave Denny some tips on blending in with the environment. What to wear when trying to blend in and when to leave a place. Denny thanked him and they agreed to meet up in a few weeks after his shooting trip.

The day of the trip arrived and after he said his goodbyes to Elke and Maria, they were off. He did think that Maria looked a bit down, but he was just imagining it. Max had said that it would take about half an hour or less depending on traffic, so they just sat chatting.

"Denny please tell me to mind my own business, but I have noticed that you're spending a bit of time in the bars in the town. Are you okay with that considering what your darling mother went through? "

"Don't worry I'm well aware of how much I'm drinking Max. I really do enjoy your German beer. I'm sure I won't end up like mum. "

As they went through a small village Max pointed out that this is where Otto comes for the provisions. Denny noticed there was a small bar on the outskirts of the village, but just put it out of his mind.

When they eventually arrived at lodge the sight of it blew Denny away. He had imagined it to be some sort of log cabin, but what was in front of him was something else. He thought it was about four times the size of his house on Durma. A wooden structure erected on stilts with a staircase leading up to the front of the building. He reckoned there must be five or six bedrooms. At the side of the lodge was an annex where he thought the caretaker must live. He could only stand and stare at the beauty of the lodge.

Eventually a shout went up. Denny knew right away that this must be Otto as he was dressed like a gamekeeper. Denny had seen a group of them in a picture his dad had on the wall of his study. Otto was an impressive man. Standing just as tall as Denny and looked like he had muscles on top of muscles. He was big with a goatee beard and moustache that had been waxed and turned up at the corners. What Denny saw beside him was just as impressive. A German Short Hair Pointer. He thought he was stunning. He clapped his hands for the dog to come to him, but it just looked at his master.

Otto came forward and introduced himself to Denny. He then

introduced his dog Ottar. German for otter.

"Max here says you can shoot a bit Denny. Although I think it will be fun to see who the better shot will be. Oh, and as for Ottar not coming to you it's because I must tell him that it's okay. Ottar go to Denny. "

The dog happily trotted over to Denny and was grateful for his ears being rubbed. Otto told him all about the lodge and surrounding acres and how it was rented out to some extraordinarily rich clients who came from all over Europe on hunting trips. He said he ran the lodge himself with the help of Frieda an older woman who came to the lodge each day from the village to help with the housekeeping and cooking. Otto suggested they head into the lodge as Frieda had prepared some food for them. When they were seated at the table a woman who he guessed must have been in her eighties walked through with plates of cheese, meat, and pickles. Otto must have seen the look on Denny's face and told him when Frieda had left, not to go on appearances as she worked harder than any woman half her age. After lunch Max said he was returning home and that he would come back for Denny in four days.

Denny was taken to a bedroom in the lodge and Frieda told him there were no more guests booked in as the hunting season had ended for the year, but as the Trust owned the land all around, they could shoot all year round. Like the rooms in the house in Zwiesel his bedroom was massive and decorated just as opulently. When she was gone, he took his shoes off and lay back on the bed. He tried to register everything that had happened to him over the last few weeks, but he struggled. Denny Foggerty a multi-millionaire? No, there had to be a catch somewhere he thought, and he told himself he didn't want all this in his life anyway as he felt he was too young, much too young. His thoughts drifted to back home. Wondering how everyone was getting on, especially Helen.

When he went downstairs, he asked Otto if he could go for a walk in the surrounding woods.

"Only if you take Ottar, Denny. There are some nasty surprises in there, but don't worry he will make sure you aware of them."

As he walked outside Otto was waiting with Ottar. He asked

111

Denny if he could whistle loudly and when he said he could. Otto told him. One long blast to get his attention. Two blasts for a recall. Three quick blasts for danger.

He started off with the dog keeping pace by his side. This felt good for him. The forest was thick with spruce, beech, and fir trees. Many of them incredibly old and gnarled. He could see a lot of streams and bogs. Max had warned him in the car to stick to the well-worn tracks as there would be less chance of bogs.

He felt so exhilarated just strolling until Ottar started barking furiously at him. He knew to trust the dog's instincts, so he at once stopped. He couldn't see what the dog was barking at until he took another step and saw that the banking had given way and taken the path with it. If Ottar hadn't sensed it, then he could have fallen down a forty-foot ravine. He praised the dog before moving on. He would have to tell Otto about it. It was just then that the dog just stood, raised his front paw up and stood stock still with his head never moving. Denny hadn't a clue what was happening until through the trees to his left he saw an adult deer being stalked by a young wolf who was absolutely beautiful. He stood watching until a noise from up in the trees startled the deer and it took off. The wolf knew he had no chance of catching it.

It was time to go back so he recalled Ottar who was out in the trees looking for birds with two whistles. When they got home it was time for the dog to be fed. Otto asked Denny to give him his bowl and then come into his house attached to the lodge.

"Denny, I thought you would like to go hunting tomorrow, but first we must get you kitted out. "

Half an hour later Denny with a beaming smile had all the clothes for the hunting trip tomorrow. It was then that Otto opened a large metal cabinet on the wall. Denny's breath was taken away as there were seven hunting rifles of all calibres clipped to the back of the cabinet. He thought they were beautiful. Each one had been meticulously looked after.

"I suggest you take the second one from the left if you can work a scope son. We'll be leaving at three thirty am tomorrow, so I suggest that after supper we retire to our beds so that we are fresh for tomorrow. I don't tolerate shoddy shooting Denny. "

Denny had assured him that he had used a scope before, and he would be up and ready. Before they went to eat Denny asked

Otto a question.

"Otto I was wondering if you like your job and enjoy where you live? "

"I love my job Denny and I do have a small cottage in the village where my wife stays as she says guns scare her. However, I am sixty-five now and can't do this forever. Why do you ask? "

"No reason Otto. Just wondering. "

Things were churning in his brain.

Next morning Denny was up and running ready for his first shoot. Otto was outside waiting and when Denny walked out, he couldn't believe what he was seeing. Otto was standing holding two majestic golden chestnut Haflinger ponies. Denny's mouth dropped open.

"Otto, we have a problem. I've never been on a horse in my life."

"We must use them son as some of the trails are only passable with them. We have ATVs, but you can't use them as the animals can hear them from miles away."

Otto told him that the horses were gentle, and he only had to hold on plus Ottar would walk alongside him. As they set off Denny was holding on tight as if his life were dependent on it. After a while he felt at ease with the horse and began to enjoy it. It wasn't long after that Otto announced they would leave the horses at a small cabin and go hunting on foot. Denny carried his rifle holster and not much else as they started to walk through the dense forest. Otto was leading and had told him that if he gave the sign of one hand raised then to stand still immediately. The dense forest made seeing in front difficult, but eventually Otto held his hand up and whispered to Denny,

"Look over to your left and you will see a large hare. Let's see what you can do with that rifle son. Remember you only get one shot. "

They then lay on the ground and Denny took out his rifle and loaded it. He adjusted the sights, aimed then fired putting the bullet dead centre through the head of the animal. Ottar had been standing watching while drooling at the mouth until Otto gave him the command to fetch the animal. He sped off through thick brush until he picked up the hare, brought it back to Denny's side and sat down with it in his mouth. Otto explained that the dog

113

would only bring it back to the person that shot it and would only release it into his hands.

"Impressive Denny considering that must have been about seventy-five metres. Where did you learn to shoot like that? "

He explained about the times he spent on the island shooting rabbits and hares. Otto told him that there will be bigger animals to hunt in these forests. To Denny the next few hours just flew by and their haul by the time they had finished was impressive. Otto had to go back for one of the horses as he had shot a red deer at the end of the hunt. Ottar stayed with Denny as if he were watching over him. When Otto arrived back with the pony, they quickly put the spoils of the hunt onto its back and headed back for the other horse.

When they arrived back at the lodge, Otto told Frieda to put the small animals in the old shed at the back of the house and he and Denny would carry the deer. He would bleed it now and leave it hanging until tomorrow ready to be skinned. Denny felt tired but elated. The rest of the day was spent looking after the horses and cleaning all the tack and guns. Otto asked him if tomorrow he could help Frieda to skin the animals they had shot today. Gladly he replied to Otto. After a lovely supper Otto broke open a bottle of Jägermeister and asked Denny if he had drunk it before to which he replied that he drank it with a friend of Max in a bar in Zwiesel.

"That will be Felix then. He's a legend in Bavaria son. A very brave man indeed. People know truly little about his exploits. I drank Jägermeister with him one night and the next morning I didn't know where I was, yet I heard he was seen entering one of the bars in Zwiesel at eleven am. "

By the end of the night, they had finished one bottle and had started on another. Before Otto went to the annex, he asked Denny if he could look after the lodge with Frieda for a couple of days as he and his wife were off to Munich to see their daughter. Denny said he would be glad to and just to leave Ottar as he fancied going out either exploring or shooting. Otto said he was fine with that, but he made Denny promise that about the shooting then safety would be paramount. Next morning after Otto had skinned the deer he left to go to Munich after picking up his wife.

Denny asked Frieda if he could give her a hand cutting up the hares and rabbits. They were then bagged and stuck in a freezer which was in the tack room. He had wondered where the electricity had come in until Frieda explained that an underground cable had been laid from the village. Whilst cutting up, Frieda had turned to him and said,

"I knew your mother and aunty Anna when they were young son. They often came up for weeks at a time and they were in their element when running and playing through the woods. They often came out covered in mud, but happy and smiling. Both were beautiful girls especially your mum with her captivating smile and long black hair. However, both never wanted anything to do with the Trust. They were both heirs to the billions of monies involved."

Denny stood working away while contemplating what she had just said.

"Now hang on Frieda, I just picked you up wrongly. For a minute I thought you said billions. "

She started laughing and Denny thought she wasn't going to stop.

"Son it's obvious that they haven't told you the extent of the Albach empire because that's exactly what it is son an empire made on other people's suffering. "

Denny was lost for words until she told him that he had to be aware of poachers in the forest at night as it would only be him and the dog in the lodge. Talk about changing the subject.

After they finished Frieda told him that she would leave his meals in the kitchen as she was heading back to the village as today should have been her day off. He thanked her and told her to head off. He wanted to be on his own thinking about what she had just said. As he wandered into the forest, he found a tree where he could sit down and lean his weary head against. More information for him to break down. He didn't notice, but Ottar had silently crept up on him and waited on Denny telling him to come and sit beside him As the dog lay with his head on Denny's lap he said,

"Well Ottar, what do you think I should do? Now I feel I need to escape to a place where nobody knows me. Before I came to your country, I was plain old Denny Foggerty, the young lad from Durma. A few weeks later I'm a multi-millionaire. However, I have no doubt that my life will be turned upside down many times in the future. So, I'm not going to let it bother me. Just live a little. "

Ottar just looked up at him with eyes that suggested he agreed with him. After walking the dog for an hour, he decided to head back to the shooting lodge. Night was drawing in, so he decided to eat a hearty dinner that had been prepared by Frieda. He thought that the German people didn't half like their meat and cheese, but it was delicious, so he wasn't complaining.

Night had now fallen and there was a bright, full moon so the forest had a ghostly light shining through it. Shadows were being cast by the giant trees which gave an eerie appearance. He thought how beautiful a place this was.

He had thought about retiring to his bed but knowing sleep would be at a premium he was just sitting when he remembered that Otto still had an almost full bottle of Jägermeister in the cabinet. He had no qualms about pouring himself a large drink. One led to another until only a quarter was left. He then started to reminisce about back home, but after a while he realised that he had made a lucky escape from the island. He still missed Helen and thought about her a lot, but he had to look forward.

A drunken sleep had come over him and it was a few hours later that he was awoken by Ottar barking. He sat bolt upright but couldn't get his thoughts together as he felt a bit groggy. Still half asleep with his mouth parched. Nearly finishing the bottle of Jägermeister wasn't his best idea, but he didn't half enjoy it. Ottar was still barking and growling so he got up and started to check all the doors and windows again. While sleeping he had dreamt that he had heard gunshots but put it down to the drink he had consumed. Surely nobody would be out shooting at this time of night. As he checked the front door a loud crack of a gun rang out. This was no dream. Nobody should be shooting in the forest at this time of year and Otto would have told him anyway.

He dressed and went to get his gun. A high-powered lamp would be useful too. He thought about leaving the dog at home, but he might have stressed himself by being left on his own. They left the lodge wondering where the shots were coming from, but Ottar new exactly so Denny ran keeping a steady pace with the dog.

116

Denny was starting to feel nauseous and a couple of times he vomited while running. After half an hour he could see some lights in the distance. He heard people laughing with music being played. He didn't know how many there were of them and as there were firearms involved, he knew he had to be cautious. Slowly moving forward, he dulled the lamp. He tried not to make a noise as he crept through the undergrowth, but he wasn't making a particularly decent job of it. The sweat was lashing off him. However, Ottar was stealth personified. Denny never heard him break a twig as he crept forward with his belly only a few inches of the ground.

They came to a small rise where they could look down on the intruders. Three guys and one girl sat around a small campfire drinking bottles of beer. Bottles were strewn all over the place. Their transport was a pickup truck that had seen better days. Lying near to the fire was a young red dear that they had shot earlier. One guy who was obviously drunk was taking more pot shots at the dead animal with the others clapping and cheering when a bullet hit the mark. With every shot Denny was beginning to feel that tonight wasn't going to end well for all of them.

Denny's problem was how he was going to get close enough to take their rifles off them without putting himself and Ottar in danger. He could make out three rifles, but you never knew if there was any more. He made up his mind it would be best if he approached them from the back of their truck. As they started to circle around the campfire, he couldn't help but admire the concentration on the dog's face. One look in front and the next look at Denny.

Due to all the music and laughing they made it to the back of the truck without being noticed. Denny was waiting for his sixth sense kicking in to let him know if he should just walk away from all this. Another bullet was fired into the dead animal which made up his mind with or without his sixth sense. He signalled for Ottar to stay close to his side and then walked to the front of the truck. His priority was to grab the rifle off the drunk. It wasn't that hard as they were taken by surprise. He grabbed the rifle and smashed it off the front of the truck breaking one of the headlights. The girl let out a scream and before they realised what was going on Denny had his own rifle pointing at them. Two other rifles were lying up against the truck, so he quickly stamped on them breaking them in half. The whole scene was becoming so surreal now as a mist was working its way over the forest floor. Nobody said a word for a while until Denny asked if any of them could speak English. They all looked at each until an unelected spokesperson walked forward with a swagger and said,

"I can speak English very well thank you. Better than an animal like you. You owe us for three rifles and if you weren't holding a gun at us, we would take the money out of your nose if we had to. Who gave you the right to interrupt our hunting trip you moron?"

"My right to stop your little illegal hunting is a long story. Too long for me to tell idiots like yourselves. Also, I doubt you would believe me. What I do know is that hunting is out of season, and you shouldn't be lighting a fire in this forest. It's not safe. "

Denny thought how arrogant these people were. After the initial shock of Denny surprising them, they seemed to gather themselves and he could see more confidence in their demeanour. Even the girl's body language was telling him she was feeling more confident about the situation. He walked over to where the young deer lay. His anger was beginning to rise, and he thought his sixth sense was trying to tell him something, but he didn't pay any attention to it.

"You have put six shots into this animal just for the sake of fun. Even if it was hunting season one shot should have been enough, but you are all so full of alcohol you think it's just a game. Pretty pathetic if you ask me. "

"No one asked you dummkopf. "said the spokesman.

Denny's head was beginning to hurt, and he knew it was only a matter of time before he exploded. When that happened, he had to make sure that Ottar would be safe.

"Here is what going to happen so listen carefully, very carefully. You are going to clean up your mess, but firstly put the fire out by pouring the remains of your lager on to it. Then put the rest of your belongings into the back of the truck, head out of the forest and never come back. That is going to be the best scenario for all of you. "

As they started to pick up their mess, he could see them whispering to each other with their backs to him. He knew something would happen at any time. It was then that the loudmouth said that Denny should get rid of the gun and if he thought he was man enough then why didn't he make them leave. Denny knew it was time to end all this, so he walked towards a nearby tree never turning his back on them. He stood on a couple of lower branches and stretched out hanging the gun up as far as he could. He motioned for Ottar to sit at the bottom of the tree. The dog sat there fully understanding what his job was.

They started to laugh before the drunk threw a rock hitting Denny on the side of the head. He must have picked it up while cleaning up. The girl had picked up another and threw it at Ottar, but it only caught him a glancing blow.

It was then that Denny's rage overtook him. They made the mistake of coming at him one at a time. The drunk who was tall, but fat made the first move. He tried to grab Denny in a wrestling hold by using his bulk. Denny took a step to the side and put his elbow into the side of his head. He hit the ground with a thud. As he was going down the mouthpiece lunged forward with a punch that caught Denny on the side of the head, but he kept focused and smashed the guys nose upwards. Blood started spraying everywhere, but although he went down, he was trying to get back up on his feet. It was then that the third guy ran at Denny swinging one of the broken rifles. He was being egged on by the girl who was shouting and screaming which was grinding into Denny's head. He was totally overcome with rage now and when the guy got close enough, he deflected the swinging rifle butt and landed two rapid punches to the guy's mouth. His teeth flew out in all directions.

To incapacitate him he gave another punch to his throat which left him on his knees struggling to breath. As the mouthpiece started to get up Denny ran and kicked him in the face. More blood and teeth were landing on the forest floor. Just because he could and wanted to, he gave the guy another kick that almost took his head off. The girl was continually running up to Denny and screaming in his face. Several times he told her to get lost, but she was incandescent with rage.

Denny was starting to feel the rage leave him. He grabbed the fat one and hoisted him into the back of the truck. Not even a whimper was coming out of him. The next was the one whose

119

throat he had punched. As he started to put him into the truck, he thought the guy was saying something in German. No doubt it wasn't very pleasant so just in case Denny punched him on his nose. Two down, one to go. Now it was the turn of their so-called spokesman. As Denny lifted him up the guy spat blood at him. It missed Denny's face but landed on his shirt. Denny punched and punched his face until he couldn't remember what the guy looked like before. He threw him into the truck.

Denny's head was really pounding now, and his heart was racing. Only the girl was left now. She was hysterical and screaming into his face. He had to get her to stop as he didn't want to inflict his rage on her.

Calm down, calm down for God's sake. Please listen to me. Can you drive the truck? If not, you have a problem. "

He thought he saw a slight nod in between her rants, but as he wasn't sure he could only hope for the best. She wasn't like calming down so there was only one thing he could do and that was to kick her between her legs. He hadn't wanted to do it and wondered if it had the same effect as it did on a guy. It worked as she fell to her knees on the ground holding her vagina and started to retch.

He walked away and retrieved the gun from the tree. As he sat down next to the tree with Ottar he put his face into his hands and smiled. When the smile had disappeared, he sat rueing what had just gone on.

"Why do I have to do this Ottar? It's awful. Why can't people just walk away when I ask them to. It's like they must prove themselves against me. Why have I been cursed with this demon inside me. "

Ottar just sat there looking at him. Just then the girl was tentatively getting to her feet. Denny walked over and helped her get into the truck. He checked that the three guys in the back were still breathing. When the girl turned the key in the ignition he leaned into the window and said,

"Tell your friends when they wake up that if I ever catch them in this wood again, I won't punch them, I will shoot them. Do you understand me? "

She nodded, reversed the truck, and headed down the rough track they came up. He knew there would be ramifications about what had just happened, but no matter what he would not lie to Otto. He slowly wandered back to the lodge keeping his breathing shallow and trying to clear his mind. Ottar never took his eyes off him. Denny knew it would be tough to leave him when it was time for him to go. After tonight it would happen sooner rather than later. When they reached the lodge, it was just a case of feeding the dog and heading to bed for a few hours.

Denny was woken up with Frieda banging about in the kitchen and the noise of a vehicle outside. He thought that it must be Otto arriving home. As soon as it was possible, he was going to tell him what had happened. Frieda rapped on the door and shouted that she wanted the bed sheets to wash, and that breakfast was on the table. He quickly showered and was at the table fifteen minutes later. It was a mountain of eggs and toast today. Otto walked in and sat down at the table. He started to ask Denny if anything had happened while he was away. Denny wondered if he knew, but how could he?

"Don't worry Denny I saw the empty Jägermeister bottle out the back. I wasn't here to offer you any, so it was fine to help yourself. However, what is not fine is drinking by yourself. Hasn't your mother's experience taught you anything? "

All Denny could say was that he could manage his drinking to which Otto just raised his eyebrow.

"Otto, I must tell you about an incident last night. I'm not sure I managed it the right way, but I won't tell you any lies so here goes. "

Denny told him exactly what had happened.

"My god Denny that was something that you shouldn't have had to experience. How are you feeling? In the cold light of day would you have done it any different? "

"I've ran it through my head repeatedly, but I can't come to a different conclusion. "

Otto sat there without saying a word until he said,

"Firstly Denny, thank you for making sure Ottar was safe, but may I ask how badly were the guys hurt? "

Denny just sat there not saying anything. His head in his hands. A few minutes passed before he looked up and said,

"Very badly Otto. "

Otto had thanked him for his candour and told him that it

121

would be best for Max to come and pick him up before it became a police matter. Otto told him not to worry. Denny agreed, but he wanted to speak to him on a different matter. Later as Denny was packing, he looked out of the window and saw a police car arrive. Otto shouted upstairs for him to stay quiet and not to come down.

Denny left his door slightly ajar so that he could try and hear what was being said. It was obvious that Otto new the officers as there was a lot of laughter going on. When the officers left Otto shouted for Denny to down to the kitchen.

"Come in Denny and let me tell you what was said and what was decided. Both the officer and I agreed that these people were hunting illegally, and they met another hunter who should not have been there as well. What I will say is that two of the guys are in hospital with injuries, although not life threatening, their faces will need a lot of work done on them. You must be some fighting machine when you get going Denny. What was it you were going to speak to me about? Max will be here in a few hours. "

"Otto, do you remember I asked you before if you liked your job and you know about my association with the Albach Trust. Well, I am putting it in writing to the lawyers that you will remain in position here for as long as you want to stay. Also, when it is time for you to retire the Trust will buy you a house wherever you want no matter the cost and provide you with considerable pensions for you and your wife. Also, Frieda will be provided for when she decides, if ever, to retire. Also, it will be up to you as to who will take over from yourself when the time comes. "

"Denny, I hardly know you and yet here you are being so kind and generous. What is happening here? "

"Let me tell you a story Otto. It has been difficult for me to understand what I have been told over the last few weeks. I would give away everything I supposedly own to get my darling mother back. I would do it in a heartbeat. I also want to make Max and his family comfortable for the rest of their lives Otto. If I can make a difference to other people's lives before I screw up my own, then fine. I have too many incurable demons in the mind of Daniel Rey Foggerty. My name I was born with Otto. I seriously don't know how long I will live as I self-destruct too many times.

"Please accept my offer, will you? "

"Denny your generosity has almost left me speechless. Yes, I will accept your offer and on behalf of my wife and I thank you so much and God bless you son and if it's any consolation I would have been tempted to shoot the filth you had to deal with never mind punch them. "

Denny walked up the stairs to his room and lay on the bed. He knew he was going to leave Bavaria as much as he loved it. He didn't want to hurt any of the people that had been so kind to him. He went downstairs and asked Otto if he could phone home. When his dad finally answered he said he was so pleased to hear from him. Denny told him that he was coming back to Scotland but would not be returning to Durma. His dad had sounded disappointed, but suggested they meet up for a weekend in Edinburgh on his arrival back. It sounded good to Denny. After they talked for a little longer, he said goodbye to his dad. Just then he heard Max's car pulling into the lodge. He went downstairs to say goodbye. Frieda came out of the kitchen and walked over to Denny.

"I loved the times I spent with your mother son, and I have enjoyed my time with you here. I may never see you again, but you will come good Denny. I promise. "

She walked away wiping her tears with her hankie. Otto came in from being outside with Ottar. He put his hand out and Denny shook it. Denny made strong eye contact with him and smiled. Next was his special friend Ottar. He knelt and asked him to come into him. Denny hugged him and gave him a scratch behind one ear. Ottar licked the side of his face.

"Otto please don't let his bloodline disappear will you. "

"Way ahead of you son. He has already sired four dogs and two bitches. Two months old. "

Denny smiled and walked out. He was surprised to see Maria behind the wheel. His spirits were at once lifted. When he was in, she leant over and kissed his cheek and told him she was so glad he was coming back. He thought she might not be so glad when he told the family he would be leaving shortly.

He sat back and enjoyed the conversation with Maria. They stopped off at a small cafe and Denny was surprised to find how hungry he was. Maria just laughed and asked him if Frieda hadn't been feeding him. He laughed with her. When they arrived back at Zwiesel he immediately took his bags upstairs. He didn't want to prolong his discussion with the family.

After asking them into the lounge he proceeded to say,

"Firstly, I would just like to say how grateful I have been for your unbelievable hospitality. I arrived as a stranger, and I hope I will leave as a friend. What you have told me Max about the Albach Trust has been mind blowing so here is what I want to happen. I presume there is a solicitor in the town, so I want what I am about to say put down in writing. If as you say I can make any decision I want, then please listen. I want it drawn up that both you and Elke will be provided with a considerable pension each and a house will be purchased for you when you decide to give up the caretaking of this house. The house can be of any size and located anywhere. Maria, a generous sum of money will be deposited in any bank you see fit. It will help for when you want to buy a house or just live off it. It's for you to spend however you wish."

"Denny, I presume that this means you are leaving us to go home. Your offer to us is most generous, but you shouldn't worry about us as we have a little money put aside for our old age."

"Max this is something I want to do. I have spoken to Otto and Frieda and said I want to look after them as well. I hope I can consider you as my family and I would be welcome back any time. Dad is making arrangements, but he did say it could be a couple of weeks due to his work commitments. If you can organise the solicitor as soon as possible Max I would be grateful. You can all talk this through and let me know at your convenience. "

Denny smiled and walked away. He knew that there was a great possibility he would ruin his own life, but he would try and improve the life of others.

The few days were taken up with helping Max as best he could and getting to know Maria better. One night he was lying in bed struggling to sleep when he heard the door being opened very quietly. It was pitch black, but then the moonlight shone through the window. There stood Maria with a small negligee on. She let it fall and stepped out of it and slipped under the covers. Denny was about to say something, but she just put two fingers on his lips as if to say don't say a word. As she cuddled into his body,

124

she put her hand on to his penis. He was erect immediately and he put his hand down to her hairy vagina and started foreplay with her. He could feel she was wet, and she started to give off slight moans as he played inside her with his finger. He leaned over and put one of her nipples into his mouth which made the moaning louder.

"I have to know what it feels like for you to make love to me Denny. I have done this before, but please show me everything you can and don't hold back. "

Denny slipped on top and entered her. As he was a well-endowed, she let out a muted squeal and he had to put his hand over her mouth. Worried that her parents might hear. Over the next few hours, he made love to her in every imaginable position, with Maria loving every minute of having multiple orgasms. It only took the slightest touch from her on his penis to get him erect again. She felt a power surge through her body every time he entered her Their bodies were stuck together with sweat when they finished. As they both lay back feeling elated but exhausted, they fell into a light slumber. When Denny awoke Maria had gone. As much as he had enjoyed it, he couldn't help thinking how it had complicated matters. It was never easy for this young boy from Durma.

Next day Max had said they had an appointment with the solicitor in the town at two o'clock. They both left it up to the solicitor to suggest figures for pensions and lump sums. However, Denny wasn't happy with the amounts and said,

"Mr Muller can you take all the amounts you have mentioned and treble them and treble your fees for today. "

Both Muller and Max sat there with their mouths slightly open until Max had asked Denny if he was sure about what he was proposing. Denny reassured them both that he knew what he wanted. Also, I would like a small payment for me until I can earn for myself. Mr Muller advised Denny that he needed a copy of his birth certificate and confirmation from the Albach Trust that he was now the sole inheritor. Denny said he would send the copy to Max and he in turn would get all the relevant information from the trust.

As Max was driving back Denny thought his driving was a bit erratic. Denny mentioned this to him in a jocular way only for

Max to say,

"Denny, do you understand the magnitude of what just went on? It's exceedingly difficult for me to comprehend it all, but may I say a big thank you from the bottom of my heart. "

As they parked up at the house Denny left Max to go and tell his family what had just happened. He wandered around the gardens feeling a bit sorry for himself as this might be the last time he would ever see the Bauer family and he might never get to see the white stag in the flesh. He sat on one of the benches and put his head in his hands. Until a hand rested on his shoulder. Maria sat down beside him and linked her arm through his.

"Denny that was a very generous thing you did today. Please don't be hard on yourself because of what happened at the lodge. You're a lovely caring man and it's been my privilege to know you even although it been for a short while. "

She leaned into him and whispered,

"Oh, and I fully intend to be keeping your bed warm for the next few nights my beautiful lover. Hopefully, your dad won't get your travel sorted any time soon. "

Denny just looked at her and thought how things might have played out between them if drunken yobs hadn't intervened. He kissed her even though he saw Max and Elke walking down the lawn.

"Well folks I bet you didn't think our meeting was going to end like this. My sixth sense is telling me that I will see you again, but when, only God knows that. "

Elke walked up and put her arm around his shoulders and said,

"Denny I would be proud to have you as my son, but it would be a little creepy as you are sleeping with my daughter. "

Maria and Denny just looked at each other not knowing what to say. Elke just laughed as did Max and told them they were old enough to just get on with it.

It was only two days later that Lachlan phoned him to give him details of his return flight for the following day. The next morning Denny was up early and had his bags packed before breakfast. It was a very solemn meal and Denny was putting a brave face on it as was Maria. When the meal was finished, Denny put his bags in the car. He then gave Elke a hug before Maria hugged him through floods of tears. He had been through this when he left Durma, so he just went and sat in the car while waiting for Max.

Not a lot was said on the journey to the airport. When Denny got his bags out of the car Max had come round and gave his hand a shake and told him he hoped he would see him again.

The flight seemed to last forever until the fasten your seat belt sign went on. As he walked through customs, he spied his dad waiting for him. They hugged and then went to get his dad's hire car. Lachlan had booked them in to Robert's hotel for two nights so that they could catch up.

Over the two days they went sightseeing with his dad showing him the old haunts where he and his mum used to hang out. On the second night Denny told him why he was back early from Bavaria. He also explained about his generous gesture to all the people over there and asked his dad if he could do the same for him. Also, could he send a copy of his birth certificate to Max. Lachlan had said he was fine with his own money, but thanked him very much and hoped he would return to Bavaria someday.

Denny then told his dad of his intentions to travel around Scotland before applying again for the police force in Edinburgh. Lachlan was a bit sceptical about his intentions but didn't want to burst his bubble. Denny saw his dad off the next morning with the usual hugs and promises to keep in touch.

Denny then thanked Robert and made sure his dad had paid this time. He walked towards the train station and bought a map of Scotland. After getting a coffee he studied it to decide where he was going.

He thought about Dunfermline but as he wasn't sure he decided to give it a miss as well as Dundee due to the incident in Edinburgh. He shut his eyes and when he opened them the name of Arbroath stuck out. Sorted. It would be a one-way ticket to there as he had all the time in the world.

He felt good just sitting watching the world go past. An hour and a half later the train rolled into the small station in Arbroath. When he got off, he wasn't sure this had been the right decision. He walked towards the harbour where he found a hotel called Jimmy Bells. It would suit him fine. He guessed that most off the activities would centre around the harbour. So, he just strolled until he came to a pub. The only similarities to the kneipes back in Bavaria were that they both sold beer.

Denny ordered a pint of lager and asked the young barmaid if they supplied food. She said that they only had pies and sausage rolls and she would gladly heat them up for him. Denny ordered one of each and after chatting to the young girl for a while he went and sat in the corner and minded his own business. Soon four young lads came in. To Denny it was obvious they worked on the fishing boats and were worse for wear with drink. There was always one louder than the others and who thought he could say and do as he liked. Denny sat with his head down and enjoyed his pint. Time for another he thought so he went up to the bar. He returned and sat down sipping his beer and thinking about the lost opportunity of Bavaria.

A shout came from the bar, directed at Denny,

"Hey, you in the corner. This is my girl so keep your eyes off her or you will have me to deal with. Do you understand? "

Denny just gave him the thumbs up and continued with his pint. This time his sixth sense did kick in telling him to drink up and leave. When there were more comments directed at him, he just finished the lager and started to walk out the door.

"Don't come back, "came the last shout.

Denny wondered if the world was going to be full of these types of people and today, he was proud of himself for just walking away. He thought he might just head back to the hotel and do a spot of thinking about his future. When he went down for his evening meal he asked the waitress if there was any pubs with music on that night. She suggested the Baron and gave him directions. After his meal he went into the public bar and found himself conversing with some of the locals. Something he never thought he would do, but he really enjoyed it.

At about nine thirty he decided it was going to be the Baron for him. He liked music a lot depending on what it was. His money had started to come through from the Trust, so he didn't have to worry about how he was going to afford anything. When he went through the doors of the Baron it was if he had walked into the Arbroath version of Scroggies. One guy was being thrown out by two bouncers who resembled gorillas. The place was mobbed, and it was a struggle getting to the bar. There was a live band doing covers and they weren't half bad thought Denny.

He had just got his pint when he felt a hand on his arm. It was the girl from the bar this afternoon. She apologised for her boyfriend's behaviour, but Denny told her not to. He asked her why she was with him, but she couldn't or wouldn't give him an answer. They chatted for a while before he asked her if she would like to dance. She was surprised but agreed. It was a slow tune, so he just held her tight and let her perfume intoxicate him. Her breasts were pressing firmly into his chest as they just managed to dance with the drunks falling around them on the dance floor. The bouncers were run ragged trying to keep everyone in check. After the music finished, they went back to the bar, and he ordered a drink for the both of them. Denny thought he would try a whisky for the first time.

They chatted for a while before Denny said,

"What happens if your boyfriend shows up Moira? "

"Don't worry Denny he never comes in until nearly closing time to pick me up. "

Denny felt at ease with her and kept asking for a dance so that he could hold her close but keeping an eye on the clock at the same time. Just when he thought he might have to disappear in case the boyfriend arrived she turned to him and asked if he would like to walk her home. He didn't need to be asked twice so they both left holding on to each other.

She suggested that they walk along the beach as it would be deserted and be more romantic. Denny wasn't sure if he knew much about this romance thing, but he thought why not. They walked and chatted until he pulled her in and started kissing her. Slowly at first then more passionately. Moira was shaking slightly but responded by pressing her body hard up against him. At the far end of the beach there was a small area covered in bushes, so they quickly headed there. When they got there and made sure they couldn't be seen they started to undress each other.

Denny could see her give a little gasp as he removed his underwear. They were soon making mad, passionate love with Moira giving out loud screams each time Denny was thrusting into her. After they finished, they lay there holding each other until Moira said,

"I know it's getting a bit cold, but before we head home can we make love one more time, anyway you like. "

Denny's response was to turn her over and hold her tight while slowly making love to her. If he thought she was very vocal the previous time, then this was way louder. Loud enough to wake the dead. When they finished and were lying looking up at the sky Moira said,

"Denny, I wish I had known you earlier in my life. You're such a nice guy and your lovemaking is so beautiful. You are the first person that has ever made me climax and it's made me wonder what I've been missing. I fully intend to ditch my boyfriend as soon as possible, but I realise you'll be leaving soon, and I will never see you again. "

The cold made them dress quickly and they started to walk briskly to where Moira lived. As they neared her house, they saw her boyfriend sitting on the garden wall. He seemed out of it, so Moira had said,

"Best if you just leave me here Denny. I'll deal with him, but if you hear him shouting then don't turn back just keep walking. I can sort him out. "

Denny smiled at her, turned, and walked away.

When he got back to his hotel, he heard noise coming from the public bar. He put his head through the door to be met by several men all in a state of drunkenness. The owner shouted for him to come in and although reluctant at first, he wandered into the bar. The whisky was flowing, and he was getting a real taste for all the various kinds. He mingled with the men even although he struggled at time with some of their words.

Denny thought he had too much to drink so he decided to head up to bed, but not before making a local hero of himself by putting enough money behind the bar to give each person three drinks each.

Next morning, he didn't feel good, and the only explanation was the drink. He had never felt like this before and thought it best to try and vomit up the drink from last night. It was obviously the whisky that was giving off a sour smell, so he opened the bathroom window. He knew that this didn't feel right, and his thoughts went back to his mum. He said to himself that he was only drinking now and again so he wasn't going to end up like her. At twenty-one he was fit and healthy and he could stop drinking anytime he wanted. Or so he thought.

130

He struggled a bit with breakfast but the more he ate the more he was starting to enjoy it. Two Arbroath smokies and bread and butter washed down with thick black coffee. As the owner, who had been waiting tables, walked by him he gave Denny a slight nod and walked into the kitchen.

Time to leave Arbroath. He walked to the station before he realised it would be at least two hours before the next train was due. He sat on one of the benches feeling tired. This is what drink did to you he thought. His thoughts drifted to Moira wondering if she had been all right. His sixth sense had been right in that he should walk away from what had been going on over the last two days.

Chapter 13

He had looked at his map before he got on the train and decided that Dornoch would be the next port of call. Arbroath hadn't impressed him very much, but hopefully this town will be different. He lay back and did a lot of thinking. Wondering if his plan to tour Scotland was one of his better ideas or not. He had just drifted off when the carriage door opened. In walked what Denny could only describe as one of the landed gentry. He looked at Denny and quickly said,

"What a stench of alcohol in here. Is it coming from you young man? If it is may I suggest you remove yourself to another carriage. Well? "

Denny just shrugged and shut his eyes again.

"I'm speaking to you so answer me or I will call the guard and he will remove you at my insistence. "

Denny opened his eyes and said,

"I hope this guard has half a dozen friends to try and help him. "

The toff started to shout at Denny and threaten him with the police at the next station. Denny was getting fed up with all this rubbish from people. He was trying to keep calm.

"Why are you like this. I cleaned my teeth this morning. Not sure if you could with all the nicotine you have on yours. "

The man wasn't for calming down. Denny then felt the train slowing right down for signals he presumed so he jumped up, grabbed the man by the hair, opened the outside door and promptly threw him out. He watched the man tumbling down the banking and then threw his briefcase out after him. He saw that the man was trying to get to his feet, so everything was fine. I won't suffer idiots any more he said to himself.

The train was pulling into Aberdeen which to Denny looked a better prospect than Dornoch.

Aberdeen to Denny was a grey looking place where lots of businesses were just catering for the oil industry. He had read about it in a magazine that his dad had. He wondered what would happen to a place like this if the oil ever ran out. Did people care or were they happy when it was the good times and not to think about it should the tough times descend on them. After finding a hotel he promptly walked down by the docks. Large ships were being unloaded by men from all nationalities.

His eye was being drawn to a pub just along the road. He thought he might just have a couple. No harm in that.

Denny spent three days visiting as many pubs as he could. A few times he was very nearly fighting with some of the locals. The only thing that stopped him was that if he received a criminal record then he could forget about joining the police force. Whisky was becoming his best friend.

Denny planned to continue his train journey North, but truth be told his heart wasn't in it. Again, he had no structure to his life and on awakening each morning he felt bored and down. He wondered if this was how his mum had ended up. After telling himself a few times that he was overthinking things through he just continued as normal. He had phoned his dad to be told that Helen had been informed by Dr. Henderson that her gran would have to go into a home on the mainland. She had quite advanced Alzheimers, and it would only get worse. His dad explained that the Parish Council had a dilemma on their hands. The rule was that if Maisie left then it was not automatic that the house would go to Helen.

"Dad there is a simple solution to this. Why doesn't Helen come and stay with you? The house is big enough and can be converted in to two separate units. Top and bottom. Helen could help with the running of the house and I'm sure you would be glad of her cooking. "

"I never thought of that son, maybe I should go and see her and have a word. "

He told Denny that his acceptance had come through from the police force and he had to attend the police training centre in Edinburgh in six weeks. This came as a bit of a shock, but maybe this is just what he needed. He had told his dad not to speak to Helen as he wanted to phone her. After he and his dad finished, he phoned Helen. She eventually picked up. Before he could say anything, Helen had said,

"I thought it might be you Denny. It's a good job I didn't hold my breath waiting for your letter. Can you make this quick as I have a lot of work to do?"

"Please give me a few minutes Helen. I am sorry to hear about your gran and the problem it may cause with the house. I have spoken with my dad, and we would like to offer you a solution. Why don't you move in with my dad? The house is big enough for both of you to have your own privacy. Dad thought it would be a great idea. "

There was silence on the end of the phone until Helen had said, "I'll give it some thought and speak to your dad. What happens if you decide to come home? "

He told her about Edinburgh and that there was no chance of him coming home so not to think about that. They said their goodbyes and that was that. He still had feelings for her, but that ship had sailed.

The next rail ticket he bought was for as far north as he could get. John O' Groats. He knew this would be his last stop, so he was mentally preparing himself to try and stay a while. There were to be a few stops on the way, so he lay down on one of the seats and tried to sleep. Too many thoughts were going through his mind, and it seemed like one in particular kept raising its ugly head time and time again. Was he taking too much alcohol? He told himself again that he could stop anytime he wanted, and he wasn't going to worry about it. He had just drifted off when something woke him up and for him to look out of the window. Only to see a sign by the side of the track saying Helmsford.

He knew that the train wasn't stopping here, but something in his head was telling him he had to get off. Why? He didn't have a clue, but he was going for it. He grabbed his bags and moved into the corridor. Blast, the train was picking up speed and they would be through Helmsford in a few minutes. There was only one thing for it. He pulled the emergency cord and the breaks started to screech and he saw people being thrown about. He knew he had to get out quickly, so he exited the corridor door and jumped onto the siding although his momentum took him down the banking. The train was at a standstill, so he quickly jumped the fence into the farmers field and ran. It wasn't easy running as whatever crop he was running through was waist high. Shouting was coming from the train, and he could only assume it was the conductor.

At the far end of the field, he found a small path leading to the shore. He sat and watched as the train pulled away and then it dawned on him that he might have to get this train back again. After sitting for a while, he got up and strolled along the beach still not knowing why he had got off here. There were a few funny looks from people as he left the beach and wandered up to the small town. His first introduction to Helemsford was standing on the road bridge that spanned the river watching two guys trying to blast the life out a seal that swam up from the sea. They weren't particularly good shots as the seal seemed to be toying with them and was floating back to the sea with what seemed like a salmon in its mouth.

His first thoughts were that he had to get accommodation and as he walked into the small square, he spied only two hotels. He walked up to the one at the top end of the square. Denny was about to go through the front doors when they burst open, and a man came flying out and landed on the pavement. It was obvious that he was drunk and just wanted to move on, but an overweight barman with his filthy apron walked down the steps and started to kick him.

"Can't you just leave him alone. You can see he is in no fit state to fight you back. You have won so why don't you just walk away. "

"Listen you, just piss off and mind your own business or I will make you, my business. "

By this time, several customers had come out and were egging the barman on. Denny walked straight up to them, looked them all in the face and said,

"If at any time you wish me to be your business then I will gladly accommodate you and only one person will come out if it intact. That will be me. "

He stood his ground and stared them down. The drunk was crawling along the road. Denny went over to him and picked him up. Once Denny got him steady on his feet the man thanked him.

"What brought that onslaught on mister? "

The man had told him that the barman who is the owner's brother was just an out and out bully who makes fun of people and if they give it back, he snaps. He always has his sycophants hanging on his every word. Denny asked him if he could manage

135

to get home and the man said that if he took it slowly then he would be fine. Denny watched him for about five minutes and decided he would make it home. He thought the sensible choice was to try the other hotel for accommodation, so he walked on over.

When he went over to the Royal Hotel, he walked into the bar and the clientele all started clapping. Denny was bemused by this until one of them explained that they had been watching out the bar windows and had seen what had just happened. The guy explained that there was no love lost between the Royal and the Crown. When he said the word Crown he spat on the floor. Just then the owner walked through and asked Denny if he could help him.

"I'm looking for a room for about three or four weeks, but I will pay you cash for four and if I decide to leave early then you can keep the money. "

He could see he was getting strange looks from the other customers. The owner George had said he had a spare room at the back of the hotel and would only charge him for the nights he stayed. After he put his bags in the room Denny went back into the bar and ordered a whisky with a beer chaser. By the look on the guys' faces he had at once ingratiated himself into the Royal's daytime drinking gang. After a while of introductions, he realised he didn't know what anybody's real name was. Everyone was called by their profession. Sparkie, Chippie, and Plumber were only some of the nicknames. One guy had walked in and 'afternoon lazy fat bastard' was shouted out. His massive belly was a dead giveaway as to what he did for a job. Nothing.

Over the next couple of weeks, he did a bit of exploring around the place and couldn't believe the number of adders he had encountered while out walking. It got to the extent that he wrapped a couple of thin brochures which he found in the hotel reception around his ankles. However, he wasn't sure that would work. He tried to keep out of the bar through the day, but that tended to be hard. He kept having this urge to have a whisky and it was becoming hard to ignore it no matter what.

There was always this niggle in his head as to why he had ended up in Helmsford. It was one night that it suddenly came to him when sitting drinking with the guys.

136

"Does anybody know Time Bomb?" he asked out of the blue. It was as if he had let off a bomb himself. Drinks were put down and everybody just stared at him. Nobody was prepared to ask him how he knew Timebomb. Even the wee dog Midge hid under the seat his owner was sitting on. It seemed on mentioning his name it got everyone extremely nervous. Eventually plumber said,

"Why do ask that young man? Do you have business with Willie? Before we continue this conversation, you're going to tell us why you ended up in Helmsford and if we're not satisfied with your answer then we will be asking you to vacate your room and get the hell out of Helmsford. "

Denny sat and looked at them and realised they were deadly serious.

"It's quite simple folks. Willie's brother Ian comes from the same island off the west coast as I do. We became good friends, and he asked me if I was ever in Helmsford to look up Willie and to say hello. Unfortunately, Willie and I suffer from the same curse. Explosive rage. "

After that revealing fact some of the men just sat shaking their heads. One man got up and walked to the door, but before he went out, he muttered,

"Bloody hell we have one Timebomb in the village, but now it seems we are going to have two soon. I'm going home to my bed and pull the sheets over my head and see what tomorrow brings. If anything. "

Denny couldn't understand what was going on and what all the fuss was about. He asked if anybody could explain why his arrival was causing a problem.

"Well son a few months ago the Royal and Crown got into a bit of a feud to say the least. There was a running battle over there in the square. Feelings had been running high for a while due to one young lad being kicked out the Crown, but not before being given a severe beating by that coward that serves in the bar and his cronies. One Sunday afternoon Willie had decided enough was enough so he downed his whisky, ran out the door, stood in front of the Crown, and shouted for all of them come out so he could give them a beating. All the Crown bar emptied and came after him. He was doing a grand job of knocking the crap out of them until somebody produced a baseball bat and knocked him to the ground. We all ran out to help him hence the running battle. "

He explained that it had calmed down and everyone went back inside until Timebomb decided otherwise and ran alone into the bar and inflicted serious injuries to some of the drinkers and then tried to wreck their bar.

"Is Willie around? I would like to meet him and let him know his brother said hello. "

They told Denny that if he stuck around for a couple of weeks, he would meet him as he is being released from Peterhead jail then and only supposing he comes back to Helmsford.

"He was jailed for fighting. Why? "

They explained to him that the owner of the Crown was friendly with the local constabulary and told them a completely different story from the truth. Hence, he got three months in the jail. As usual the police never came near the Royal for their statements. Denny was a bit shocked at all the this and decided to keep it to himself of his intention to enter the police force.

He spent the next two weeks running over the hills in and around Helmsford, but any good he was doing was outdone by the nights in the Royal bar. Whisky after whisky was being poured down his throat and he was struggling each morning and was forcing himself to go out running.

Some days he felt that bad he would just wander down to the shore and sit watching the sea until it was time for the bar to open. He wasn't sure meeting Willie would be a clever idea, but as he was here, he thought he might as well. The bigger problem was how he was going to curtail his drinking, but it was something he enjoyed so why should he. The days were becoming longer, and his thoughts often drifted back to both Durma and Bavaria. One day he phoned his dad and felt quite emotional talking about what was happening on Durma. His dad had said that Helen was going to move in soon as her gran was going to the care home within a couple of weeks. Denny asked if he could phone him more often to which Lachlan had said he would be delighted. Next was the phone call to Max.

Maria answered the phone and Denny seemed to be a bit lost for words to start with. She was happy to hear from him and said it had been a bit quiet without her handsome Scottish boyfriend. She laughed and then passed the phone to her dad and Denny and Max had a lengthy conversation about everything and anything.

Next was a call to Otto. He told Denny that it was life as normal in the forest. However, one day he had the most beautiful moment when the white stag appeared in front of him. It had stood and looked at him before nonchalantly walking away. Just before they ended the call Otto had said,

"Denny please tell me to mind my own business, but are you keeping your drinking in check? "

Otto must have known by the silence on the other end of the phone that it was a touchy subject.

"I've got a slight problem Otto, but I'm sure I can manage it. Don't worry about me Otto. One day I will get to see the stag. "

"Denny I'm not worried just concerned so if you need to speak to someone about it then phone me anytime. "

After Denny had made his calls, he lay on his bed and decided. He thought it only polite to meet Willie, but after that he was going to head to Edinburgh and get himself sorted out with living accommodation. That was the plan anyway. The night of Willie's return there was no party organised as all the guys wanted this to be low key.

Denny had sat himself at the end of the bar and at eight o'clock Time Bomb walked through the door. Nobody said a word until he shouted,

"Don't tell me that you haven't missed me? Get the bloody drink up. "

A cheer went up and they all started to ply Willie with whisky. Denny thought there was nothing to him and couldn't understand how he could give out all these beatings. A crew cut and scars on his face made him a bit menacing, but other than that he was just an ordinary guy. After a few bottles had been quickly 'downed' Willie looked over at Denny and said,

"Who is our esteemed guest sitting hiding in the corner. Is nobody going to introduce me? "

Willie just stood and looked at Denny. Nobody said a word. They couldn't think of anything worse than two Time Bombs exploding.

"My name is Denny, and I wasn't hiding in the corner. I don't have to hide from anything or anyone. What's your name? "

The men started to make a big gap between them. Ready for a quick exit. There was a silence until Willie said,

"I'm Willie and where are you from pal? "

"I'm from a 'shithole' of a place called Durma and at this point I don't know if I am your pal or not. Oh, and your brother Ian sends his regards. "

It had been a long time since the regulars had seen Willie lost for words. He just stood there looking at Denny. All of a sudden, he threw his body at Denny grabbing him around the waist and pushing him back against the wall. The bar emptied through to the lounge expecting the worst. The walls of the bar were shaking, but Denny got hold of Willie and threw him into the middle of the bar. They stood looking menacingly at each other until Willie burst out laughing which set Denny off.

"Two whiskies Angus and keep them coming as its going to be a long night. "

Angus popped his head up from under the bar where he had been hiding. The other clientele started to filter through from the lounge with a look of relief on their faces.

When everyone was back in the bar Willie announced,

"Right folks this is my brother's pal from Durma. He wrote to me while I was in jail, and he did mention that a mad bastard called Denny Foggerty might call in and see me if he was ever in the area. He did warn me however not to get him mad as it would end up in carnage. "

Denny and Willie started to laugh as did the other guys, but theirs was a nervous laugh. The drink started to flow for real and before long the whole of the bar was well and truly drunk. It was then the owner came in and started to help a few of them out and point them in the right direction to get home. Then the owner George asked Willie and Denny through to his office, just off the bar.

"Right lads I think it might be time to call an end to the feud with that scum across the road. What do you think? "

They both looked crestfallen until Willie said,

"Easy for you to say George, but what happens if they don't want to end it? "said Willie.

George had said to Denny that it had nothing to do with him, but George was covering all eventualities. Denny thought he had better head up to bed. He said his goodbyes, but just before he left Willie pulled him aside and whispered in Denny's ear.

"It isn't over pal, there is a time of reckoning coming for these bastards over the road. Nobody gets me jail time and gets away with it. Trust me. "

Next morning Denny felt worse than he ever had. He spent an age trying to vomit up the whisky from the previous night. An idea came into his head. He skipped breakfast and ran a cold bath. He lay down in it and twice nearly fell asleep or passed out. Once he slipped below the water and came too spluttering and coughing up water. He knew he needed help as this couldn't continue so he thought he would wait until Edinburgh, but he wasn't going to let on to his dad as that could end up killing him.

He dried himself and put his clothes on and returned to his room and lay on his bed contemplating his life in front of him. He had told himself he needed help too many times and finally he realised he was ashamed. It hadn't taken long, but he knew he couldn't do without the whisky. He didn't have a clue how he could help himself or who to turn to for help which he desperately needed.

This would be his last day and night in Helmsford. There would be help he could get in Edinburgh. When he walked past the bar, he heard Willie's voice. It was his intention to go out for a long walk and disappear early tomorrow morning, but Willie saw him and came out and virtually dragged him into the bar. Willie wanted to know all about Durma and how he got to know his brother. Over a few whiskies Denny told him everything about his life. Although he swore him to secrecy about the Albach Trust.

"You've had a hell of a time pal and I really feel sorry for you. I thought I had a hard life at times, but it pales into insignificance compared to yours. What the hell are going to do with your life now especially with the Trust. Hell, your head must be ready to explode. "

"Willie I've never had a decent night's sleep in years. Please don't take this the wrong way, but I have been accepted into the police force in Edinburgh and I start in a few weeks. Also, I told you about my mum and I am sure I am going the same way and

141

without help I don't know what will happen to me. I have enjoyed meeting you Willie, but I will be leaving early tomorrow morning. "

They both sat in silence just looking into their whisky glasses. Denny told Willie he would see him later for a few drinks, but he would not be late in heading to his bed. Although filled with whisky he told Willie he was off for a long walk to get his mind in some semblance of order. That night Denny had a large meal and told George his intentions for the next day and on no account would he accept any money back. He thought it only prudent to have his last few drinks with the guys in the bar. As he walked in Willie was sitting on his own in front of a side window. Denny sat down beside him, and they were just chatting when suddenly a boulder came through the window hitting Denny on the jaw. Everybody was shocked, but one guy had the foresight to stand on the seat and shout,

"Whoever it was just ran into the Crown. Guy with a shaved head. "

George ran through and tried to calm everybody down, but Time Bomb's fuse had been lit. George didn't know if he could contain the situation until Denny stood up and shouted,

"Willie this is not your problem it's mine and I'll sort it out." Willie was about to kick off as Denny could recognise the signs.

"I'm going over the road myself and if I don't come out then your free to do what you want. Do you hear me Willie? "

Willie's chest was heaving, and his eyes were glazing over. So, Denny knew it was time to end this once and for all. As he started to walk over the road Time Bomb appeared at the door, but Denny roared at him this time to get back inside. As he walked Denny kept thinking how cursed he was. Always someone or something else dictating the outcome of his life.

His rage hadn't kicked in yet and deep down he was hoping the situation could be resolved without too much violence. After all he only wanted to speak to the bald-headed guy.

As he neared the front door of the Crown, he could see someone trying to bolt both doors. He took off and ran at the doors smashing into them and nearly taking them off their hinges. When he stepped through them the guy who had tried to bolt them was literally splattered up again the back wall with the

142

imprint of the lock on his forehead. He was trying to tell himself to be calm but found himself laughing at the same time. Slowly and casually, he walked through the doors to the bar and stood in the middle.

"By the look on your faces I presume you were expecting Willie. I'm sorry to disappoint you all, but you'll just have to put up with me. I only came for the guy who threw the boulder. That same boulder that hit me on the chin. If you give him up, then nobody else will get hurt. What's it to be then? "

Nobody said a word until the bully behind the bar piped up,

"You're getting nobody from this bar you little 'scrot' Go back to your arseholes from across the road. "

"You have just made the biggest mistake of your life calling me a 'scrot.' "

It was then that the bald guy appeared at Denny's back and swung at him with a baseball bat. Denny saw him in the mirror at the back of the bar at the last minute and although he deflected it still caught him on the same jaw that the boulder hit. Denny was now full on with his rage. The doors to the bar burst open and Willie walked forward and stood shoulder to shoulder with Denny. For the guys in the bar, it must have been menacing. Two maniacs ready to go off on one.

"Did you think you were going to get all the excitement big man? "

They both started to laugh with an evil grin on their faces. Then the carnage started. Denny jumped at the barman dragging him on to the top of the bar while pounding his fist into his face repeatedly before taking the water jug and hitting him over the head. He left him lying on the bar only to turn round and see Willie smashing two guys over the head with a chair. Denny picked up a table and threw it behind the bar wrecking all the bottles on the gantry. Another two guys who must have had a brainstorm ran at Denny, but Willie intervened and put the one on the right onto the floor and started to knock hell out of him.

Denny duly dispatched the other one with a flurry of blows that sent the blood spurting out the of guy's mouth and ear. For good measure he burst his nose with his trademark haymaker punch.

Denny turned round to see Willie picking up a six-seater table

143

and throwing it at the large bay window. The whole window, frame and all landed on the pavement outside. This was the opportunity that some of the older guys needed. They just jumped on the bench seating and went out the gap that was left. Some headfirst. There were a few men left who couldn't make up their minds whether they wanted to be in this fight or not. Willie and Denny made up their minds for them and with a combined attack punched them into submission.

The floor was becoming slippery with the blood. Just then the owner who must have been keeping quiet in one of the upstairs rooms came running behind the bar. He was shouting that he was going to call the police, but before he could say another word Willie shouted back saying,

"There will be no police this time. Do you hear me? I'm not doing any more jail time for a 'dick' like you, but if you do call them, I will come and burn your hotel down and make sure you can't get out. "

Willie then pulled him by the throat on to the bar and continually smashed the owner's face until he was unconscious. He left him lying next to his brother.

When the two stood looking around all they could see was mayhem. Willie then walked behind the bar and poured two large whiskies. As they drank, evil smiles come over their faces. They were about to leave when Denny grabbed Willie's arm and said,

"Hang on something isn't right. Where is the guy with the shaven head? "

They both walked up to the end of the bar only to find shaven head hiding below the hatch at the end. He had his hands over his ears and had obviously been crying.

"Leave him to me Willie. "

Denny opened the hatch and grabbed him by his collar. He then pulled him up and forced his head onto the edge of the bar. Taking the hatch lid, he went ahead and smashed it down on the guy's head for quite some time. He turned to see Willie with a look of disappointment on his face probably because it wasn't him that was doing it. Eventually he let the guy fall on to the floor.

Then came a shout from the front door. It was George.

"Get yourselves out the back door, walk up the river and in the back door across the road. Don't argue just do it now. They moved quickly out the back and headed for the path that ran by the river. They eventually came to the steps that led into the Royal. George met them at the door. He sat them down and explained that he would cover for them as much as was humanly possible, but there had to be a limit. He said that all the guys in the pub would swear that you were in the bar all night.

"Can I say one thing though lads. I looked through the Crown bar door and all I could see was something akin to a bloody war zone. Look at your hands for God's sake. They are scraped to hell. Just in case the ' polis ' come looking put some effort into cleaning them up and wear gloves for a while. Denny, I will give you a pair before you leave and that will be on the first bus tomorrow to Inverness at nine o'clock. "

Denny thought he had better go to his room and forget the whisky for one night. No matter how hard that would be.

For once Denny had slept and his internal clock woke him at six in the morning. He started to think about what had happened last night, but what had gone on couldn't be undone. After a long soak in the bath, he packed and went downstairs for breakfast.

Amazingly causing mayhem and destruction never spoilt his appetite and George had done him proud by making up a packed lunch for his long journey. As he was about to leave George shook his hand and whispered to him,

"Try and get some help for your drinking son but drop in anytime you are up here. Take care. "

"Thanks George I'll try hard. Oh, and look after Willie will you. "

He could still hear George laughing as he closed the hotel front door. With his gloves covering his war wounds he walked up to the bus stop at the main road. As he sat in the shelter, he looked over at Helmsford. Another place where his demons had got the better of him. While he had his head in his hands, he heard someone saying,

"Is this anybody's seat? "

Willie started to laugh, and Denny thought to himself what a cracking guy this would be without his rage. After chatting for a while Denny saw the bus coming down the hill. He stood and shook Time Bomb's hand and said,

"Willie I am sure I'll need your help again so I know I can just phone the pub to get you. Oh, and don't dare wave me away. I have an image to protect even although it's a terrible image. Or I might just jump back off the bus and then we'll see what would happen. "

As he sat on the bus seat, he knew exactly what would happen. The bus started to pick up speed and Willie started to give a silly wave and started to do a little jig. Denny started to laugh. He made a mental note to try and laugh more.

The following year the Crown was purchased by George and converted into self-contained flats for the tourists. An exceptionally large cheque from Germany paid for all expenses. The accompanying note with the cheque only said it was from the other Time Bomb. George had told everyone in the bar one night about the cheque which he realised had come from Denny. He had said he wasn't sure he was going to accept it, but Willie had told him that he should take it as Denny would have wanted him to have it and as sure as hell, he could afford it. Nothing else was said.

Chapter 14

Denny knew that this journey was going to be long as he was going to try it without getting off at some point for a whisky. By the time the train had reached Edinburgh he jumped off and ran like hell till he hit a pub in Rose Street. When he was on his second whisky, he suddenly realised how bad he was getting. He got up and walked to the phone in the snug at the end of the bar and phoned his dad. Lachlan was delighted to hear from him and told him he had taken the liberty of securing a flat for him. It was in Learmonth Grove which wasn't far from Fettes Police Training College. He borrowed pen and paper from the barman to write the address down as after a few whiskies he might not remember. His dad asked him how his health was, and Denny told him he was feeling great. He was getting into the habit of lying to people. It became second nature to him.

After Denny moved in to his flat, he had to get kitted out with new clothes. So, a shopping trip along Princes Street was in order. He said to himself that he would try and only drink the whisky when he finished work or his days off.

The day had come when he had to attend the college to become a police officer. Weeks went by with Denny making a great impression on his training officers, but he was struggling to get through the days. If the days were interesting then he could cope, but if not, then his brain was in turmoil trying to think of ways to get him through till leaving time. He often thought that he would have to resign, but the thought of telling his dad he had failed wasn't a possibility.

Denny had been assigned a partner in Patrick Laing. A tall soft-spoken Irishman who seemed capable of handling himself. They got on well together until one day when investigating a fight in a pub from the previous night Patrick had saw Denny accepting a whisky from the owner when he thought his partner wasn't looking. When they were outside Patrick had told Denny he saw what had happened and never to do that again when they were working together. Denny apologised and said it was a one off. A silly mistake. One day he had noticed a leaflet in a shop

147

window while out pounding the beat. It was for Alcoholics Anonymous and made a mental note of the phone number as he didn't want to write it down while Patrick was there.

His only escape from work was heading to the pubs either at night or on his days off. Money wasn't a problem as he was still receiving a payment from the Trust. One of his favourite pubs was the Strachan Arms which was only a few minutes' walk from where he lived. It pretended it was an upmarket establishment, but the same class of working girls plied their trade there as they did elsewhere. For a while one of the girls took a shine to Denny and a few times he took her home with him at the end of the night. There was always an argument the next morning as to whether Jennifer would accept payment. He always insisted that she accept more than the going rate. Much more.

Denny started to go out running and do exercises to try and keep fit and keep his body in good condition. He thought that this would keep the effects of the whisky at bay. However, it didn't last long, and he knew he was just kidding himself on. He even tried taking the neighbours cocker spaniel for walks, but he just ended up taking the dog to the pub with him. The neighbour found out and put a stop to it.

After one drunken Saturday night he woke up feeling awful and doing his bouts of vomiting the whisky up. He said to himself that he loved the drink, but the drink didn't love him. While lying on the sofa feeling sorry for himself, he remembered he had written down the number for the AA. He was surprised to get an answer on a Sunday, but a lovely sounding girl called Gail spoke to him. She gave him the address and time of the next meeting and encouraged him to come along. It was in four days, so he had plenty of time. Especially for some more whiskies. Despite his drinking Denny was getting rave reviews from his handlers at college and they had asked him if he would like to be attached to the C. I. D. He wasn't sure as this was more responsibility, but after some thought he had said he would as it could be a bit more interesting.

It was Acting Detective Constable Foggerty that walked through the doors to the AA meeting. When he looked through the glass door and saw everyone sitting there, he turned around and started to walk out. Then a voice shouted,

"Is that you Daniel? Please don't be shy. Just come on through. "

Denny had used the name Daniel as he didn't want anybody knowing he was attending these meetings. Especially the Police Force. Denny just sat in the circle of attendees not knowing what it was all about. People from all walks of life. Some with their heads down while others were putting a brave face on it and looking everyone in the eye. He wondered if this was the help that his dad wanted to get his mum. Then it was his turn to give up his story. All he could say was,

"My name is Daniel. My mother died not so long ago through being an alcoholic. Now I am that same alcoholic. It's just that I like the whisky too much. Up until now my job has not been affected, but for how long I don't know. "

They all clapped, and Gail put her hand on his shoulder and gave a little squeeze. It was over an hour before everybody had their say and Denny felt he needed to get into the fresh air. As the meeting broke up Gail said,

"Daniel this will be hard, but we are all here for you and we will do anything we can to get you off the alcohol. "

She gave him a note of her personal phone number and told him to phone at any time if he needed help. He thanked her and walked out the building looking for the nearest pub. After a few whiskies he made up his mind that he would try his damnedest not to let his illness affect his job.

As the weeks passed Denny found himself learning more about detective work and began to enjoy it. However, night times were often just a blur with the drink, and he found himself buying a quarter pound of fruit drops most mornings to cover up the smell of his breath.

It was while he was on an operation one night that he excelled himself. The police had surrounded a warehouse down Leith knowing a gang of robbers were hiding out after they set the alarm off. Denny was told to stay at the back and see the experienced officers as they entered the building.

At one point a member of the gang burst past the front line of the police, but Denny took him down with a flying tackle and then proceeded to give him a couple of punches to the chin. He felt someone pulling him off the guy and telling Denny to ease

149

off. The gang had been rounded up and were being led out of the warehouse. At that point Denny's sixth sense kicked in and he shouted to his superior that there was still a man hiding.

"Get a grip Foggerty we have them all. Don't spout your nonsense. "

"No disrespect sir, but I am not talking nonsense. There is one more guy hiding out. Take my word for it. Just trust me. "

His senior officer stood there looking at him until he announced to the team that he wanted one more sweep of the warehouse. The police team grudgingly agreed and started to search again.

"I hope your right Foggerty, or we will be having words. We are already into our overtime budget. "

Denny told them to look at the far end of the warehouse. It wasn't long before a shout went up,

"Got the bugger sir. Foggerty was spot on. This could be the gang leader as his face rings a bell. Works for Thomson, I think. "

That name sent a bit of a shiver up Denny's back and as the robber was led past him, he put his face down so that he couldn't be recognised in the future.

"Well done everyone. Let's get back to the station and get this wrapped up. Foggerty, well done and be in my office at eight o'clock tomorrow so stay out the pub. "

Denny wondered what the hell that comment was about. Did he know about his drinking? Was he just saying it as a matter of fact? Or was Denny just being paranoid?

To hell with it he would have a few whiskies on his way home.

The Strachan Arms was still open when he got there. The barman told him they wouldn't close for another hour, so he had plenty of time for a few. That night while trying to chase sleep he thought he was at the crossroads of his life. He knew he had to stop drinking, but how could he as he really enjoyed the whisky. This was another time he wanted to put his face in the pillow and cry. There was nobody to help him as he had tried hard to keep it a secret.

Next morning, he headed for his boss' office not knowing what to expect. His boss had asked him to sit down.

"Well Foggerty, that was sterling work you put in last night.

Well done. One thing I would like to explore is how did you know there was another guy hiding? Before we talk about that though I must pull you up about your unconventional way of apprehending a suspect. Fine that you tackled him, but then punching him twice on the face is not standard practice for a police officer. As much as you feel like it, please don't do it. Denny then explained about his sixth sense which certainly raised his boss's eyebrows.

"Does it work every time Foggerty, and can you give me another example? "

Denny told him about looking for Isla and how he still thinks about it. He said that it wasn't full proof, but when it kicked in you could always rely on it.

"I'm sure we will have a lot of use for your talent son, but a word of advice. Lay off the drink. Pounds worth of fruit gums or whatever they are don't hide the smell of the alcohol. Your training instructors picked it up right away and if you hadn't been an excellent student then you would have been kicked out on your ear a long time ago. Get it sorted Foggerty, but look after this."

His boss handed him his new warrant card. Acting Detective Foggerty carefully putting it in his back pocket as if was overseeing a million pounds. Denny couldn't bring up his dependency on whisky as he was sure it would be instant dismissal, but he needed desperately to speak to someone but who? He couldn't speak to his dad or even Ian as they would be so disappointed in him. Bavaria was a no go as he didn't want to drag them into his life which was spiralling downwards at a rate of knots. When he thought about Willie he just laughed.

It was then he realised that Gail had given him her personal number. That evening he tried a few times to get a hold of her, but it just kept ringing out.

There was nothing else for it he told himself. A drink was in order. He walked past the Strachan and eventually found a pub near Dean village aptly named The Dean. First impression was it was a bit rough. Second impression was that it was a 'dive' of the first order. That suited Denny though. He just put his baseball hat down low and got stuck into the whisky. His plan was to try and slow down and pace himself. As he sat at the end of the bar a fight started over someone accusing the barman of short-changing him.

This fight was going to really kick off which wasn't good for Denny as it would involve the police. He walked around the bar and suggested to the accuser that he should take his trade elsewhere. A small part of Denny's six sense had kicked in and he knew the barman was a thief. The man started to protest, but Denny just took his arm and lifted him out of the bar. Denny went into his pocket and took five pounds out and gave it to the man. Telling him he believed him, and it wasn't worth getting arrested for. As the man started to protest Denny produced his warrant card from his back pocket and showed it to the man. The man looked at the size of Denny, then the warrant card, turned and walked away.

Denny thought about walking away too, but instead walked back in and found the barman laughing with a few of the regulars. As he sat down a whisky appeared in front of him.

Denny grabbed him by the apron and pulled him towards him before saying.

"Listen you slimy bastard I know you short changed that guy. You're a low life so I suggest you never do that again. "

The barman started to swear at him, so he pulled him closer and then poured the whisky into his ear. Denny released his grip and then gave the guy one punch that sent him flying to the other end of the bar before ending up on a couple boxes of crisps. Denny walked out and headed home which was a bit strange for him. He was sober for once in a long time.

When he arose the next morning, he saw that there was a message from Gail saying she would love to meet him. Before he went to work, he phoned his dad to give him all the news. His dad was delighted for him. He asked his dad to put Helen on and she sounded quite happy. Denny was pleased for her and when she hung up, he felt a pang of regret never knowing if he would ever see her again.

Unfortunately work that day was just boring paperwork and he noticed his instructors hanging over him at times. Presumably checking out his breath for the smell of alcohol. A good breakfast and mouthfuls of mouthwash had done the trick. Wrigley's spearmint chewing gum being chewed all the way to the station completed the cover up. When Saturday came, he was getting quite excited about meeting Gail. He thought he could do with a whisky but thought better of it. There would be plenty time for that afterwards. He took the forty-seven bus up to the Grassmarket. This was an area he never really frequented so he just ambled around. He was early so he was enjoying making a mental note of all the interesting pubs. The Cafe Rio was bigger than he thought and when he entered, he struggled to see her. Finally, he saw her waving from a table at the back.

As he approached the table, he couldn't help thinking what a lovely looking girl Gail was. Short, cropped jet-black hair, blue eyes with a pert little mouth. He had never noticed her at the meeting, but that was due to him always keeping his head down. Once they had ordered, Gail had said she was glad he had contacted her. However, he had to quickly realise that this meeting was about his alcohol addiction and nothing more. They talked for a while before Denny revealed why he had contacted her. He needed help. Lots of help.

She was straight to the point saying that as much as she was there to help him it was only Daniel Foggerty that could get himself out of the mess he was in.

"Daniel, I saw your body language at the meeting and I'm not sure you really want to help yourself. You've got to be strong and have the will power otherwise you're wasting both of our time. "

He knew she was right but wasn't convinced he could.

"Now is not the right time or it may be highly inappropriate, but can we meet up for a coffee another time then? "

She was a bit hesitant but said she would think about it and tell him at the next AA meeting. After they went their own way Denny thought he would have a look at some of the pubs he had noticed. It was only the afternoon, but one whisky led to another, then another until by six o'clock he was really feeling a bit worse for wear. After buying his next whisky he looked into the glass and just laughed. He knew there wasn't a hope in hell of him giving up this beautiful drink. His laugh drew somebody's attention round the bar. A guy who was regaling some girls with his tales of how much of a great guy he was.

"Keep it down pal we are trying to enjoy ourselves here without listening to you laughing into your whisky glass. So, pack it in or else. "

Denny knew he couldn't afford get into trouble, but this ' prick ' had just annoyed him.

"Listen you 'prick' if my laughing is causing you a problem then I suggest you move further along the bar with your entourage or go to another bar. Also, what do you mean by or else? "

"Or else means I will take you outside and give you a good kicking. Understand? "

"Why don't we have it out right here and now and the ladies can see what a blowhard you are although there will be a lot of blood coming from your nose so the ladies might want to stand clear. "

The guy took off his jacket and walked around the bar. Denny had his feet on the bar at the bottom of the stool so when the guy came into range, he lifted himself up and launched a punch on the guy's nose. The cartilage must have disintegrated even before he hit the ground. As he lay there moaning Denny walked on top of him leaving a footprint on his forehead to get to the door. Just before he exited, he turned to the ladies and apologised if he had spoiled their night. He took a cap that he kept for these purposes, pulled it down low and hailed the first taxi he saw.

Next day he just lay in his bed until later in the afternoon when he got himself up and wandered out for a few whiskies. However, he struggled to keep them down and headed back to his flat. He went straight back to bed and never surfaced until his alarm went off at seven am. Over breakfast of toast and coffee he thought how easy it had become for him to lift his fists. Was this another demon with which he was cursed? He thought he should add it to the list and just shook his head. When he got to work his boss had asked him into his office. Denny was beginning to panic a bit after the skirmish the other night.

"Come in Foggerty and sit down. You haven't been with us long, but I have a job for you, but if you don't feel up to it then it's not a problem. It could be dangerous, but only if you make mistakes. "

He went on to explain that they were trying to set up an undercover operation on young Billy Thomson. As soon as he said his name Denny started to feel a bit dizzy. His boss explained

154

that they needed someone to shadow him whenever he left his house in New Town which wasn't far from Denny's flat. He explained that over the next few weeks Denny would be taught how to do surveillance. He was told that he would only report to his boss as they couldn't be certain that Thomson wasn't paying off police officers. This was all about drugs and Denny had to try and find out how it was arriving in Edinburgh for Thomson to distribute it.

Denny had been told to go away and think about it, but his first impression was that he was the lamb to the slaughter. Next day he walked into the boss's office and told him he would do it, but he wanted as much training as possible. Over a few whiskies the previous night he thought that this might be a terrific opportunity for him to rise up the ranks. There was one minor problem, however. Denny didn't have a driving license although he had driven his dad's van since he was a youngster, but only on Durma. His boss had told him not to worry as they would fast track him through the DVLA process which was standard practice for the police force.

Denny was quite excited about all this, but he was worried about one thing. The whisky. He then thought to hell with it as he wouldn't give up the whisky and just try and do the assignment as best as he could. It wasn't that he didn't want to give the alcohol up, he couldn't and the quicker he realised this the better. He had asked his dad to send the relevant books he had back on Durma. Books he had bought on surveillance, camouflage, and basic survival techniques. He thought he would try and contact Felix in Germany and ask his advice. There was no way he was leaving anything to chance.

That night after he had been out on the ' drink ' he had come back to a message on his answer machine from Gail. She was just reminding him about the next AA meeting and how was he doing. He phoned her back and explained that there was a chance he might not make it as he was going through some intense training now, and it included night - time work. However, he was making great inroads into cutting out the alcohol. She told him she would phone next week to organise a meet up for a chat and coffee. When Denny came off the phone, he realised just how easy it had been to lie to Gail about his drinking. He just shrugged his shoulders and forgot about it.

The following two weeks had been manic with the training and when he went home, he felt he needed to have whisky before he got there. His head was buzzing each day and thought it justifiable to drink the alcohol to relax. Denny new that this was rubbish, but it suited him to think like that.

After eight weeks of training and learning to drive his boss thought he was ready to start the surveillance operation. Denny knew exactly what he was going to do. Intelligence had said that Thomson drank in the Thistle Bar which wasn't far from where he lived so Denny sat in the undercover police car most nights watching who he went in. It turned out to be the same two goons he had beat up in Rose Street. Small, but relevant information. He knew this wasn't going to be a quick investigation and said to himself ' slowly wins the races ' Denny. For two weeks he noted everyone that he thought looked suspicious. Especially the ones that went in and came out a few minutes later. He knew it was time to change tactics.

When he was reporting back to his boss, he had said to Denny that he needed to take time off and then get back to the job in hand.

Denny decided that he was going to explore some of the pubs in the town especially the ones up the Grassmarket. Somebody at work had told him to explore the 'Pubic Triangle' for a laugh. After having a drink in a few bars, he realised why it had been given that name. Every pub seemed to have a 'stripper' tucked away in some part of the lounge or bar. This was new to him, but he found it amusing as the girls were of all shapes and sizes. He sat at the bar watching all the guys ogling these girls and some of the comments that were shouted were hilarious. "Put your clothes back on. You've got more tattoos than a drunken sailor. You need a couple of pies to feed you up. "

Nobody seemed bothered about the overpriced drink that was being served. Until Denny was in the Port Bar, and he noticed the price of his whisky was going up every time. The next time he bought a whisky he challenged the barman about the cost. The barman was a bit threatening and told Denny to take his custom elsewhere. Denny asked to see the owner and eventually a guy walked through from the back.

"Are you the arsehole that's causing problems? "

"Firstly, I suggest you curb your language pal, "said Denny.

The guy just laughed, but Denny went right back at him. He took his warrant card out of his back pocket and said,

"DC Foggerty at your service sir. "

Denny smiled and watched the guy's face turn to grey as he started to mumble what he thought might be an apology until Denny said,

"Please listen to what I am going to tell you. There are some decent guys in your bar for a bit of entertainment and you and the barman are ripping them off. So, I will be back in and if I catch you at it again then this place will lose its licence. Got it? "

Denny realised he shouldn't have produced his warrant card, but instead just walk away. However, he seemed to be becoming less capable of thinking things through. Not good for a police officer. He headed home and sat in his flat just mulling things over in his head. He wondered where his life going and could he see himself doing this for the next twenty years.

Next day he got up early and went for a run around a park close to his house, but he was only half an hour in when the vomiting started, and he had to sit on one of the park benches and put his head between his legs until the sickness died down.

After he walked home, he thought about phoning Durma, but it wasn't long since he did that. It was obvious he needed help, but he couldn't understand his refusal to accept it. It was Monday again, and Denny sat at his desk doing some boring paperwork when his boss dropped a set of car keys on his desk and said,

"We need to start upping the ante on the Thomson case Foggerty so get a move on. You are free to do your own hours but make them productive and remember to report to me only. He left early that day to prepare himself for his night surveillance.

He sat in his Ford Escort watching The Thistle Bar and Thomson finally arrived with his cohorts. Denny was starting to get a bit fed up just sitting around noting faces, so he decided a more direct approach was needed. He put on a large duffle coat which he had obtained from the lost property office at the station. Next was his cap and then he added a pair of spectacles with clear lenses. On entering the bar nobody seemed to bother about him and he sat at the bar near to where Thomson was entertaining

157

several people. It was obvious that he thought he was the king pin, and they were all laughing and nodding their heads when he said anything.

"Are you looking for anything for tonight big man? "came a shout from one of Thomson's crew. This was Denny's way in, so he replied,

"I might, but I'm not sure I have enough cash so how much is two lines of the cocaine? "

Thomson piped up that there was no cocaine, but he would have plenty on Saturday night. Denny thanked him and said he would call in on Saturday. This meant that he would be getting a delivery on Friday, so he had to find out where. He had to be watching his house most of Friday. Denny had another couple of whiskies before he realised he was driving. At home Denny tried to think of a plan to snare Thomson. Eventually he concluded that he would do this one way. Play on his vanity. He obviously thought he was untouchable and that would be his downfall. He had to make his plan full proof.

He watched Thomson's house each day, but he never surfaced until after midday and never looked like he was into anything illegal.

It was Saturday and Denny knew he had to be on top of his game today. However, he had woken up with his usual cravings, but today of all days he was struggling to keep them at bay. He did the usual and parked along the road from Thomson's house and waited. It seemed like an eternity before he walked out the door, but this time with three other guys. These guys looked in a different league from his usual goons. Denny likened them to three gorillas and their faces were covered in scars. They had obviously seen a bit of action and Denny thought this changed his plan considerably. They all jumped into a car and headed off at a steady speed.

Denny followed a bit behind, but he wasn't afraid of losing them as they were in a racing green Jaguar. He sensed this was Thomson's car. Eventually they headed down Leith Walk and turned into an industrial estate. Denny stopped and decided to walk a bit. He carefully looked around the corner only to see them enter a warehouse. The door had been open so there must have been someone in before they arrived. He waited on the corner

158

until the doors opened and a white van appeared as did Thomson and his men and got in the Jaguar. He watched the van pass, and he recognised the driver as one of Thomson's goons.

He didn't know who to follow so he opted for Thomson. The Jaguar was only driven as far as the Thistle Bar where they all got out. Denny knew he had made the wrong choice.

He decided to go home and regroup. He dropped the car off and headed for a little pub just down the road from the Strachan. The whisky was hardly touching the sides. When he was finally drunk, he staggered home and went to bed. Next morning, he was lying in bed smelling vomit. He looked over the side of the bed and saw a patch on the carpet where he had thrown up. Although this was not a good sign, he just buried his head in the sand about it and cleaned up his vile smelling vomit. On the Monday he had went to his boss and told him about the problem he had trying to follow two vehicles and suggested it would help to have somebody with him when he was on a surveillance. His boss had said he would think about it, but due to the sensitive nature of this case he couldn't guarantee anything.

Denny continued with the surveillance but was getting nowhere and was becoming quite frustrated. He had thought about the frequency of the drugs being delivered to Thomson, but he could only guess it would be an as and when situation. One night he got the breakthrough he was waiting for when Thomson's goons had brought a guy out of the pub and dragged him around the corner and had given him a beating. He waited until it was clear and crossed the road and started to help the guy up. He walked him along the road into a small park. Sitting the guy on a bench he quickly engaged in conversation with him.

Denny pretended to be a good Samaritan and asked him what that was all about. The guy whose name was Johnny told Denny he owed a lot of money to Thomson. Unfortunately, Johnny had said he was a gambler and never had much luck on the horses. Thomson had told him he had to pay off his debt by working for him if he didn't have the cash which Johnny had quickly realised would be the distribution of drugs around the streets and pubs.

"How would you like to pay off your debt in one go Johnny? "said Denny. He saw the guy's eyes light up and Denny told him all he had to do was find out who was supplying him with drugs

159

and when and where they would be arriving in Edinburgh.

"That first part is easy son. It's his dad in Dundee that does the supplying but finding out when they will come into Edinburgh is the hard part, but he has two warehouses which he uses. You see son, Thomson likes to boast about how big a man he is, but he is lightweight compared to his dad. Are you the police? "

"No not the police pal. I'm trying to muscle in on Thomson's patch. So, I want as much information as I can. How much is your debt to him? "

Johnny had told him it was a hundred pounds. It was quite a bit of money, but Denny could cover it.

"Okay here is what we will do. I'll meet you here in a couple of nights and give you what you owe him. For every piece of relevant information after that I'll pay you twenty pounds. To get near him keep borrowing small amounts and I'll cover it. "

Denny told him he would be outside the Thistle bar every second night after their first meeting. Before they parted Denny said,

"Johnny if you double cross me, I'll slit your throat and dump you in the water at Leith Docks. "

Johnny just nodded as if he understood.

The next day when he was sitting at his desk his phone rang. It was his boss asking him to come through to his office. When he walked in there was a woman standing against one of the walls.

"Come in Foggerty and meet Pc Shonagh Slater. She will be your new partner for the duration of the Thomson surveillance. She will answer to you, but you will both be under my command. Both of you will have a car and I will be expecting some satisfactory progress soon. Oh, and don't put her in any danger Foggerty. "

When they left the office Denny asked if she would like a coffee so, he could bring her up to scratch. They got their drinks and went into one of the interview rooms so that nobody could overhear them. He spent about half an hour giving her an update. Denny noticed what a good-looking girl she was with a great body. He had to concentrate though as this surveillance could get nasty. Shonagh asked what he wanted her to do and he said to bring the car and park about one hundred yards up from the

160

Thistle Bar at one o'clock tomorrow.

The next day he was sitting in the car looking in his rear-view mirror when he saw her pulling in up the road from him. He got out of the car and walked up to her car and sat in the passenger side. It was idle chit chat between them as they kept an eye on the comings and goings at the Thistle. Shonagh quickly realised that to do this surveillance was a case of mind over matter as she had only been at it for a few hours, and she was bored.

Thomson had arrived with his goons at three o'clock. Ten minutes afterwards they both saw a car going around the back of the bar with several people in it. Denny waited a while and strolled over the road holding a street map of Edinburgh. Another of his props. He went around the back and a few minutes later he was starting to walk back until someone walked out the side door. It was the barman carrying an empty beer barrel.

"Can I help you pal? What are you doing around the back of the pub? "the barman asked in a gruff voice. Denny explained he was looking for a short cut to the Strachan Arms. The guy looked at him suspiciously before saying,

"Your bloody miles away so go back up that road and keep walking. Now bugger off and don't let me catch you here again. Understood? "

Denny thanked him for his help and walked up the street and continued past the car where Shonagh was waiting. He knew the barman was still watching so when he was out of sight, he waited ten minutes before he walked over the road and headed to Shonagh's car. He told her he had noticed an expensive car tucked in behind the bar. They started to work out their next move, but Denny thought he had blown it as the barman would recognise him if he went in, but they had to know who was in there. It was then Shonagh had said she had an idea. She would go in and ask to use the toilet and check out all the people in there. Denny thought it was simple, but it meant exposing her face to whoever was in there.

"Nice idea, but they might recognise you in the future. "

"Denny I've been in amateur dramatics since I was young so give me a few minutes and I will change my face completely. Denny watched as she removed her make up bag from under the front seat and got to work. He wondered why she would have a

161

makeup bag on a surveillance, but then again nothing surprised him about the fairer sex.

By the time she had finished he was convinced this wasn't Shonaugh that was sitting next to him.

"Be careful Shonagh. Remember just in and out. "

"Denny my pretence is to ask to go to the toilet so hopefully somebody will agree as I'm about to wet myself sitting in this cold car. "

As she walked through the door there were only a few regulars in and there was no sign of the barman. She could see where the doors to the toilets were at the far end of the bar. She kept on walking until she came upon several men all seated in a small area which they thought would give them privacy.

"Excuse me I was going to ask the barman, but as he is not here do you think he would mind if I used the toilet? "

"Get lost you hooker this is a private meeting, "said young Thomson.

She stood there putting on a look of shock until an older guy said to young Thomson,

"Shut your mouth Billy you wouldn't know manners if they jumped up and bit you on your arse son. Good job your mother can't hear you. On you go lass. Don't mind him. "

Shonagh went through the toilet door, but she was sure somebody had followed her and was standing outside the ladies' door. She continued as normal and after she finished, she momentarily stood behind the toilet door leading back to the bar. All she could hear was young Billy arguing about why it should always be a Friday. As she went past them, she stopped and thanked Thomson senior. She was however trying to memorise the faces. She smiled and walked out the bar. She followed Denny's example and walked up the street and round the corner and waited for a while before heading back to the car.

Once she was back in the car, she told him what had happened. Denny was really pleased with the news and told her she had done a fantastic job. They discussed what their next step should be. Denny had said he would meet Johnny tomorrow night and take it from there, but firstly he wanted to see what Thomson senior looked like. Shonagh thought that might be a bit risky, but Denny was in charge. He told her to head home, and he would

162

contact her once he had formulated a plan. They parted company and Denny put his disguise on from the previous time and walked over the road and into a side road and waited. Eventually they all came out the back door and he walked up past them. He memorised the face of Thomson senior and his henchmen, but just then young Billy shouted,

"Hey, you I thought you were coming in for something the other night? "

"I was sir, but unfortunately, I didn't have any cash. "

Billy told him they would come to an agreement if he was strapped for cash. Denny thanked him and said he would see him soon. Denny made a mental note of the car registration and walked away.

As he drove away, he decided that he needed a drink and returned to his flat dropping the car off. He had a couple of hours to pass before it was time to meet Johnny, so he found a bar within walking distance of the Thistle. He sat drinking the whisky until a working girl came up to his side. She smiled and soon he bought her a drink. It led to several drinks, and he was enjoying her company before he realised, he had to run for the meeting with Johnny. He told her that he would come back and if she was still there then they would go for a drink. She agreed and then Denny had left.

At first, he thought Johnny hadn't turned, but eventually he saw him in a doorway in one of the side streets. He walked over to him and gave him the hundred pounds.

"Listen Johnny I need information and I need it fast. Where is his other warehouse and if possible, the exact day of the month when he gets his deliveries? Okay? "

Johnny just nodded and then thanked him for the cash. He left and walked down and into the Thistle. Denny waited for a while just up from the bar until he saw him coming out. Unfortunately, he was holding his jaw. Denny new that this was meted out because of overdue payment so that others wouldn't do the same.

He quickly walked back to the bar only to find the girl sitting with a couple of her friends and some guys. Denny didn't blame her, so he sat at the bar and ordered a whisky. When he was on his second, he felt somebody sidling into him. It was the girl from before. He asked if she would like a drink. Vodka and Coke was her answer. A few minutes passed before one of the guys she had been sitting with shouted,

"Hey 'slag' get yourself back here as your in our company. Don't let me come over and give you a slapping. You hear me bitch "

Denny thought please not another loudmouth. He just whispered to her to stay where she was as she was safe with him. Another few minutes passed before the big mouth got up shoving the people at the table out of the way and came over to the girl. He lifted his hand to strike the girl, but Denny grabbed the guy's hand and squeezed it until a pained expression came over the guy's face. He deflected a punch from the guy's other hand before sticking the head on him. His mates jumped up and started towards Denny.

He pulled the girl out of the firing line and waded into the guys. After the hit on the second guy Denny's rage was in full flow. The girls at the table were screaming and getting sprayed with blood. They were jumping over each other to get out of the way. Even although there were four of them, they didn't put up too much resistance and soon they were either lying on the table or passed out on the floor. He was breathing hard, and he needed to get his heart rate down. What came into his head was why did he stop punching them so quickly? He leaned on the bar until his rage was dying down. Eventually he picked up his whisky and drank it. Denny asked the girl if she would like to come back to his place. She nodded and they started to leave the bar, but not before Denny picked up the water jug from the bar and smashed it over the first guy's head. Denny found that was a great encore. He stopped and turned to the barman who was physically shaking and gave him five pounds.

"I hope this covers the cost of the broken water jug and if you value your health, you will tell the police you were hiding and couldn't identify me. "

As they were walking out the usual big evil smile appeared across his face. The girl had seemed a bit perplexed by this. When walking to his flat Denny said,

"Seeing as I've just laid out four guys to protect your name would you do me the courtesy of telling me your name. Your real name please. "

164

She told him it was Dianna and asked what his name was. He told her it was Max as he had no doubt that the pub incident would be reported and investigated. With no alcohol in the house, he suggested they skip the niceties and head to bed. Denny spent all night making love to Dianna and by the sounds that were coming out of her she was thoroughly enjoying it. Her fingernails kept digging into his back and she thought this was the best love making she had ever had, but every time she had moaned the name Max, he felt a bit awkward. Just before they drifted off to sleep, she turned to him and asked,

"Max, can I ask you why you smiled when you beat up these men? "

"It's a long story Dianna and my name isn't Max, but that is an even longer story. "

They then fell asleep with Denny holding on to her until he awoke at about five o'clock. She was gone. She had drawn a heart on the top of the bedside cabinet with her lipstick before she left. Little did she know that he had slipped fifty pounds into the inside pocket of her jacket last night. He was desperate for a whisky, and he knew it was getting harder to refrain, but today he had to give his boss an update on the inquiry into Thomson. He got up and tried to go for a run, but after twenty minutes his heart wasn't in it, so he just walked home. Pretty disillusioned about the state of himself, but he did his usual and just shrugged and forgot about it. Denny sat in the incident room with Shonagh waiting for their boss. When he came in he wasn't looking best pleased.

"Right Foggerty let's get this part out the way. There was a report of a fight in the Links Bar last night and when uniform investigated, they took a report from one of the victims and he gave a description of the assailant. Unfortunately, what he gave described somebody like yourself Foggerty. Where were you last night? "

"Well sir there must be tens of thousands of people like me and what you must think about was the person possibly concussed and did he tell you what the incident was about? "

"Don't get smart with me Foggerty and answer the bloody question. "

"Well, that's easy sir I was tucked up in bed with my friend

Dianna until five o'clock this morning. If you like I can tell you what we got up to. "

Shonagh was standing with a smirk on her face and Denny was praying the boss didn't ask for her full name and address. The boss then wanted a full update on the Thomson case and asked him how far away he was from a result. Denny had said it would be at least a month away if it all went to plan. He also asked for two radios so that they could communicate between the cars. Also, he wanted access to the lost and property office for the both of them. They both went for a coffee and sat in interview room three to throw ideas back and forward.

"Tell me Denny did you just make up that story about being in bed with that girl. "

"No Shonagh that was definitely true."

He saw a look of jealousy on her face, but that was up to her. She could take him as she found him. Denny explained that for the next four weekends they would have to be on surveillance Friday, Saturday, and Sunday. He asked her if she had a boyfriend and if so, he was sorry, but this was at a critical part of the case. She said she had no boyfriend, so they worked out how they were going to do this. He had said the most important part was trying to keep an eye on the warehouse at Leith and the other premisses when he gets information from Johnny which meant separating. He told her they wouldn't get lucky right away, but anything was possible.

He told her to get as much clothing from the lost property as possible. Clothing that could make her out to be a working girl. She understood where he was coming from as Leith was a well-known area for the working girls. Denny said he would meet her in Albion Road on Friday night at six and to prepare herself for a long shift. The whole of the weekend was a bust, but one thing Denny thought he noticed was a guy walking about aimlessly. Just up and down the street and occasionally walking around the warehouse. He thought this guy was security for Thomson and next weekend he would find out.

It was Monday morning and Denny was called into the office of his boss and told to sit down.

"Foggerty you once told me a story about your sixth sense enabling you to find the body of a young girl on the island you came from. Remind me of the name of the chap who was suspected of killing her. "

Denny jumped up and said,

"Before we go any further sir, he wasn't suspected of killing her. He bloody well did kill her by smashing a hammer over her head. Proven by the Pathologist Dr Neala Belmont. So where is this leading as I'm now starting to get angry. "

"Calm down lad it's just that I have been contacted by the Highland and Islands police asking if we had any information on a chap called Hamish McLure. "

"Please tell me they have found him sir. "

"Unfortunately for him they have. However, he hasn't much of a head left as it has been caved in by some blunt object. He was found floating in the sea off Dunnet Head and was named by a photo displayed on posters in the area. "

Denny jumped up shouting and punching the air with his fists. His boss told him to calm down and eventually Denny sat with that weird smile on his face.

"This might be a stupid question Foggerty but have you any suspicions as to who might have done this. Anyone from the island? "

Denny started to laugh and said,

"Any one of the four thousand people living on Durma would have gladly wielded the object that killed him sir and if I find who did it, I will gladly shake his hand and buy him a whisky. Thank you, sir. For making me a happy guy. "

His boss thought him to be a mixed-up lad and he would have to keep an eye on him. Denny couldn't wait to phone his dad and although he wasn't allowed to make private calls, he went into a side room and dialled. When his dad answered he asked him if he had heard the news. Lachlan had heard, but it was only yesterday that the whole of the island heard the news. Denny asked if he should phone Scroggies and speak to Ian, but his dad had said Ian hadn't been seen for a few weeks.

A big smile came over Denny and it was at that point he knew who it was that had sent McLure to Hell. Ian and Time Bomb. He told his dad he would phone him soon and hung up.

It was celebration time and he headed out on the pretence of speaking to his confidential informant. Denny ended up drunk for two solid days not even going home to shower and change. He was lying in bed on the third day when there was loud banging on the door. Eventually he got up to answer it without any clothes on. When he opened the door Shonagh was standing there with an angry look on her face.

"Come in Shonagh I can see your angry. Have a seat. "

"This is not about how I am Denny Foggerty. I am angry because I haven't heard from you in two days. Not even a message left at the station for me. You could have been in big trouble, but you know what Denny you think it's all about you. Look at the state of you and by God you smell. It stinks like a brewery in here she shouted at him. "

He asked her to give him ten minutes and he walked into the bathroom. She could hear the shower going and after a while he walked out towelling himself down and went and put some underwear on. He then opened the windows and asked her to give him some time to explain as to what is going on. After making them coffee he started to tell her about everything from when he was young until now. He didn't leave anything out. Shonagh was shocked to say the least. She just sat there unable to take it all in.

"I'm not in a clever way at the moment, but I'm trying hard to fix it he lied. However, I promise I won't let my drinking jeopardise our working relationship and promise I will never put you in harm's way. You have every right to go back to the station and tell them how you found me today, but all I can ask of you is to hold back until we have nailed Thomson. What do you say? "

She just sat staring into her stone-cold coffee wondering why the hell she had ended up in this situation. After a while she looked up at him and said,

"I appreciate you have been through some terrible times Denny, but I am at a loss as to what to do. You say it won't screw up our working relationship, but all it needs is one drink too many the night before for it to go up in smoke. I'll agree to work with you until we take Thomson down, but after that I don't think so. I won't say anything to our boss unless you blow it in anyway Denny, and then I would. "

That night he had met Johnny and he had produced the information Denny had wanted. Thomson had another warehouse down at Bonnington. Johnny told him how to get there so after he had given him his money Denny headed off to check out the other warehouse. When he got there, he immediately felt that this wasn't right. It was too far away from young Thomson's comfort zone. Still, he would check it out for any security later.

As he was sitting in his car his sixth sense was telling him this was just a front and the warehouse in Leith was the hub of their operations. There was still one thing to check and that was any security. He parked the car further away and got out putting some old clothes on which made him look like a bit of a tramp and then walked to the warehouse. He pretended to be drunk and he was staggering around which came easy to Denny. When he got there, he banged on the big double doors several times. If anybody came out, he would ask if this was the Y. M. hostel. After banging the doors for several minutes nobody appeared so he continued staggering back up the road. He headed home hoping Johnny would produce a time and date and then they would be on the final stage.

When he got home he noticed three messages on his machine. The first was his dad. The second was Gail from the AA asking if they could meet up sometime and the third was just someone laughing. When he redialled the third one it was George from the Royal in Helmsford who answered. George asked him how he was, and Denny had replied fine and was cutting back on his drinking. The lies were coming thick and fast now. George had said it must have been Willie that had tried to speak to him. Denny didn't understand why Willie would have his phone number, but he must have contacted Ian who in turn had asked his dad for the number.

At work the next day he updated Shonagh on what he had found, and they had sat down and talked over what they thought the next stage should be. They both agreed that if Johnny came up with the information, then they should go ahead and finish what they started. Denny had said that as they didn't know when or if that information would come through then they should continue with the surveillance to see if a pattern of people visiting the warehouse could be established. Shonagh said she was up for it. Denny had a plan for the next night, and he shared it with her.

Denny parked his car a bit before Shonagh was to turn up. A while later he got a bit of a fright when his door opened and someone got in. He didn't recognise her as she was dressed as a prostitute, and he could easily have walked past her in the street.

"Don't say a word, Denny. I don't like dressing like this and please refrain from asking me how much I charge for fear of getting a punch on your nose. "

"Would I ever? "said Denny while laughing.

He had decided that they must know the security at the warehouse so tonight was the night. He drove the car down to where they could easy see what and who was coming in and out. He thought he was too close, but at this stage they had to take a small risk now and again. As they sat talking it was Shonagh who suddenly said,

"Quick Denny somebody just came out and is walking towards us. Please just follow my lead. "

She lifted her tops up exposing her breasts. Hitched her skirt up and grabbed his hand and put it up between her legs. She started to kiss him with Denny keeping one eye open to see what the man was going to do. They both feigned surprise when he rapped on the window with Shonagh sorting her clothes. Denny rolled the window down and the man shouted,

"Take your whore and get as far away from here as possible and don't come back. Got me? "

Denny just muttered an apology and started the car. He then drove off and eventually he started to laugh. A few minutes later Shonagh had said,

"I don't want to go home yet Denny. Please take me somewhere and make love to me. Will you? "

She didn't know how he would react to that, but she got her answer when the car started to speed up. He drove to a deserted area he had passed while going to Bonnington. There was a mad rush to get their clothes off and he then climbed over to the passenger side. He rolled the seat back as far as it would go, tilted the back rest, and then lay on her and slowly entered her. There was to be no foreplay tonight. Shonagh was loving every minute of it and Denny felt her climax several times. When they finished Denny climbed back to the driver side, but neither of them got dressed. They just sat looking at each other's naked body with the rain hammering down on the roof of the car before Shonagh said,

"Denny, I needed that and loved every minute of it. You're such an enthusiastic lover, but we must remain professional about our work so it can't happen again. "

Reluctantly Denny agreed, but deep down he hoped she might change her mind in the future. When he went to see his boss the next day, he was full of praise for Shonagh's part in the surveillance last night and his boss said that it would be noted. He had high hopes for that girl he said.

"What are your thoughts on a timescale for the conclusion of this operation Foggerty? "

"Well sir if my confidential informant comes through with the final bit of the information then we are good to go."

His boss started to shout,

"What bloody informant Foggerty? Are you telling me we are relying on the word of some drug addict to conclude an operation that has been going on for months?" Why was I not informed?"

"No disrespect sir, but it was you that wanted to keep this as secret as possible. Plus, he is not a drug addict just a guy who borrows money from Thomson."

"For your sake son I hope you are right about all of this as there is so much riding on it."

Denny knew there still a lot of hours to do sitting in his car waiting for Johnny to turn up. If he turned up. After his boss was finished with him, he told Shonagh he had things to do, and he would keep in touch. She knew where he was going, the pub.

Denny's life was starting to go into freefall, and he felt there was nothing he could do about it other than to stop drinking. He always had these great ideas in his head about what kind of life he had wanted for himself, but these ideas were now just becoming pipe dreams. He had his sexual needs, and he was becoming quite ashamed as to the number of working girls he was bringing back to the flat each week, but they knew of his sexual prowess in bed plus the amount of money they paid him. Even his flat was becoming a mess and at times he never even thought about opening a window for fresh air.

One Saturday he saw an open top bus offering tours around the city, so he thought that as he had always wanted to see more of Edinburgh, he would go for it. When he exited the bus at the end of the tour, he felt thoroughly ashamed as the only thing he

171

had done was to make a mental note of the bars he had spied.

That night while waiting to see if Johnny would turn up he thought that he might have to leave this beautiful city. However, it would be the same wherever he went. The whisky would still drag him down. Johnny was a no show, so he headed home only to find Shonagh sitting on his doorstep. After asking her in he made coffee, and they sat chatting about work until the phone rang. It was Helen. Shonagh asked him if he wanted her to leave, but he just shook his head, walked into the kitchen, and shut the door. After asking each other how they were she told him that his dad wasn't well. He had a heart problem, but Dr. Henderson was giving him drugs to keep it at bay. Denny asked how serious it was and should he come over, but Helen had said his dad didn't want any fuss and there was no need for him to come over. He explained that he would have struggled anyway as he was in the middle of a big investigation. Before they hung up Helen had gone quiet before saying,

"Denny, I know about your drinking and how bad it is. So please don't come back to Durma while you are like that. It would break your dad's heart into pieces."

"Helen I'm not going to deny that I'm in a bad way at times, but my work has not been affected, for how long I don't know. I'm getting great praise from my boss, but everything rests on the outcome of this investigation on which I am working. I have no doubt if you have heard about my drinking then you will know that my rage episodes are still hanging over me."

He had said goodbye and told her he didn't know when or if he would see her again. She just put the phone down. When he went into the living room Shonagh had left. He then phoned his dad who was glad to hear from him but reassured him that he was fine and not to worry about him. Denny suggested that his dad give up work altogether as Denny would organise a payment from the Albach Trust meaning that he wouldn't have to worry about money again. His dad had said that on no account was that to happen. After a bit of small talk Lachlan had asked him about his investigation. Denny had said it was going very well and would soon conclude. At least that wasn't a lie. His dad said he was proud of him and then hung up.

On hearing that Denny lost it and started smashing ornaments around the room. Ashamed again. He grabbed his jacket, locked the door, and got a taxi to the Grassmarket to look for some new pubs. While wandering around he walked past a phone box outside a bar called CC Blooms. Packed into the booth were four middle aged people. Two guys and two women all smoking a joint. Denny thought he needed cheering up, so he approached them and shouted,

"Police. What the hell is going on here? How old are you lot?"

He produced his warrant card for effect before the four of them mumbled some sort of apology and headed off, heads down, into the throngs of revellers going from pub to pub. The right type of smile came over his face this time. Denny visited several bars, but he was becoming frustrated at the need to have naked women dancing on everything available. Invariably his thoughts always drifted to his dad's health. His sixth sense was telling him that his dad wasn't fine, and he was worse than he made out. Unfortunately, now there was nothing he could do about it. He was consuming whisky after whisky until he was struggling to focus, and his legs felt weak. He hailed a taxi, but after a while he thought that hadn't been the right idea as he was feeling nauseous. He wasn't far from his flat before he shouted to the taxi driver to slow down, threw the door open and vomited. The driver started to shout at him, but Denny was feeling too ill to argue with him, so he just got out the cab, threw some money in the window and walked home. In the morning he sat having his usual coffee and made a big decision. He wasn't going to beat himself up about his drinking anymore, but just continue the way he was living and to hell with it. He knew he was good at his job, and he had to try hard not to let the whisky interfere with it.

At the police station he met up with Shonagh to discuss their next steps over the coming days. He told her it was a priority to get the information from Johnny and as much as Shonagh agreed she was getting worried that he was stringing them along. Denny had said he felt otherwise but would give it another week and if he hadn't come up with the information then they would have to think again. He had a suspicion that she was becoming less and less enthusiastic about the whole thing.

That night while waiting in his car at the agreed rendezvous he was startled by a knock on the window. It was Johnny. He told him to get in. There was a look of excitement on Johnny's face that said he had the information.

"I've got what you need, but this time it will cost you one hundred quid. The information is genuine as I got it from a guy who was in Thomson's organisation but was kicked out for making too many mistakes. The shipment will arrive next Saturday night usually between seven and eight o'clock depending on traffic over the bridge. It will be a large, white van with the words Medical Supplies painted on the sides."

Denny suddenly grabbed him by the throat and started to squeeze to the point where Johnny was about passing out.

"Listen to me you low life. Don't you ever try and extort money from me again or you won't have long to live. Understand?"

He took one hundred and fifty pounds out of his pocket and stuffed it inside Johnny's jacket and told him nobody was to hear of this. Johnny was still recovering but managed to nod his head. As he got out of the car Denny had grabbed his arm and asked what his surname was. Johnny had replied it was Scott.

Next night he knew he had to try and find a way into the warehouse. He asked Shonagh to go with him and they cruised around the streets next to the warehouse without trying to attract attention to themselves. They were just ready to give up when Denny said to Shonagh to go to the other warehouses and stop the car. It was that simple. All the warehouses in the road had the same adjoining roofs. Each with a skylight front and back. Denny reckoned that there would only be a single brick divide in the loft space between them. He got out of the car and walked along to try and get a look through the windows of the next warehouse. This was empty, but Denny wouldn't be surprised if Thomson didn't own both places. Satisfied he told Shonagh to head home and he would tell her and their boss his plan tomorrow, but not all the plan to their boss. When he had been dropped off, he made something to eat and mentally started to prepare his plan. It all depended on him getting in to one of the skylights so after eating he phoned Shonagh. He told her they would have to meet up tomorrow night where he was going to try and get into the warehouse.

"Denny that's extremely dangerous due to the hight and we

both know one of Thomson's men will be in there."

"Shonagh this is the most critical part in my plan. Trust me.

The following night she picked him up and they set off to the warehouse. She parked up the road and Denny got out and walked to the far end of the next warehouse. There it was. A large wall which butted up to the wall of the warehouse next door. A burnt-out van gave him a lift up and he walked along the wall until he could grab a hold of what was left of the original metal fire escape. The fire door had been welded up so he pulled himself up on to the roof, scrambled up to the apex and walked quietly along until he came to the skylight. He needed to see if he could open it. When he looked in, he was in for a shock. There were two of Thomson's men sitting around a table with a flask in front of them. He had planned on one, but it didn't matter as it looked like one of them was old. He lifted the skylight, and it opened easily due to the rust having done its job on the lock. This was going to be his way in so he pressed the skylight down with a little bit force to make sure it wouldn't bang in the wind. He then made his way back over the roofs and walked up to where Shonagh was waiting in the car. He told her all about what he did and saw. She queried whether the second person would be a problem. He told her he could manage it and not to worry.

It was time to go home for both of them and after being dropped off at his flat Denny realised, he hadn't been for a whisky. He stood on the doorstep contemplating what to do. Eventually he turned the key and walked into the flat. That night he lay in bed with sweat running off him until the alarm went off. As he got out of the bed he realised the sheets were soaked through, all because of one night with no whisky. He couldn't care less.

When he walked into the station the next day, he motioned for Shonagh to follow him. They both entered the boss's office and sat down. Denny told him that all the relevant information had been gathered and this was to be his plan. His boss had tried to tell him what he thought, but Denny had said,

"Look sir I appreciate your help, but if this is going to work it has to be my plan and mine alone. If it doesn't work, then I will take the blame. Even resigning from the force but you must trust me. Can you organise ten officers to be here on that night. Ten officers that can look after themselves and it would be best if they were armed. I can't be armed for obvious reasons, and I want you to issue an order to every armed personnel that if a firearm is aimed at them then they take the shot. A few other things sir is that I don't want anybody being recognised and putting them or their families in danger in the future. So, I want balaclavas issued to everyone and there will be no exceptions. I also want to restrict these officers from using a phone after they have been told about the target. Lastly, I don't want Pc Slater anywhere near the action when it goes down. Shonagh quickly said.

"Listen Foggerty, if you think I have sat in a draughty, cold car freezing my arse off to not be in on the action then you can think again."

Denny just looked at her and burst out laughing. His boss said he would take everything on board and speak with the two of them within a couple of days. Denny then explained to Shonagh that they would still have to do surveillance on the warehouse right up to the night before just in case something out of the ordinary came up. Deep down he was always hoping that she might be up for more love making sessions.

He phoned his dad every two or three days and after a while he realised how much he missed him. At the moment there was no chance of visiting him so he would just have to accept it. The day was drawing nearer, and Denny was trying hard, or so he thought, to lay off the whisky but he was struggling. He was worried that too much alcohol might affect his judgement and put lives in danger. At times he just wished the operation would be over and he would get back to having no pressure on him. Three days later, Shonagh and him were called to the boss's office. He went through everything Denny had spoken to him about and agreed to everything except the shooting. He was worried that it might lead to trigger happy officers.

"Look sir. Firstly, why would you arm officers if they can't protect their lives. Are you telling me Thomson's gang wouldn't hesitate to fire. They know that if they are caught then they will be going down for a long stretch so they will have no qualms about shooting. However, if you don't agree with me then I'm out of the operation. Take it or leave it."

Shonagh could see that Denny was angry, but there was nothing she could say to help defuse the situation. She knew he was right.

His boss just sat staring at the both of them for what seemed like an age until he said,

"Okay Foggerty I'm going to go with what your proposing, but if there is any indiscriminate shooting then both our jobs are on the line. Do you understand?"

Denny just nodded his head and thanked him. Shonagh also thanked their boss, and they walked out and sat at their desks. Denny was sitting looking pensive for a while until he spoke to Shonagh and said he would see her tonight at the usual time and place. His head was hurting what with his dad not being well and the pressure of this operation. He had made up his mind that if this didn't go to plan, he would resign and head for pastures new.

That night as he and Shonagh sat in the car she had asked if everything was all right. He told her about his dad. She had asked if he shouldn't be heading home to see him, but Denny said he would try after the operation. He told her he was afraid to go back home in the state he was in with alcohol. She told him to take one step at a time and if he needed help afterwards then she was here for him.

The day of the operation was here, and he had woken up drenched in sweat again. He had wondered if it had been a clever idea to lay off the whisky last night or not. His head hurt and he felt a little dehydrated, so he had forsaken his usual coffee for a bottle of water. Everybody involved had been told to turn up at the station for mid-day. This gave Denny plenty of time to go over his plan in his head. On checking the local weather forecast he found the wind was to increase over the day. They didn't call Edinburgh the Windy City for nothing. After Durma he could manage any wind conditions, but when he saw it was to rain, he started to get a little concerned. Thirty feet up on a slippery slate roof was a different matter. When he arrived at the station there was a lot of activity going on. This was obviously the policemen drawn in from other stations. There was a nervous energy coming from them. They knew they were in for some action, but not knowing what was getting them a little jumpy.

Denny didn't introduce himself as he wanted just to mingle among them to see if his sixth sense kicked. It did. He couldn't pin down exactly what was happening but was sure one of the men should not be in the group. They were to use three of the offices which were kitted out it with food and beverages. No names had to be used to make it difficult for reprisals. One guy in particular was asking a lot of questions as to what the operation was. Denny was staying close to him, and his sixth sense was in full flow. The guy was engaging anybody he could in talk about what they were to be expecting. By late afternoon he had pulled his boss aside and told him about his sixth sense and suggested the guy be removed and kept away from a telephone. His boss had said he couldn't virtually lock up a serving officer on Denny's hunch.

"Okay sir here is how we do it. Before we give them the details, we tell them that they must make a trip to the toilet as there would be no time afterwards. If I am right, then when you name the target, he will make up some lame excuse about stomach problems and he needs to rush to a toilet, but I'll be waiting outside."

His boss agreed and when it was time for a briefing, they all sat around a couple of tables, and they were told the name of the target. Denny had been looking in from a side window when suddenly the guy stood up complaining of an upset stomach and started to go out the door much to the amazement of the others. The boss just ignored him.

When the guy was outside Denny saw him in a blind panic looking for a phone. He found one in a side office and started to dial, but Denny was watching through the window. As soon as the guy had finished dialling Denny walked through the door and put his finger down on the cradle. The guy went pale. Just then the boss entered and asked the guy who he was phoning. He had said that he was trying to phone his ill wife. Denny picked up the phone and asked the switchboard to redial the number and when it was answered to put the phone down. After a minute, the girl phoned him back and told him it was the Thistle bar. The boss had then told two burly officers to take the guy away and lock him up and on no account was anybody to have contact with him. Denny then went back to the room and told everyone what had happened. They were raging as this guy could have put their lives in danger.

When the boss passed over the floor to Denny it raised a few eyebrows. Here was a young officer who seemed in charge. He explained the plan down to the last detail before telling them that he would be leaving on his own to the target to be inside the building when they arrived. Denny asked if there were any questions. His boss spoke up,

"Just one officer. When were you going to tell me about you being in the building when we arrive?"

"I just did sir and anyway somebody must neutralize the two men in there or it won't work. Trust me sir. Oh, and remember I will be the guy upstairs with the balaclava on so try not to shoot me."

The look on the boss's face was a picture. Denny wished them well and said he would see them later and headed off.

At the agreed time the men were seated in the van waiting for the go ahead. Denny had been there for a while struggling to walk along a wet roof with the wind howling. As he went through the skylight, he accidently let the window slip and it banged down in the frame. He quickly dropped down on to the floor which was further than he thought. One of the men was asking the other what the noise was so Denny quickly put his balaclava on and waited. He heard one guy saying it would be the skylight blowing in the wind, so he positioned himself behind some boxes and waited. The guy coming up the stairs was the same person that had told him and Shonagh to remove themselves the other night. Denny waited and waited. The guy walked over to the window before shouting to his mate that he was right it was the window.

Denny moved quickly and punched him on his chin. The blow knocked him out, but Denny caught him and lowered him to the ground. He slowly crept down the stairs and walked up behind the other guy and before he turned round Denny grabbed his head and smashed it off the table at which he was sitting. Denny then placed him as if he were sleeping with his head on his hands. It was then that he heard vehicles coming to the entranced to the warehouse. It was time to head back up the stairs.

Thomson was following the van in his car and started blasting the horn for the doors to be opened. When there was no reply, he started shouting about what he was going to do to his men if they had fallen asleep inside. Eventually, he got a spare key from the car and opened the side door before opening the shutter doors by pulling on the chain. When the door was fully open the van was driven inside. Then all hell broke loose as the police cars arrived and armed men exited from their van shouting for everybody to get on the floor.

From the top of the stairs Denny could see it all unfolding. Then one of Thompsons's men produced a handgun and started to fire. He was taken down at once, but not before getting a round off. It struck someone but Denny couldn't see who. Thomson had run for the stairs and went up them two at a time. Denny knew that this was his escape route. Through the hole in the wall at the far end and exiting from a door in the next building. He wasn't going to let that slimy toad get away. Just as Thomson got to the top step Denny surprised him and smashed his face with his fist. Denny wasn't finished there. He gathered all his strength, picked up the inert body of Thomson and lifted him over his head before launching him as far as he could down the metal stairs. There were a few noises of things breaking, but Denny knew it wasn't the metal on the stairs. He smiled and smiled.

He walked down the stairs and stepped over Thomson's prone body, but not before putting his heel on to his nose and squashing it. When he got to the bottom, he could see that it was Shonagh that had been shot. He knelt beside her and asked how she felt.

"I'm okay. It's my shoulder that has taken the bullet, but I'll be fine. Good result partner."

Denny was trying to smile but was struggling. He knew he was good at his job, but he didn't want this.

When the crime scene was tidied up, they all ended up at the station and the boss told them to be back there at seven in the morning for the paperwork to be completed. Denny had been in the office for two hours before anybody appeared. He was halfway through his paperwork when his boss shouted him into his office.

"Firstly, Foggerty you have been exceptional organising this operation and I'm putting you forward for a commendation. Shonagh went through an operation last night at a private hospital. Obviously for security reasons. She is well, but it is feared that she won't have full mobility of the shoulder and arm in the future. I know this hasn't been easy for you, but before you make any rash decisions, please hear me out. This has been one of the biggest drug busts in the whole of the United Kingdom."

He told Denny he would like him to consider undertaking a similar operation to the one they had just finished. The Dundee police was peppered with corrupt officers whose allegiance was to Billy Thomson senior and they needed them routed out. Plus, Thomson was to be taken down. His boss had said that it would be a massive undertaking and he would be on his own again.

"Sir, I will think about it as I'm not sure I can do this, but there is one thing I can categorically tell you is that after the operation I will no longer be in the police force."

"Okay Foggerty just stay connected. Oh, and you know that the medical people reckon that young Thomson will be paralysed from the neck down. What exactly happened up there on the staircase as his jaw is broken and his nose is beyond all recognition?"

"Well sir, it doesn't pay to run upstairs taking the steps two a time. He must have fallen when he missed the top step and it's a long way down. Oh, and no disrespect sir but I don't give a damn."

Denny turned his back on him and smiled.

He was posted missing for three days and all officers were told to look out for him, especially in the bars.

Chapter 15

Denny had jumped in his car and headed off to Dundee to try and get the feel of the place by staying in a hotel. The only places he got to know were the bars and nightclubs. On the second morning he woke up in a strange bed. He looked over but there was nobody there and he had no idea who he had met last night. A note was lying on the bedside cabinet which said,

"I'm off to work so just let yourself out. By the way last night was awesome."

There was no name on it, so he just lay back and started thinking as to whether he wanted to run this new operation. He knew he had to start soon as the whisky was taking its toll on his body. He needed a knew identification as over the last few nights a plan had come into his head that might just work. On the third day he walked about Dundee to see what type of city it was. He guessed it had been a vibrant city at one stage but now it was getting rundown. He took a taxi and asked the driver to take him around the no-go areas for respectable citizens. The driver said he was mad, but it was his money, and in certain areas it would be a quick drive through.

Denny's overall impression was that there was a lot of unemployment by the number of youngsters on the streets. This place was a paradise for drug dealers.

Before he left Dundee, he phoned his boss expecting the usual bollocking and he wasn't disappointed. After his boss finished Denny then asked if he could speak without being interrupted. His boss said,

"Don't get impertinent Foggerty as I could still put you on a charge."

"But sir, if you do that then I can't clean up Dundee making you a hero and the possibility of me getting shot would mean I would be out of your hair for ever. What do you think?"

On arriving back at his flat in Edinburgh he noticed that his answer machine was flashing with four messages. He thought the messages would be from his boss, so he ignored them. Eventually after staring out the window for a while, he decided to check the messages. The first one was from Helen saying his dad had taken a bad turn and was extremely ill. He was hungover from last night and her message didn't sink into his brain for a moment. He noticed that the message was three days old so panic set in, and he at once lifted the phone and dialled Helen although he knew that this wasn't going to be good news.

When Helen picked up, he immediately asked about his dad.

"Denny, I am so sorry, but your dad died last night. If it's any consolation he died in his sleep. I knew you were on an important investigation and thought you couldn't reply to my first message."

Denny sat down, put his head in his hands and thought that this can't be happening. His world had just gone into meltdown. He could hear Helen asking if he was still there.

"I'm still here Helen. I just can't take it in. It was as if he was indestructible. Oh God Helen why him? I will phone you later as I need time to gather my thoughts. Thank you for being there for him at the end."

Before he put the phone down, he was sure he could hear Helen sobbing. He then phoned his boss and told him. His boss was very sympathetic and told him to take as much time off as needed.

"Look sir, I am coming in today to speak to you about Dundee as I want everything to be in place before I come back from Durma."

His boss had said to be there for two o'clock and they would go over it. Denny then lay down on his bed and felt like crying. His head felt like it was going to implode, and he wondered if his demons would ever leave him. Maybe in death he would be free.

As he sat in the office of his boss he contemplated getting up, walking out, and never going back to the police force. However, he needed something to stop him killing himself with the whisky. He had read somewhere that if you stop heavy drinking before the age of twenty-five then your liver has a chance of recovering. Only a year and a half to go he thought.

When his boss came in Denny told him what he needed for the operation. Accommodation which he would choose himself, an untraceable car, and a high-powered camera. The most important thing he needed was a new identity and a reason for him being transferred to the Dundee constabulary. He then started to tell the boss his plan.

"Bloody hell Foggerty that is going to be dangerous. If you get caught you could end up being killed."

"It's worth it sir to get the best result. Anyway, I'm well on the road to dying sir. Oh, and I would like a contact here and that is Pc Slater. As long as she has one functioning arm and hand, she can answer a phone and keep in contact verbally with yourself. Nothing is to be written down for obvious reasons."

The boss had said he had to think about it, but Denny told him he would be back from Durma in a week and if he hadn't approved it then he would walk away.

Denny had arrived back at his flat via a couple of pubs and a load of whisky. He knew he had to sleep it off before he spoke to Helen. Two hours later he phoned Helen and when she answered he asked how she was.

"I'm fine Denny, I know it can't be easy for you. Just to let you know that due to the logistical nightmare of getting your dad's body to the mainland for an autopsy and then back again the authorities have decided to forego the autopsy and just continue with the burial with your consent? It would be in three days assuming that would suit you?"

"That's all fine with me Helen and can I ask you to organise a simple sermon from the Rev. McGlashan please. Also, if I phone you as soon as possible can you pick me up from the ferry? Oh, and Helen just to let you know I am not the same Daniel Rey Foggerty that left a few years ago."

They ended the call and Denny had thought he should try and cut back the whisky for the next few days, but that would be tougher than anything he had done before.

He phoned and booked the ferry for later the next day as he had to drive all the way up to Mayfort. He had a few smart clothes in his wardrobe so they would suffice. Denny decided he would leave early enough to make sure he did not miss the ferry. Before he left, he phoned Helen and told her what ferry he would be on. The drive was boring and only made palatable by the music from the radio. He made a mental note to buy an expensive music player when he got back and take time out to listen to every type of music there is.

When the road sign for Mayfort came into view a sense of

foreboding came over him. He was scared. Scared to meet people who most certainly judge him. He didn't even know how Helen and Ian would react to him. It was a certainty that Time Bomb would have been in contact with his brother so there was every possibility that Helen would react badly as well. His only hope was that his dad hadn't found out.

On the ferry over he started to feel nauseas from the swell and all the whisky he had been having lately. Twice he had to throw up over the side. When he disembarked on Durma he felt like weeping. It was still the same dour, cold piece of rock that he knew. Helen came running over to him and threw her arms around him. She then took a step back and looked at him. Denny sensed a look of disappointment from her.

"Let's go Denny it's freezing. The van is just over there."

As they were heading towards Kismay he caught her looking over at him a few times.

"I hope you're not too disappointed Helen although I did warn you. However, life has been good to you as you look as lovely as ever. You'll have to tell me everything that has been going on with yourself. Not about your boyfriends though as I might get jealous."

A smile came over his face which was a relief for Helen as she didn't know if he was serious or not. It was then that he asked Helen to pull over and he then got out and vomited by the side of the road. When he got back in, he could see a shocked look on her face.

"Denny, how bad is the drinking? I would like to know. I'm not blaming you in any way, but if there is anything I can do to help then please just ask."

"There is only one person that can help and that's me. My drinking is bad Helen, unbelievably bad at times. Can I just say though that as soon as dad has been buried, I am off. I have unfinished business at my work. Also, if you want me to stay at one of the rooms at Scroggies then I understand."

Helen had told him that he would be staying at the house, and she wouldn't take no for an answer. As they drove through the village, he found himself slinking down in the seat. Why? He didn't know but thought it might be embarrassment. When they arrived at the house waves of emotion came over him and he

185

asked Helen if he could have a moment before going in.

"I'll take your luggage in and just you come when you feel like it. I have prepared some food for us, and Denny please listen to me. If you feel the need for a drink then please go for one, but don't you bloody dare be ill for your dad's funeral or drink will be the least of your worries. Understand?"

Denny just nodded his head and smiled. God, he had missed this lovely girl. He went into the house, and it felt strange with his dad not being there. First his mum and now his dad. After struggling with something to eat he asked Helen to tell him everything that had been going on. He was genuinely shocked when she told him about her gran who had died a year ago. He asked why his dad or her had not told him. She just shrugged her shoulder and said he hadn't even sent her a letter or tried to phone her. He couldn't argue with her. She told him what her life had been like for the last few years.

He felt guilty as her life had been uneventful compared to his. It was then Denny's turn to tell her what had been happening. When he explained about the Trust, she asked him to explain it to her again. She couldn't take it in. This was too much for her.

"Are you telling me you left here as plain Denny Foggerty and you arrive back as Denny Foggerty multi-millionaire? Bloody hell Denny this is incomprehensible. My brain can't take all this in."

As they sat on the sofa together you would have thought that there would have been a lot to talk about, but there wasn't. They hardly said a word to each other until Denny had said he was going to walk down to Scroggies for a drink and see Ian.

She told him that when he came back, he would be having the top floor of the house and on no account to come into her bedroom later.

Scroggies was still the same. As he walked through the doors everyone stopped drinking and just stared. He stared back at them before going to the bar and ordering a whisky. They quickly lost interest in him, so he sat down at the back of the bar. Ian walked in a while later and spied him sitting on his own. He got his drink and sat down beside him.

"Not the best circumstances to be meeting up in Denny, is it? "How are you feeling son? I was sorry about your dad."

"Not in the best shape Ian. I presume Willie would have told you all about me and my drinking. I thought I could manage it, but it was not to be. Anyway, how are you?"

Ian told him that life on the island goes on as normal, but he was having a lot of problems with his boat and money was getting tight. No mention was made of Hamish McLure. He had said that he and Dr Neala Belmont had been an item for a few years, and she comes over whenever she can.

"Ian, how much would a new boat cost?"

"About one hundred thousand pounds to get a top quality one. A lot of money. Why do you ask?"

Denny said he was just wondering and after talking for a while and a few more whiskies he made his leave and walked home. Even the weather was the same as the rain started to pour down, but as he walked through the door Helen came over with a hot tea and a towel for him to dry off. It wasn't long after that he had said that he needed to speak to her about money and the house, but not to worry as it would be all good. He then headed off to bed. During the night Helen had heard him shouting in his sleep and at one point she thought about going up to see him but had decided against it.

At about six o'clock the next morning Denny was up and dressed and he headed out for a walk. He walked up the North track until he came to a rocky out crop where he sat letting the wind hit his face. After a while he heard someone coming. It was Helen.

"Did you not think to ask me if I wanted to walk with you Denny? Just as we did many times before."

She smiled and sat down beside him and put her arm around him.

"Helen, I have something to say to you and please don't argue. The house will be yours for as long as you need it and if or when you don't then we can dispose of it however we want. There will be an amount of money deposited into the bank at Mayfort that the island uses, for you. If you want to continue working, then fine, but with that amount of money you don't need to. He knew she was going to argue but he quickly asked her not to.

"Helen I am going to ask you to do something for me and I have no right to expect you to agree to it. Before you arrived just

187

now, I decided. I have one last job to do in the force and then I'm finished. It's my intention to get myself sober if I can but I need help. What I'm saying is that will you help me if I arrive back on Durma? It would be difficult for both of us and if you tell me to get lost, I will just walk away and you would never see me again. It could be a few months and to be honest I won't try and stop drinking before the police operation is finished. For reasons particular to myself."

"Of course I will Denny, but at any time you decide not to come back then please phone me right away. If I don't want you back then I'll do the same. Agreed?"

He just nodded and then asked her if she wanted to walk a while with him. They linked arms and all the old memories came flooding back. Denny was in Scroggies that night and Ian had sat beside and said,

"Do us all a favour son. Have a few whiskies, but please don't get drunk. Get a half decent sleep for the funeral. After that when your back on the mainland you can do what you want. Do it for me please."

Denny nodded, finished his drink, and walked up the road.

Helen had heard him shouting again during the night, but she didn't know how to manage the situation.

The day of the funeral was here, and Denny had said he would just go along with what she said. When it was time to walk to the cemetery there was knock on the door. It was Ian. He asked if he could walk with them. Denny thought this was just like his mother's funeral and he appreciated what Ian was doing. They were just waiting for Helen now. As she walked down the stairs Denny felt faint and grabbed on to Ian. She was wearing the lace black dress of his mother.

"Sorry Denny I should have told you. Your dad gave this to me, and I had Mrs Scougal alter it. Do you mind?"

"I don't mind at all. Thank you for this Helen. You look beautiful."

Ian had said it was time for them to go so they locked up and started walking. Denny couldn't believe it. It was just a sea of people walking to the cemetery. Helen explained she wanted everyone to be able to pay their respects, so the service was to be held outside. This surprised Denny and he looked up at the grey sky, but then just shrugged.

The funeral service was short but fitting for a proud Scotsman like Lachlan. Ian grabbed Denny's arm and led him to the casket which was just at the church door. Three fishermen walked with them. Denny thought there would be a problem with the odd number, but Helen walked forward and stood with the men. This was a bit of a shock for the mourners as the ritual of carrying the coffin was always the job of the men. After his dad was laid to rest, he sat at the graveside until everybody had gone.

"As bad as I am dad, I'm still going to make you proud. Say hi to mum for me. Love you both."

He went to his room after the funeral and didn't come out until the next morning which had Helen worried all night.

As got into the van he asked her if they could stop off at the harbour so he could say goodbye to Ian.

They shook hands and Denny then said,

"Ian please keep an eye on your letter box over the next week or so. Oh, and please just accept my gift to you."

The return journey to Seahaven wasn't making Denny feel good at all and he tried hard not to have Helen stop the car for him to vomit. While they sat in the van waiting for the time for embarking Denny had turned to Helen and said,

"Thank you so much for organising dad's funeral Helen. It was very moving. I am not going to be too deep about this Helen, but I know I made a big mistake in leaving you. I've never loved anyone as much as I have you. I meant what I said yesterday. I am going to try hard to get back to you."

Helen then leaned across and put her arms around him and gave him a kiss on the lips. She didn't have to say anything. When Denny was on the ferry Helen stood watching and waving until the boat was a small dot on the horizon. Only then did she breakdown. Wondering if she would ever see him again. She had been down this road before.

When Denny got back to Edinburgh, he went straight to the police station. No matter how hard it was going without the whisky. That would come later. As he walked to his boss's office he got such a lovely surprise as Shonagh had walked out from a side office. He walked forward and gave her a hug watching her right arm as she was still in rehabilitation. They both smiled at each other and agreed to meet up for a coffee tomorrow before they both walked into the boss's office. Discussions went on for about two hours and it was agreed that Denny's plan would go ahead.

After telling Shonagh he would meet her at a coffee shop they both knew the next morning. He headed out to get some whisky inside him. As he sat drinking, he did a lot of thinking and realised that the success of this operation had to be quicker than the previous one due to his addiction. Next morning, he did his usual and went to the bathroom to vomit up the whisky from the previous night. He wondered how he was ever going to break this habit. Anyway, he had to go and meet Shonagh so he showered and headed out the door.

She was waiting for him and after she told him how sorry she was about his dad they started to work out how this operation was going down. Once business was sorted, he turned to her and said,

"Shonagh, how bad is your mobility in your arm and will you ever get back to full duties?"

"No Denny I'll be stuck behind a desk for the rest of my working life in the force. Another problem I have at present is I am being evicted as my landlord wants to sell the house my flat is in."

He just looked and looked at her until he asked,

"Shonagh, you have been in my flat and how do you like it?"

She told him it was a lovely flat but could do with a cleaning from top to bottom. She then laughed. He told her that as soon as he was in Dundee the flat was hers to keep and he would contact his dad's solicitors for papers to be signed. Also, a sum of money would be deposited in her bank account if she would furnish him with the details. Enough so that she could leave the force if she wanted and embark on any other career, she would be happier in.

"C'mon Denny what are you trying to do here. I appreciate what you're doing, but your offer is massive. How could I accept a gift of this size?"

"Look Shonagh. My head is hurting from too much whisky last night as you've probably guessed. I am doing this because I can, plus there is no guarantee that I will be alive at the end of this operation. It will either be me or Thomson that will be in Hell. Hopefully, him."

She started to cry, and Denny told her to get a grip as he couldn't be bothered with people crying. She smiled and thanked him from the bottom of her heart.

The next few days for Denny was organising accommodation in Dundee and finely tuning his plan. He was being seconded to the Dundee police as a liaison officer between them and Edinburgh to see if their intelligence data bases could be merged. Accommodation was a one-bedroom flat at the back of the Wellgate and to call it spartan was an understatement. His new name was Danny Bauer and he had dyed his hair black and wore black rimmed spectacles with clear glass in them. He was confident nobody would trace him back to Denny Foggerty. On the third day his phone rang twice, the first was Ian.

"Denny what the bloody hell is happening here. I'm standing with a cheque for one hundred thousand pounds in my hand from Germany and a brief note saying happy fishing Fish."

"It's a long story Ian and you wouldn't believe it. If I ever get back to Durma I will make you that cup of tea and tell you all about it."

They spoke briefly before Denny had said he had to go. The other phone call was Shonagh telling him that his informant Johnny Scott was found floating in Leith Docks with his head bashed in. It couldn't be determined when he was put in the water. Denny was so angry, but it made him realise that Thomson senior was playing for real. As much as this operation was two-fold, finding the corrupt police officers was going to be second to him eliminating Thomson. He wasn't going to have him arrested just eradicate him like the bug he is. He thanked her for the information and reminded her for security reasons he didn't have an answer phone. The following day he reported to the police headquarters in W Bell St. in Dundee.

He had to report to a D I Francis Broomhill who was holding a meeting with several officers in attendance. As soon as he walked in his sixth sense kicked in telling him that this was 'corrupt central' and he thought this was going to be easy to route them out. D I Broomhill stood there with his three-piece wool suit, brogue shoes and hair slicked back with Brylcream. He couldn't afford to dress like that on a policeman's wage. Broomhill was telling the officers about a drug bust that was to go down tonight. Denny thought how amateurish the guy's planning was. Denny could have been anybody. The guy in charge then made a speech as to how they were going to take down the drug dealers tonight. Denny thought that wasn't going to happen. After the meeting Broomhill introduced himself along with his brown-noser called DC Brian Lancaster who was dressed as a spitting image of his boss. They told him in no uncertain terms that he was only here to watch and listen and if he was asked out on an operation he was to sit in the car and do nothing. That night he was to report to the station at seven o'clock to go on an operation. Plenty time for Denny to have a few drinks. When he got to the station with five minutes to spare, he was told to travel in the last car.

When they got there Denny thought this was going to be a botched job. They were going for a drugs bust and acting on an anonymous tip off according to one of the officers sitting beside him. This was going to be one almighty 'cock up' so he just put his head back and shut his eyes. He was awoken with people shouting and running around like 'blue arsed flies' with nobody knowing what they were supposed to be doing. After a while Broomhill called a halt to the proceedings.

Back at the office Broomhill held a debriefing. Denny had never heard as many excuses for tonight's debacle and the boss seemed happy that it hadn't worked out. From the back of the room Denny suddenly said,

"Maybe it was because they were tipped off by someone in the room or the anonymous tip off was crap."

Everyone turned to face him with faces that weren't exactly friendly.

"Who asked you Bauer? I told you to sit at the back and keep quiet, didn't I?"

"Just saying the bloody obvious sir, but as I am not part of your team, I will take my leave. Goodnight gentlemen."

Denny could still hear Broomhill shouting after him as he left the station. He was a bit startled when Broomhill had said Bauer, but he would get used to it. It was back to his flat now via a pub just over the road from him.

That night Denny lay awake working out how viable his plan was going to be. No matter how many times it went through his head it came back to one thing. Thomson would be a different proposition to his son. Every time he thought about him one word came to mind. Eradication. In the morning he phoned Shonagh and asked her to speak to their boss and see if it would be possible to get into the bank records of the officers in Dundee, especially Broomhill and Lancaster. She said that it would be difficult but would try and persuade him.

As Denny walked into the station he was mentally preparing himself for a backlash from Broomhill. He would just apologise and get on with the job. He wasn't disappointed. As soon as he got to Broomhill's office he was shouted on to come in. When he entered Broomhill was standing with his lackey sitting down at the desk. He started to shout at Denny before he stopped him and said.

"Okay let's get this straight sir. I will stand here and take your reprimand but not while he is in the room. As he is of equal rank to me any reprimand must be done by a senior officer with a union representative present. However, I wave my right to have a union representative to assist me. So, he goes. Is that clear?"

Denny was trying hard not to laugh at the expressions on their faces. Eventually the boss gave Lancaster a nod which was for him to leave the room, but as he passed Denny he gave him a look of contempt. Denny then stood and took the reprimand from Broomhill while trying not to walk forward and punch him in the face. As he was about to leave he stopped at the door, turned and said,

"Permission to speak freely sir?"

"If you must Bauer."

"Not that I have been on any stakeouts, but it appears to me that whoever you were trying to catch was one step ahead of you."

Denny walked quickly out of the room knowing that Broomhill was rattled. Such a good start. He spent the rest of the day going through files, especially to see if there was any mention of Thomson in them. There wasn't any. Denny thought that for Thomson being the biggest drug dealer on the East coast there had to be something. Unless somebody was making sure his name didn't appear anywhere. Another plan came into his head. A girl was assigned to do all the filling so he asked her if she would like a coffee. Over the coffee he asked her if she would like to go for a drink that night and she readily agreed.

She suggested the Rendezvous and they met there at eight o'clock and when she had come in, he had said how lovely she looked which wasn't a lie. She introduced herself as Katherine which Denny already knew from examining the files. Katherine Martens. They spent a nice three hours just talking and listening to live music although Denny was drinking doubles, unknown to Katherine or so he thought. As they stood outside waiting for taxis as they lived in opposite directions, he turned to her and asked,

"Is there any chance we could do this again Kath?"

"That would be nice Danny, but next time if you ply yourself with whisky like you did tonight then I'll walk away. Did you think I wouldn't realise you were buying doubles for yourself? Oh, and by the way its Katherine, not Kath."

All he could do was stand and smile. The first taxi arrived, and she headed off home. After waiting for a while, the second taxi arrived which was just as well as a bitter wind was starting to blow through Dundee. While sitting in the taxi he thought he would take a chance.

"Is there anywhere I can get a 'spliff 'around here pal?"

"The drug dealing in Dundee and surrounding area is controlled by Billy Thomson senior and God help anyone who tries to muscle in on his business. Let's put it this way there is a car crushing plant on the Arbroath road and it's rumoured that a few people are ensconced under thousands of tons of scrap metal. You could try and get something from one of the pubs like Sinatras or the Number One, but watch out as lots of pubs are run by gangs from different areas around Dundee. Most are not a bad lot it's just that they are always looking for a scrap. It's rumoured that Thomson uses some of the gangs for distributing the stuff."

As they drew up to the Wellgate Denny took out two twenty-pound notes and handed it to the driver. He got a bit flustered and tried to tell Denny it was only three pounds, but Denny said it was for the information in keeping him safe. The driver thanked him and gave him his card with the number of the taxi control on it.

Denny walked along the close to the stairs leading to his flat with a slight stagger on. He had been noticing that lately it wasn't

194

taking as much whisky to get him drunk. He made a mental note to ask Katherine about the gangs in Dundee, but it had to be casual as he wasn't there for anything to do with drugs.

It was late before he got to the station as stomach cramps and vomiting had held him up. As he approached the same room he was in the other night he heard Broomhill laying down the law about them not catching any drug dealers. He was putting on a good show and should have been in amateur dramatics which reminded him he had to phone Shonagh tonight.

On walking through the door, Lancaster walked up to him and said,

"You can get out Bauer as you're not needed here. This is real police work."

He put his hand on Denny's chest and tried to push him back out the door. Denny grabbed his hand and with all the strength he could muster squeezed his hand until Lancaster was screaming in agony. It was obvious by the intensity of the screams that bones were being broken much to Denny's delight.

"That's enough Bauer let his hand go. You will be up on a charge of assaulting a fellow officer just as soon as I am finished in here."

"I doubt that sir as I am sure you as well as all the officers in here saw him put his hand on me and try to push me through the door and it wouldn't look good on anybody's record if they are caught lying about the incident. Would it?"

He walked out the door before turning round and popped his head back in and said,

"By the way, I will be working my own hours from now on as okayed by my boss Deputy Chief Thomas Shearlaw and if I may offer some advice, I would get somebody to take Dc Lancaster to the hospital".

As soon as he was out of the station he headed to his flat and phoned Shonagh. He gave her an update and told her he was beginning to irritate the top brass but was living dangerously. It was obvious that the DI was in Thomson's pocket and there was going to be some retribution to try and force him out of Dundee.

"Shonagh, I need those bank records sooner rather than later so what's happening."

"Denny, I keep chasing the boss, but he says it isn't easy."

"Shonagh can you not just lift your top up for him. It worked for me."

"Foggerty if you ever say that again I will personally walk to Dundee and punch you in the mouth and by the way the money you put in my bank account is scary."

Denny knew he had to find out how Broomhill was in contact with Thomson. Every day Denny would wander through the police station just so that he was seen to be working. He was in a side room when Broomhill popped his head in and said,

"Several of us are going for a drink after work, but you're not invited."

"Please tell me what pub you will be in so that I can avoid it."

"It's called the Copper Beach so steer clear. We don't want your kind around. Hear me?"

"Loud and clear and I hope Lancaster can hold his pint with his left hand."

Denny laughed and walked out the station. He had to get home and change into a disguise that he wasn't going to be recognised in. Long coat, scruffy shoes, flat cap and new pair of spectacles would have to do for the night. More clothes and hats would have to be bought.

He took a taxi and was in the pub well before they came in. Broomhill, Lancaster and three others entered and went and sat at a table beside what looked like two thugs. Denny sat at a table further away with his head on his hands as if he drunk but his face couldn't be seen. A double whisky in front of him. In his pocket was his camera, but it was going to be difficult to get pictures. One of the thugs went into his pocket, threw a bundle of notes on the table, and said something whereby everybody just laughed.

As Denny walked to the bar, he noticed some lads sitting in the corner wearing knitted jerseys. Blue with a yellow strip across the front. He wondered if they were part of one of the gangs he had heard about. He stood at the bar with his back to the police crew and slowly walked back at times to see if could hear anything, but he was too far away. Another whisky was bought and again keeping his face hidden walked back and sat down. It was then that the two thugs decided to leave, but before doing so an envelope was passed under the table to Broomhill who quickly put it in his jacket pocket. Denny thought how stupid they were. As the two thugs walked to the door one of them walked over to the table where the four lads sat. He put his hand out and one of the lads gave him a wad of cash. In turn the guy peeled off what looked like a twenty pound note and threw it on the table and walked out of the pub.

Broomhill's crew were starting to enjoy the free drink, but Denny didn't think there was anything else he would see or hear so he got up and left. He hailed a taxi and headed home. He asked the driver to drop him off about a couple of streets before his flat. His sixth sense was telling him something wasn't right. As he neared the flat there was guy in a car over the road who was watching the close leading to his flat. Denny was still in his disguise, so he crossed the road and walked past the car while memorising the number plate. Further up the street he walked into the next close and climbed over a wall next to his flat. On entering the flat he immediately wrote the number plate down. He stripped off all his clothes and headed to bed, but not before moving the heavy wardrobe behind the door.

It was just a matter of waiting for the nausea and stomach pains to arrive and they came with a bang that night. The next morning, although it was the weekend, he phoned Shonagh to ask her to try and trace the number plate. She said that somebody would still be working and she would have an answer today if not Monday morning. When she asked how he was his answer was,

"I'm bad Shonagh. I think I previously told you that unless I wrap this operation up quickly then due to my health it just won't happen. I'm making inroads, but to try and snare Thomson is going to be very difficult so I have decided as to how I'm going to deal with him. However, you don't want to know what the outcome is going to be. Everybody knows he is at the heart of the drug dealing, but nobody will give up any incriminating information on him."

They finished their chat with Shonagh telling him to be careful and to think about walking away from the operation. Denny was going to try hard and keep off the whisky during the day as he needed to be reasonably sober for the start of the night. Katherine had mentioned that she often went running along the front at a place called Broughty Ferry so he got a taxi out there in the off chance he might bump into her. All he could do there was to walk a while, sit on a seat and watch the water which was where the North Sea met the river Tay in the estuary. Once somebody had told her that dolphins often came inland as far as this, but she reckoned he had been winding her up as she had never seen any in all the time she had been running there. Denny could only agree with her.

It was a struggle to keep the whisky down from last night and people passing by would stop and ask him if he was okay, but he knew a monumental effort had to be made. He sat for lengthy periods of time until the wind chilled his bones, and he took a taxi home. As normal he asked the driver to stop a street before his address. Denny had no disguise this time so he walked up an adjacent street and approached his flat from several closes and jumped over the walls until he could walk up the outside steps and into his flat. He gently looked out the curtains and saw the same car and driver. He must have been getting bored as he was reading a newspaper and not paying much attention to Denny's flat.

He decided that he would go and see other parts of the town tonight. Which to Denny was different drinking establishments. Later when he jumped into a taxi, he asked the driver to take him to a night club which had a bit of life about it. The place he recommended was called the Palais which seemed a bit run down, but it suited him fine. It was on two levels, so he went upstairs and sat overlooking the dance floor. Denny just sat thinking about what was going to happen to him in the future. Nearly twenty-five, an alcoholic, a job he might be killed in and a bucket load of money that he couldn't care less about. After a few whiskies he thought that the night was going to liven up as he looked down and saw several groups of young lads coming in resplendent in their coloured knitted jerseys. It was obvious that by the look on their faces that they were intent on a fight of some sort. He wondered how long it would take to kick off. He recognised some of the jerseys that the lads had worn the other night in the Copper Beach, but there were at least three other coloured jerseys in the crowd. As he sat back, he wondered who would start the fighting.

It didn't take long before a shout went up.

" Lochee Fleet Rules Ya Bass, go on Stevie "

At this point an angry looking bastard ran forward and started punching hell out of other gang members. Everyone joined in and it was a melee of young blokes with different coloured jerseys trying to knock hell out of each other. The bouncers waded in, but they were on a hiding to nothing as it looked like a coming together of several packs of wild dogs. After a while it all seemed to calm down with the gangs retreating to their own relevant sanctuaries on the lower floor. Waiting for round two.

Denny had felt the need to relieve himself, so he headed downstairs to the toilet. When he entered he found two lads beating the hell out of a young lad who had been part of the Lochee Fleet gang when the fighting had started. He couldn't care less who was fighting with who, but the two lads were a lot bigger and giving the lad who Denny didn't think was old enough to be in here, a right kicking. Denny grabbed the first one by the hair and smashed his head off the cubicle door who then fell to his knees.

"C'mon pal its now one on one so let's see what your made off."

Denny wasn't sure if the other lad was making a run at him or the door which was behind him. It didn't matter anyway as the door burst open and four Lochee Fleet wild dogs ran in grabbing the two lads from the other gang and started to beat hell out of them. Denny went into a cubicle and relieved himself. As he was leaving the guy who he thought was Stevie said,

"Appreciate that pal and if you ever need our help, you will find us in the Pillars Bar in Crighton Street and remember Fleet rules."

Denny gave him a nod and walked out back up to his 'perch' upstairs. The fighting continued at intervals throughout the night and Denny wondered if this was a normal Saturday night for them. He went down to the bar for another whisky, but as he stood at a packed bar something came over him. His sixth sense had kicked in big style. It was as though somebody was watching him, but the place was so busy he couldn't pick anybody out. The only thing was that he thought he saw two burly guys leaving the front doors. It was only the back of their heads he saw so he couldn't be certain, but they looked like the two guys from the Copper

Beach who had been drinking with Broomhill.

There was to be no more whisky for him even although he could have done with a few. It was time for him to head home, but before he got a taxi he went and sat on a bench in a small community garden over the road. He sat and watched and was about to hail a taxi until he saw a car draw up at the front of the Palais. The same car and driver that had been outside his flat for nights on end. Out came the two guys from the Copper Beach pub and they headed into the Palais. After fifteen minutes they left the nightclub shrugging their shoulders to the driver, got in the car and sped off.

Denny knew this was about him and he had been made. The guise of being a liaison officer between here and Edinburgh hadn't worked. He had been poking around into files that had nothing to do with what he was supposedly there for. The right thing to do was walk away from all this, but Denny never walked away from a fight in his life. It was time to get everyone rattled and that included Thomson.

He hailed a taxi and as he neared his flat his sixth sense was at boiling point. The driver was told to head into the next street and drop him off. As Denny strolled back, he saw the car sitting over the road as usual. He knew that his pals would be waiting for him up the close, so he came over the back walls as quietly as possible. As he looked over the last wall, he could see three of them standing in the shadows, but he wasn't convinced that he could see them all. Very slowly he climbed the back wall with a brick he had lifted from a bucket lid.

When he was on top of the wall, he launched himself off at the first available guy and smashed him over the head. He went down like a fallen tree. The surprise gave him the advantage and he started to punch the other two ferociously as his rage was in full flow. Unfortunately, he had made a mistake as another goon came out of an old coal shed and hit him with a spade landing just above the eye leaving a deep cut. He grabbed the spade and with all his strength swung it at the guy's head breaking the spade in half with the force of the spade cutting deep into his skull. These people came to hurt Denny, so he was going to hurt them by letting his rage take over. He started pounding the guys on their faces with what was left of the spade for a while before smashing their legs. He wanted them out of commission.

Denny then sat on the cold ground and for the first time in his life thought how evil he could be when he wanted. That thought quickly passed as these people weren't here to give him a warning, they were here to end his life. He sat for a while until he felt blood from his forehead dripping on to his cheek. He had to move and move fast. He ran upstairs and got a kitchen knife, ran down and climbed over the walls at the back and onto the street. The guy in the car had fallen asleep so Denny walked over the road, punched in the window, and grabbed him by the throat.

"Tell Thomson if that is the best he can do then his best isn't good enough. Let him know in no uncertain terms that I am going to come looking for him. Before I knock you out please try and remember that your pals are lying up the close and they won't be dancing for a while."

He then proceeded to smack him twice on the jaw. Once to knock him out and another time because he could. He put a hole in the tyres before he turned away and smiled. As big a smile as he had ever done. It was obvious that he could no longer stay in his flat. So he ran up the close stepping over the men and up to his flat. He quickly packed, went into the bathroom, and found a needle and thread. He looked in the mirror and went about sewing eight stitches into the cut just above his eye. His work wasn't very pretty as he struggled to see for the blood. On grabbing his bags, he had a quick look around before walking to the phone and ripping it out of its socket.

His car was parked up the road, so he threw his bags in the boot and headed in the direction of Arbroath. As he passed the breakers yard he saw that the flood lights were still on and somebody was still working the grab and crusher. Maybe it's one of Thomson's victims going to their death.

Chapter 16

He remembered where Moira lived in Arbroath. So, he drove up as near to the house that he felt was safe. Nobody would recognise his car, but he sat in the street looking in front and behind for about half an hour just to make sure he hadn't been followed. He couldn't make up his mind whether to knock on her door. There was nobody else. He had to do it. When he knocked on the door there was no answer the first time or the second time, but when he knocked again, she opened the upstairs window and asked who it was.

"It's Denny, Moira I really need your help so can you please let me in? I'm sorry it's so late."

The door opened a few minutes later and Moira stood there in her house coat.

"God, Denny what's happened to you. Have you been in an accident or what? Get yourself in."

She showed him into the living room and sat him down on the sofa. She made tea for the both of them. As they sat drinking, she lifted his head and said,

"Denny if I had put a hem on my skirt with stitching like that, I wouldn't wear it in public."

Denny just knew he could trust her and told her as much as he thought she could handle. The look on her face said it all. She took time to take it all in. He told her he needed his face patched up and a place to sleep for the night. She told him he was lucky as her mum and dad were away for the weekend however after looking at his cut again, she said,

"There is only one way to fix that cut Denny and that is to take out all your botched stitching and start again, but it would be sore and I don't want to inflict that type of pain on you."

He asked her to get on with it and he promised he wouldn't cry as he was a big boy and laughed. When she came back, she had a sewing box and a small kitchen knife in her hand.

She started to cut away his attempted stitching and it wasn't long before the wound would be exposed again. She cleaned it with disinfectant and a ball of cotton wool.

"Okay Denny I'm going to start stitching, but if it gets too sore then please tell me to stop."

He just laughed. After twenty-five minutes she asked him to look in the mirror on the living room wall. He turned and said,

"Thank you, Moira you've done a brilliant job."

She told him he could sleep on the sofa, so she went to get him a couple of blankets.

"Denny, I would love you to share my bed, but I am seeing a really nice guy so I'm sure you understand."

He reassured her he did, stripped off and got under the blankets. Seeing him stripped off again she almost changed her mind, but she had to be sensible. When she got up the next morning he was gone. He had showered and left several lipstick kisses on the bathroom mirror. Gone but never forgotten. Priority now was to find a place to stay. As he was driving, he noticed a sign that said holiday cottages for rent so he pulled into the road. The road seemed to go on forever, but eventually he arrived at a row of very basic cottages.

An old lady came out from the first one and asked if she could help him. He asked about renting a cottage for a few weeks and she was glad of the trade. He paid four weeks upfront and she gave him the keys to the last one in the row which suited him fine as he could get the car hidden at the gable end. He walked to the top of the road where there was a telephone box and phoned Shonagh. She had still been in bed, but gathered her senses when Denny started to tell her about last night.

"Denny, enough please. You can't go on like this."

"Shonagh please trust me as my plan is working. Once I have the bank details, they will make mistakes as they will be rattled so I need that by mid-day or I will walk and that's what I want you to tell the boss. Nothing else."

He told her he would have to phone from a phone box and also, he wanted the addresses of the officers as well. As he put the phone down he wondered if his boss would come through. When he wandered back to his cottage he found bread, milk, butter and eggs on the small table in the living room. God bless the old lady he thought and made a mental note to thank her and introduce himself. As Danny Bauer though. Denny had struggled through last night as his usual stomach cramps were getting worse. He needed a whisky so there was only thing he could do, and he would head out to a place called Forfar which had been sign posted in Arbroath. If anybody was looking for him then Arbroath would have been the next obvious place for him to hide out in. Drinking and driving was a risk, but a risk he had to take.

As he drove through Arbroath, he noticed a small corner shop on one of the side streets. He suddenly decided he couldn't risk the drinking and driving, so he stopped at the shop. He came out with three bottles of whisky. He had to bribe the shop keeper with a twenty-pound note as being a Sunday he was too early to buy alcohol. As he drove back Otto's words of not drinking on his own kept coming into his head, but he wasn't naïve enough not to realise he was on the slippery slope and had been for a while. The whisky had to be kept to a minimum and as long as it was keeping the cravings at bay then he could manage. The next morning, he felt lousy. Was it too much whisky or not enough.

During the night of just lying on top of the bed he formulated his final plan. Assuming the information from Shonagh came through. It was imperative he had to get photos of Broomhill with Thomson but that wasn't going to be easy. Firstly, he was going to go to Well St. station and really rattle the corrupt ones. He went to the top of the track and into the phone box. It was eleven o'clock, so he was hoping that the information he needed was ready. When Shonagh answered her phone extension her voice sounded a bit excited.

"Good news Denny, the information has come through and the boss and I have gone through it and there are four officers who have been putting illicit amounts of cash into their bank accounts over a period of years. We even managed to get a judge to let us look into the bank accounts of their wives and one showed interesting reading. Oh, and the car was registered to a scrap metal company which is on the road between Dundee and Arbroath."

This was great news so after noting down the names of the four officers he thanked her and to tell her boss to organise a squad to come to Dundee for their arrests on short notice.

Broomhill, Lancaster, Briggs, and Hill. They were the ones in the pub taking bribes from Thomson's men. Briggs looked like he had been told to be there as he didn't look comfortable that night. His wife's bank account was the one that made interesting reading. She would be the person he would break first and then it would be the domino effect. They would all come tumbling down.

Denny phoned Shonagh back and asked her to give him the home address of all the officers. On the journey back to the cottage he went to a supermarket, filled up with petrol and stocked up on food, but the whisky had ruined his appetite so he knew that a lot of the food would be spoiled. As he entered the cottage his senses were on high alert. Someone had been in when he had been away. It was only when he put the groceries down that he noticed the shepherd's pie on the table. He laughed, but still checked the kitchen and bedroom. It had been the owner of the cottages and she must have thought that Denny needed feeding up. The rest of the day was spent making sure his plan was as full proof as possible. It all rested on Mrs Briggs.

That night the owner who he had found out to be Mrs Watson had knocked on his door looking for her pie dish and was disappointed that he had barely eaten half of it. He asked her in and to be honest he was glad of the company.

"Tell me to mind my own business son, but you have an empty bottle of whisky in the bin and two full bottles in the kitchen. What is going on with you?"

"Well Mrs Watson it's a long story, but I'm sure I am an alcoholic. My mother was one, but that is not my excuse. I only have a few weeks to complete my job here in Tayside then I'm going back home to try and get clean. I'm a mess at times."

"I had an idea son as my husband Bertie liked the whisky and I suppose you could have called him an alcoholic, but God rest his soul he never missed a day's work. I'm going to give you a tip which may or may not help you. He drank a lot of water. Not in the whisky but glasses and glasses of the stuff each day. Sometimes he could 'pee' for Scotland, but he reckoned it made him function better. At the back of this cottage there is a large stone which covers a well. There is a spring several foot down and a bucket attached to a rope for pulling up the water. It is the most beautiful water you will ever have tasted. Try it."

Before she left Denny thanked her for her advice and said he would try it.

After having something to eat he went round to the back of the house, found the stone, and easily rolled it away from the well. He dropped the bucket in, heard a splash, waited a moment, and started to haul the bucket up. When he lifted the bucket out, he took a cup he had brought out and dipped it in the water. As soon as it touched his lips, he knew this was something special. Maybe this could be the extra help he needed to get him through this operation, but then again it could just be wishful thinking on his part. Just clutching at straws. After drinking several cups of the stuff, he went inside and grabbed a couple of bottles with tops and filled them up. He left them outside as the chilly wind blowing from the sea would keep them cool. He might have been imagining it, but he felt a bit more refreshed.

However, he was up early next morning preparing himself to put the last pieces of the jigsaw into place. He had to be waiting up the street from Dc Brigg's house when he went to work. He hoped he had got the address right, but then Briggs walked out of the front door, kissed his wife, and jumped into his flash car and drove away. Denny waited for about half an hour and then walked to the front door and ran the bell.

Mrs Briggs answered the door with a smile on her face. Denny produced his warrant card and said,

"Mrs Briggs I am a new colleague of your husband, and I would like an informal chat if you don't mind. Nothing to worry about."

She asked Denny in, and he sat in the chair while she was sat on the sofa.

"You have a lovely house here and your husband drives an expensive car. How is it you can afford all these trappings when I am on the same wage as your husband, and I can struggle with the rent for my poxy flat at times. Did you come into money at any time Mrs Briggs?"

"What are you trying to say Dc Bauer?"

"What I am saying Mrs Briggs is that we know your husband has been receiving kickbacks from a certain drug dealer in the town. You have been complicit in his actions by depositing some of the money in a bank account in your name."

The colour drained from her face and the smile disappeared, replaced by tears. She knew they had been caught.

"What will happen to us detective? Is there any way you can help us out? Please, I'm pleading with you."

"There is one way and that is for your husband to turn Queens evidence so we can convict the other corrupt officers on the force. It will go an awfully long way to keeping your husband out of jail and he could end up with just a suspended sentence."

Denny had lied about all that, but he had to convince her that there was a chance for her husband. Slim to none.

"I'm going into the station now to ask your husband to come home on the pretence that he is ill so you can discuss what you want to do. Let me tell you though Mrs Briggs if your husband doesn't agree then you will both spend a considerable number of years in prison and as a police officer he will have a terrible time. I doubt he would last a couple of months in there. I will be back here at eight o'clock tomorrow morning for your answer and on no account is your husband to inform the other officers or I will ask the judge to give you both the maximum sentence he can. Do you hear me? Oh, and don't think about trying to dispose of any money from your accounts as they have been frozen."

Denny left her sobbing into a cushion and was sure he had put it over strong enough and she would convince her husband to cooperate with any enquiries. He then went to his car and drank a large bottle of water to see if it could stave off the whisky cravings that were starting. The traffic was busy, and as he sat waiting in the traffic jams, he thought that this was a good start, but there was a long way to go. At the station he locked the car and walked in along the long corridor. He noticed Briggs was working in one of the side offices which was a bonus. As he entered, Brigg's mouth dropped open, but he managed to say,

"What do you want Bauer? Get out I don't want to see you."

"As I can see by your face Briggs seeing me was a bit of a shock for you, but please listen carefully to what I'm going to say to you."

He told him he had been to see his wife and she had confirmed that the money they had in their accounts were from him taking kickbacks from Thomson and she knew several other officers were involved. His face had gone white, and he was struggling to put two words together. Denny put a hand on his shoulder and squeezed with the pain bringing Briggs back to reality.

"Okay, here is what's going to happen next. You're going to go home because you're ill. Stomach upset. That lovely wife you have will let you know exactly what I said to her, and I will be at your house early tomorrow morning for an answer. Remember though, the first person to 'sing' gets the best deal from the courts. Now I'm going so I suggest you head off and speak to your wife, but don't come back in here and don't answer your home phone to anybody."

Denny left the building, jumped into his car, and sped off. He eventually parked up the road from the Brigg's house and waited. After a while, the car drew up into the drive and Briggs virtually ran into the house. Denny spent most of the day on surveillance making sure they didn't do a 'runner'. He took a break later in the afternoon and walked to a pub where he quickly drank a couple of whiskies. When he got back to the car, he could see their car in the driveway. He wasn't going to spend much more time there.

When he returned to the cottage he parked and went up to the post box and phoned Shonagh. He told her about his day and asked her to phone their boss tonight and ask for him to organise the squad to be on the road as soon as he telephoned early tomorrow.

"The dominoes are beginning to tumble Shonagh. If I'm still alive by the weekend, then they will be lying flat. Please stay by the phone till you hear from me."

The call was ended there and he started walking back down the track. His mind was elsewhere as he was startled when a car slowly passed him by. It was only Mrs Watson who gave him a wave and continued, but this was not good from Denny's point of view as that could have been one of Thomson's men. When he got to the cottage he picked up a bottle of whisky and walked down to the beach. He sat on the sand taking sips of whisky until the cold beat him again. However, he thought it would be good practice for a return to Durma.

Over the last few weeks, he had thought about Durma a lot and decided that he would return only until he had beaten the booze and then he would leave again. With or without Helen. It was now time for something to eat and try and get an early night even if it was only to give his body a rest. The next few days were both critical and dangerous, so he had to try and get his act together. He felt a bit lightheaded from the whisky so at about nine o'clock he drank two large bottles of the spring water and went to bed.

At three in the morning, he jumped out of the bed and ran to the toilet as he thought he might end up wetting the bed. As he stood there urinating, he felt something was strange. He had actually slept for about six hours. This was unprecedented. There was hope for him yet.

Next morning, he was up early and forced himself to eat and took one glass of whisky then went around the back and filled up the water bottles. He took the car and parked in his usual space just up from the Brigg's house. Their car was still in the driveway so if they had ran then they didn't take the car. Denny felt a bit nervous just waiting and waiting. At five minutes to eight he walked to their door, and it was the wife who opened it and let him in. He asked her to double lock it before going into the lounge. The husband sat there and didn't even look up as Denny sat over from him.

"Right let's cut to the chase. What have you decided? Remember there is no going back. Talking is going to be in your best interests."

It was Briggs himself who said he would give him everything he needed but would want protection for him and his wife and a deal for both of them as well. Denny nodded his head as if in agreement, but he knew fine there would be no deal whatsoever and he couldn't care less. He went to their phone and called Shonagh and said it was on and he needed the squad there as soon as possible. He also asked for armed police to be outside the Brigg's house for however long it would take. Also, he wanted the doors of the police station locked and guarded at nine o'clock once he was inside. The squad had been waiting in a layby just over the Forth Road bridge from the early hours, so it wasn't long before they were traveling through Dundee.

Denny walked through the main doors to the station and asked Sargeant Dunn to lock the place down. He said he wanted Broomhill, Lancaster and Hill put in separate interview rooms and if they resist he was to cuff them with force if need be. The Sargeant had that look of what the hell is happening here but did

209

as he was told. Everyone in the building was looking bewildered and Denny went through the place announcing that it would all come clear soon.

It seemed an age before two cars came into the car park and his boss DC Thomas Shearlaw stepped out of the first one. Seven more officers followed him and walked towards the main door. Denny shouted to the Sargeant to let them in. Once in the boss walked forward to Denny and shook his hand and said,

"Great work Bauer. Did you manage it without the whisky?"

"Don't be bloody silly sir. You know I don't touch alcohol" said Denny with a massive grin on his face.

"Right Bauer you and I are going to interview the suspects while all the other officers will take this place apart. The other suspect and his wife are under police guard and will be interviewed by one of my best officers in this field."

The boss asked which one they should tackle first, and Denny had said it should be Hill as he will probably crack first. When they went into the interview room they sat over the table from Hill. It was Denny that took the lead.

"Right Dc Hill, whoever informs us about the connection between this station and Billy Thomson first will more than likely receive something like a suspended sentence. You see Hill I don't think you can do jail time. We have your bank account details and what we must know is who gave you the kickbacks. We know they came from Billy Thomson but were they passed to DI Broomhill and then on to you or did you get them direct."

He mumbled something with his head down before Denny slapped the table giving Hill and the boss a fright.

"Look Hill, DC Briggs is being interviewed as I speak and he's probably singing like the proverbial canary so you had better get in before him to get the lesser sentence or my boss here will make sure you rot for a long time in jail. We will leave the room and give you exactly five minutes to think about it, but when we come back in, we better have the right information or you're a goner Hill."

They left the room and while waiting outside the boss turned to Denny and said,

"Interesting interrogation techniques Bauer. From which manual did you learn them."

"From the 'I couldn't care less' manual if it gets done sir."

They went back in, and Hill gave them all the information they needed. Times, places, and amounts and it had all come from Broomhill.

Next was Lancaster and as soon as they went in, he had said, "You have nothing on me so get lost and get me a solicitor."

The boss had immediately said,

"Listen you lowlife, Hill and Briggs have given us enough information to put you away for a long time so shut up and tell us everything we want to know."

Denny couldn't help himself and chipped in,

"Your only hope of getting a pal in the jail is if you end up in the same cell with Broomhill, but you will be on the end of many 'incidents' during your long stretch there. How long is up to you so just talk."

It was then that Lancaster started to cry, and Denny really wanted to smash his head on the table, but it wouldn't go down well with the boss being there.

After another few hours the boss had told everyone that the interviews were concluded, but he told everyone to be very wary as it seems there is little concrete evidence to pin on Thomson. They had to stay together and not to leave the hotel in which they were staying. The boss looked at Denny, but knew he was speaking to himself. Denny gave him a slight nod of the head as if to say I want a word with you. Denny walked down the corridor and found an empty room and waited for the boss. With the door firmly closed Denny went on to say,

"Sir, you and I know that Thomson, with a top lawyer, is pretty much untouchable so I'm telling you this now. I haven't spent all the months in Edinburgh and now here to let him walk away. So my work here isn't done so I will be staying here for a few more days anyway."

" I hope what you are planning to do is legal as we both could be in a lot of bother."

"Trust me sir, nothing will come back to you and after I have written out my reports then hopefully you will never see me again. Now I have one person to speak to and I'm going for a whisky."

The boss just looked at Denny knowing that no matter what he was going to do he couldn't be stopped. Denny headed to the main offices and went and sat on the edge of Katherine Marten's desk. The look on her face said she knew what was coming.

"Katherine it was a lovely night we had in the Palais a few weeks ago, but there was one thing that I couldn't get my head around. It was the number of times you were pumping me for information about myself while you thought I was out of it with the drink. At first, I put it down to you being nervous on our first date, but I linked it to the lack of information there was in the files about the biggest drug dealer on the West coast of Scotland. So, I am assuming that at some point Broomhill told you to get rid of anything relating to Thomson. No matter how small. I can see by your face I am correct so here is what I think should happen. After about two weeks I think you should resign from the force citing reasons that you have been embarrassed by the corruption here and you need a fresh start. It will give you more time to look for your imaginary dolphins in the Tay estuary. This will remain between you and me. Okay?"

Denny walked out of the station with his boss shouting to him that he had better be in at eight o'clock tomorrow morning. He got in his car and drove to the Pillars pub. It was empty at this time with only a few of the regulars in. He asked the barman if Stevie had been in. He had said not tonight, but he could get him on the phone if he would wait. Denny nodded and ordered a whisky. The barman went to the phone at the end of the bar and phoned Stevie.

An hour later in walked Stevie with two of his gang. Denny asked them to go into the lounge for a chat. The three of them were a bit wary but went through. Denny got the drinks in and then asked Stevie for his help.

"I need some information from you please. Firstly, I need the address and the street layout around Billy Thomson's house. Secondly, I would like to know how he is bringing the drugs into this area and beyond."

The three of them looked a bit frightened when Thomson's name was mentioned. Denny reassured them that they were safe and once he got this information, they would never see him again. Stevie said the first part was easy and told him what he needed to know. He said his two pals would find out about the drugs as he was fairly sure they come into the small harbour in Arbroath.

"What will happen is I will take Levi and Bodhi up to Arbroath tomorrow and I can assure you they will find out. Why are you going after Thomson though that's a suicide mission?"

"Trust me lads there will only be one person to come out of this intact and that will be me. If it all goes to plan, I will be back here to put a considerable amount of money behind the bar for all the gang to enjoy a drink for a long time."

Denny gave Stevie the number of the phone box at the top of the road and asked for an answer at eight o'clock sharp tomorrow night. Just as he was leaving Stevie said,

"I take it you're a cop then?"

"After what I'm about to do I doubt it."

Denny laughed and walked out. He headed home to drink some whisky with loads of the 'magic' water. The water was so 'magic' that he did wet the bed that night. As he sat on the edge of the bed at about three in the morning, he was so ashamed. He remembered his dad's words about his mum's organs not working very well and he was scared. The first time in an exceptionally lengthy period.

After washing himself he ran water into the bath and soaked the sheets. Nothing he could do about the mattress. He wondered how he was going to tell Helen if it was the whisky that had just made him wet the bed. He would worry about that later. As soon as he got into Well St. police station, he heard his boss shouting on him.

"Good morning, Bauer let me tell you what is going to happen today. Thomson will be brought in for questioning and then we will take it from there."

"No disrespect sir but you know as well as I do that, he will flaunt in here with a big fancy lawyer and half an hour later he will be out the building laughing his head off. However, I might have some good news about his drug operation. At eight o'clock tonight I could have the information on how he brings his drugs into the country and where he lands them. So how about we prepare to raid him tomorrow, just like Edinburgh?"

"How good will this information be Foggerty, sorry Bauer?"

"I will bet my life on it if the intel comes through. If it goes flat then you can sack me, but please remember that in a couple of weeks I'll no longer be a police officer."

213

They left it at that, and Denny went into a side office and started the massive amount of paperwork that had accrued. He hated this part of the job. As he sat there, he looked out of the window and saw an expensive car pulling into the car park. He knew it had to be Thomson with his lawyer. He looked from the side of the window as he didn't want his face seen.

After about an hour Thomson and his flashy lawyer came out of the station laughing and Denny had spoken out loud saying,

"Laugh all you want you moron. You won't be laughing in a few days."

His boss walked through the door and told him he had been right, and Thomson's lawyer had tied them in knots, and it looked like Thomson would get away with it.

"Please sit on that chair sir and let me tell you a little story. I haven't busted my arse off not to let him get away with it. Soon you will never see or hear about him ever again. Understand?"

"Bauer, I hope you're not thinking about doing anything drastic or for that matter illegal."

The boss looked at Denny and thought he had never come across such a person in life never mind his career as Denny Foggerty. If that was really his name. It appears he just couldn't care less. Denny just got on with the laborious paperwork. That afternoon the four corrupt officers were to be transported to Saughton Prison in Edinburgh. As they were being escorted out Denny stood at the far end of the corridor. He then smiled and started clapping until his boss shouted at him to stop. When they passed him, they gave him a menacing look, but Denny just laughed. Another rebuke came from his boss. For Denny this was a satisfactory outcome, but it wasn't enough. He wanted the big prize. Thomson.

His boss said that he would keep the men in Dundee for another few days but not indefinitely if his information comes through. Denny had said he would come to the Queens Hotel at eight thirty tonight and speak to him personally, but he had to leave the station now to follow up on the lead about the drugs. What Denny really meant was he was desperate for a whisky. He kept to some of the pubs he still had to explore as Thomson was still free and dangerous.

After four whiskies he thought it more prudent to head home

and wash the sheets from his bed. He stopped at a bank and withdrew a considerable amount of money. When he got back to the cottage his sixth sense told him somebody had been in again, but it wasn't shouting out at him. Denny was still being careful, so he walked around the back only to see his bedsheets hanging on the washing line. How embarrassing was this. Just then Mrs Watson walked around the corner.

"It'll be another couple of hours before they're dry. Don't worry son I often had to do this for my Bertie. Sometimes he had to decide which was causing this. The whisky or too much water. Come in, I've left some food on the table for you. You must eat." she said with a raised voice.

As they sat at the table Mrs Watson suddenly asked him if he had a wife or girlfriend. Denny was truthful and said he didn't really know as it was his intention to go back home to get sober, but he didn't know if his girl would want him back. She asked him where home was, but he said he would prefer to keep that a secret due to the nature of his job. She told him if she really loved him, she would take him back.

"Let me tell you this young man it won't be easy to get clear of the drink and as much as people will help you ultimately it will be you and you alone that can kick the habit."

Denny gave her a hug and thanked her for her advice, and he told her he was going out tonight and might be back late. At just before eight o'clock Denny was sitting in his car next to the phone box when the phone rang giving him a bit of a fright. He got out and answered it.

"It's Levi pal. Stevie asked me to ring you. There is a fishing boat due to come into Arbroath harbour on Wednesday night. It's called the Fortuna and will berth at the far end of the harbour next to a small warehouse marked Ab 21. It's expected about nine o'clock and if you're looking for the drugs then search under the fish in the boxes. Before Denny could say thanks, the phone went dead. He went back in the car and headed to the area that Stevie had told him Thomson's house was found in. After touring about for a while he was just about to call it quits when he came across the house. For God's sake it was massive. How did he miss it the times he had been back and forward. The arrogant bastard had even put the name Thomson on his wrought iron gate. He must think he is invincible.

Denny checked for cameras but could only see one overlooking the front door and there would be one at the back door. He reversed and waited a while taking in the surrounding. He was about to start the car when a side door in the wall to the right opened and Thomson walked out. On a lead he had his small dog which looked to Denny like a rat on a lead. Denny kept low and watched his movements. Thomson walked to the bottom of the street and let the dog off. He lit a cigar and just stood watching the dog urinating over everything above the ground. He stood for about twenty-five minutes before putting the dog back on the lead and walking back through the side door.

Denny waited another half an hour before he left his car and walked down the short road. There was nothing at the end just a wilderness. Unfortunately, it was a dead end, so the only way out was the street he came along. That wasn't good. On walking back to the car, he remembered about going to the Queens Hotel for a meeting with his boss.

All the men were sat in the lounge having a drink when Denny walked in. There were the cursory waves and nodding of heads until the boss got up and walked through to a small empty snug bar. As soon as they were in Denny had told him the information he had received from Levi. His boss didn't seem that convinced, but Denny assured him that the intel was spot on.

"Okay Bauer, I will get everything ready except I won't tell anybody the finer details and we will all be here till Friday morning."

Denny thanked him but refused his offer of coming for a drink with the rest of the men. He felt that it would be a long hang on till Friday, but decided he didn't want anything to do with this operation. Edinburgh had been enough for him. He had his own agenda. He stopped at a bar for whisky before heading home. When he reached the phone box up from his cottage he stopped the car, went in, and phoned Helen. When she answered he asked her how she was and apologised for not phoning, but he had been undercover for a while, and he didn't want to get anybody dragged into his murky world.

"Have you made up your mind about what you're going to do Denny? Are you wanting to come back to Durma, and will I see you again?"

"I want to see you again Helen more than anything, but the next week will be so critical. My three options are I will be buried with a bullet in my head. Next it might be me spending the rest of my life in prison. The third would be that this alcoholic would return to Durma and try and get dry, but it would not be pretty for either of us."

"Denny, you are beginning to scare me, but out of the three I would take the third choice in a heartbeat. I know it won't be easy, but I am sure we can work through it. Here is the thing though Denny. If you do get dry and then decide to go back on the drink, then you can 'bugger off ' from the island and I hope that I would never see you again. Is that plain enough?"

Denny started laughing and told her that if he couldn't kick the habit he would be off the island. He would choose the island's highest point and take himself off it. Never to be seen by anybody again.

That seemed to end the conversation, but Denny then told her he would be on Durma in about a week and a half. He would phone her for a lift from the ferry. He told her he needed to go now. One last thing was Denny telling her,

"It's bad Helen, my drinking is very bad."

Denny put the receiver down and drove down to his cottage. The first thing he did was to go to the whisky bottles only to find he was out of the stuff. What was his plan now? Either go for more bottles of just visit some pubs in Dundee?

He decided to use the next few nights on surveillance at Thomson's house and mentally make notes of his movements. Sitting around in a car for hours at a time wasn't playing well with his mind. Too much time to think. One night sitting there with the chilly wind blowing through the gaps in the doors of the car he thought how things were going to play out on Durma. He knew it was his last chance and he hadn't been pretending to Helen about going off the cliff. He didn't like the person he had become through the whisky and wasn't going to ruin other people's lives. He wondered if he would ever get better.

Thomson was a creature of habit. He was so arrogant thinking he was untouchable just like his son. He came out the side door of the garden wall every night at the same time and went through his routine of letting the dog off the lead and then smoking his cigar before going back in. Denny wondered what age he was and guessed that he would be mid to late fifties. This was his second last night in Dundee. He liked the place and really hoped that the city would receive some real investment and bring it back to its former glory. He was hitting the whisky bad for the last few nights, but he knew that tomorrow night he had to lay off even if it made him a bit jittery. However, he knew his plan would work as it was simple.

Chapter 17

Denny rolled into work on Wednesday morning at about ten thirty with his boss shouting,

"Where have you been for the last couple of days Bauer? We have an operation to plan."

Denny walked forward and said,

"Look sir, I don't have any operation to plan. I have given you all the details. All you must do is act on them and you will be a hero just like Edinburgh. Unfortunately, I have other matters to deal with and as from right this minute please accept my resignation from the police force. Then my actions can't come back to haunt anybody but me. One thing I would ask from you sir and that is for Pc Slater to come and pick me up tomorrow morning."

"Okay Bauer, but what about your own car?"

Denny started to laugh and said,

"Remember that one of the items I asked for was a disposable car? Well, it will be disposed of tonight. Anyway, it's a rust bucket."

The boss shook his head and thought he will miss this enigma, but maybe for the force's reputation it would be better this way.

Denny was struggling to fill in his day and the shakes were starting so he headed towards the Pillars pub. The place was empty, so he sat at the bar and ordered a whisky. After a couple more he knew he had to watch the alcohol intake. After the third one went down, he ordered a fourth and just sat sipping with his plan for tonight going round and round in his head. However, there couldn't be any room for slip ups. On finishing his whisky, he handed a large envelope to the barman and said,

"This is for the Fleet boys and tell them to enjoy it and if I find out you have been skimming from it I will come back and rip your throat out. Understand?"

The barman gave a faint nod. Denny thought he was just warming up for what was about to happen tonight. He told himself to keep focusing and no matter what happens he shouldn't deviate from the plan. He couldn't rely on Thomson

219

walking the dog at the same time every night, so he drove and parked in the road adjoining Thomson's. The nerves were starting to make his stomach churn. Either that or it was the whisky.

He felt his hands shaking as he gripped the steering wheel and tried to relax them. An hour later Denny's sixth sense kicked in more intense than he had ever felt. Thomson came out the gate and started walking down the road with his dog. Denny had kept the ignition running and slowly he reversed the car and turned the steering wheel so that he was facing down the road Thomson was on. His heart was pounding but there was no rage this time. Slowly he started to drive without putting the headlights on. When he thought Thomson was more interested in his cigar Denny floored the car and aimed it to hit the 'scum bag' dead centre. Thomson flew up and over the bonnet with his cigar still clenched in his teeth. He landed on the boot with an almighty thud and slid off onto the ground. Denny quickly got out and ran round to the back of the car. The first thing he did was to check for a pulse from Thomson. Although it was faint it was exactly what Denny wanted. Denny lifted him up, put him in the boot, and then stuffed an old rag into his mouth. Then he tied his feet and hands with old rope he had found on the beach.

As he got back in the car his heart was still pounding but he couldn't hang around. He drove very carefully through the town before turning off onto the Arbroath Road. When any car came up on his tail, he was expecting it to be the police but he didn't have far to go. He saw the floodlights from the breakers yard not too far ahead. As he turned off onto the track leading up to the large gates. They were locked so Denny started to blast the car horn. Soon an elderly guy came running up and opened them. Denny drove in and when he parked up, he got out and said to the guy,

"I've got a special one from Mr Thomson. He needs this one crushed to a cube then put in a hole and buried before the cars are put on top. He said you would know what to do."

Denny handed him a bulging envelope and told him Mr Thomson had said for this amount of money it had better be done right.

"Don't you worry son. For this amount of money, I would

220

bury Thomson himself."

Denny was trying not to laugh and then he asked the guy where he wanted the car. He pointed over to the large mechanical grab and crusher. Denny drove over to where he had pointed and got out. He faced the car towards the crusher. The guy was already in his cab when Denny signalled to him to wait a moment. He went to the back and opened the boot. Thomson wasn't quite awake, so Denny slapped him hard a few times to make him come to. When Thomson focused, he looked out and all he could see was scrap cars. His eyes were bulging, and Denny leaned into the boot, took the rag from his mouth, and whispered in his ear,

"Oh, it was me that threw that rat of a son of yours down the stairs smashing his spine. See you in Hell arsehole."

Denny closed the boot lid and waved for the guy to start work with the grab. Denny got out of the way, and he thought he could hear Thomson screaming but with the noise of the grab and the crusher starting up the guy had no chance of hearing anything. Denny stood and watched the powerful grab sink its teeth into the car before it wheeled round and dropped the car into the crusher. After a few minutes, the side of the crusher opened and what was once a car spewed out the side. He turned and walked away with that evil grin on his face. As he walked down the track, he felt he was at peace with himself. The first time in ages. He knew that taking someone's life was wrong for most normal people, but Denny felt he wasn't any normal person. His demons made sure of that.

He crossed the main road and trekked over the brush to get to the beach. He didn't know if he could get through the night without a whisky, but no car meant no chance of whisky. As he walked along the shoreline the heavens opened, and the rain came down to dampen his mood. It seemed like an age before he came to the cottage. He was totally soaked through and with his hands shaking he struggled to get the key in the lock.

Just then Mrs Watson came out of her cottage and took the key off him and opened the door. When he got in, he couldn't believe what he was seeing. This beautiful angel of a woman had been in and put on a log fire and now it was glowing red.

"Get your clothes off and put them on that screen over there I'll be back in a minute."

221

Denny did as he was told and sat in the seat next to the fire before his guardian angel came in with a few blankets and a bottle of whisky which had about a quarter left in it. She poured him a large one and sat in the opposite chair. Denny then asked her if there was anything in this world, she could have then what would it be.

"Where did that question come from son? I have been saving up for a while to see my grandkids in Australia for what would possibly be my last time, but the cottage rental business has been poor this year and it's been a struggle to put money away."

"Well Mrs Watson if I were you, I would be booking your flights. Trust me."

Denny's eyes then closed, and he was sound asleep. Next morning, he awoke to find all his clothes neatly folded so he quickly dressed and packed his holdall. It was time to leave. After locking up he knocked on Mrs Watson's door. When she came out, he thanked her for looking after him and said he was off.

"You have been an angel to me Mrs Watson and I wasn't joking about booking your tickets. I have left something for you beside the bed."

Denny then gave her a big hug and a kiss on the cheek and walked up the track to the phone box. When Mrs Watson went into his cottage she could not believe her eyes when she picked up an envelope and hundreds of pounds fell out. She ran and opened the door to say thanks, but he was away up the road. She thought that was one troubled boy.

From the phone box he phoned Shonagh at her house. He explained for her to pick him up at a café that sat just over the Tay Bridge at eleven o'clock, but if he wasn't there, she was to wait fifteen minutes and then go home. Denny wasn't going anywhere near Well St. so he decided to walk over the bridge to meet Shonagh, but first he would stop off for a few whiskies. One pub was right over from the entrance to the public walkway for the bridge. At ten o'clock he decided he had better make a move.

As he walked, he was starting to get cold as a bitter wind was blowing in from the North Sea. He thought he would try and jog a while, but that was a bit of a joke as he had to stop now and again to throw up the whisky he had consumed. When he reached the middle of the bridge he stopped and vomited the last of the whisky into the Tay. As he was looking over, he thought how easy it would be for everybody if he just took a topple over. However, he came to his senses and walked quickly over to the other side.

When he got to the café, he saw Shonagh sitting in her car. She got out, ran over and put her arms around him.

"Let's go for a hot drink Denny you look frozen. When was the last time you ate?"

Denny followed her in and although he didn't feel like eating, he knew he had to try. He tried the famous Forfar bridie and Shonagh the bagel with cream cheese. A large pot of coffee sat in the middle of the table. Shonagh was desperate to tell him about the raid up in Arbroath. All the intel that Denny had given them was spot on and a massive amount of drugs recovered. More importantly the four crewman they arrested were 'spilling the beans' and it was now going to be an Interpol operation. Denny was trying hard not to listen as he was concentrating on the his famous bridie.

"I heard you quit Denny. Are you happy about that?"

"Of course, I am Shonagh. I was never cut out to be a police officer. To many rules to stick to. Too much don't do this and don't do that for my liking as you know. There was no way I could continue the way I am. The drink has got the better of me and I must return home to try and get sober. If I don't get clean, then I will hopefully see my mum and dad in heaven."

Denny paid the bill and just before leaving Shonagh had told him that young Billy Thomson had died due to breathing difficulties. Denny turned to her and said,

"Well, him and his dad will be sitting next to each other at the dining table in Hell now."

"Oh, Denny please tell me you haven't done anything to Thomson senior have you?"

"Now Shonagh what makes you think I would do something like that?"

He walked out the café laughing.

The hour and half drive was a bit strained. Denny just wanted to sleep and a couple of times he asked her to stop the car so that he could bring up the famous Forfar bridie. At the police station in Edinburgh he phoned Helen and asked if she still wanted him to come home although he did say he was a mess. She told him she wanted him home as soon as possible and no matter how bad he was they would get through it together. He told her that he would book the ferry for late afternoon tomorrow but would phone her as soon as he knew the time.

This was it for Denny. He was going. Just then the boss walked through and said,

"Well Foggerty, I would like to say something before you leave us. Your skills as an undercover police officer have been second to none. However, your disregard for authority has been a big pain in the arse both here and in Dundee, but it has been my pleasure to have known you son. I don't suppose you will accept a commendation, will you? I take it from your laughter that it's a no then."

Denny walked forward and started to shake Deputy Chief Thomas Shearlaw's hand and said,

"Sir, if you ever need any other parts of Scotland cleaned up then whatever you do don't come looking for me."

Denny took two steps back and for once in his short police career saluted his boss. The boss saluted back and walked into his office a bit emotional. Denny then turned to Shonagh and said,

"Pc Slater it has been my pleasure knowing you young lady and I hope that I might see you again, but if I do then please don't be lifting your top up for me."

Denny just got through the door before a desk tidy hit the frame. Shonagh could hear him laughing and she just smiled with tears in her eyes. She realised there would never be another Daniel Rey Foggerty in her life.

He got a taxi to Waverley Station and bought his ticket to Inverness. It wasn't till five o'clock so he went hunting for whisky. Plenty of places for a drink but he had to keep an eye on the time. He made the train by the skin of his teeth. Too many whiskies. He found an empty carriage and tried to sleep. He was awoken when the train came into Dundee with people coming on and others getting off. Sitting back, he thought about everything that gone on and would he have done things differently. Probably not. He thought that one day he might get back to Dundee and get to know it better. He shut his eyes and was soon sleeping again.

After what seemed like an eternity the train pulled into

Inverness. He got the last bus which was going to Mayfort, but not before 'sinking' a few whiskies for the trip. As the bus was nearing Mayfort he started to become agitated. Not really knowing if it was the whisky losing its effect or he was getting near to Durma. Both left him a bit afraid. The bus entered Mayfort and Denny knew there was no going back. There was time for more whisky, but he thought it might not be a clever idea going on a ferry plus it wouldn't be nice for Helen.

The crossing was the worst he could ever have imagined. The boat wasn't sailing it was rolling from side to side and struggling to get any head way. He had phoned Helen before the ferry sailed to tell her what time he would arrive in Seahaven, but he thought she would be sitting in her van for a while.

The wind was whipping up the waves and Denny could only sit on the forward deck and focus on a point on the horizon to stop him from vomiting. There were black clouds hanging over the 'rock' that was Durma. The way he was beginning to feel he couldn't have cared less if the ferry had taken a nose dive and sunk to the bottom of the sound.

When they finally docked, he went to the toilets and made himself sick. By the smell of vomit coming from in there a few people had the same problem. He washed his face and rinsed his mouth out before putting a few fruit gums in his mouth. Habits die hard. As he walked down the gangway, he spat out the fruit gums and looked across to see Helen waving furiously. She ran across and wrapped her arms around Denny and wouldn't let go. He had to prise her arms off.

"Thank you so much my beautiful boy for coming back to me. I really hope we can work this out. Let's get in the van."

Denny was quite surprised how okay he felt on the journey to Kismay. Even the bumps and holes didn't seem as bad.

"I have been reading up a lot on your addiction and realise that you won't be cured overnight so if you want to get off at Scroggles I fully understand. Also, I think we should take our relationship slowly and at the moment keep out of each other's bed until we feel it is the right thing to do. What do you think?"

"I won't be going anywhere tonight, Helen. I don't feel well so a hot bath and bed sounds good to me, but I must tell you something about my condition which is not very pleasant."

Denny told her about the time at the cottage when he wet the bed. Although he still didn't know what had caused it. Either the whisky or the water. She just sat there and seemed to take it in her stride.

"I don't care what problems you have. I know we are both strong enough to get through this. Oh, and remember you said that if you failed you would take a 'flyer' of the highest point on the island? Well let me tell you Foggerty I will be standing at the back of you with your dad's gun and I'll make sure you go over. Agreed?"

Denny could only laugh and headed for a bath. Helen brought some towels into the bathroom and was quite shocked as to how the whisky had ravaged his body.

"Here is the deal, Denny. I will let you into my bed when your body gets back to the magnificence it was when I last lay beside you."

Denny splashed her with some bath water and they both laughed. Something they hadn't done for an awfully long time. When Denny looked out the window the next morning the same grey skies were still there, and he thought that was one thing he had to forget about. How dull and boring the island was and not to let it get to him again. Just when he was finished dressing there was a loud knock at the door and he shouted to Helen that he would get it. When he opened it there stood Dr Neala Belmont. She saw the look of shock on his face and quickly said,

"Don't worry Denny I'm not here as Dr Belmont the pathologist, but as your GP. I take it Helen hasn't told you yet?"

Denny asked her in and Helen came through with a tray of coffee and breakfast rolls she had just baked. She 'mouthed' sorry to him. Neala told him that she now lived with Ian here in Kismay and she had qualified to be a GP as Dr. Henderson was about to retire. Denny found it hard to accept that somebody would want to come and live on Durma. The coffee and rolls went down a treat before Neala had said,

"Well Denny, I'm not just here for Helen's lovely baking. I'm here to see if I can help you with your problem. I can see you looking at Helen as if she has told me something that was supposed to be a secret. Denny, there are a lot of people on the island that know about your problem so don't be embarrassed about it. About fifty percent of the fishermen down there in the harbour have a problem, but most just don't care. I will come back tomorrow, and we can talk about what plan you have to try and get clean. If you don't want to talk about it, then fine, oh and Ian would like to see you sometime."

He had said that he would be happy to see her and it was left at that. Denny knew that one of the main hurdles in ridding himself of the alcohol was keeping out of Scroggies. At this stage of the recovery he knew it would be virtually impossible for that to happen. As Helen was working, he decided to try walking around the coastal path and as long as his sixth sense didn't kick in anywhere then that would be fine. He took a couple of canteens of water and a large meat pie in his ruck sack. As soon as he was on the path he didn't feel well and had to sit on a rock. His stomach was cramping up, but not even the water was helping. He walked on just holding his stomach and telling himself he couldn't give in to the pain he was feeling. After another half an hour of walking he had to stop and lie down just of the grass. The pain was so bad that he couldn't even raise himself up to urinate so he just lay on his side, opened his trousers, and relieved himself.

When he felt it was okay to do so he got up and went down a path leading to a small inlet. He sat on a washed up tree trunk and ate his pie wondering how long he could hold it down. Denny made a mental note as to where he had felt unwell just to see if he could go further the next time. Time for home he thought, but today was a bit of a lesson for him. He had to eat and drink as normal as possible and increase his exercise small steps at a time as it had surprised him how bad a shape he was in.

Helen greeted him as he walked through the door with a big hug and asked him where he had been.

"Denny I will be involved in your recovery as much as you want me to be, but please let me know where you are going every time you go out for obvious reasons."

Denny nodded and was going for a lie down as he was struggling without the whisky. He was embarrassed to tell Helen he needed a whisky. She could see his struggle so she suggested he walk down to Scroggies and see if he could see Ian. She smiled and he walked forward and gave her a big kiss. Helen thought how much she had missed that, but she wasn't being naïve as she knew she could handle the brunt of several relapses to come.

Although it was August, Denny had to put a coat on to walk to Scroggies. When he got there, he decided to keep walking down to the harbour. There it was. A brand 'spanking' new boat was docked there. He stood looking it over and it did look a bit special. He couldn't see Ian, so he shouted,

"Permission to come aboard skipper?"

Ian popped his head out of the engine hatch and gave him permission. As Denny landed on the deck Ian walked over and gave him a hearty handshake. Ian made the tea, and they sat chatting for a while with Ian asking how Denny could afford to buy him a new boat. When Denny explained everything about him, and the Albach Trust, Ian spluttered into his cup. Denny just laughed and said he found it hard to comprehend himself. They sat talking as if Denny had never been away, but Ian never once mentioned his drinking. Denny said he was going to Scroggies for a whisky. Ian said he would go with him if he gave him ten minutes to complete the oil change.

As they neared the doors of Scroggies Ian had turned to him and told him to get his head high as he went through the doors. Denny found it hard to try and pace himself as Ian was drinking pints and he was trying to sip his whisky so as not to finish too quick. After a couple of hours and a few drinks later Ian said that he was going home and the look on his face suggested that Denny did the same. Not once had the name Hamish McLure been brought up. When Denny went through the door Helen shouted to him from the kitchen that tea was ready and would he like to go and freshen up.

After eating, Denny realised this would be the hardest part of the day. There was nothing to do on Durma. Nothing at all. That night Denny sat Helen down and told her what he intended to do and when, not if, he was clean then he wanted her to be part of his long term plan. It was all too much for her and she suggested they concentrate on one thing at a time which was the alcohol. Denny said he understood but told her he would implement his plan with or without her.

The knock on the door the next morning reminded him that Neala was coming to speak to him. As they sat in the lounge

Neala had said that she would prefer if Helen took part in the conversation to which Denny nodded his agreement. She asked Denny to give him a history of his drinking and his plan to try and combat it. He told her he would take it slowly and after a few weeks if he was still drinking the same amount or getting worse then he would go 'cold turkey, and if that didn't work then he was going off the cliff.

"I take it by the serious look on your face you aren't joking Denny? There is one thing I will say and that is there no medicine I can give you apart from painkillers to suppress the stomach cramps. It will be all up to you."

"Neala, I do appreciate what you are doing, but I don't want any sympathy from anybody. I don't want any help from anybody when I relapse and struggle to walk home. No pep talks from other people apart from yourself. I just need to try this myself along with Helen by my side. As for me going off the cliff I am deadly serious. No pun intended."

Neala left after telling him he could call in on her anytime he wanted. He left Helen to get on with the baking and got his dad's gun out and started cleaning it with the gun oil that was still in the drawer of his dad's desk. It still felt good in his hands and decided to pass the time away by going hunting for rabbits. He told Helen what he was going to do and where he was going to do it. In his rucksack was a canteen of water and some of Helen's scones. As he walked to the coastal path it felt strange being back on the island and he knew he was at the most crucial part of his life. What a waste of a life if it didn't go past twenty-five years.

It was supposed to be summer, yet he felt the cold wind creeping in to his body. On finding a sheltered area he lay down and started to adjust the scope and wait for the rabbits. One popped it's head up, but Denny was too slow. It must have been half an hour before another appeared and Denny got it in his sights. He was just about to pull the trigger when he started to shake uncontrollably. There was no way he could squeeze the trigger. The stomach spasms then started and all he could do was just lie there and wait till it all passed. It seemed like an age before he felt okay but he knew that the rabbits would be safe for another day. As he walked home, he told himself that he didn't think his plan of cutting down gradually would work. It was going to be all or nothing. Just before he got to the house there was something niggling in his head about August but after thinking for a while, he just forgot about it. When he got in Helen asked how he got on. He told her about his thoughts on his plan which scared her a bit and she tried to tell him to give it a chance

"Helen, is there anything about August that is important as there is a niggle that keeps coming into my head about it?"

She had said that she had no idea and was going to put the tea on and would run him a bath to see if that would help his cramps. As Denny lay soaking himself Helen came in with warm fresh towels. She looked down at his penis and as much as she had missed his kisses, she also missed him being inside her but she was going to stick to what she had said. He had to get his body in shape before they would share a bed together. Giving him something to work to. The next morning Denny sat at the kitchen table and Helen walked through with one of her baked bread rolls with a lighted candle on it. Denny was stumped as to what was going on until Helen gave him a long lingering kiss and wished him a happy birthday. He knew then what the niggles in his head had been about.

Denny gave her a hug before there was a knock on the door. When Helen opened it, Mike Stewart was standing there asking if he could speak to Denny. She asked him in and went to make more coffee. As he sat down Denny was eyeing him up warily. Mike wasn't here to pass the time of day he thought.

"Denny I am going to get right to the point. As you know I am the police contact between here and the mainland, Edinburgh to be exact. They have contacted me to give me some information they had got recently from a drugs bust. They think drugs may be coming into several islands off the West coast of Scotland and distributed throughout the mainland. There have been reports that a couple of young girls have been offered drugs in Seahaven but nothing confirmed yet. This is all new to me and I was wondering as you were recently in the force if you could help us in anyway?"

Denny started to laugh and said,

"I know where this has come from Mike. It was that old bastard Shearlaw wasn't it? Mike I would love to help you but just look at me I can hardly help myself. As you know I am an alcoholic and if it means helping you out or going for whisky then the whisky wins hands down. It is my intention to get clean Mike and part of that regime is trying to exercise more which means more walks around the island to start with. So, as I'm doing that, I will put a bit of thought into where and how drugs could be landed here, but apart from that I can't promise anything."

It was Mike's turn to laugh and said,

"Your spot-on son. It was Deputy Chief Shearlaw that had said you might be of help. Denny, he spoke very highly of you and wished he still had you on the force."

When Mike had finished Denny saw him to the door and told him to give DC Shearlaw his regards. Denny had a grin on his face when he had said it. He started his planned daily walk with his rucksack filled with things to eat and water. Although, as he walked, he thought that whisky would have been better than water. When he came to the place where he had his stomach cramps yesterday he felt he could go further so he carried on remembering he had to walk back. After another mile or so he felt his stomach starting to tighten up and knew the cramps would start soon. He sat down on a large rock and waited.

Ten minutes later he started to vomit and had to think as to what he had been eating yesterday. He thought that what he had brought up had a red tinge to it. Tonight he knew he would end up at Scroggies for a few but this wasn't getting him off the drink. He knew that. When he got home he immediately got on the phone to his bank in Mayfort. The last of his salary from the police force had been deposited but he got a bit of a shock when the manager told him that a bank in Edinburgh had transferred seven hundred and fifty thousand pounds into his account today. After ending the call, he sat and thought that the money was the sum that his dad had promised him on his twenty fifth birthday. It had to come from the Albach Trust on his late mum's instructions. He phoned the bank back and told the manager that an amount should be paid monthly and transferred to the Post Office in Kismay. He would let him know the exact amount later. Strangely he thought that although he was worth a massive amount of money or so he has been told, it really didn't mean anything to him. He had plans as what to do with it.

That night in Scroggies he had spent too much time drinking

whisky and there wasn't Ian there to suggest he headed home. When he got in the house Helen was sitting reading and he could see that she wasn't pleased although she just kept on reading and avoided eye contact with him.

"Helen can I please speak to you. My plan to tackle the drinking looks to be a non-starter. I just can't say no to another whisky. My idea to try and reduce the alcohol down gradually is ill thought out and I have decided tonight while sipping whisky ironically is that I have three weeks to make a difference, or I will take more drastic action. I'm sorry."

Helen didn't utter a word as he headed off to his bed.

Denny went on his daily walk with his usual provisions and although he had walked further again the craving for whisky was as bad as ever. His body was feeling fitter, but his stomach wasn't getting better and each time he put a whisky inside himself it was a real setback. Today was just the same except he had carried his dad's scope with him to look for areas where a boat could possibly come in. Denny told himself that he was kidding himself on as he knew every inlet around the shores of Durma. As he approached Nest Point he thought that this could an obvious contender. The track ran right down towards the sea before turning sharply and heading towards Sea Haven. When he was getting nearer, he saw tyre marks coming and going from Sea Haven. It was possible that he was reading too much into it as it could be someone using a trailer to pull an inflatable to be used for diving. He looked at the trees up on the rise and some large sand-dunes on the other side of the track with a small stream running alongside then meandering to the sea.

Denny started for home with the cramps gnawing at his insides. He never even contemplated eating or drinking which he knew to be wrong as at least there would be something to vomit up. He thought there was something about Nest Point but if there was then his sixth sense wasn't telling him very much. Just a little perhaps. On returning home he found Ian having a cup of tea and chatting with Helen.

"Hi Denny, how far did you get today? Were you trying to help Mike with surveillance of the island?"

Denny thought this might be Ian trying to find out how he really was, but he did tell him about his suspicions at Nest Point.

Ian had said it was a possibility for a boat to get in quite close. Also there had been an inflatable moored at Sea Haven with diver's gear seen in it. Quite easy for anybody to sail around the headland and meet a boat.

"Anyway son, I need help for the next few days. I have increased the number of pots for the boat, and I need a hand checking for flaws before and after I use them. I hope you don't think its beneath you just because you bought me a hundred thousand pound boat do you?"

Ian laughed.

" I'll be there at whatever time you specify Ian and I'll even make the tea just as you like it if you can do one thing for me. However, I can't tell you what it is just yet. Agreed?"

Ian just gave him a nod and the deal was done.

That night Denny had decided to try and not go for whisky. During the night Helen had first heard him moaning and groaning before shouting in his sleep. She had gone upstairs and slipped into his bed and held him tight.

"This is awful Helen. Please make theses pains go away."

All Helen could do was to hold him for most of the night and when the morning came only then did she realise how bad a state Denny was in. He sat at the kitchen table with his head down and ate very little. She packed his rucksack as he was helping Ian today but she knew she would get most of the food back. As Denny walked down to the harbour, she looked out the window and saw someone who was a shadow of his former self. She refused to cry.

Chapter 18

Denny sat on the seat outside Scroggies waiting for Ian to sail in. The weather was cold as usual, so he was warmly wrapped up. Having such a bad night was making him feel very tired but he knew that if he fell asleep Ian would wake him. It only took him a few minutes for him close his eyes and drift off. It must have been his six sense that alerted him to a 'presence' sitting next to him. He didn't open his eyes but thought as to how he was going to address this. Denny quickly opened his eyes and grabbed the person by the shirt. The boy couldn't have been more than eighteen years old. Just sitting there with just a shirt on, a pair of jeans, and shoes that had seen better days.

"Hi I'm Archie. I'm Archie. What's your name? What's your name?"

Denny didn't know what to make of him and he only wanted to shut his eyes for a few minutes. He thought if he shut his eyes again then when he woke up, he would be gone. No such luck.

"I'm Archie and I'll just sit here with you. Just sit here. What's your name. "

Denny knew it was pointless ignoring him, so he said,

"Archie my name is Denny so now will you go away. Please let me suffer in peace."

"I'll just keep you company Denny. Keep you company."

It wasn't long before Ian's boat came into the harbour and tied up near to where Denny was sitting. As Denny rose to walk to the boat, he turned to see Archie shivering from the cold. He took off his coat, handed it to him, and told him to button it up. He greeted Ian and asked for permission to come on board. By the look of the catch this had been a good morning's fishing. Ian had asked him who his pal was sitting on the bench. Denny had said his name was Archie and he was from the mainland but other than that he hadn't a clue. They worked for about an hour checking and repairing the pots before Ian had declared it was time for a cup of tea and something to eat. When they were just about to start, they both looked towards Archie before Denny shouted for him to come down onto the boat. Archie must have been listening to what Denny had said so he said,

"My name is Archie, my name is Archie, permission to come aboard sir?"

Ian just smiled and waved for him to step on board. Denny made the tea and Ian produced enough sandwiches and pies to feed a navy. Which was just as well as Archie had the appetite of the whole navy and he started 'wolfing' down what was on offer. Ian asked Denny how he was, and he had said he wasn't good, and his drastic action was getting nearer to taking the drastic action they had talked about.

"Look Denny, I will give you all the help I can but I refuse point blank in helping you to jump off the cliff. There is not a hope in hell."

"Don't worry my friend I have agreed with Helen that it will be her that will help me end it. If I end up that bad, I don't want to die like my mother did."

"Archie will help you. Archie will help you jump off the cliff."

Ian and Denny burst out laughing followed by Archie who didn't know what they were laughing at. They then asked Archie what his surname was, and he had replied, Doull. The only thing they could make out was that he had sneaked on to the ferry to come to Durma. He couldn't tell them anything else apart from he had a dog that had died. All his possessions were what he was wearing.

Ian could see that Denny was suffering so he suggested he went for a drink while he took Archie to Neala for a check-up and then see if old Mrs Carruthers could look after him for a few days until something could be sorted out. Denny was glad of Ian's suggestion and couldn't get the first whisky down his throat fast enough. After four whiskies had been consumed, he held back as he planned to go out tonight with his scope to see if any small boats were coming to shore. As he left Scroggies he saw Ian coming out of Mrs Carruthers and he gave Denny the thumbs up. Denny walked home and found Helen cleaning the house.

"Helen, can I speak to you please. This is very important to me and hopefully you as well. When, and I repeat when I am clean I would like us to leave Durma and go and live in Bavaria and have a more hands on approach with the Albach Trust. Our home would be in our shooting lodge on the estate which I have

235

owned since mum died. I know Durma has been a big part of our lives but I couldn't live here for the rest of my life. More importantly I want to spend the rest of my life with you. Take your time to think about it and we can speak when the time is right for you."

She seemed shocked as to what he had just said, but she told him that she would give it a lot of thought but told him that there was one contributing factor. That he was clean and would never ever relapse. Denny agreed but what she didn't know was he had already spoken to Maria and Otto advising them that he no longer wished for the lodge to be rented out and he would speak to them at some point. Maria had told him that she had taken over the running of the big house with her boyfriend Micke and Denny had said that was fine and to wait until he came over to hear his plans for the whole estate which included them.

Denny then started to tell her about Archie which reminded him to get his coat back and to look out some clothes for the young lad. The sun was starting to set when a knock came on the door. Helen answered it but got a shock when a lad standing there said,

"My name's Archie. What is your name? What is your name?"

Denny came to the door and asked him in if only because he had Denny's coat over his arm. They both knew that Archie struggled a bit with his mental health, but he seemed a likeable young lad. Helen offered him a cup of tea and asked him if he had eaten. Archie had said in his roundabout way that he had eaten but would accept more if it was offered. Helen thought that she would need to be up early to make more pies the way this young lad was 'scoffing' them. Denny had asked Archie if he would like to explore the island with him tonight and Archie's rapid nodding of his head was a clue. He gave him a heavy knit sweater and told him to keep the coat. Before they left the house Archie took Helen by surprise and gave her a hug and said,

"The pies were lovely. The pies were lovely. Thank you."

When they started walking Denny gave him a torch and told him in no uncertain that he should not go near the cliff's edge. Archie nodded and asked Denny what they were looking for. Denny explained the best he could that he was to keep his eyes open for any lights on this track or on the shoreline. Twice Denny grabbed the back of his coat before he took a tumble off the cliff. Where was Ottar when you needed him. His mind wandered back to the Bavarian Estate and wondered how old the dog would be now or even if he was still alive.

Denny was brought back to the present when Archie started pointing excitedly. Denny pulled him into the side of the hill and put his finger to his mouth indicating for Archie to stay quiet. Denny switched both torches off and kept still watching the light. That was definitely a boat leaving the shoreline and he thought he could hear a van heading on the track to Sea Haven. Too late. It was then that he started to throw up which surprised Archie and the lad seemed frightened.

"Don't worry lad I have a problem with alcohol, and I have to vomit the contents of my stomach up now and again."

"Archie look after you. Look after you."

They started back with Archie putting his arm around Denny whenever he had to stop and vomit. When they arrived back Helen seen the state of Denny and suggested he go down to Scroggies for a few to take the edge of his stomach pains. He said he would and take Archie home. Denny spent more time than usual in the pub that night and Helen heard him come in after midnight and he seemed to be bumping into everything in his way. She was woken several times that night with the noise of Denny vomiting the whisky up. After that, his shouts and moaning meant she didn't get any worthwhile sleep and in the morning she felt awful. This was to be a nightly occurrence and she didn't know how long she could manage it.

Every night Denny went out at the same time each night with Archie tagging along as usual to try and see if there was a pattern to the visits of the boat they had seen previously. Archie was becoming a liability as no matter what Denny was telling him he was doing the opposite. Over a three-week period, Denny had realised a pattern, but he needed definitive proof as to the name of the boat and who was involved.

Denny's drinking was getting worse and his relationship with Helen was starting to deteriorate although she had refrained from saying anything so far. One night with his side kick at his side he started to walk towards Nest Point and his sixth sense started kicking off. As strong as it had been in a long time. He knew he should have told Archie to go home but it would have been an argument so he just forgot about it. Denny took a different route as he didn't want to be seen coming along the track. They headed towards their target from inland where they could look down on any activity at the shoreline. When they got there Denny had to pull Archie down into a hollow and told him quietly not to say a word.

Denny could see that the boat couldn't get fully to the shore so that was what the inflatable was for. On looking through the scope he could see the name of the boat was Endless Summer and there was one guy piloting the boat and another handing bales of what he presumed were drugs over the side to the guy in the inflatable. A white van sat on the track, and he could see a guy sitting in it with the engine running. He was so busy trying to see what was going on that he hadn't noticed that Archie had disappeared. This wasn't good he told himself. Hopefully, he was bored and headed back the way they came. The guy on the boat was handing over the last bale and he then stood up and stretched while facing Denny.

Oh my God thought Denny. The face he was seeing in the sights of the scope was none other than John Scougal, Scoug. He couldn't believe what was happening. Surely this can't be right he kept telling himself. On looking through the scope again it was definitely Scoug. The gap in the front teeth and the big ears were unmissable. Denny's heart felt like it was going to pound out of his chest, but he knew he had to move away quickly before he had to vomit, but where was Archie? He kept telling himself that Archie would be tucked in bed by the time he got home.

He just took his scope in and then headed off to Scroggies not even acknowledging Helen. He sat there on a mission to drink the bar dry of whisky. Seeing Scoug had un-nerved him and he was visibly shaking. He made a vow to himself that he wasn't going to tell anyone. Not even Mike Stewart. He would deal with it himself.

Denny came too lying on the beach with the cold surging through his sweat covered body. His mouth so dry that his tongue was stuck to his palate. The cheek that he had lay on was frozen to the damp, salty sand. As he tried to open his eyes, he quickly shut them again as the cold sea breeze was making them hurt. He didn't know what had woken him. Whether it was the noise from the squabbling seagulls or the waves crashing over the seaweed covered rocks at the bottom of the sandstone cliff.

Denny was kidding himself on as he knew damn well what had woken him up. It was the drink that was starting to wear off from last night and reality was beginning to kick in. The stench of putrid vomit burnt his nostrils so that every time he inhaled, he felt nauseous. He made the effort to get up on one elbow and see if he had been sick down his shirt or on his jeans. By a miracle he had missed both although he did notice a wet patch on the front of his jeans. He lay there just watching the mesmerising ripples of the emerald green sea. So clear, but his alcohol fogged brain wasn't. He looked along the path only to see his house about one hundred yards away. When he looked at his knees, he realised that he had tried to make the last hurdle of his alcohol soaked journey on his hands and knees.

Denny asked why he was doing this to himself, and the simple answer was that he was an alcoholic.

It was impossible to go on like this, so he made his mind up there and then that the time had come to take the drastic action he had been talking about. Little did he know that today would bring such devastating news.

As he walked through the door Helen was waiting for him. If looks could kill he was a dead man walking.

"Where the hell have you been you arsehole? Don't tell me. That cesspit of a place you all call a pub no doubt. I have been up all night worrying about you. Why am I doing this? We said we would try and get through this together, but you haven't even tried."

Denny couldn't say anything as she was right, so he just stripped his clothes off and put them through for washing and went and lay on his bed. It was a couple of hours later that there was a hammering on the front door. Helen answered it and there was Mike and Ian along with a few of the fishermen standing there. Denny had quickly changed a went downstairs. Mike then said,

"Denny was Archie with you last night as he hasn't come home. Mrs. Carruthers has been worried sick."

Denny wasn't going to tell them whole truth but just said they

239

had been scouting out Nest Point and it seemed they had been too late as all they could see when they got there was a ship's light heading off in the distance. They had lay in a hollow up the hillside waiting for any more activity, but none had come. That was when Archie had snuck away without Denny noticing. Presuming he had headed home.

"Are you in a fit state to retrace your footsteps from last night Denny?"

He nodded and got his boots and coat on. They left the house. He took them inland and walked to where they would come down onto Nest Point. After a while Denny had asked them to stop so that he could vomit behind a tree. The look on Ian's face said it all. When they arrived, Denny showed them where they had ended up lying and gave them a rough time as to when Archie had disappeared. They decided to follow the tracks around the shoreline with Denny and Ian using their scopes. It was Denny who saw his lifeless body floating face down in the shallows at the shoreline. He ran down and grabbed Archie's lifeless body and pulled him onto the banking. He hoped there would be a pulse until he saw a large hole at the side of his head and new it would be futile checking for one. The men stood and held their usual silent prayer then lifted wee Archie and started carrying him back to Kismay.

When they got back to Denny's house it was suggested that they put the body in the back of Denny's dad's old van. Nobody wanted to see a body being carried through the village. While the body was being loaded into the van Ian quickly walked down and told Mrs Carruthers what had happened. The body was taken in to the Icehouse to wait for Dr Belmont carrying out an autopsy.

Denny went back home and spoke to Helen.

"I blame myself for his death Helen. It was up to me to look after him and look what has happened."

"Denny you weren't his keeper so stop blaming yourself. He probably slipped on the slimy rocks and bashed his head. Don't you think? By that look on your face that's not what happened was it. I don't want to know Denny as it's beginning to scare me."

"All I will say is that Archie, God rest his soul, will get retribution and I will be the one to do it."

Helen just sat with her head in her hands and thought how her little world was beginning to unravel before her eyes.

"Helen, please listen to me please as this is particularly important. It's now time for me to take the drastic action to help me beat my addiction. Here is what I would like you do." Denny went on to tell her how he wanted to live for a few weeks in the room at the back of the house. It had never been used for a long time. It was so basic. The base of a bed, a fireplace, toilet and a large ceramic wash basin. There was a small serving hatch to the side of the door and a small window at the side of the house looking out towards the sea. He gave her a list of items he wanted for the room. A mattress and bed clothes from one of the spare bedrooms, his radio, several changes of clothes, bottles of disinfectant and a bucket. He told her several books would be arriving so could she pick them up.

"As soon as we are ready, I am going into rehab by going 'cold turkey.' I'll make a list of foods I will need you to prepare for me please. I'll need to speak to both Ian and Neala before I go into that room. Helen, please don't be afraid as I'll come through this so that we can get on with our new life together."

Over the next few days Helen and Denny worked hard at getting the room habitable at best. Logs were stacked up next to the fire and a comfy chair placed at the side of the bed. Helen didn't have a clue as to what was happening, so she just went along with whatever Denny said.

The books arrived and Denny had asked Ian and Neala up to the house for a chat that night. Ian had an idea what it was about. When they arrived Denny said,

"Why the glum faces folks it's not as if I'm asking you to throw me off the cliff into the sea. Well not yet anyway."

He explained everything he was going to do which raised a few eyebrows from everyone. He asked Neala if Helen could spend a few nights in their spare room if the noises from the room were getting too much for her and then lifted his hand to stop Helen protesting. Neala said that Helen could stay anytime, and she would check in on them periodically but then said,

"Denny, it looks like you have looked into all this but a word of warning please. You will no doubt have heard of 'Delirium Tremens' or commonly known as the DTs. These can be very serious and give you some very nasty symptoms so be aware."

241

"It's your turn next Ian. Did you think you were going to let the girls do all the hard work? I would like you to help me by popping up tomorrow night with a hammer and a bucket of large nails to nail the door to the room I will be living in completely shut so no matter what I can't get out."

"Oh, please don't Denny. I don't know if I can do this. My heart is aching as it is."

"Helen, I know you are strong and I'm not asking you to stand with that gun we had talked about at my back while I try to fly."

He started to laugh. Helen started to shout,

"Foggerty if you say that once more, I'll shoot you right here and now. Understand?"

The evening was finished off with tea and sandwiches along with some small talk which seemed a bit surreal. When they were leaving Ian took Denny aside and asked him if he knew exactly what had had happened to Archie.

"Ian, I trust you completely so what I tell you doesn't go any further. John Scougal murdered Archie. I didn't see it happen, but I did see Scougal and his men dropping off what looked like drugs at Nest Point that night. One thing though Ian is that I, and I alone will get retribution for wee Archie. You will not be involved. Is that understood Ian? Not like the demise of that bastard McLure. If you still have your rifle on the boat and you find it missing one night, then don't worry it will be gone for good."

Ian looked a bit shocked, but he shook Denny's hand and he and Neala walked home. The next day was taken up by Helen giving Denny endless hugs. Not that he was complaining mind you. Bang on six o'clock that night both Ian and Neala arrived. Denny was keen to get on with it as he had refused to go for any whisky that day. As Denny went through the door Ian got to work at once. Hammering the large nails through both the door and the door frame. He left the heads of the nails slightly proud so that he could get them out easier when the time came. When Ian was finished Denny spoke to them through the hatch and said,

"No matter what sounds you will hear from this room on no account should you try and open this door and thank you for your help."

Ian and Neala didn't hang about and left telling Helen they

242

were just down the road if she needed them.

The next few days weren't easy for either of them but when it was the fourth day Denny found the stomach pains to be horrendous and the sounds that were coming out of him resembled an animal not a human being. Helen continued with her work and tried to blank out the noises from the room, but it was hard, very hard. Every couple of hours she would take a small step from the kitchen and stand at the window and try and engage him in conversation but often it was one way. The smell of vomit coming from the room was often very pungent although she knew Denny was trying to keep the toilet and his bucket clean.

If it wasn't for his music on the radio and his books along with trying to speak to Helen he knew he wouldn't make it. Denny was trying to do exercises and although the room wasn't big, he kept walking back and forward until his feet ached or he had to stop to throw up. Even although the fire was going constantly, he often felt cold and edgy. It was during the tenth day that he started to get agitated and would often punch the wooden door with Helen having to fix his hands up later threw the window. He knew the next five days were critical and he was making sure he was trying to eat as much of the food that he had asked Helen to make. Glasses of water were being 'downed' each day and he was continually looking for a sign that this detox was working.

That sign came on the sixteenth day. While urinating he noticed that the colour of his urine had gone from a dull orange to a shade of green. He also noticed that when he emptied his bowls the smell wasn't as pungent. He wasn't prepared to share this with Helen as he didn't want to give her false hope, but he did mention it to Neala when she came to ask how he was. She had said these were good signs, but he wasn't out of the woods yet. Not by a long way.

The next morning, he couldn't get comfortable lying face down and when he turned over, he found he had an erection. The first time in many weeks. Even then he didn't tell Helen, but all these little signs were telling him to keep at it. He thought he might have to ask her to buy some more books on the subjects he had been learning about, Woodmanship and Forestry Management. However, he had decided that his exercise regime was going to be increased and he was trying for hundreds of press ups and sit ups each day but still fully aware the stomach cramps and vomiting were still there.

Neala came to see him on the eighteenth day, stood outside on the step and asked him for an update on how he was feeling. He explained everything that was happening even the erection which she had laughed at. He didn't know how to take that. When she was doing her best to examine him through the window, she told him that all his vitals were looking good, and his complexion was a better colour. Not the dull grey it had been.

"Denny, I think I need to tell Helen about your progress as that girl has been going through hell these last few weeks. She needs to have her spirits lifted or she will be the one that is ill. I promise I won't mention your 'morning glory' and I will play your recovery down a bit. Remember Denny you must be sure that you are fully detoxed before you even contemplate coming out and even when you do you will still have the stomach cramps and some tremors."

Denny thanked her and asked her if she wouldn't mind working with him towards his day of leaving the room. She said it wouldn't be a problem a problem and she would be back in a couple of days for another examination and hopefully it would be the last. At last Denny felt his appetite was about back to normal and it was nearly ten days ago that that craving for alcohol had gone.

Day twenty arrived and he got out of the bed and did his usual before putting his clothes on. Stretched. What he didn't see was Neala standing on the step looking in the window. She laughed and said,

"Good morning 'big boy' you're looking good. Don't be embarrassed as I have seen many men's naked bodies in my time. Unfortunately, most were on a 'slab.' Get dressed and I'll give you a quick check over and decide on a course of action."

Just then Helen appeared at the window and said,

"Showing off again Foggerty?"

Whereby they all laughed, and the ladies went inside for breakfast. Neala came up with Ian the next morning. No boats were out due to the bad weather forecast of high winds and heavy rain. Neala gave Denny a quick check up through the window and she then walked through to the kitchen. Helen was standing in front of the door and Ian had his hammer at the ready. Denny shouted that it was time and Ian got to work removing the nails.

A tall good-looking guy walked through the open door and Helen walked forward with Denny waiting for his hug. Instead, she slapped him on the cheek which surprised everyone, especially Denny.

"Don't ever do that to me again Daniel Rey Foggerty. Next time I will shoot you myself."

Her tears started to flow, and she hugged Denny then went to Ian and Neala and did the same and thanked them from the bottom of her heart. After a lovely breakfast they were about to go when Denny said,

"What about a celebratory drink before you go?"

The three of them looked at Denny in disbelief but he quickly said,

"Just joking folks, just joking. Where is your sense of humour?"

"With you Denny it's long gone. Trust me."

Over the next few weeks Denny kept his recovery going and one night he was trying to get off to sleep when the bedroom door opened, and Helen slipped in naked. She got into bed and straddled Denny and for the next half an hour she rocked back and forward until they were both satisfied. It was lovely for both of them to wake up together. This was their first love making together in a very long time and wouldn't be their last. They now shared a bed and they were going to savour every moment. Denny went and helped Ian with his pots, but he couldn't stop thinking about Archie. He spoke to Ian about him and he had said that Denny should have a long hard think before he did anything.

Denny thought he needed more info as it would be difficult to prove who killed Archie. So a few times he took his dad's old van and drove to Sea Haven. He was looking for Scoug and his cronies and also the white van. It was on his third trip he found everything he needed. A white van was parked up at the pub and an inflatable boat on a trailer next to it. Denny was parked in a side street where he could see everyone who might be going to the Crown pub but for some strange reason today it was closed. The rain started so he retrieved a coat from the van and stood watching. About an hour later he saw the doors to the pub open and several regulars made their way over the small car park. He was beginning to feel a little nervous which he thought was good as it would heighten his senses. No matter what was going to happen he couldn't afford to get the police from the mainland involved. Well not yet anyway.

He was about to give up when he saw Scougal and his three cronies walking to the pub. Denny was a bit startled by the fact that there were three cronies until it suddenly dawned on him. He thumped the van in anger leaving a large dent. How could he be so stupid. The fourth had to be a 'spotter' watching for anybody coming along the track. Obviously, Archie had. Another dent appeared in the van.

The time felt right so he slowly walked towards the pub when he started to feel slight pains in his stomach. He prayed that they wouldn't last long. When he went through the doors, he saw that the bar was horseshoe shaped and Scougal and crew were over the far side where they would struggle to see him. One guy was sitting at the door where you went in. Obviously still being the 'spotter' but Denny would deal with him later. He walked around the bar and right up to Scougal's table, slammed his palms down, and stared at them.

"Stay calm lads as this is an old friend of mine from a long time ago. They tell me you're a drunk now Foggerty is that right?"

"I have never been your friend you 'toad' and here is how this is going to play out. I know you are bringing drugs through this island and to be honest I couldn't care less. However, in doing so you murdered a friend of mine. His name was Archie. So, what is going to happen is that I will kill at least one of the four you in revenge for him. Probably the only good thing you have in your favour is you won't hear the bullet coming but it will have your name on it. He didn't deserve it."

"What are you talking about Foggerty there are only three of us are you still drunk?"

"Listen Scougal, I have never felt better and no longer touch alcohol and I'm not stupid. Do you think I wouldn't notice your 'spotter' over there at the door. You forget that I know you were in the army. You have been warned."

Denny walked to the doors whereby the guy sitting there made a slight movement towards him. Denny pushed him down on the seat and punched him hard on his cheek which left it lying at an awkward angle. Next was a punch to the guy's left eye which must have smashed the socket with the ferocity of it. Just then the barman decided to intervene. He ran around the bar and tried to grab Denny but found himself with Denny's hand around his throat and being lifted against the wall with Denny telling him,

"If you want to ever breathe again then go back behind the bar and leave me alone. Do you hear me?"

The guy gave a slight nod and Denny threw him back against the bar. Scougal and his men just stood watching. Denny was about to leave but turned and smashed the nose of the 'spotter' spreading it over his face. Denny wondered why he just did that and then thought 'because I can.' He walked out and over to his van and sat waiting to see what would happen. Meanwhile a large evil grin came over his face. It wasn't long before Scougal's crew came out half carrying the injured guy hoping that Dr Henderson will still be practicing or sober. Dr Henderson would have to be a plastic surgeon to fix that face.

He had seen enough so he headed home content in his days work.

Denny knew that worse was to come for them, but he also knew that he had to be very careful not to screw up his new life. What he was going to do had to be full proof. Each night he headed out for a run to get his eyes accustomed to the dark and also check out Nest Point. He took his dad's rifle and shot a few rabbits if there was nothing happening from the sea. This was all good cover if somebody had seen him. He thought he knew Scougal's pattern for getting the drugs delivered but he had to be sure. He had went down to Ian's boat one night and searched for the same type of gun safe that was in the old boat.

He was struggling to find it until someone at the top of the stairs shone a torch on him and said,

"Would it be the rifle your looking for Denny?"

He got a fright before Ian walked down the stairs and asked him if he was sure about what he was going to do. Denny said that he was never more sure in all his life. Ian made a cup of tea and Denny teased him by asking for a splash of whisky in his. Ian asked him how he was feeling and said he was having his ups and downs but was generally okay.

"Ian, can I ask you if it's your intension to be on this island forever."

"Forever is a long time son but probably yes. I'm settled with Neala and we're both happy. Why?"

"Just me and my thoughts Ian. Nothing to worry about."

Ian showed him where the rifle and ammunition were and wrapped them in an old waterproof coat and told Denny to be careful. Denny left Ian and walked home. As he walked he was trying to work out when he thought that boat would be back and it realised it would be in two nights. Drug dealers are arrogant and think they are invincible he thought but in two nights he also thought they would be going to Hell. That night he had a heart to heart with Helen and asked her if she could give him a definite answer as to whether she wanted to leave the island and move to Bavaria with him.

"Listen Denny Foggerty, if you're going then so am I as I won't lose you again. I shed too many tears to last a lifetime when you disappeared the first time. Now please tell me all about it."

For the next two days he went out shooting rabbits. It was important to gauge the wind and the light. He needed to try out Ian's gun, so he put it beside his dads in the same gun case. He had to use his rifle as Ian's would blast the rabbit to pieces. When he used a tree as target practice he was impressed by the ferocity of the shot. This gun was going to make some mess of a human body. One night his sixth sense was tingling so he got up and told Helen he was going on reconnaissance for Mike Stewart and not to worry if he was late. Denny started to hurry along the track as his sixth sense was telling him that this was the night. He moved of the track and came to the small rise looking over Nest Point where he watched from the last time.

From his look out he could see a light in the sea, but it seemed to be getting closer. Next he heard a van coming down the track from the Sea Haven end. Three guys got out the van and started to get the inflatable off the trailer.

Denny was looking through the scope but even without it he could see it was Scougal and his crew. The boat came as far as it could and Scougal and one of the other guys went to meet. It sat about fifty yards from the shore and Denny could see there was only one man in the wheel house. There was music coming from the van and it looked like the third guy was trying for a short nap. Scougal had gone onto the boat to unload. Passing the bales down to the man on the inflatable.

Denny lay down and decided that the guy on the inflatable would meet his maker first. There was noise from both boats and the van engine was still running. The guy looked at his chest and wondered why a red dot had suddenly appeared on it. Denny gave him the answer when his chest exploded, and he fell with blood still pumping from the massive hole in his chest. Scougal got down on his knee looking as to where the shot had come. Eventually he stood up and being the arrogant bastard he was, he put his arms out and shouted,

"I know it's you Foggerty, but you know what, you won't do it because you're a drunken coward."

Those were the last words that John Scougal ever uttered on this earth as the red dot sat on his forehead and Denny squeezed the trigger. Scougal's head was almost taken off his shoulders and he then toppled into the sea. The guy in the car was sleeping through this but the pilot in the boat realised what had just happened and pushed the boat to full throttle. Denny wanted to give him a fright and started firing at the boat. Suddenly the boat exploded in a fireball, and it was Denny who got the fright. Several further explosions lit up the sky. He realised there must have been extra fuel barrels tied down on the deck. He thought it was just tough luck for the pilot. It was only the explosions that woke up the guy in the van and he got out to look at the carnage playing out in the sea. He jumped in and took flight going as fast as he could up the track. However, he made a mistake in not taking the trailer off the van and when he got to the top of the incline the van was slewing all over the place and eventually toppled off the road and landed on the rocks at the bottom of the cliff.

When Denny went to see the van, he saw the driver lying through the windscreen with the side of his head caved in.

Denny walked back to his vantage point with a beautiful evil grin on his face, lifted the gun above his head and shouted at the top of his voice,

"Vengeance for wee Archie you bastards. I warned you but you ignored me. Rot in hell."

Denny turned and walked home but first he went to a high point on the cliff, took a hankie out and cleaned the gun. With all his might he threw it as far as he could into the sea. It wasn't long before he got home and yearned to be cuddling into Helen but he knew he had to go to Mike Stewart's house and tell him what had happened. Well, the abridged version anyway. Half the village was up as they must have been wondering what the explosions had been. He met Mike at his door and was asked in. Denny's version of events was that while watching what was going on another fishing boat arrived and all hell broke loose. Shots were being fired from the newly arrived boat and Denny had saw two guys topple over and one landed in the sea. It was then that the original boat took off before it exploded after he had heard more gunfire. He said that a white van with a trailer headed towards Sea Haven but didn't know what happened to it. Mike quickly said,

"It sounds to me Denny that you witnessed a drug feud. You were lucky not to have been caught up in the firing."

"Your right Mike but I tried to keep my head down when all that mayhem was going on."

"I presume you will swear to all this Denny. It is likely that the police will be here tomorrow after my phone call as this is very serious. I will get some men to come with me to secure the crime scene, but you should go home and we'll speak later after you have had a sleep." Denny went home smiling and went into the bedroom where Helen was lying there still asleep. Bless her she had slept through it all until Denny woke her up with his cold hands under her pyjama top.

Chapter 19

After a long lie and a very energetic lovemaking session they both crawled out of bed whereby Helen bathed and started work on her orders for baking. After he washed Denny went to the kitchen and Helen had said,

"Oh, by the way Daniel Rey Foggerty why is there an obscene amount of money in my bank account? I checked the balance the other day and was rather surprised to say the least."

"Well Helen, I did it before you agreed to come with me. Or it could have been the 'cash fairy.'"

Denny walked away laughing and suggested they go for a walk tonight after tea when he would tell her about the drug feud he was caught up in last night. Helen didn't know if he was joking or not.

Denny walked to the harbour and waited for Ian to sail his boat in. He sat on the bench at Scroggies and wondered about wee Archie. His body had been taken to the mainland for autopsy and a burial in a pauper's grave somewhere where nobody would visit him. He wasn't going to let that happen. He could see that Ian's light was on in his cottage, so he went over and knocked on his door. Neala answered and when she saw it was Denny, she asked him in.

"Neala I'll come straight to the point. I don't want wee Archie buried in a paupers grave where people don't know him and won't even attend his grave never mind visit it. I don't care how much it costs as I'm sure Ian has told you I can afford it."

"Don't worry son I'll make it happen and can I ask if you had anything to do with the explosions we heard last night?"

"As if Neala, as if."

Instead of waiting for Ian's boat to appear he walked back home and got on the telephone to Maria in Bavaria. He explained about his ideas for the house in Zwiesel and the hunting estate as well as his plans for the Trust. He explained to Maria that the plans were a massive undertaking and would she be prepared to help him along with her boyfriend. Maria said she would love to help. Denny told her that a salary for both would be agreed and when she started to protest, he had said that nobody would ever work for him for free.

His next call was to Otto, and he was surprised to find he was actually at the lodge instead of in the woods. After the usual greetings Denny had said,

"Otto I have something to ask from you. I know you want to retire but how about I employ you to tutor me all about woodmanship and teach me everything about the forests that I'm coming to live in."

"Your right Denny I do want to retire but I would be up for coming here two or three times a week to teach you as I know I would be leaving the estate in good hands. If there is no payment from you."

"Then we have a problem Otto. You won't be working for me for nothing. So even if it's a small salary then I'd be happy as I want it to be you Otto."

After a while of discussion they came to an agreement both were happy with. He also told Otto that there was a possibility he would be bringing help over at some point. Otto had told him that Frieda's great niece had taken over the looking after of the lodge and he asked Denny if he wanted to keep her services. Denny had said if he had chosen her then that would be fine by him. He told Otto that he expected to be over in a few weeks but would give him and Maria plenty of warning.

Denny then made his way to the harbour leaving Helen to carry on her baking. Ian was just tying his boat up so Denny got about sorting out the considerable catch.

"I've just come past Nest Point and you've left it in some mess Denny. There is even a van and trailer lying on the rocks with loads of debris floating in the sea. I hope it was all worth it."

"Every single minute Ian and if needs must I would do it all over again. Neala will tell you about wee Archie's body. Now let's get on with this catch as I'm expecting visitors from the mainland."

They worked until it was all finished before Denny left and walked home for a bath to get the smell of fish off him. It was just before five o'clock, so he walked down to the bench outside Scroggies, and waited. Wondering who the police would send this time. He wasn't worried about what they would ask him as he had gone over the fictional story time and time again until he was word perfect. After all he was once a police officer.

At half past five he saw what he thought was an official car for Durma coming over the hill. As it drew nearer, he didn't recognise the driver and passenger but as it got close a huge grin spread across his face. It drew up just a few yards from where he was sitting. The first person to get out was DC Thomas Shearlaw followed by Pc Shonagh Slater. This was a lovely surprise for Denny.

"Well, well. They really have sent the big guns over this time haven't they sir. It was also nice of you to bring my favourite police constable with you."

They stood and looked at Denny for a while before Shonagh walked forward and gave him a hug with her boss protesting that Foggerty was still an active witness and not to be fraternised with.

"Oh give over sir and if you call me Foggerty again I'm going to throw you in the harbour. It's Denny or you can go to Hell. Nice to see you too."

The boss didn't know if he was being serious or not, but Shonagh just laughed incurring a stern look from her boss.

Mike Stewart arrived just as Denny asked them where they were staying, and Mike had said he didn't know as to how many people were coming over. So he would have to find a room for them all.

"May I suggest Mike that the two officers go to Scroggies as I'm sure they will be glad of a pint at the end of the day. The boss and Shonagh will come and stay with Helen and I. Sorted."

When that was agreed they all took their bags and walked up the road. Firstly, to Scroggies and then to Denny's house. When Denny walked through the door with his unexpected guests Helen was slightly taken aback but after introductions, she was happy for the company. The boss wanted to see the crime scene as soon as possible and asked Mike if he could organise transport and they would get started. While waiting for Mike Helen showed the boss and Shonagh to their rooms and made a pot of tea with biscuits she had baked this morning. When the two other officers arrived, they got tucked in to Helen's biscuits and didn't look keen to move away from the open fire. It was the boss that roused everybody when Mike had tooted the horn.

"I would appreciate it if you came with us Denny and tell us how it played out. While your mind is fresh."

Two four by four trucks took them to Nest Point and parked on the track just before it swung towards Sea Haven. Denny started to tell them what had happened and pointed to where he had seen it all unfold. The two fishermen keeping an eye on the scene had managed to rope the inflatable with the guy still lying inside it. After Denny had finished, he noticed one of the officers climbing up to where Denny had been.

"I don't know what you're expecting to find up there other than some of my urine as it was a cold night. If you're looking for any shell casings then my rifle scope doesn't fire bullets."

"What type of rifle do you own Denny?"

This came from Shonagh, who after Denny told her it was his dad's rabbit hunting gun walked over to the inflatable and looked at the corpse. She pulled back the tarpaulin. Looked at the corpse and shook her head.

"Sir, it's like he has been hit by a cannon. His chest is totally caved in."

They all walked around the shoreline to where the van lay on the rocks and started to take details. Denny kept an eye on the sea and the shore just in case Scoug's body had been washed up. He knew the tides and if his calculations were correct then Scoug's body would be floating somewhere in the Atlantic Ocean or hopefully lying on the bottom being eaten by the crabs. DC Shearlaw had said that all the drugs that were in the inflatable and any that had been washed up had to made secure. The men put all the surviving bales into back of the trucks along with the two bodies. Before they left the boss turned to Denny and asked,

"I don't suppose you got the name of the boat before it blew up did you?"

"Are you having a laugh with me? Have you forgotten I was once a police officer. A disobedient one at that but then again somebody once asked if I would accept a commendation. The name of the boat was Endless Summer."

It was then that Denny said that if they weren't starting back now then he was off as he was hungry and then told everybody they would eat together at seven thirty. Shonagh asked her boss if she could walk back with him to see how rugged the island really was. The boss just gave a slight nod.

They walked the same route Denny had taken when he had come to dispatch the drug runners to Hell. They had only walked ten minutes before Shonagh said,

"I hope you don't mind me asking but how are you coping with the alcohol?"

"After a struggle I'm finally free from that poisonous stuff. It was hard but for the first time in a long time I have a better focus on my life."

"When you left Edinburgh, I never thought I would see you again."

Shonagh smiled and put her arm through his and they walked home with Denny pointing out all the dangerous inlets to steer clear off. As they got near to the village he pointed out the school he went to and the cemetery his mum and dad lay in. He told her about how life was so hard at times and how the weather influenced everyday life. As they got near to the house, she slipped her arm from his and said,

"Circumstances apart it's been a real pleasure."

She then kissed him on the cheek.

Everyone was there when they got back, and Helen had told them that if they wanted to wash up then go ahead as dinner would only be half an hour. Mike had excused himself even although Helen had said he would be more than welcome to stay. As they sat around the table the talk was a bit strained until Helen produced a large pot of lamb stew with her scones she had baked earlier. They all started to tuck in to their meals and there was even less talk now as everyone seemed to have their mouths full. For the sweet course Helen produced an apple pie and homemade custard. Denny watched as the boss discreetly opened the top button of his trousers.

Coffee was then served in the living room where talk of work was banned at the insistence of Helen. The boss then asked Denny what he was doing since he came back to Durma and what were his thoughts were for the future. Denny didn't try and hide anything.

"Well boss when I worked for you, I was an alcoholic and I can see by your faces that has surprised you all. I struggled most days with the whisky but the days without it were awful although

I vowed not to let it affect my work. The only person that truly knew about my condition from the force was Helen, but I swore her to secrecy so no recrimination from you sir or I will come over and throw you in dock at Leith. I did enjoy my job, but it was untenable with the way I was."

Denny went on to tell them all about inheriting the Albach Trust and what his plans were for the future. They sat there in silence with a stare of disbelief. He didn't know if they believed him or not until Shonagh confirmed what he had just said as he had confided in her in one of his darker moments. He told them how he had detoxed himself by going 'cold turkey' with the help of Helen and two friends from the village. Next was Denny explaining to everybody about his Intermittent Explosive Disorder which certainly raised a few eyebrows.

"It appears to me Denny that you've not had your troubles to look for but I'm glad you tried to keep a hold of your rage while working for me but to be honest I'm not sure you did. How the hell did you get into the force anyway?"

"That was easy sir, I lied."

DC Shearlaw thanked Helen for her wonderful hospitality before excusing himself as he was retiring for much needed sleep. The two men headed off for a well-earned pint at Scroggies while Shonagh helped Helen clear the table and do the dishes. Denny sat wondering how much did the boss believe of his story. No point in worrying.

Denny was up early next morning and went for a run around the cliffs and he couldn't believe how good he felt. By the time he got back everyone was up and washed ready for the day ahead. Breakfast was warm breakfast rolls with butter and jam or marmalade and a large pot of coffee. It looked like the sea air had given the boss a hell of an appetite by the amount of rolls he was devouring. After they had eaten the boss had said he would like to get on with Denny's statement as he didn't want to impose on Helen's hospitality any longer.

Denny suggested that they use his dad's old study, and the boss should phone Mike Stewart to come up and witness it. He didn't want Shonagh involved. Denny also wanted to have a witness so he phoned Ian but it was Neala who said he was still out but she would only be too happy to come and help him. The four of them sat in the study and it wasn't long to take down Denny's version of events and he was quite happy to sign the statement.

"You know Denny when I came over here, I immediately thought that this might be Thomson trying to get a toe hold in again."

Denny took the pen the boss was holding and put it down on the desk and said,

"I will tell you this once and once only. Thomson will never ever come back to haunt us. The ghosts in Hell are not allowed out so no more focus on him."

The boss looked at him and then gave a slight look of resignation as to what Denny was trying to say to him. Mike said that he had a phone call from Edinburgh saying that a transporter was on its way to collect all the evidence and they phoned him because they couldn't get DC Shearlaw. It was now time to go so after they packed the two officers came up and thanked Helen for looking after them. Denny shook the officers hands before giving Shonagh a hug that almost squeezed the life out of her. He then walked over to the boss and shook his hand and gave him a slight nod. Helen had given Shonagh a warm cuddle before going to the boss, who was standing on ceremony and gave him a Durma hug. He seemed a bit embarrassed but gave her a lovely smile. Denny had told Shonagh and the boss he would contact them with his new phone number in Bavaria and hoped they would come over for a stay.

Denny walked them down to the harbour and they got in the car. However, the boss got out again and looked over the car at Denny and said,

"Tell me Foggerty, what did you do with the rifle you used? It was some yarn you spun us this morning."

"Somewhere that nobody will ever find it sir."

The boss smiled as he got in the car and they departed Durma with Shonagh blowing him a kiss with another little tear in her eye. When he got back to the house, he took Helen in his arms and said,

"Thank you, and have I ever told you how much I love you."

The next few weeks were making sure all loose ends were tied up from the Durma end before they left. Helen had spoken to

257

Jinty and asked her if she would like to take over the baking and cleaning business she had and Jinty had jumped at the chance. According to Helen she had been a major source of comfort for her in Denny's missing years. Helen had asked Denny about the house, and he had said he had plans for it and just to trust him.

Denny had phoned both Otto and Maria to say they would be over in three days. Helen's passport had arrived, so it was all go as they planned to have a nice quiet meal with Ian and Neala before they went. That night with the meal prepared, they sat waiting for them to arrive. Denny was having a cup of tea when there was a knock on the door. Helen opened the door, and a shout came,

"Is that mad bastard Foggerty about. Sorry, the rich mad bastard Foggerty."

Helen got such a shock at this stranger standing on her doorstep and Denny dropped his teacup spilling its contents over the table.

Oh know, this can't be happening thought Denny. He knew the voice and thought he must be dreaming. He ran to the door and there stood Willie McLean aka Timebomb. Denny couldn't speak.

"Are you not glad to see your pal from Helmsford?"

It was then that Ian and Neala came round the corner.

"Sorry Denny, but he just appeared on our doorstep a few hours ago. If you don't want him to come in then no worries."

Denny had said that everybody was welcome but wasn't sure he hadn't said that while in shock. When everyone was seated Denny introduced Helen to Willie whereby she said she was pleased to meet him and then clipped him over the back of his head.

"What was that for Helen?"

"For using that type of language in my house."

It was a lovely time with Willie getting several clips over the head for his language. Supper was exceptional and Willie had said,

"Well Denny, if you ever leave this bonnie girl again, I will personally hunt you down and give you a good beating."

Ian just sat shaking his head. Willie had come out with tonight's biggest revelation. He hadn't touched a drop of alcohol since the fight in the Crown hotel. Denny thought that was a near miracle. It was time to get the business out of the way.

"Ian, Neala there is one thing both Helen and I would like to do and that is we would like to give you this house. Neala, you need more space than you have for your surgeries, and we would hate to have to try and sell it so if you say yes my solicitor will contact you to have signatures exchanged. There is also my detox 'cave' for when Willie comes to stay. Neala, I also have a proposition to put to you. It is my intention to set up a Western Isles Trust whereby money from the Albach trust will be invested for the regeneration of the islands and I would like you to oversee it in your spare time. Of course, with a suitable salary."

"Denny I know there will be an argument if we said no but you have already bought me a new boat at great expense and now this. I'm lost for words."

"Take it you bloody numpty. I'm going to need some place to sleep when I come over."

Willie just waited on the clip on the back of the head which duly arrived. Neala had said she would be privileged to be a part of the new trust and would look forward to working with her counterparts in Germany.

Denny hoped they would be back over every three or four months to see how any regeneration program was coming along and that they could stay with them as the house would be big enough for him and Helen coming back over.

"There could be a problem there Denny. There will more than just you and I."

"Helen we will not be bringing anyone else with us at this stage so what's the problem?"

"The problem Denny Foggerty is that I'm pregnant."

"What do you mean pregnant?"

"It means you've done the business Foggerty. You've done the business."

After Helen had given another clip to Willie there was a palpable excitement in the room. Nobody said a word until Helen mentioned that Neala was looking after her. Denny just sat staring at the floor until he rose and walked over to Helen and said,

"I can't believe you're having my baby."

"Well, there might be a problem there Denny as Neala tells me there are two heart beats. We're having twins' sunshine of my life."

Both Ian and Willie got up and shook Denny's hand and gave Helen a hug. Denny asked Helen why she hadn't told him, but she said she only found out this week. Denny was shocked and he had to take a moment to gather his thoughts. Ian had suggested that this was a good time to leave but not before Denny said,

"Willie, please don't think you are getting off lightly. I have a proposition for you. I need someone to help me in the forests when I get over there so I was wondering if you would be interested in coming over to stay at least for a while. Ian said you once worked in the forests on an estate up near Helmsford. You would have to learn all about the forests over there as I will have to do from a guy called Otto and if you don't do as he tells you then he will shoot you."

"I would love to Denny, but we have the problem of me getting a passport and then getting entry into Germany."

"Don't' worry about that as the lawyers that run the Trust are some of the finest in Europe. Plus, the British Government would be glad to get rid of you."

Denny told him to leave his details with him. It was then that they all started to leave, and Denny felt emotional as he shut the door. He was leaning on the table trying to take it all in when the door flew open and Willie shouted,

"Are there plenty of women over there Foggerty?"

Denny picked up a scone and hurled it at the door missing Willie by an inch. As the door closed, he could hear him laughing as he tried to catch up with his brother and Neala.

Next morning he asked Helen if she would like to walk down with him to the school. They timed it so that the kids were on a break. As they walked in Miss Glover and Miss Bryant met them and gave them a hug. After a while of idle chitchat Miss Glover said,

"Denny, I heard about your problems and I'm so glad you're now free from that wretched stuff. Well done."

"One of the reasons we are here is that although it's a long story the shortened version is that my late mum left me as the sole heir to a massive fortune through a trust in Bavaria. I won't

260

go into it all but what I am proposing to do is set up a Western Isles Trust to help regenerate any island on the West coast. It is an idea of mine to build a new school at both Kismay and Sea Haven and I would like you both to have a big input as to how it should turn out. Neala your GP will contact you with regards to your thoughts as we will be leaving Durma tomorrow morning at ten o'clock. The best news however is that Helen is expecting twins. We have only found out so it's a bit overwhelming at present. We must go now to start packing but may I say,

"Thank you so much for being our teachers. Without you we wouldn't be the same people we are today."

Miss Glover started to cry which set Miss Bryant off closely followed by Helen. After hugs were exchanged, they said their goodbyes and Denny was glad to get away from all this crying.

Denny had already phoned Bavaria a few days ago confirming flight times so now it was time for packing. He suggested that they take the bare minimum in clothes as Zwiesel had some good clothes shops. A couple of change of clothes and any pictures of the family along with toiletries was the order of the day. There was a knock on the door and in came Jinty.

"I came to see you before you left. I'm going to miss you Helen and it will be heart breaking not seeing the 'bairns' growing up."

"Well Jinty why don't you have some serious thought about coming to stay in Bavaria. Plenty of work and I'm sure Denny would buy you a house, wouldn't you Denny? Denny? Denny? Where are you?"

Denny had escaped to the kitchen and was making a cup of tea for the three of them. He knew it was only a matter of time before the tears would flow. After a while they started to say goodbye and Denny was spot on with the tears. Jinty gave Denny a big hug and he whispered into her ear that of course he would buy her a house for her and her boyfriend. He had to do his usual when Jinty gave you a hug and that was he had to prise her hands off from around his neck. When Jinty left it was only a matter of time before they left the next day so it was just a case of relaxing. Denny took Helen's hand and suggested they go for one last long walk along the cliffs. As they stood overlooking the sea they both reflected on their time on Durma. Denny wondering what his life would have been like without his mental demons. Helen thinking about how fate brought them together. Then pulled them apart and now bringing them back again.

They were up early next morning ready to go on their big adventure. Denny had said he had organised a car to take them to Inverness rather than the bus, but it would still be the train to Edinburgh. He explained that they would stay over at Robert Trapps hotel before their flight the next morning.

At ten o'clock Ian arrived to take them to the ferry. As they passed Ian's house Neala was out giving them a cheerful wave. When they looked over to the school there was a large banner displayed saying,

"Good luck Denny and Helen."

All the school children along with Miss Glover and Miss Bryant were waving frantically. They put the windows down and waved back with Helen in tears. When they arrived at the ferry terminal, they had to wait half an hour. They sat on one of the benches and Helen went looking for a toilet.

"Ian, I keep having this little niggle in my head. Throughout my life I have maimed and killed a lot of bad people and it's in my head that it might come back to haunt me. I don't think it has made me a bad person but that is not for me to judge."

"Denny stop beating yourself up about what you have done. I suppose I don't know half the things you have done and to be honest I don't want to. However, I think you may have rid the world of some terrible scum. Anyway if anybody comes looking for you then you have the perfect ally to watch your back. Timebomb."

They both laughed and then Helen arrived back. It was time to board so Denny took Ian's hand and said,

"Thanks for everything pal and don't hang around when we board."

Helen went to Ian and gave him a huge hug with tears thrown in. As they both walked away Denny turned and said,

"Is that tears I can see Ian?"

"Get lost Foggerty."

As the ferry started to leave, they walked up to the top deck only to see Ian was still there. When Helen started to wave Ian got in his pickup, blasted the horn and drove away. The journey was a bit choppy and it reminded him of what his dad had said about his mum and his first journey over. He said to Helen they should stay on the front of the boat and look forward not back. When they disembarked at Mayfort the taxi driver was true to his word and came and met them and put their bags in his car.

The journey only took half the time that the bus would have taken which was a bonus.

When they got out at Inverness, Denny gave the driver a wad of cash with him protesting it was far too much. However, Denny told him that they as well as others would be back over periodically and would require his services. The driver had said to phone him anytime. Denny went and bought four tickets next to each other for the train to give them privacy. He asked Helen to sit looking out of the train on the left as it would be more interesting. This was a different world to her and although she had lived in Glasgow this world was a much nicer place. Suddenly, Helen said,

"Did you go and see your mum and dad's graves before you left Denny?"

"Yes, no worries I went down a couple of times last week and Ian is going to tend the graves."

As they came through Dundee he started to sweat a little bit wondering about everything he went through. Even wondering if he would ever see the Gangs of Dundee in action again. A story to tell the twins someday. Maybe not. It didn't seem that long before the train was rolling in to Waverley Station in Edinburgh. When they started to walk to Robert's hotel, she kept on saying how beautiful the city was. There was no argument from Denny about that.

As they walked into the hotel Robert came bounding down the stairs and shook Denny's hand and after being introduced to Helen he gave her a lovely welcoming hug. He put them in the best room in the hotel and told Denny how sad he was hearing the news about his dad so soon after his mum. He said that dinner would be at seven and what were they going to do till then. Denny had said they might like to go and wander about Princes St. gardens and then go for a coffee. Robert said it would be nice for a catch up after dinner.

As they sat in the gardens Helen remarked how she could live here if there wasn't as many people. Denny just laughed.

At about six thirty they wandered down for dinner. When the plates came Denny had half a cow as before on his with Helen having the other half. After they were finished Robert had said they should go through to the lounge where he would bring coffee and they would have their catch up. On the tray was a bottle of cognac and as Robert lifted it Denny just put his hand on his and said that neither of them drink.

Again Denny didn't hold back and told him about his time abroad and then back in Scotland. He explained about his addiction and told Robert all about his inheritance of the Albach Trust. Robert sat their mesmerised as to Denny's life story and didn't say a word. Until he mentioned that he was involved in the young Billy Thomson bust. Denny just smiled and Robert said he didn't want to know anything. A walk later on took them around the streets near to Prices St. gardens again When they walked along Rose St. He felt a shiver up his back with Helen asking him if he was all right. He said he was fine and suggested they head back as they had an early flight tomorrow.

After breakfast they were about to put their bags in Robert's car when Denny had said that he wished to settle the bill. Robert was about to do his usual when Denny said,

"Robert we fully appreciate your help but this time I will pay and there will be know argument."

Denny handed him a cheque and Robert stood there looking at it in amazement.

"Denny, I don't make this in two years. I can't take it."

"Please just take it and can I tell you that we, along with several other people, will need to stay in your hotel over the year. To and from Bavaria."

There wasn't much conversation going to the airport as Denny thought Robert was a bit bewildered. They said goodbye and both walked through customs with Helen due to her pregnancy being searched by hand. As they sat waiting, they were both wishing they were in Bavaria now. The call for the flight was announced and they proceeded through the departure gate and onto the plane.

The flight was as uneventful as Denny's first one was and he hadn't realised that this was Helen's first flight. Eventually they arrived and he knew she was getting a little bit excited. The baggage reclaim was slow but there was no hurry. When their bags came through, they collected them and walked to arrivals.

It was easy to recognise Maria as she was the one jumping up and down excitedly. She ran forward, grabbed Denny and hugged him and then kissed him on the cheek. When Denny introduced Helen she hugged her just as warmly

"I am so glad to have you over here and I am so excited about your news Helen. Let's get out of here and get back to Bavaria. Helen marvelled at the size of Munich but didn't think it matched Edinburgh for beauty. It had been a long day, so she eventually drifted off with Maria and Denny catching up in the front. After a bit of a delay due to heavy traffic they were nearing the Estate. Helen had woken up and when they approached the house she had said,

"Denny, you told me that we would be coming to a very large house. What I see is a small bungalow in front of me."

Denny and Maria just laughed before he said,

"Wait two minutes darling as that is just the annex."

As they came round the corner there stood the magnificent house he had been telling her about.

"Bloody hell Foggerty you didn't tell me how beautiful it was."

Helen could only stare with her eyes bulging. She didn't say a word. She couldn't. They drove up to the side of the building and Denny got out and put their bags out of the way. Otto and Gertie walked out the main doors and down the steps with Otto introducing themselves to Helen and Gertie to Denny. Helen was still in a bit of shock until Maria said that she hoped they didn't mind but there was to be a small party at the big house tomorrow night as her mum, dad and boyfriend would be there as well as Otto and his wife.

"In case I forget Denny all my guns are now yours so look after them please." said Otto.

"Mr Denny, I don't know if I am invited to the party but I haven't got a nice dress to wear."

"Listen Gertie, his name is Denny unless you are angry with him and then it's Foggerty and tomorrow we will go into town and look for clothes for the party. You are one of the family."

Denny excused himself and walked to the edge of the forest and stood a while looking at that mist creeping along the forest

265

floor. He knew he had made the right decision.

As he walked back, he was about ten yards from the stairs when Otto said,

"Denny, I have brought a present for you, in fact two presents."

Just then he gave a low whistle, and he stood aside to let two stunning German Pointer pups come up and sit beside him. They looked up at Otto and he gave them a nod. They ran towards Denny who sank to his knees as they snuggled into him. Denny unashamedly cried floods of tears. The pups licking the salty tears from his cheeks. He thought his dad would understand. Otto said,

"I thought you might want to see their father, Denny."

He gave another low whistle and stood out of the way to let Ottar through. Another nod and Ottar walked forward and growled at the pups giving them a telling off. They scattered away into the trees. Ottar snuggled into Denny to get his ears scratched.

More tears flowed and it was then that Denny knew he would all right.